Invitation to Scandal

BRONWEN EVANS

BRAVA

KENSINGTON PUBLISHING CORP.
www.kensingtonbooks.com

BRAVA BOOKS are published by

Kensington Publishing Corp.
119 West 40th Street
New York, NY 10018

All Kensington titles, imprints, and distributed lines are available at special quantity discounts for bulk purchases for sales promotions, premiums, fund-raising, educational, or institutional use.

Special book excerpts or customized printings can also be created to fit specific needs. For details, write or phone the office of the Kensington special sales manager: Kensington Publishing Corp., 119 West 40th Street, New York, NY 10018, attn: Special Sales Department; phone 1-800-221-2647.

Brava and the B logo are Reg. U.S. Pat. & TM Off.

ISBN-13: 978-0-7582-5921-9
ISBN-10: 0-7582-5921-2

First Kensington Trade Paperback Printing: May 2012

10 9 8 7 6 5 4 3 2 1

Printed in the United States of America

For my fabulous Beta readers—Diane, Carrie, Kelly, Dani, Katrina and Cathy. The book is stronger because of the wonderful feedback you gave me. Thank you!

ACKNOWLEDGMENTS

Writing can be such a solitary process but in writing this book I've never felt alone. I have such a wonderful support group of friends and family. Special thanks go to Jem Stanners for giving me a male point of view. As always, thanks go to my Book in 50 Days team, especially Gracie and Karen, who encouraged me on the days the words wouldn't come, and who held my hand through the editing process. Thank you to my wonderful editor, Megan Records, and my ever patient agent, Melissa Jeglinski. I was very green about this industry and both of you have kindly eased me through the process.

Chapter 1

T he things I'm prepared to do for my country, Rufus
Knight, Viscount Strathmore, thought wryly. Thank
God his plan was working. He'd laid his trap and the weasels
were taking the bait.

He'd been aware of the two men the instant they'd entered his room, even though his head was buried between
the serving wench's slender thighs. Normally he preferred to
take his pleasure without an audience, but tonight he welcomed the intrusion—had planned on the intrusion . . .

"Rufus—please . . . Lord Strathmore, yes, oh, God, yes . . ."

If Lucy's moans were anything to go by, he was perform-
ing more than adequately for the inebriated gentleman he
was portraying.

Perhaps too well.

Thankfully the thieves were overly bold.

The open window in the tavern's bedchamber allowed no
ventilation on this humid, still night. The scent of sex and
cheap perfume clung to the air, adding to his body's thrumming tension. With grim determination he suppressed his
burgeoning arousal at the woman's near orgasmic cries. He
was grateful that her breathy entreaties were not loud
enough to blanket the soft thud of clumsy tiptoeing feet. He
knew the exact location of the men searching his room.

Pushing desire aside, Rufus concentrated on his performance while keeping an eye on the rummaging thieves. He knew he'd have to act soon. He hated to leave a woman unsatisfied, but he looked forward to a lengthy, all night apology afterward.

He'd picked this inn, not just because of Lucy's obvious charms, there was only so much he'd do for his country; the lass at least had to be pretty. He'd picked the tavern because it was located next to the Deal docks. The Bosun's Inn was full of undesirables—cutthroats, ruffians, and drunkards. Just the sort of men Rufus sought.

One of the men moved closer to the bed. The taste of woman and the edge of danger fed his tension. *Patience. Don't act too soon.*

One of these brigands, currently rifling through Rufus's belongings, was going to provide him with the intelligence he sought. In his line of work it paid to find leverage. A thief would often squeal when faced with a choice between freedom and transportation to the colonies.

He'd set up this intimate scene to perfection.

As with most of his adult life it was all an act.

Tonight's role was not about a man sating his lust between a pair of willing thighs. Enjoyable as that would be, and indeed, it was something he intended to do with lovely Lucy before the night was over, it was about gaining much needed information. One of these thieves was going to provide it.

Provide it—right—now—

He lunged for the nearest man, whom he noted with heart sinking was the largest. Luckily, the man's hand was deep within the pocket of Rufus's discarded trousers. Rufus's punch landed squarely under the man's jaw, snapping his head back. Before the man could even shake his hand free, he went down like a shot grizzly bear.

Heedless of his nakedness, Rufus turned toward the second man. He wasn't quick enough. Two muscle-bound arms wrapped around his bare torso from behind.

A kick of adrenaline gave him the strength he needed. He still held the advantage. His nakedness meant the robber had nothing to hold on to, whereas Rufus was able to wrench free of his assailant's hold, grab the man's shirt, and fling him over his shoulder. He watched with satisfaction as the thief slammed to the floor, flat on his back, winded.

Before he could move, Rufus placed a bare foot firmly on the robber's neck. He ruthlessly repressed his excitement. The capture of an informant was only the beginning . . .

"Lucy, my dear. Would you be a love and bring me my right boot?"

The buxom redhead eased from the bed. Conscious of her own beauty, she swayed provocatively toward his Hessians, and both Rufus and the man on the floor followed the beauty with their eyes.

As she handed him his boot, he gave her a wicked smile and patted her bottom. "Thank you, sweetheart. If you'd like to wait on the bed for me I won't be but a minute."

Ensuring his weight was still on his captive's neck, Rufus slipped his hand inside his perfectly polished Hessian and withdrew his dagger. At the sight, the man at his feet began to whimper.

He applied more pressure, until the man's eyes began to pop from their sockets and his hands clawed at Rufus's bare feet.

Rufus calmly stated, all hint of drunkenness vanishing from his posture, "You and I are going to have a pleasant little chat. A chat about the smuggler known as Dark Shadow."

The man's eyes widened in alarm. He knew the name. Every villager in Deal knew the name. The minute "Dark Shadow" was mentioned, the townspeople clammed up as if the grim reaper would strike them down.

Rufus waved the knife even closer and applied more pressure for good measure, his eyes gleaming with threat. The man started to shake.

The vermin beneath his foot should be afraid. Rufus had

sacrificed most of his life in the pursuit of only one thing: to reclaim his family's honor. Sensing how close he was to achieving his goal, nothing and no one would stand between him and the truth about his father.

Over the years he had risked his life for his country countless times, driven by the need to prove to the world he should not have to bear his father's sins.

Rufus was nothing like his sire.

The Foreign Secretary, Lord Ashford, thought Rufus took risks for God and country. That was partly true. But more important he did it to bury the stench of disgrace that had been his father, and to block from his mind the guilt eating him from the inside. He should have accompanied his father to Hastingleigh all those years ago and stopped him from betraying his country.

Now he had the opportunity to lay the past to rest. Dark Shadow would lead him to England's most prolific and deadly French spy. A spy who'd stolen British secrets and, if not caught, would prolong this war for several years.

Rufus, however, wanted more. He prayed the spy could tell him about his father. About his father's rumored betrayal of his own class, if not people—the French Aristocracy. Rumors Rufus longed to prove false.

Only then would he be free.

Watching his prey squirming below him, Rufus kept all his senses attuned. The man's accomplice still lay unconscious, and Rufus's comely bedmate sat naked and unsatisfied on the bed, clutching the sheet to her bosom.

Rufus bent down until his head stopped mere inches from the crook's face. "I think it only fair to tell you I'm an evil man. A part of me hopes you won't talk so I can put this dagger to good use." Rufus slid the cold steel down the man's front, stopping at his groin. "With women like pretty Lucy in this world it would be a shame to unman you."

The man's mouth opened and closed like a dying fish. Rufus eased the pressure on his throat so he could at least talk.

"What do you want?" his captive croaked.

Rufus hid his smile of triumph. "Thieves stick together. I want all that you know about the infamous smuggler, Dark Shadow. Preferably where he's based and"—he dug the point of his dagger into the man's groin—"who he is."

Fear quavered in the thief's voice. "No one's ever seen him. The men of Deal have no idea who Dark Shadow is. Most think he's not from around here, while others think he's one of you lot—a nob fallen on hard times."

He pressed his foot down harder. "You expect me to believe he might be local gentry?"

"Believe what you will. No one wants to know," the man choked out in a hoarse voice. "They're scared to know too much."

Rufus pressed the tip of his dagger through the layer of clothes to bare skin. "Oh, come, surely someone has seen him. Someone must want to collect the bounty on his head. I'll even double it."

In his previous dealings with thieves and cutthroats, most informants' tongues loosened with the added incentive of money. Yet the man looked more frightened instead of interested.

"There ain't no way I'd tell you anything even if I knew somethin'. I'd be dead before I could spend it. The villagers think Dark Shadow's a modern-day Robin Hood. They'd harm anyone who thought to inform on him. They want his coin. Most of what Dark Shadow makes goes back to the village. God bless him, he gives to the elderly, the widows, orphans, and children."

"He gives the money away?" Rufus asked dubiously.

Lucy sat up, clutching the sheet to her ample bosom. "Aye, my lord, he does. He sent me mother ten pounds to look after me brother, little Jack, so that Jack wouldn't be forced to work as a cabin boy on one of them ships. He slips her something almost every month."

Rufus straightened and ran a hand through his hair. He

needed time to think. He found it hard to believe that a smuggler who took care of women and children would knowingly harbor England's most notorious spy. This put a different slant on how he should proceed. Dark Shadow could be useful. Perhaps having him arrested was not the best plan. He lifted his foot off the man's throat. "We're done—for now."

The man on the floor gingerly sat up. "He doesn't even run his ships from one particular cove. It's a different place every time. The Revenuers almost captured him once, but he disappeared like a ghost racing the dawn. That's how he got his name."

Rufus knew how easy it was to be a ghost. Men of his standing, men with money, found it easy to disappear. Perhaps Dark Shadow *was* a nobleman down on his luck. If so, he'd be easy to find. He knew this from experience. No matter how hard you tried, past sins always found you.

Twelve years ago, at the age of twenty, upon his father's death, Rufus and his family were ostracized. Faced with Society's scorn, he'd had no alternative but to try to regain the family's honor and position in Society. Especially if his mother and sister were to survive. Pride was a luxury he and his family could not afford.

He'd learned to push aside his own identity and portray a character the *ton* wanted to see. An honorable man trying desperately to atone for his sire's shortfalls. A man prepared to demonstrate the correct penance in order to earn Society's forgiveness.

He was sick of trying to earn their respect.

Self-loathing pulsed through him, and despair. He was afraid if he didn't ascertain the truth, and soon, there would be no honor left to restore.

For the past twelve years he'd worked tirelessly chasing a phantom. Chasing the truth about his father. The father he could have sworn would die on his sword before dishonor.

The father he obviously hadn't known.

At twenty, Rufus had ceased his life of aimless leisure and gentlemanly comfort to ferret out the fact from fiction. Most nights he prayed he'd like what he found. Each time he thought he'd glimpsed a facet of truth, it vanished like the mist when the sun rose. So he continued to play his part, the part of a nobleman, even though he was deemed a tainted one.

A nobleman no one wanted. Due to his father's fall from grace, he became an embarrassment. He drifted in and out of Society like a bad smell. A person of note, a person to be put up with, but not one you would openly welcome and acknowledge for fear of retribution.

He inwardly chuckled in self-mocking amusement. He was not worthy of knowing.

He was a man who ruthlessly pursued his goal without heed to others. A man who knew the rules of gentlemanly conduct and ignored them as it suited. He was a man who fought to restore his family's honor, while conveniently forgetting, when it suited, what the word meant.

Perhaps he was exactly like his father. The thought pushed stinking fear into every pore.

He pulled the man to his feet. "Off with you. Take your friend with you when you leave." Rufus went to his coat and withdrew some coins. "Apologize to him for the jaw. I hope it's not broken. Here's something for your trouble. If you do hear anything, anything at all, you'll let me know." His voice indicated it wasn't a question but a command. "I will be staying with Lord Hale. Do you know where his estate lies?"

The man nodded. "Aye. I know where Hastingleigh is, my lord."

Still pondering the new information, Rufus watched, mind whirling with this newfound intelligence, as the man dragged his partner out the door. He'd get no more out of them. Dark Shadow was not all he seemed, and that worried Rufus. He didn't like the fact that a supposedly deadly, dan-

gerous smuggler helped people. Something about this situation was monstrously wrong.

Of all the damnable luck. Robin Hood. Rufus arrogantly thought spreading some coin around would loosen the Dealites' tongues. Now he didn't know how to proceed, and time was running out. At the end of summer the spy would be gone. The winter storms made sending messages through smugglers too risky. They took too many chances in order not to be caught, and the loss of a ship meant the loss of intelligence. His spy would have to find other, more traditional ways to send Napoleon his traitorous communiqués.

He rubbed the back of his neck, trying to ease the tension. He was close. So close.

Perhaps his friend Christopher Canthorpe, the Earl of Hale, would be able to furnish him with the names of the local gentry fallen on desperate times. History showed that many noble families of Kent resorted to smuggling when the need arose. It was a good lead. As good a place to start as any.

What reason could he give Christopher for needing this information? Christopher was not particularly astute; one could almost call him simple. Perhaps, Rufus thought, he could suggest he was looking for an estate in the area and would start with those who may need to sell. Yes. That was it.

Besides, he could always say he would like to be closer to the Hales. He hoped Christopher would ask for his sister's hand in marriage. Madeline's prospects were limited by their sire's sin, but the Hales had always stood by them because their mothers had been firm friends, and still were.

Christopher was nearing forty, and being a bit of a bumbling idiot, was also not so in demand. His title and wealth drew some interest, but his tendency to spend most of his days at Hastingleigh, his portly figure, and lack of intelligence did not raise him to prominence with the mammas of the *ton*.

Madeline would not be happy with his choice of husband,

but she was only eighteen and there was no rush to send her to the altar. Lord Hale was a safe choice. She would be protected by Hale's name and standing in Society. Once she married it would be one less thing for him to worry about.

Rufus stooped to right the chair that had fallen during the scuffle. He'd have to talk with Stephen Milton, Marquis of Worthington, his co-spy master, in the morning and regroup. He was too close to capturing the spy and finding out the truth about his father to let a supposedly saintly smuggler get in the way. He knew he could do nothing more tonight.

Just then Lucy moved, stretching like a sleek cat on the bed. The sheet slipped to lie at her waist, exposing her bountiful breasts. He could do nothing more about Dark Shadow, so he approached the bed with his thoughts at the moment on more carnal delights. With a rakish grin, he faced the woman now sitting up naked in his bed.

She gave him a "come and take me smile."

He feasted on the sight and felt his body stirring once more, and this time he didn't try to stop it. No point wasting the rest of the night, he thought, walking the short distance to lock the door, thus ensuring there would be no further interruptions.

Turning back toward Lucy, Rufus suppressed a shiver of need, hoping her body would help him forget how trapped in this life of intrigue he really was. With cool precision he inwardly calmed the rutting beast.

He reined in his cravings and crawled up onto the bed. Rolling Lucy onto her front, he said, "Come, my beauty. Now that my business has concluded I feel a tad amorous."

With that he placed practiced kisses upward, along her slender limbs. Upon reaching the plump globes of her bottom, he grasped her hips and set her on her knees, opening her to him. Soon her giggle of delight turned to a crooning moan, as his tongue and wicked mouth set about finishing what he'd previously started.

This time there was no audience, and he had all night.

Chapter 2

Three days later

R*heda Kerrich,* she inwardly scolded, *you're a fool. Your current predicament ventures well beyond stupid.*

For the umpteenth time she thumped the unmarked barrel of French brandy that had kept her pinned against the fat tree trunk for the past three hours. The humiliation of her predicament hurt almost as much as her feet, which were being crushed by the heavy barrel.

"Oh, just move, blast it." Never one to admit defeat, she let out a yell of frustration and pushed at the barrel once more with all her might. It mocked her efforts by not budging a snail's trail from its position wedged in the tree roots at her feet. All she'd managed to do was awaken the pain in her numbed legs.

"Bloody inconvenient," she growled under her breath. "Where is a man when I most need one? Normally they're a nuisance, yet, now—now when I am in desperate need, one cannot be found. Typical."

She turned her head and once again scoured the countryside for help. The green meadow stretched from the road on her left, downward to the jagged cliffs on her right. The sea sounded as angry as she felt, the waves crashing against the rocks below. Although trapped, she was thankful she'd stopped

the barrel from rolling off the cliff's edge for its contents meant food for her friend Meg and Meg's four young sons.

That's if she delivered it to them before nightfall.

How could she have been so stupid? Swiping at the hair obscuring her eyes, Rheda said, in a voice she used when scolding her horses, "This is beyond maddening."

Perspiration trickled down between her breasts. She didn't have much time. The Revenuers would pass through at dusk. Surely her brother must have missed her by now. She prayed Daniel would come before the Excise men.

She dropped her head to her chest and sighed. Her brother had gone fishing, but no fish ever resulted from Daniel's fishing trips. She'd determined "fishing" was Daniel's excuse for spending the day in bed with one of the local lasses. It would be dark before Daniel even realized she was missing.

She lifted her head and cocked it to one side. Were those horses' hooves thundering toward her? She stretched her neck, but she couldn't see past the bend in the dirt road. *Please let it be Daniel.* She'd had enough trouble today without having to explain the barrel to the Excise men. Worse, she couldn't rely on her name to get her out of this mess. In her disguised rags it seemed unlikely they'd even recognize her.

She wiped a hand across her forehead and tried to push the errant strand of hair out of her eyes. She must look a mess. She wore no bonnet. She'd donned her oldest dress, tied her hair roughly behind her neck, and had on her old work boots.

Daniel would be furious. He hated it when she ran about the countryside dressed like a local doxy. Last year, on his eighteenth birthday, Daniel decided to reestablish their family's good name. His focus on restoring the barony meant Rheda was supposed to conform to Society's expectations, and unfortunately, also to his. Being dictated to by a brother who was six years younger infuriated her, especially since

she'd singlehandedly run the estate ever since their father had died over eight years ago. Luckily her guardian, the late Lord Hale, had bowed to his wife's wishes and let Rheda prove she could manage the estate on her own. She would forever be in Lady Hale's debt.

She'd had to fight Daniel as well. He hated her decision to help the women of the village. She provided brandy for the widows to sell at market. If she didn't they'd starve. He'd ordered her not to move this latest barrel on her own. Rheda squirmed against the tree. She did not take well to orders. Now she'd have to admit her so-called transgression. She hated it when he was right. She gave in to her growing anger at her own helplessness and thumped the tree behind her.

"It's his fault I'm in this mess."

The wind rustling through the trees was the only reply to her murmured censure. If Daniel had delivered the barrel as she'd requested, she would not be in this embarrassing situation. Meg needed the barrel to sell tomorrow, or her children would go hungry this week.

Meg was a local Deal widow, her friend and confidante. The one person Rheda could count on to protect, help, and guide her. Although only a few years older than Rheda, Meg was like the mother she'd never had while growing up. Due to the life she had lived, Meg was wise beyond her years.

The thundering hooves focused her back on the problem at hand. Horse and rider appeared around the bend. The horse was galloping so fast she wondered if its accomplished rider would see her. Her heart missed a beat. The man wasn't Daniel. Daniel didn't own, nor could he afford, a magnificent beast such as this.

Please, she prayed, *let him fly past without noticing me.*

Like every other aspect of her day, she was denied her wish. The rider pulled on the reins, and the powerful steed came to a sliding halt in the middle of the road, gravel spraying through the air.

Her shoulders drooped. "Perfect," she uttered to no one but herself.

The stallion pranced on the road in tune to the pounding surf, its owner stroking its neck with a large gloved hand. He took in her situation and seemed to whisper something in his horse's ear. Rheda licked her lips nervously. Would he be friend or foe?

The pair trotted across the field in her direction and halted in front of her.

"Are you in need of assistance?" His voice was velvety smooth, yet commanding.

She saw two dark eyes rimmed with lovely long eyelashes, and a wide soft mouth. With a mouth that soft he would be very responsive. She might even be able to control him. The stallion before her was impressive. He would make a fine mate for her mare, Desert Rose.

"He won't bite," the man added, misinterpreting her interest in his horse as fear.

With some reluctance she lifted her gaze to the owner of such a beautiful piece of horseflesh. Her heart tumbled in her chest, flipping and flopping as if caught in the thundering surf behind her.

Beautiful.

She shook her head. The word applied equally to the stallion's rider. She had never seen such an arresting man. Her pulse hitched as she drank him in, the pain from the barrel momentarily forgotten. When she reached his dark eyes she shivered. He had a look of danger about him.

His eyes were almost the same color as his horse's glossy coat, a luminous rich brown. His breeze-swept chestnut hair was fashionably cut and softened the hard planes of his handsome face. His countenance screamed he was a man not to be messed with.

Like his regal mount when he sought his mares, this man could mesmerize any female he chose to conquer—she was sure of it.

Rheda tried to move her foot so the pain would distract her from the knowledge that this man's beauty disturbed her more than it should.

To hide her reaction to him she bit out a reply. "Of course I need some help."

His good looks sharpened as anger washed over his face. She bit her bottom lip anxiously. Pain did not lend her to manners, but with nothing more than a blink his anger disappeared to be replaced by a heart-skipping smile. He looked truly splendid.

"You appear to be stuck." His expression turned curious and his voice held amusement. Yet underneath his cool, refined composure there simmered a dangerous, exciting energy.

She would not be intimidated. She raised her head in a show of daring. Rheda Kerrich did not frighten easily. Besides, the man wore the appearance of a gentleman, not the uniform of a Revenuer. Rheda usually found gentlemen easy to handle. Men rarely kept up with her sharp wit, and her intelligence baffled them. They could not tell if she was joking at their expense. It was enough to drive most away.

Fueled by this logic, she uttered, "Oh, well done. What great powers of deduction." He still did not move. "Do not just sit there. Get off your fine mount and help me move this barrel."

Her boldness hid the small tremors of fear pulsing through her blood. They were alone on a deserted road. She was now at the mercy of this stranger.

He dismounted in one graceful move. Standing, he stood head and shoulders above her. His broad shoulders were garbed in an expensive riding coat that looked like he'd slept in it, but the covering could not camouflage the muscled physique hidden beneath. The cut molded and enhanced. He radiated strength. This man was not a typical aristocratic fop.

She should be careful.

Her gaze dropped and took in his powerful thighs. She

followed them down to where they disappeared into knee-high boots, covered in a fine layer of dust. He must have ridden some distance. Where was this beautiful stranger from?

Her breath seemed to catch in her throat.

She glanced back to his face, held speechless for once in her life by the power of his beauty.

He finally spoke. "You are uncommonly rude to a person who has stopped to offer assistance." His tone implied hurt.

"You have been here several minutes," she said between clenched teeth, "and yet you still have not made a move to help."

He walked toward her. "How rude of me. I'm Rufus Knight, Viscount Strathmore, at your service," and he bowed low.

Rheda felt her stomach squirm, as if it were filled with wiggling worms. He might be worse than a Revenuer. She recognized the name. The Strathmores were prominent friends of Lord Hale. Rufus Knight was a favorite of his mother's, Lady Hale. Countless times she'd sat and listened to Lady Hale's indulgent tales of her godson, seemingly oblivious to the rakish exploits surrounding him in gossip of the worst kind. Viscount Strathmore's reputation preceded him. His appetite for sins of the flesh was known to be insatiable. He was a notorious womanizer, devoted to pleasure and seduction. He was like her father in that regard, and she'd learned to loathe rakes of his character early in her life.

Worse, Lord Strathmore's father died amid rumors of treason, so the *ton* kept the son at a distance. That must be tiring for him, because the rumor was he was looking for a pious young lady to become his wife. A woman who was well connected within Society and who would help dilute the scandal attached to the Strathmore name.

A woman so different from herself, Rheda felt a minuscule ounce of safety. Whatever happened here, he would do everything in his power not to end up betrothed to the likes of her.

Good. She doubted he was more determined than her in this matter. Wedlock was exactly that—a life under lock and key, figuratively speaking. Freedom curtailed. And that would not suit her at all. Marriage was not in her future.

Besides, she needn't worry about being disgraced. She had so little reputation left, one further strike would not alter her situation.

She drummed her fingers on the top of the barrel. Given the circumstances, it was best she did not inform him of who she was. Self-preservation kicked in. Her clothing would fool him anyway. He would assume she was a local farming wench, not the sister of a baron. She gave a silent prayer and hoped he was just passing through. She knew the village of Deal held little attraction for a man of his ilk.

So she decided to remain mute regarding her identity.

His gaze swept her ragged appearance. He gave a decidedly rakish smile. It was the reaction of a man who knew how to take advantage of the opportunities life presented. His eyes combed over her in an almost physical caress. "Come, what is your name, pretty wench."

She turned her head to look at the sea. Silence reigned for a moment before Rheda, growing impatient at her trapped state, swung around to issue a command for freedom, only to pause when observing the critical glint in his dark eyes. He was not happy at her refusal to give him her name. Nevertheless he approached the barrel and tested its weight.

"How is it that I find you in the middle of a field with a barrel, obviously full of something, brandy perhaps, and pinned against this oak tree?"

She struggled to form a reply that wouldn't sink her deeper into trouble. "Just unlucky, I guess." This time she could not hide her grimace.

"Don't be flippant. I can see you are in considerable pain. I'm here to help you."

Her mouth dried. Lord Strathmore's considered gaze roamed her person before he lowered his eyes to study the

heavy cask, obviously trying to work out how to move it without causing her additional harm.

He was very close. He smelled of sweat, leather, and dust, decidedly masculine. He glanced at her and caught her stare. Gloved fingertips gently brushed her hair off her cheek. She turned her head away, but not before a pleasant shiver swept down her back. He did own the most arresting eyes. They declared his interest was decidedly back on her. He was pressing his advantage. She held her breath and prayed his fingers would not roam elsewhere.

She blushed at the effect his proximity was having on her. She had thought him a big man when he sat upon his stallion, but standing next to her, she realized he was enormous, well over six feet and all muscle. He stood taller than Daniel, and her brother was considered a tall man.

He crouched down and gripped the barrel with two large hands. "I look forward to a reward for my services."

"A 'thank-you' will suffice."

His lips curved into a wicked grin. "Surely, rescuing a damsel in distress is worth more than mere words?"

She tried to calm her racing heart lest he see how his threat unsettled her. She needed to shift his thoughts in a different direction. "I do not have any coin on me."

He looked up at her. "You have very succulent lips. A kiss from them would be worth any amount of coin."

She pressed back against the tree. His eyes betrayed him. He was trying to distract her. He was purposely taking her mind off the pain to come.

"That is not funny." She scowled at him.

His laugh was rich and deep. And infectious.

"You think I am jesting," he replied.

She watched completely enthralled as he lifted the heavy cask pinning her legs. The muscles of his shoulders grouped and rippled under his tight coat as he set about moving the barrel. It was infuriating that it took him only one almighty heave, and she was free.

Blood rushed back into her numb legs. She gritted her teeth and held in the tears. Her legs buckled under the excruciating pain. She opened her mouth to scream. Instead she did something she had never done in her life.

She fainted dead away.

Rheda's eyes slowly flickered open, and she saw a canopy of blue sky above her. For several minutes, while she recovered her senses, she lay on the fragrant grass, enjoying the sunshine and the sensation of firm, strong hands expertly stroking her legs . . .

She bolted into a sitting position and tried to slap off the far-too-familiar hands.

"What do you think you are doing?" she forced out in a wobbly voice, her body heating with shame. She'd actually been taking pleasure in his touch. She tried to gather her legs to her chest, but his hands tightened around her ankles.

"I am merely trying to help the blood flow back into your limbs." He flashed a smile so roguish, it had Rheda nearly succumbing to his charm. Then he added, "It has been the most pleasant of tasks. You have extremely pretty legs."

Don't blush. Don't give him the satisfaction.

"Shall I continue?" Without waiting for a reply he slid his long, lean fingers up under her dress.

She followed their path with her eyes. She seemed frozen— his touch calming her into submission—much as her touch did with her horses. He stroked up her stocking-covered leg, the sensation very seductive. It was shockingly so, once his fingers met the bare skin of her thigh.

Rheda felt a sudden warmth pool in her stomach. She had never experienced such a purely primal, feminine reaction to a man's touch before. But then she'd never allowed any man such freedom with her person.

She dragged her gaze from his hands, up his broad chest and wide shoulders, onward past his perfectly tied cravat.

This man was too handsome for her own good. Like a poisonous eel, he looked harmless, but a touch could be deadly.

His eyes darkened, reminding her of the hot chocolate she'd drunk this morning. They locked with hers, causing heat to sear along her nerve endings, where previously she'd had no feeling at all.

"Your legs may experience some tingling once the circulation starts working properly."

Oh, she tingled all right.

"That is enough, thank you." He did not loosen his grip on her ankles. "My legs are perfectly fine."

"Now that I have freed you," he said in a voice as smooth as the fine French brandy she held in her barrel, "you will return the favor by helping me."

The hairs on her arms prickled. This could not be good. If he discovered her true identity, it would get back to Daniel. If that happened, Daniel would definitely put an end to her activities. She needed more time . . . Not only that, they could be in serious trouble, accused of participating in free trade.

His next words threw her off balance.

"You're very tempting, you know." His voice and the fire in his teasing eyes were having a similar seductive effect as the alcohol would have.

Who was she fooling? She'd been off balance the minute he'd gazed upon her.

"Your beauty cannot be disguised by these rags. I see someone has given you fine silk stockings, your lover perhaps. He must be a wealthy man."

"I have no lover."

Rheda could tell by the quirk of his brow that he did not believe her. A woman dressed as she was, with hidden silk stockings. No wonder he had jumped to the wrong conclusion.

She shook her head. "Besides, I had nothing to do with

the face God bestowed on me. It is not meant to entice you. I cannot help how I look."

He nodded. "No more than I can help wanting to glory in it."

With those husky words, he rose over her, slowly pressing her back into the fresh green grass. She felt every inch of his lean, hard body, and his masculine scent filled her nostrils. Rheda's body betrayed her, welcoming the feel of him; the aroma of sandalwood and virile man became a heady rush that enhanced all her senses.

His lips hovered by her ear as he ran his hand slowly up the inside of her leg. His fingers found the top of her thigh, and with a small cry, she pushed her hands against his shoulders and squirmed beneath him. She tried to twist away from his touch, but he captured her wrists in his other hand and thrust them on the ground above her head.

"Come now, do not play coy with me. You are old enough to know the games men and women play. I would give you great pleasure. I would satisfy you more than any of your other lovers."

She'd had no other lovers. How could she make him believe that?

Before she could respond, his lips found hers in a drugging kiss. The slight stubble around his chin was abrasive on her skin—Rheda decided she liked the feeling. He played with her lower lip, sucking it between his, gently nipping. It made her light-headed. His tongue probed the entrance to her mouth until she surrendered and opened to him. His tongue swept in, and a tremor rocked her. He tasted divine. Like the waves crashing on the rocks, something wild and wanton unlocked and broke free. She embraced the madness his kiss was unleashing within her.

She'd never experienced a kiss like it. With each heaving breath she could feel her breasts pushing against a solid wall of muscle, and to her horror, her nipples hardened. Her gasp formed a tangled knot in her throat. She could not speak.

She could only feel the heat of his hand burning her skin where he touched her, igniting bewildering forces in her blood.

Finally he drew back. "What is your name?" he murmured as he lightly tickled the back of her knee.

Rheda's brain spun. She could not give him her name; things had gone too far. She could barely think with his hand stroking her leg. Her heated skin turned maddeningly sensitive to his touch. It was humiliating to have one's body react wantonly at the mere touch of a stranger, even if he was the most attractive man she'd ever clapped eyes upon. She shivered and jerked involuntarily, the movement causing his muscled thigh to slip between her legs.

He flashed a smile full of sin and pressed his thigh against the most intimate part of her. Sizzling warmth flooded her lower body, making her burn with mortification. Her heart pounded in a frantic beat as she realized for the first time in her life she was aroused—aroused and infuriated.

"Do not . . . Get your hands off me."

Ignoring her words, Lord Strathmore's lips pressed lightly to her neck and he whispered, "Where did you get the barrel?"

Rheda froze at his words. The haze of frightening desire swirling around her vanished. This was not about a man wanting to pleasure a woman; he was trying to seduce her for information.

Why did he wish to know about the barrel? He was obviously not a Revenuer. Her eyes narrowed. To atone for his father's treason perhaps he was a government man. There had been an increase in patrols in the area. His Majesty was rumored to be annoyed at the smugglers. The king felt trading with the French was helping to line Napoleon's coffers.

She choked back her anger. Smuggling actually kept the king's own people fed. Most of the inhabitants of Deal would starve without the income from this illicit activity.

She stared back at Lord Strathmore, his handsome features

a blur. His head lay so close that his hair feathered disturbingly over her cheek.

Lord Strathmore hadn't really wanted her. His focus had been on the barrel. Why that annoyed her, she could not guess. She usually never welcomed the attention men gave her. And she attracted plenty of attention.

She would have to be careful. "Stop. Get off me."

He pressed closer. She stiffened in fright. She could feel his erection against her thigh. Perhaps this wasn't solely about interrogation.

He groaned. "You cannot mean that. If I replace my thigh"—he rubbed his leg familiarly against her mound—"with my hand, I'm sure I'll find you wet with your own need." He pushed his hips forward. "I know you can feel my desire for you."

She definitely felt it. It was hard to miss.

Rheda fought against her own longing, trying to deny she wanted to feel more. At the age of five and twenty, she'd seen and experienced more of life than most young ladies. Yet her station in life meant his current seduction would have consequences. Consequences he would not want to pay any more than she did. She was not naive. If he compromised her, he would be forgiven, she would not. Society's rules were devised by men, for men. Men like her hedonistic father.

She gave a small snort. The mess her father left upon his death meant she'd had little chance of doing what Society expected. Not if she'd wanted to save Tumsbury Cliff Manor for Daniel.

Lord Strathmore pulled her slightly off the ground and reached behind her. "Let's get rid of some of these clothes. I want you naked, skin to skin, when I take you."

Naked.

Naked! Take her . . .

She shook her head and began to struggle in earnest. This was a mistake. A dreadful mistake. He couldn't really want to

"take her" in an open field where anyone could stumble across them. Were all men pigs? Slaves to the animal hanging between their thighs?

However, he did seem to have forgotten about the barrel.

Her hands rose between them, to batter against his chest, forcing some space between their bodies.

"No. Don't. Please . . ."

At her word "please" he hesitated. Rheda held her breath, feeling her heart race with trepidation. With a man of Lord Strathmore's ilk, she may have already gone too far to appeal to his noble self. She could not rely on his honor, because he did not know her true identity.

Now he never could.

His face was disquietingly close to hers. She found herself transfixed by his mouth, a mouth she could still feel and taste.

God help her. She wanted him.

Rufus could see where her gaze rested. The feel of her eyes upon him . . . If anything, his desire for her grew. He was so hard, so aroused . . .

This woman was all softness and curves. She had an air about her that teased and confused—a combination of innocence and siren. Her beauty caught him in her web, and he could not break free. He had an overwhelming need to stake a claim on the wild gypsy woman lying panting in his arms.

After the amount of riding he'd done today, searching for any clues as to the area Dark Shadow used for his illegal activities, he would have thought sex was the last thing on his mind. His body obviously thought differently.

He had not been looking for a further dalliance. Lucy had been willing and very obliging. But the barrel meant he needed this woman. What better way to ensure her cooperation than seducing her, using pleasure to conquer any reluctance in revealing the source of her barrel.

He could take her, here and now. He saw it in her eyes. She wanted him. Why then did she hesitate?

Rufus's arms tightened around her. The flowery scent of her filled his nostrils. He inwardly cursed. He wanted her, but this wasn't about giving rein to his baser instincts. He needed information. Information about the origins of her barrel. With the utmost reluctance he tempered his desire.

The barrel could hold the key to his mission. A traitor was using a Kent smuggling operation as cover. His capture would help the war effort. The spy sending vital war intelligence to Napoleon had to be stopped.

When he'd rounded the bend in the road, the barrel was the first thing that had drawn his attention, after which he'd become enchanted at the sight of the golden-haired goddess prone against the tree. His hunger for her was growing, as was his admiration. She'd faced him with bravado, trapped. She would have been hurting, yet she faced him down like a tigress. But when she lay in a dead faint in his arms, he'd felt every soft sensuous curve.

A powerful, overwhelming desire swept through him again. He immediately pictured her silken tresses falling over his bare skin as she rode naked above him. However, at present, the most powerful aphrodisiac was the chance her seduction could lead him to Dark Shadow.

He frowned. If Dark Shadow was a down-on-his-luck noble, perhaps she'd been given the barrel—payment for services rendered. To have a woman of her beauty, he'd pay almost anything, and he was sure other men would, too.

His eyebrow rose. Perhaps that is what she was after. Why had she stopped him when he could tell the sensuous beauty before him was as aroused as he?

By the state of her drab dress, money was in short supply. He could pay her. He was certainly wealthy enough, and he'd paid for the pleasure of a woman's body numerous times before. In his line of work, working for the government, it was almost impossible to keep a mistress, so his liaisons were frequent and fleeting, often in exchange for money.

He shook his head to clear the desire clouding his judg-

ment. With iron-willed control, he set her away from him and forced his desires back into check.

She lowered her eyes, and with a flush staining her creamy skin, she began to straighten her clothes.

"Will you look at me, darling?" he managed.

She tossed her glorious mane of fiery-gold curls over her shoulder and gave him a mutinous look. He kept his tone disarming. "What has caused your sudden about-face? I know you were enjoying my attentions. When we are fully joined, flesh to heated flesh, I'll give you such pleasure your screams will be heard over the pounding surf."

She sat back on her heels, her eyes weary. "I don't doubt your skill as a lover, but I am not read—that is, I am not yours for the taking."

He smiled. "Perhaps an incentive is required. How remiss of me to expect to sample your bountiful favors when I have offered nothing in return."

Chapter 3

A frown stole over her poignant heart-shaped face. Lord Strathmore felt himself harden further. God he wanted her. He resisted the urge to push her down into the long grass and forget his troubles by sinking deep within her hot, welcoming body.

He couldn't help one further attempt at getting what he wanted—knowledge about the cask of brandy. He reached for her and pulled her back into his embrace. "Name your price. I am an extremely wealthy man, and I shall be very generous." He paused and gently kissed her lips. "Especially if you tell me about the barrel."

Rheda was beginning to hate the barrel.

She couldn't look away; there was something warm and tender in his eyes that seemed to be lulling her toward her own demise.

"How does five guineas sound?" He paused and ran his finger gently down her cheek, tracing the outline of her lips until they parted on a soft sigh. "I'll double it if you tell me where you found the barrel."

Her heart beat a wild pulse in her throat. A man just bartered for her as if she were a whore. She shouldn't be surprised. Her actions were deplorable. She'd let him touch her, kiss her . . . To her great shame, she longed to do more. With him. With this beautiful, dangerous rake.

Remember your mother.

Rheda twisted within his firm grip. "I am not for sale at any price, my lord." With her pride hurt she uttered, "Let me go."

His arms tightened. "Is the sum not enough? One hundred guineas?" She was shocked at the small fortune he'd offered, yet the purring quality of his husky voice quieted her alarm.

Vaguely Rheda realized she was letting him caress her again, stroking with hushed delicacy the column of her throat, her bare shoulder, her tingling breasts . . .

Slowly he bent his head, his lips following the path his fingers had taken, his soft caress sending desire shooting through her body. A tremor shook her as he tugged her bodice lower, deliberately exposing her breasts to his heated gaze and wicked tongue.

"Two hundred," he said, his voice husky with want, before his tongue played in a leisurely erotic dance on her skin.

Rheda came to her senses just in time. Just before his mouth latched on to her nipple. Just before she forgot everything except what this man could make her feel.

She struggled in his arms, trying desperately to pull out of his tight embrace.

"Don't be afraid, angel . . ."

She felt the soft brush of his breath on her ripe swells. If he suckled her she'd be lost, so she suddenly found her strength. Spying a heavy stick, she grabbed it and swung it at his head. It connected with a sickening thud, and he let her go. She fell backward on the grass as he struggled to his feet with a roar of injured pride.

"What the hell was that for?"

Rheda hid her fear, pulling up her bodice. She scowled up at him, refusing to let her own helplessness conquer her. "I am not for sale and you would not listen. You wouldn't unhand me." She lowered her voice. "Perhaps rape is the only way you can take a woman."

He stood staring down at her, his breath coming in ragged pants. "We both know it would not have been rape. Even now I can see the desire in your eyes."

"Yes—a desire to be left alone. Not to be molested by a brute stronger than me simply because he feels like it. Not all women are whores. Or is monetary incentive the only way you know how to get a woman?" She all but spat the words at him.

Shock flared in his eyes. He glared down at her, his rigid stance indicating how livid he was.

She followed his angry stare, only to gasp as she quickly lowered her skirts from where they were bunched around her waist, her legs exposed to his heated gaze.

He was breathing heavily. She could not quite meet his eyes. She had been enjoying his touch, his fingers' caress, and his lips' soft trail. Her eyes could not meet his knowing gaze; instead, they roamed downward and came to rest on the great cylindrical bulge in his trousers. He was still hard for her. She could not tear her gaze away.

"If you keep staring at my trousers like that, I'll think you are lying and you do in fact want me as I want you."

His words brought more heat to her cheeks.

"Are you going to put me out of my misery?" When he spoke, his voice was an intimate murmur designed to coax the deepest secrets from her. Her eyes were drawn back to his bulge. "I meant were you going to tell me about the barrel?" His voice grew heavy with sarcasm. "Unless you were thinking of some other way to end my obvious suffering. I wouldn't want to touch you again and be accused of rape."

She shook her head and looked away. With a strangled sigh, Rheda leaned back on her elbows and looked up into his ruggedly handsome face, trying to still the sparks of heat flaring in her veins. She had to tell him something. She knew from experience that a man of Lord Strathmore's fortitude would not leave her alone until he had his answer.

"We had a big storm pass through here a couple of nights

ago. I found it washed up on the beach this morning. It must have fallen off a ship. I thought I'd roll it home."

"On your own?"

"I couldn't risk leaving it. Someone else might take it. Selling the contents of this barrel could feed us for a month. Unfortunately, as I was rolling it, the barrel slipped off the road down this little slope. I managed to stop it from going over the cliff, but became pinned against this oak tree."

She kept her features blank as the lies rolled off her tongue. If Lord Strathmore was with the government he'd learn nothing from her. Smuggling was punishable by transportation to the colonies, but finding goods washed ashore after a storm was merely salvaging.

His voice became resolute and dropped an octave. "I do not think so; the barrel is not even wet." He dropped down to kneel on the grass beside her, making any idea of escape ludicrous. Besides, with his stallion there was no way she could outrun him. "Do I need to coax a better response from you?" He reached to cup her chin in his hands. He lowered his face until their lips almost met. "I ask again, where did you get it?"

Rheda swallowed her fear. "On the beach, my lord."

"You will tell me the truth. It wasn't in the water, was it? What beach? Where did you find it exactly?" His words flew at her with urgency.

She stammered, his nearness affecting her more than she liked. "I—I cannot remember exactly which beach, but it was near here. The cask is heavy, and I hadn't rolled it very far before I became pinned."

He eyed her wearily as if judging the truth of her words. Her heart began to pound as his eyes darkened from deep brown to almost black. He lifted one hand to stroke her hair as it lay flowing loose on the ground. In a low, deadly tone he said, "Perhaps I should summon the Revenuers and let them extract the truth from you since my methods of persuasion do not work."

Meg always told her to work with the devil you know. She would be wiser to place herself in this man's hands than let the Revenue men get her. But she seethed with indignation at having to beg. She crossed her fingers behind her back and lied. "Please, Lord Strathmore, I swear on my father's grave that I found it on the beach."

"If you tell me which beach, I shall not hand you over to the Revenue men. Do you know what would happen to you if I do? They'll likely not care about my being accused of rape."

She lowered her eyes. "I will tell you."

His hand continued to cup her chin, forcing her to look at him. "Well, I'm waiting." His eyes bored into hers. "Which beach?"

She chewed her bottom lip. Which beach should she pick? It would have to be Fraser's Landing. It was the only beach with a slope gentle enough for her to have rolled the barrel up it. Besides, it was a beach smugglers never used.

"I found the barrel on Fraser's Landing. It's not far from here. Do you know where it is?"

He gave a small nod—followed by such a devastating smile she wished him to Hades. A ruthless man should not own such a smile. It made remembering the danger he represented impossible.

"That wasn't so difficult, was it?" He studied her silently. "However, I will have your name." His tone was cajoling as if she were an errant child. She tried to conceal her annoyance.

"Why do you need to know my name?"

He responded with a crooked smile. "Do not be angry just because I have demanded the truth from you. I did free you. I want the name of the woman I am about to kiss," he added.

Rheda's eyebrows knitted together in a frown. "Your at-

tempt at seduction is getting tiresome. There will be no kiss; my simple thank-you should suffice."

She tested her legs and gingerly rose to her feet. She looked down on him still kneeling on the grass. Her breath caught in her throat; he looked as chiseled and flawless as a Greek sculpture that had recently been cleaned. Then he smiled, and he looked as exciting as his prancing stallion. Untamable. Unmanageable. Deliciously dangerous. The hairs on her arms rose. She'd never met a man like him.

His contented grin, like a cat that just swallowed a bucket of cream, sent her stomach tumbling. His smile was his most potent weapon. His lips full and inviting. He no doubt slayed many a woman with such a smile, and she had to dig her fingernails into her palm to keep from succumbing.

"I should go now. I need to get the barrel home before dusk."

"You are worried about the Revenue men. There is no need. I'll protect you." He rose to stand before her. Carefully, she stepped a little away, trying to tear her gaze from his powerful body, trying to put space between them.

He considered her for a minute, and she lowered her eyelashes to hide her resentment.

"I'll help you get the barrel home. I could use some rope and tie it to Caesar's saddle. We could drag the barrel along the road behind him." He indicated his impressive stallion. "It will be less tiring."

He seemed much focused on her barrel. She was reluctant to let him help her, but it would look suspicious if she did not. Would he think she had something else to hide? Right now she didn't need any government man, if he was one, poking his nose in her business.

Besides, she could not very well leave it abandoned here while she went in search of Daniel. Someone might take it, and then where would Meg and her children be?

Like a mouse facing a cat guarding some extremely invit-

ing cheese, she instinctively knew she could not trust him. What really prickled her skin was she should have thought of his suggested transport option herself, before leaving home. She would have avoided being caught.

When she made no reply, he raised his hand again to her cheek. "You have such lovely silken skin." Lord Strathmore's husky voice sounded deeper than before, too appealing, too seductive. His eyes gazed into hers as if he sought the Holy Grail rather than the source of a barrel. She could almost feel herself compelled to step forward and reveal the truth.

His thumb stroked her jaw, his touch lingering and provocative. She knew she should move, flee his disturbing nearness, yet she was held captive by the intensity of his gaze, by the raw, powerful masculinity emanating from him.

His knuckles brushed over her moist, swollen lips. Fiery sparks shot from his fingers to her skin. She shivered.

"Tell me you don't have a lover. Tell me you do not belong to anyone," he huskily said as he continued to stroke down her throat.

Still half-dazed, she frowned, his brows were lowered, his nostrils flared. He looked like his Thoroughbred, a stallion primed for a race, but held back at the gate. His presence emitted a magnetic field that brought the fine hairs on her body upright. Struggling to clear her head, she tried to make sense of his words—belong? What on earth did he mean? She clapped her hands to her cheeks. He thought her some man's mistress.

Chapter 4

His question irked her; it was so typically male. Women, by necessity, always belonged to some man. Either a father, a husband, or, as in her case, a brother. "Yes, my lord." She belonged by her younger brother's side, Daniel Kerrich, Baron de Winter, as an equal. She did not and never would "belong" to any man.

But Rheda would not dissuade him of his notion.

Regret dowsed the desire burning within his eyes. "A pity I had not met you sooner." The rasp in his voice continued his seduction. "Perhaps you'll soon tire of your protector. I am more than willing to offer for you. You are a beautiful woman, full of passion. A man would have to be in bedlam not to want a taste." He released her and stepped clear. "You still have not told me your name."

"I don't intend to, my lord."

He inclined his head. "Are you afraid of your protector finding out about our little interlude?"

She was. Daniel would challenge Lord Strathmore to a duel for the liberties he'd taken. Or worse, insist on marriage. She couldn't allow that since she'd encouraged him. "Perhaps," Rheda acknowledged breathlessly. She certainly wasn't about to inform him that his was the first kiss she'd ever experienced. Her body's response told her how good it was.

Lord Strathmore's sensuous lips drew taut at her words.

They stood watching each other, the tension skimming

around them, until he turned and whistled for Caesar. "Come, boy. We are duty bound to see the lady home. With her barrel."

He beckoned her toward his horse.

He finished tying the barrel with rope and hitching it to the saddle so that it dragged behind his stallion, then turned to look at her, his face a mask of seriousness. "If I were your protector you wouldn't need to lug barrels found on the beach to market. I would keep you in luxury beyond your wildest dreams."

She ignored his remark, unsure what to say. He could not possibly know she'd turned down a more honorable offer than his. One that would have helped her brother and given her more wealth and status than his casual proposition ever could.

Long ago she'd vowed never to be owned, even in marriage. Her father never valued her mother for anything. When her mother died, her father spent the rest of his life whoring, gambling, and drinking to excess. It was as if her mother had never existed.

So she'd made plans of her own. Plans that Lord Strathmore's stallion could well advance, if only she could—what was the term—borrow Caesar for a day or two. Suddenly she hoped Lord Strathmore, or rather Caesar, would be staying in Deal.

They walked in silence beside his horse. The sound of the barrel scraping over stones and holes in the dirt road filled the air. Their progress was slow. The cask couldn't be bounced too hard or it would break.

"Are you simply passing through Deal, Lord Strathmore?"

"Please, call me Rufus."

She pretended to be interested in her rescuer, but in reality she was scouting a very skilled eye over his Thoroughbred horse. Caesar would be perfect to breed with her two Arabian mares.

Her dream was to own the biggest horse stud in Kent. If

successful she'd be free of any male obligations, and she'd be able to help the villagers of Deal. Smuggling was a dangerous business, and it left far too many widows and orphans.

She would breed Anglo-Arabian horses to sell to the cavalry. The idea had come to her when she'd been given two Arabian mares by Prince Hammed. It was his suggestion to cross them with an English Thoroughbred.

With consternation, she admitted the only flaw in her plan was that she lacked the money to procure a Thoroughbred stallion. Daniel refused to even consider her plan. She eyed Caesar as if he was the pot of gold at the end of her rainbow.

With a jolt, she realized Lord Strathmore had asked her a question. She glanced about her. They were at the last crossroad before entering Deal.

She could not take him to her home, so she pointed left. Meg's cottage was at the edge of town, a few blocks back from the docks. The road on the right led back inland toward Hastingleigh Estate, the Earl of Hale's property.

"You have not been listening to a word I have said. You seem much taken with Caesar."

She smiled demurely. "It's just that I have never seen such a fine horse. Is he a Thoroughbred?"

"Yes, Caesar is a purebred. He is listed in the General Stud Book, and his sire's bloodline can be traced back to Godolphin Arabian—one of the first Arabian stallions ever brought to England."

She swallowed her excitement. Godolphin Arabian was one of the finest and oldest bloodlines. Any horse bred from one of his offspring would be worth a fortune.

"Caesar looks very frightening. Does he have a nasty temperament?"

Rufus turned and rubbed Caesar's nose. "He is very much like me, friendly and easygoing unless someone crosses him." The threat hung in the air disguised as a casual statement.

She ignored it.

"Do you let your wife ride him?" She caught her breath.

Rheda hadn't heard of any betrothal, but then she did not keep up with all the Society gossip. She was annoyed with herself for being interested in his reply. Why did she care if he was married? She'd tasted freedom, and she swore she'd never end up as chattel like her mother. Besides, at five and twenty she was already considered a spinster.

Lord Strathmore laughed out loud. "I am not married, and no I do not let anyone else ride him. Would becoming my mistress be more conducive now that you know I am not married? Is your current benefactor married?"

He'd got the completely wrong idea about her question. She'd asked about a wife to test Caesar's temperament. She could hardly "borrow" the stallion if he turned nasty on her. But like most men, Lord Strathmore assumed she was interested in him.

"My protector is not married. I only asked the question because it has been a dream of mine to ride a stallion such as this one day."

"Perhaps during my stay in Deal I could allow that."

Her pulse leaped. "You plan to stay in Deal? Do you have business here?"

"Not business, no. I'm visiting a family acquaintance, the Earl of Hale."

Rheda's heart sank. She should have known he would be staying with Christopher.

Just then Meg's door opened and four little terrors swarmed toward them. Caesar whinnied and stamped his feet at the sound of the children's squeals.

"Easy, boy." Lord Strathmore's voice was calm and soothing.

Meg stood in the doorway of her ramshackle cottage, concern etched on her face at the sight of Rheda and her companion.

Rheda hurried forward. "Meg. Look what I found on the beach. We should be able to sell the contents and feed the lit-

tle ones for a month." Luckily, Meg caught her warning look.

Her boys rolled the cask around the back of the cottage as soon as Lord Strathmore had untied the ropes. Once the cask had been stowed, the boys returned to admire the stallion.

Meg played her part beautifully. "That's a good day's work, Rhe. Won't you come in and have some tea now? Come on, you lot, leave the beast alone and come inside."

Rheda looked back at Lord Strathmore. He'd made no attempt to engage either woman in conversation. He simply stood holding Caesar's bridle with one hand and resting the other hand on one narrow hip, his powerful legs slightly spread, as if he stood on a heaving ship's deck riding out a storm.

Thankfully, he did not try to come nearer to the cottage. Yet she felt no relief. Rheda was certain she hadn't seen the last of the gorgeous viscount. She must not go near Hasting-leigh until Lord Strathmore had departed. Explaining that to Daniel without enlightening him to today's events would be difficult.

With a cool look, she tried to infer their acquaintance was over. "Thank you, my lord."

He blew her a kiss, his face alight with a mischievous grin. "Until we meet again, sweet *Rhe*." He could not hide his gloat over finally learning her name.

With sinking heart, she turned and stepped over the threshold of Meg's cottage. She'd have to put the word out around the village that they were not to give the viscount any information about a woman named Rhe.

She paused before closing the door. With dread she knew she'd be unlikely to stop a man like Lord Strathmore from ferreting out the information he required. His pockets were deep, and the villagers, if in dire circumstances, might betray her. With grim determination she decided she'd have to involve Dark Shadow. No one would cross the infamous

smuggler. If Dark Shadow called for silence, not a soul would talk.

She wasn't sure if Lord Strathmore was really interested in her, a woman he desired for a dalliance while he visited the area, or if he was actively after the source of her barrel.

She pressed her hand to her churning stomach. She closed the door on his handsome face, inwardly cursing how the day had eventuated. Once he'd visited Fraser's Landing, he'd know she'd lied.

She needed to learn more about Viscount Strathmore. What was he really seeking in Deal? She'd have to find out and quickly.

Rufus watched the door of the cottage close and let out his breath in a quiet rush. The encounter had been very enjoyable and quite fortuitous. Before he'd even settled in, he'd found evidence of smuggling and another beautiful local lass whom he could seduce for information. Rhe plainly knew more than Lucy. Rhe tried to hide it, but she was a terrible liar.

He shook his head, feeling amused, a self-mocking smile twisting his mouth. He'd felt Rhe's response in his arms, so she wasn't immune to his favors. He wasn't conceited. Females, no matter what class or age, consistently vied for his attentions.

He frowned. Why did she not want him to learn her identity? She had something to hide. *Don't get too excited.* Perhaps she was scared of her protector. He would have to ascertain his name and position. He'd win her eventually. His blood heated. He was going to enjoy this assignment.

He mounted Caesar and turned back to the crossroads. At least he had a place to start his search—Fraser's Landing. If the lead came to nothing, he hoped a wild gypsy girl with hair the color of dried wheat, sparkling emerald eyes, and a body made for sin would make such a search unnecessary. She knew something.

Luckily for him she was the perfect age to be experienced enough to make her seduction enjoyable. He would enjoy having the enchanting temptress beneath him, above him, any which way a man could take a woman. He shifted uncomfortably in the saddle. With a wry flex of his eyebrow, he admitted he desired her. Everything about her was profoundly sensual, from the silky softness of her hair, to her lickable creamy skin, to her slim thighs, firm yet soft, and those eyes . . .

A man could lose himself in those vibrant green eyes. He'd have to be careful. At least he knew her name—Rhe. Who the devil was she? It was clear she did not live at the cottage, although she pretended she did.

Perhaps she lived with her benefactor and was ashamed. Rufus's stomach clenched. Or her protector was very good in bed, hence her loyalty. Rufus had offered a hefty sum for the privilege of having her, yet she'd declined. Then again, perhaps she loved her protector. Something stabbed near his heart. He scoffed out loud. A kept woman couldn't afford the luxury of love. No, it had to be something else.

He tapped the end of his riding crop on his chin. She'd make a magnificent mistress. Pity he didn't plan to stay in Deal long enough to bother needing one. Right now he did not need a mistress; he needed information. However, Rhe might satisfy him in more ways than one. She'd make an excellent informant and a succulent bedmate.

Caesar, normally sure footed, missed a step. Pain shot through him, almost making him lose his seat. Riding a horse fully aroused was most uncomfortable. However, the pain was a timely reminder. His memory subtly shifted. Marguerite. Rufus tightened his grip on the reins. He'd been down this path before, and his colleague had paid with his life.

Women could be just as deadly, just as cunning, and just as brutal as any man.

Anger surged through him at the mere memory. Mar-

guerite's kisses had been the sweetest taste of sin. He would not be fooled again. Rhe might share his bed and enjoy his body, but he'd never let himself care for a woman who could be the enemy.

Rufus swore a low oath at his continuing discomfort. He may desire the wild gypsy woman called Rhe, but he would use her, gain his intelligence, and move on. He would treat her as the enemy until he achieved his goal. Only then would he care one way or the other whether she was innocent of any crime.

He pressed a hand to his side, remembering the pain resulting from Marguerite's stab wound. Guilty until proven innocent was now his motto. To lose himself in a beautiful woman and ignore her ability to deceive was a mistake he would not make a second time.

Nevertheless, it did not mean he could not enjoy the soft, curvaceous gypsy's charms. He just had to remember what the female sex was capable of—outside of bed sport.

So how could he find her again? He loved the thrill of the chase. He would locate the woman and seduce her. With grim determination, Rufus knew he'd find a way. He needed information and she had some. Still, there was no question that her lush loveliness entranced him.

This time he would not forget his mission. Not only did he have a job to do, this traitor was the key to untangling his father's disgrace. He would not rest until he'd cleared his father's name and restored the Strathmore honor. If that was at all possible.

He grinned. Despite his mission, he would enjoy a dalliance. No, not just a mere dalliance, he felt a restless aching need to possess her. He wanted the fascinating beauty in his bed regardless of what he could learn from her.

His eyes narrowed. No. The mission must come first. He'd waited more than twelve years. His own redemption hung on his success.

Damn. He knew his thoughts were false. The vixen had burrowed under his skin. He wanted her. And Rufus Knight, eighth Viscount Strathmore, always got what he wanted.

"Are you in trouble?" Meg asked as she made the boys sit at the small table in the middle of her cramped but clean cottage. Meg might not have much, but what she did have she looked after. Rheda could see her own reflection in the rickety polished table and chairs, and the ratty armchairs by the fire, although worn, showed not a speck of dust. "He certainly looks like trouble," Meg added. She placed the children's bowls of stew in front of the hungry younger lads and turned to offer Rheda a drink of fresh lemon.

Meg's face searched hers, filled with motherly concern. Rheda pushed her hair off her face. "I'm not sure. I could be."

"Who is he? He's a gentleman, obviously. That was prime horseflesh I saw." Meg's face broke into a smile. "And he was prime man as well. Handsome as a devil sent to tempt."

Rheda's face heated, and she couldn't hold Meg's gaze. "Lord Strathmore. He found me with the barrel and stopped to help. I'd become trapped against a tree. I'm just thankful he found me before the Revenue men." A shiver skittered down her back. The Revenuers had been trying to catch anyone with unstamped goods for months. She was in no doubt that Lord Strathmore had been correct when he said they'd use any means necessary to extract information from her. Her blood turned to ice imagining what could have happened.

"You can't keep doing this, Rhe. It's too dangerous. You have too much to lose if you are caught. Not like us village folk. You've done enough for this town. And you've all but saved Tumsbury Cliff Manor. Daniel's a grown man. Let him take over the burden of providing."

Rheda glanced over to the boys. "How can I stop? Most

of the neighboring widows rely on what Dark Shadow provides them in order to survive. What will happen to them? To their children?"

Meg's face tightened. "Maybe Daniel would continue to support them?" she asked, but it wasn't truly a question.

Rheda gave a short laugh. "Daniel is becoming like most men, despite my influence. I fear he's becoming blinded by the idea of a rich and influential barony. That's all he thinks about." Rheda hung her head. "Sometimes I despair of my own brother. He grows more like Father every day." In a whisper she added, "I don't think I could stand that."

Meg turned to the stove and began dishing out more stew. Hot and fragrant, it smelled divine. Rheda's stomach pinched reflexively. She watched Meg walk and slide the bowl in front of her eldest son, Connor. When she looked up, Meg was watching her.

"What of your other scheme? Over summer all the women could pool their cut. We can live off the fish we catch and vegetables we grow. Would that be enough for stud fees?"

"Who's going to do the fishing?" Rheda said with uncharacteristic sharpness. "Perhaps their husbands? Oh, wait. Their husbands have died at sea, or are in prison for smuggling, or they've simply walked out on them. Or mayhap they have a man who is one of the better ones," she added with a brittle smile. "The sort who gambles, and whores, and provides better for their fancy women than his children."

She grabbed the next bowl from Meg's hand and set it down a bit too hard on the table. Some slopped over the side. She and young Connor looked at each other.

"I could do the fishing. I'm old enough," he interjected.

Rheda forced a smile, patted his head, and turned back to the stove.

"Eat your meal and don't interrupt," Meg said gruffly. But she bent and kissed his head, proud of her son's offer.

"I have been beating the odds for over five years, Meg,"

Rheda said quietly, "and I will not stop now. Not for the Revenue men, nor fines, nor all the rest."

Meg paused in adding more stew into a bowl. "Not even if the coin involved in your smuggling ends up in Napoleon's coffers?"

Rheda hesitated, then shrugged her shoulders. "Incidental, and not my intent. That's why I only trade in goods which I sell for coin. In any event, when I get my horse stud started, I'll be helping the war effort. I'll supply our troops the finest cavalry horses and be done with smuggling." She tried to end on a triumphant note and smiled brightly. "I just need a bit more time."

"That's what you're running out of. The government's determined to stem smuggling. And you know what they'll do to you if you're caught?"

Rheda nodded and looked away, into the bubbling pot. Yes, she knew. Prison. Or if she was really unlucky—transportation.

Meg shoved a bowl filled with stew into Rheda's cupped hands. The broth inside was warm, but Meg's next words chilled her. "There's been news, Rhe. They're stepping up their patrols of the beaches. There will be Revenue men in every port, on every beach. Any time. You need to find a way out. Now."

She looked out the window, down the path to where she'd last seen Lord Strathmore. Was her hunch right? Was he a government man? She cupped the bowl tighter, so that the warmth started to chase away the chill seeping through her bones. Whether he was or wasn't, he was still trouble. Or maybe he was just what she needed. Her brain began whirling with ideas. "I might just have found a way," she murmured.

The sound of the boys slurping their food and the crackle of the stove were the only sounds in the stuffy room. Rheda silently ate her stew, all the while thinking up her grand plan.

Glancing at Meg she stated, "I only need a few more months. I'm quitting at the end of summer. I should have enough stores by then to carry everyone until I sell the first foal."

Meg's face screwed up. "Foals? What foals? I thought you couldn't afford a stallion?"

Rheda moved to hug Meg good-bye. "I don't, but Lord Strathmore may come in useful there. Or at least his stallion."

Meg pushed her away. "I don't like that look on your face. It means trouble. What are you planning? You can hardly ask to borrow his horse when you've just pretended you're someone you're not."

She slid Meg a sly smile and made her way to the door, her shoulders straight, her step light. "Who said I had to ask?"

"Lordy," Meg said as if in prayer, "you're inviting trouble."

Chapter 5

Davy Appleton hurriedly picked up the line holding his fish. He didn't wait to clean it. He knew his mother would worry unduly if he was late home. He'd stayed out too long in his rowboat, but the fish took so long to bite in the hot weather that he'd had to wait until almost sunset to get a bite. He was pleased with his catch. He'd caught a large snapper, and now his little sister, Sassy, wouldn't have to go hungry tonight.

He glanced toward the dimming sky. The sun was about to set. He hated having to pass Jacob's Point in the dark. The knowledge that Jacob's ghost haunted the rocky outcrop sent shivers down his spine.

Perhaps he'd be better to cut through Harding's Wood.

He nodded to himself. Yes, the woods, though dark, would be preferable to a ghost. What dangers could possibly lurk in the woods? Nothing that could hurt a boy of almost twelve.

As he made his way hurriedly along the woodland track, an owl hooting to his right comforted him. He was not alone.

His stomach rumbled and his mouth watered at the thought of the fish filling their bellies tonight.

So engrossed in images of the feast they would eat, he did not hear the deft footsteps approaching swiftly through the encroaching darkness.

Before he was aware he had company, a gloved hand covered his mouth and he was lifted off his feet, his fish falling unheeded to the forest floor.

No, unfortunately, he was not alone.

Chapter 6

"I am ill, Daniel. Please close the door on your way out and leave me alone." Rheda lay in bed, propped up on a huge array of pillows, feigning ill health. There was no way she was going to Lord Hale's dinner party this evening. She had another task to complete. Her mares, Desert Rose and White Lily, were in season.

Ignoring her, Daniel entered her bedchamber and strode toward the bed. "You cannot be ill. You have never been sick a day in your life." Daniel swept a critical eye over her. "What's wrong with you?" His eyes narrowed and his hands went to his hips. She hated it when men used such an arrogant, intimidating stance. "Are you trying to avoid Lord Hale? I cannot understand you, Rhe. Christopher stood by you through the scandal, and has offered for you since. You owe him some respect, and ignoring his invitation is rude."

Rheda dramatically threw an arm over her eyes as if the light hurt them. "Lady Hale sent the invitation, not her son. Christopher's a bumbling idiot. Lovable, but such a bore. All he is interested in is hunting and fishing. He cares nothing for the villagers of Deal."

Daniel had the decency to blush. "But you'd be safe. We'd be safe. Provided for. Even with the scandal hanging over you, you know he'd still marry you."

"That's because he's too dim-witted to believe it. Sorry, that was uncalled for. I didn't mean it." She sighed. "Anyway,

I am not trying to avoid Lord Hale." This at least was true. It was the guest of honor she wished to avoid, Lord Strathmore. The mere thought of his name sent shame searing through her body and set her pulse fluttering.

"Then why can't you accompany me and lend your support? It's been a long time since the earl offered you his hand in marriage. I am sure he has all but forgotten your refusal. The awkwardness has long since passed."

She hadn't told Daniel about her encounter with the sinfully handsome Lord Strathmore four days ago, nor did she intend to. Her assumption that Lord Strathmore would look for her had been correct. So far, by threatening the mere name, "Dark Shadow," she'd managed to stop any tittle-tattle. The gypsy woman named Rhe remained a mystery to the viscount, and she wanted it to remain that way.

"I am truly sorry, Daniel. It's my monthly courses. Please go without me."

A pained look flashed across Daniel's face.

He was a handsome boy with features similar to hers, although his hair was much darker, a rich chestnut brown. She frowned. Rather like Lord Strathmore's. Goodness, why did he keep popping into her head?

She swept her eyes over her brother. At almost nineteen Daniel was still really a boy. His looks and title had the local girls in a swoon. However, his ability to find a suitable match would be greatly disadvantaged if she couldn't inflate the family coffers. Neither one of them bore any blame for their impoverished state.

Daniel originally had no idea how Rheda kept the creditors at bay, and by the time he did it was too late. He allowed her to continue only because he needed the extra money to restore the estate to its former glory. She had to give him a large portion of her earnings. Daniel was determined to rejoin Society. Once he achieved his goal he'd close her down without blinking an eye. What she needed was her horse stud profitable by then.

She loved Daniel dearly. She'd been more like a mother to him because he'd never known his own.

Rheda had been left to raise him when their mother died in childbirth—his birth. Their father took no interest in either of his offspring, too intent on drinking, whoring, and gambling.

Their family had never been affluent, but at seventeen, after their father's death, she was stunned to learn the extent of their debts. It appeared the late baron bestowed more money on his mistresses than on his children. They were certainly better provided for.

Since then Rheda had been determined to protect Daniel's inheritance. She'd worked hard, and with the help of "Dark Shadow" had managed to pay off her father's debts and maintain Tumsbury Cliff Manor in a reasonable state of repair.

Daniel bent and placed a kiss on her cheek. "Very well, I shall offer your apologies. I'll miss having you by my side."

She ruffled his hair. "You are such a liar. I know Lady Umbridge is also a guest at Hastingleigh. You know scandal surrounds the beautiful widow. She's renowned for her sexual prowess. I expect that like most young bucks you're itching to make her acquaintance."

"Rheda, you of all people know not all scandal is true. Besides, you should not know of such things," Daniel scolded, his face a mask of brotherly outrage.

"Humph. I am almost six years older than you, Daniel. Stop treating me like a child. I am a grown woman."

"An unmarried woman of advanced age. I begin to despair for you, Rhe."

She gritted her teeth and tried to hold on to her temper. Marriage was not for her. Her father had taught her that in this world of unreliable men, a wise woman dared depend only upon herself.

She wouldn't allow this argument with Daniel tonight. She needed him to leave as soon as possible if she was to get

the horses over to Hastingleigh, mate them with Caesar, and have them back home before dawn. This was not the time for an argument about her lack of matrimonial prospects.

She sighed. "Just go and have a good time."

"She's not interested in me anyway," Daniel sulked. "It's Lord Strathmore she's after. Why else would she come all the way to Deal?"

Why indeed. With a pain in the vicinity of her chest, Rheda acknowledged it *was* the barrel Lord Strathmore had been interested in all along. He'd hardly need a dalliance with a lowly maid when he could sample Lady Umbridge's delights. She thumped her pillow. Lady Umbridge could have him; all Rheda needed was his stallion.

Daniel halted at the door. "I'd best alert Cook to the fact we'll have a visitor tomorrow. You know Lady Hale will call once she hears you are unwell. She still has hopes you'll marry Christopher. She thinks you and her son are well matched. Considering your lack of dowry and your advanced years, it is a fine offer and one you should be grateful for." Daniel shook his head. "I'll never understand why you won't." Without waiting for her usual reply, he simply closed the door.

Rheda waited until Daniel left the house before throwing back the covers and racing for her wardrobe. She pulled out a pair of Daniel's old trousers; they fitted perfectly around her waist, although they were still a little long in the leg. She bent and rolled the legs up. Next, she slid a shirt over her chemise. She left off her corset, horrible thing, and finally added Daniel's old jacket. She tied her hair up in a knot at the back of her head and donned one of Daniel's caps. Having a younger brother was, on occasion, very convenient.

Within fifteen breathless minutes she was at the stables. Jamieson, the one man she could not do without, was waiting for her with the two mares saddled. He had been her mother's head gardener and now was Daniel's butler, valet, and right-hand man. The estate would have fallen to pieces

without Jamieson and his wife, Penny. They'd remained at Tumsbury Manor when things had become precarious and helped her set up "Dark Shadow" to keep them afloat. He was the one man she trusted.

"Is everything ready?"

Jamieson cocked his head conspiratorially. "It could not have gone any smoother. I gave two casks of our finest brandy stock to Ted, Lord Hale's head groom. Ted told Lord Strathmore he'd have to corral Caesar in the back paddock because there was a mare in heat in the stables. Caesar will be far enough away from the house so no one should hear the noise. We won't be disturbed."

The night was clear and the gibbous moon shone brightly. They'd have plenty of light to enact their plan. Rheda refused to acknowledge the pangs of guilt knotting her stomach. What the arrogant viscount didn't know, well . . . It was his fault for being so casual with his prize stallion. She planned to "borrow" his stallion for the evening, and as many evenings as she could over the next week, to ensure her mares were impregnated. Caesar could well be the resurrection of her dreams, if not her family's reputation, and support the women and children of Deal. With the stallion's offspring, she could begin building her horse stud. The money she'd make off two foals of Caesar's lineage would allow her to buy further stud fees and more mares.

Desperate times call for desperate measures. Her mares were in heat. She'd never been afraid to take a risk. Lord Strathmore's visit, while annoying, couldn't have come at a more opportune time.

They rode the mares the two miles to Hastingleigh Hall. They stopped outside the paddock to unsaddle the mares and to tie up their tails. Mating horses was a tricky business. If her two mares weren't impressed with Caesar, there could be a lot of kicking and biting. She wondered if her ladies would accept the impressive stallion. If not, they'd try again tomorrow night. She didn't want any of the horses hurt. Depend-

ing on Caesar's temperament, this could turn very nasty, very quickly.

Already Caesar had their scent. The mares were giving tiny whinnies of welcome as the huge stallion pranced along the fence line, rearing on his hind legs and tossing his head, nostrils flared, eyes glazed and slightly wild. The sight of the magnificent beast held Rheda immobile for a heartbeat, until she realized they'd best get the mares in the corral before Caesar broke the fence down.

For a woman starting her fourth decade of life, Lady Umbridge was still beautiful enough to have any man wanting to rise to the occasion. For a healthy, red-blooded male in need of a woman, she was indeed tempting. Lady Umbridge, seated on Rufus's left, would tempt a saint into sinning.

"I have such a sense of déjà vu," she cooed. "The last time I sat at this dinner table, I was a very young eighteen-year-old newlywed. I was sitting next to the handsome Lord Strathmore then as well."

Not Rufus. It had been his late father.

Her low throaty voice continued, "I have not had the pleasure of spending enough time with you. Having known your father I am sure we could become firm friends. If given the right incentive."

She let him know what incentive she meant. Her leg pressed his beneath the table.

Rufus tried to ignore the fact that since her arrival yesterday, Lady Umbridge had been intimating that she'd come to Kent for more than taking the country air. She was on the hunt and she wasn't after a fox. She'd set her sights on sharing his bed.

There were three reasons the sultry widow did not stir his ardor, despite her creamy skin and perfect complexion.

First, she was far too obvious, and like any hot-blooded male, Rufus excelled in the thrill of the chase. Second, she had committed the ultimate sin and mentioned his father.

His father's last deed before he died had led to the family's ruin, and Rufus did not need reminding of it. And last, she was the current paramour of Stephen, Lord Worthington, his good friend and co-spymaster.

One did not encroach on another man's property unless he'd either finished with said property or one was mad with desire. Currently, the only woman driving Rufus mad was a fair-haired gypsy called Rhe. A woman, who, it appeared, was a ghost.

Lady Umbridge leveled hard blue eyes on him. "Of course your father shot himself the very next day. I do hope history doesn't repeat itself. It would be rather a waste." And her hand found his thigh.

He reached under the table and removed her hand. "Do not fret. I'll not be shooting myself tomorrow." His steely gaze sent a clear message of his disinterest.

Ignoring her flushed face, he turned his attention to the young man directly across the table from him. Baron de Winter had been staring at Lady Umbridge as if he wanted her to become the next course.

That did not bother him. In fact, if Stephen could pawn Lady Umbridge off on this green-behind-the-ears pup all the better.

His eyes narrowed and he took another sip of his red wine. He knew this lad. He looked very familiar. Where had they met before? He could not for the life of him place the baron. He almost never forgot a face or a name. In his line of work, it paid not to. Never mind. He'd corner him after dinner when the gentleman retired.

He speculated on the empty place at the table beside Lord Hale. Turning to their hostess seated on his right, Lady Helen Hale, Christopher's mother, he asked, "We appear to be missing someone. I hope they're not indisposed."

"How astute of you to notice. Yes, Miss Kerrich, the baron's sister. She is unwell, I have been told, although I am assured it's nothing serious." She focused her gaze on the

baron and called, "Daniel, you do promise me your sister is not seriously ill. I am quite sure Christopher would send for the doctor if needed."

The baron's face colored. "There is absolutely no need Lady Hale. Rheda is simply indisposed."

"Well, I shall visit her tomorrow and ensure for myself that all is well."

Rheda?

Rufus almost choked on his mouthful. Was Rhe short for Rheda? He shook his head and took another sip of his wine, trying to halt his coughing. No, it could not be. But the proof was sitting across the table from him. Why had he not noticed it from the start? The baron's hair was darker than Rhe—Rheda's, but the features of his face and the deep green of his eyes gave her identity away.

No wonder Rufus had been unable to find her. He'd been looking in all the wrong places. He cringed at the realization he'd almost seduced a lady. But it added to the puzzle. What on earth had she been doing with that barrel?

Lady Umbridge spitefully added softly in his ear, "I suspect she's too embarrassed to show her face at Lord Hale's table in front of polite society. He supposedly proposed to her."

Rufus wasn't at all surprised. Miss Kerrich was a beauty any man would desire. Lord Hale wasn't the brightest pumpkin in the patch, and although handsome, his lack of intelligent conversation and his portly body did not endear him to the ladies. Even with his wealth, he was not inundated with marriage prospects. Keeping his question casual he asked, "But they never married?"

Lady Umbridge smiled conspiratorially, warming to her story. "I believe Lord Hale was gentleman enough to say she had refused him. However, the gossip was he withdrew his proposal once the scandal became known."

Rufus's eyebrow rose. "There was a scandal?"

"Oh, yes. A young Arab prince, Sultan Hammed, was vis-

iting here with his lordship. Miss Kerrich struck up quite a friendship with the prince and his sister. On the prince's return home, he sent her two beautiful Arabian mares. She did not return them. Everyone assumed they were payment for services rendered."

His pulse quickened at the word *scandal*. Miss Kerrich might be more experienced than he'd first thought. She might even be open to his seduction. She certainly seemed enthusiastic when he'd kissed her.

He sighed into his glass. He needed to be sure. She was the baron's sister. He could hardly compromise her if she was indeed a virgin. He did not wish to end up leg shackled—especially to a woman so inappropriate. Restoring the Strathmore good name came first. And when he had achieved that, he wasn't about to tarnish the image by marrying a woman who acted like a hellion and was surrounded by scandal.

Besides, his bride was already picked out. A demure, respectable woman, Lady Clare Browning, a friend of his sister. Clare's father, the Marquis of Lee, needed money and he was prepared to overlook the scandal attached to the Strathmore name in order to get it.

Clare was a woman who would not embroil the Strathmore name in further disgrace. Although there was no formal understanding between them, the marquis expected Rufus to offer for her.

His gut clenched at the thought. As with most of his life, due to his father's treason he was left to pay the price. A marriage to a mouse of a woman who couldn't even look him in the eye. How he'd ever get her with child he shuddered to think. If he was free to choose a wife, regardless of consequences, she would not be his choice.

Since when had he ever had the luxury of free will?

At the end of dinner, while the men were enjoying their port and cigars, Rufus moved across to the baron. "Please

pass on my sympathies to your sister, Lord de Winter. I had the pleasure of making her acquaintance."

He watched a frown play across the young man's face. "Did you? She did not mention it."

"The meeting was not of significance. She merely pointed me in the direction of Hastingleigh." A small lie but far better than the truth.

"Was she out riding Desert Rose, one of her Arabian mares? I'm surprised she did not pester you into borrowing your fine stallion. Caesar's a legend—Godolphin Arabian stock. She has dreams of breeding Anglo-Arabian horses for the cavalry."

Rufus's mood darkened. Light flashed in his brain. Mares? So, it was Caesar she had been taken with. He thought she'd been afraid of his steed, but she'd been assessing his horse's character. His pride stung. It wasn't often he had to compete with his stallion for a lady's attentions.

"Breeding horses? She sounds a remarkable young woman." Rufus did not have the heart to tell Daniel he had found her running around the countryside with illegal contraband, dressed as a gypsy. Nor that he had kissed her senseless, taken liberties with her person, and wanted more.

Much more.

Lord Hale joined the conversation. "She is quite right of course. They would make fine cavalry horses, and with the war, we need as many horses as we can get." He turned to address Rufus. "Speaking of excellent horse flesh, by Jove, for such an expensive steed, you are remarkably unconcerned with his care. Why is he not in the stable? Ted has turned him loose in the back paddock."

Rufus knew his smile did not reach his eyes, and he felt his jaw tighten. "At this time of year I was concerned you may have had mares in your stable. If they were in heat it could cause quite a mess."

Lord Hale gave a jolly laugh. "I never keep the mares sta-

bled over summer for that very reason. No, they are at the other end of my estate, well away from the stable and any stallions I may corral in the back paddock. The stable contains only two geldings, no threat to your prize stallion."

The muscles across Rufus's shoulders tightened. Annoyance coursed through his body, quickly followed by anger. "Are you sure? I could have sworn someone told me the stables contained mares." The head groomsman had told him so.

Lord Hale frowned. "I hope not. Ted, my head groom, is too experienced to make that mistake, especially when I was due to have guests arriving." Lord Hale paused for a moment. "Yes, I am sure Ted knew not to house any mares, because I'd informed him you were bringing Caesar."

Like the mechanism of his expensive pocket watch, Rufus's mind silently ticked. What was going on? Ted had definitely told him there were mares in the stable.

Still, Rufus gave him the benefit of the doubt. "Perhaps Ted thought Miss Kerrich's carriage might be pulled by her mares."

The baron laughed. "Yes, that is quite likely knowing my sister. She'd love any excuse to get her mares within close proximity to Caesar and let nature take its course. Her mares are in heat."

The cogs in his brain came to a grinding halt. He could not believe she would be that audacious. The conniving little . . . he could not think of words bad enough to do her justice. Sick? He would bet his life she wasn't sick. She had planned this evening almost as well as Wellington planned his frontal assaults against Napoleon.

He knew exactly where Miss Rheda Kerrich was, and it was not on her sickbed. He would wager his whole estate she was in the paddock with Caesar and her two mares. Stealing what rightly belonged to him—Caesar's lineage.

The room was suddenly too hot. Hell, he was not about

to let some hoyden make a fool of him. Besides, if he could catch her thieving, he would have leverage. She would have to tell him about the barrel. And more . . .

He tugged at his cuffs. Stephen, watching from across the room, understood the signal and casually strolled toward them.

"It is uncommonly warm this evening, Lord Strathmore. Could I interest you in a stroll in the garden? I have news from your mother that I should deliver as promised."

Rufus smiled at the group of men. "If you will excuse us, gentlemen." The two men bowed and took their leave.

Together they walked down the terrace and into the garden. As soon as they were out of view, Rufus turned and strode purposefully through the rose garden, down the walled orchard, toward the back paddock.

"Are you going to tell me what this is all about?" Stephen asked, trying to keep up.

"Remember the gypsy I thought could lead us to Dark Shadow? It turns out she is not a gypsy at all. She is Miss Rheda Kerrich, the baron's sister."

"So you have opportuned a lady. How distasteful." Stephen laughed. "Don't look at me with that thunderous expression. Seduction is now out of the question. We will simply have to look elsewhere for a way to gain the information we require."

Rufus could barely speak his anger was so intense. "Let's not be so hasty. I've done some investigating in the few days I have been here. The baron's father left the estate bankrupt. Yet, since the age of only seventeen, on her own, she has managed to hold off the creditors. How is that do you think?"

"You think she's involved in smuggling? Highly unlikely. Besides, Dark Shadow's organization is one of the most feared in all of Kent. A woman? Surely not."

"Beneath every powerful man, there usually lies a woman." Rufus doubled his pace. "She could be his mistress."

"Slow down. Where are we rushing off to, and what has prickled your skin tonight?"

"I believe, having seen something of Miss Kerrich's character, that she's capable of almost anything. She is not some young ballroom chit." Rufus still remembered the feel of her womanly curves in his arms. He'd dreamed last night. Reliving her response to his kisses. Her wild abandonment in his dreams—and the fact she was closer to thirty than twenty—indicated she was not a normal simpering virginal miss. "The minx has Caesar in the corral so she can secretly mate her Arabian mares with him. She has planned it all."

Stephen laughed appreciatively. "Brilliant. You would be unlikely to look for Caesar until morning. What are you so upset about? I am sure Caesar will enjoy the task."

Rufus swung around to face his friend. "For one thing she could get herself killed. Have you ever seen horses mating? If Caesar does not impress the mares, he will have the stuffing kicked out of him. Alternatively, if he takes a real shine to the mares and they deny him, God help anyone who tries to get in his way. Mating horses is not a job for the inexperienced or a woman. You need huge reserves of strength to maintain control."

"You are simply peeved because she fooled you. I have never known a woman who wanted your horse more than you. This evening is getting interesting. I am looking forward to meeting Miss Kerrich."

Caesar was being the perfect gentleman. The mares, however, were being perfect teases.

White Lily, after much fanfare, had finally consented to Caesar's ministrations. Caesar was not new to his task, and Jamieson did not even have to hold him steady. Desert Rose, however, was a different story. The first time the mare was mounted, she tried to twist sideways, almost tearing Rheda's arms from their sockets. But she managed to hold her still,

and the second mounting ended successfully, with Caesar giving one final victorious grunt.

She walked Desert Rose around the corral as she wiped the sweat from her eyes. "How long do we rest him before we give White Lily another try?" she called to Jamieson.

Jamieson scratched his head. "I'm not sure White Lily's ready. She does not seem particularly impressed by Caesar."

Rheda handed Desert Rose to Jamieson, approached the panting stallion, and rubbed his nose. "He's gorgeous, aren't you, boy? Who wouldn't be impressed by those strong shoulders and lean, powerful legs?"

"Most women are thoroughly impressed with my physique, thank you for your praise," an enraged male voice heralded from the shadows. "Caesar, here."

On hearing his master's deep, commanding, baritone voice, the stallion quickly trotted across the corral to his side.

She could sense Rufus at the edge of the field. The humid, still air, suddenly swirling with his presence. His raw virility set her pulse thudding, even from a distance.

He'd found her. Casting about in desperation for a quick escape, she realized fleeing was useless. Once Rufus reentered the house, everyone would know she had been here. Due to the story of how she came by them, her horses were infamous.

She'd have to brazen it out. Pretend this was nothing out of the ordinary, and act as if she had every right to have her horses in this field.

Even so, panic rose up swiftly, instinct readying her to flee as two men advanced into the paddock. They were dressed all in black, the look threatening in the moonlight. Her heart accelerated as she recognized the taller, broader physique, but even then she could not hold her tongue.

Irritation dribbled down her back like sweat. Dropping her voice to a lower octave and crossing her fingers behind her back, she responded, "There's nothing interesting going on here, my lords. Simply mating some of Lord Hale's horses."

His forceful gaze swept over Jamieson and her, trying to ascertain their identities. A shiver of fear sliced her insides. Damn the moon. She prayed it was dark enough, and her disguise good enough, that he would not know who she was. Perhaps he would think her one of Lord Hale's stable boys.

She ground her teeth in resignation. What was the worst that could happen? He was too late; the deed had been done, with one horse anyway.

Eyes sharp as flint slashed in her direction, and she took a step back.

Ignoring her, Lord Strathmore bent to study his horse. "Have you been having an enjoyable evening, Caesar? I hope you have not let the Strathmore name down and you have performed appropriately."

In a voice she hoped mirrored a young boy's she said, "Actually we were debating if he had enough stamina to service the second filly." Perhaps Lord Strathmore would think her being here, with his stallion, was a genuine mistake if she continued as if she'd done nothing wrong.

"I think you will find Strathmore males are perfectly capable of pleasuring more than one female in one night."

A chuckle escaped from his companion while Jamieson gave a discreet cough.

Rheda, thankful for what little darkness the moon provided, simply blushed, his insinuation not lost on her.

Lord Strathmore approached until he towered over her, menace oozing from every pore. Rheda thought the effect was somewhat spoiled because he looked thoroughly enticing with his white ruffled shirt accentuating the black of his jacket. "We shall have to discuss how you are going to repay me for Caesar's services—Miss Kerrich—Miss Rheda Kerrich—Rhe."

Chapter 7

Rheda closed her eyes, knowing in the marrow of her bones that Lord Strathmore was the sort of man who would not stop until he got what he wanted, and now he had leverage.

"Bloody hell," she muttered. He'd not been fooled for a minute. She dropped her head in defeat. Not only had he found out who she was, he had caught her in the act, stealing from him, stealing his stallion's seed.

"Yes, you can say that again, bloody hell. Although such language from the mouth of a lady." Lord Strathmore turned and glared at Jamieson. His voice, sounding more dark and dangerous, said, "At least you were not stupid enough to try this on your own."

"How on earth did you know what I was up to?"

"Your brother and Lord Hale."

Her mouth gaped. She looked up at Lord Strathmore and then across to Jamieson. The ground seemed to pitch and roll as if she had drunk to much brandy. "My brother knows?"

"Not exactly. I guessed who you were and what you were up to from their comments this evening. It was not hard to put it all together."

Her hands unclenched as she felt the ground revert to level, relief sweeping over her. Daniel must never know. He had threatened to sell her mares once before when she had

been caught riding White Lily half undressed in the sea. The swim had not been Daniel's concern; his concern was the fact she'd been indecent. Unclothed for all to see.

But she was swimming at their secret cove. The cove could not be reached except by the private path down through the cliffs. The path was well hidden on de Winter land, camouflaged as a steep cliff face; the beach below was impossible to see. It had always been her and Daniel's private place.

She had swum there almost every day of her life, thousands of times. Only this time Daniel decided to join her, without telling her, and he'd brought a visitor. Luckily, it was only Lord Hale, and he seemed more amused than embarrassed by her nakedness. Lord Hale always indulged her "quaintness," as he called it.

Daniel, on the other hand, had been livid. More than livid. She'd thought he was going to explode with rage. To this day he did not let her forget it.

If her brother got wind of what she had done tonight he might finally do as he'd threatened and sell her mares, even though the horses had been gifted to her. Daniel, being young and the baron, was trying to find his feet in his manhood. He was getting very tiresome of late, trying to take over from her and be head of the household. At the moment, he was beginning to think he controlled and owned everything on the estate, including her mares. Being a woman was so unfair.

Tonight's escapade might just push Daniel past reason. His unconventional, willful sister had again drawn attention to herself and tarnished the de Winter name—that was how Daniel would see it anyway.

She glared up at the one man who had ruined everything. Why couldn't he have stayed in the house with the other guests? How she hated his calm, smug face. What annoyed her even more was that his male beauty still made her blood gallop through her veins.

"What do you plan to do now?"

Wryly, his lordship answered, "I'll think of something."

"I don't have any money."

"I am well aware of that. If you had money you would have simply asked to buy Caesar's services instead of stealing them." He paused and gave her a sensual look that started a flicker of heat smoldering in the pit of her stomach. "As I recall, you had something infinitely more valuable to offer the last time you owed me payment for a service rendered."

She gasped—their kiss. "How dare you!"

"I dare! How dare you, helping yourself to Caesar? He could have been hurt by your mares. Do you know what you would have owed me then? Being my mistress for a year would not even begin to cover the cost."

Jamieson stepped forward. "Now see here. Lord or no lord, you will not speak to Miss Kerrich that way."

Lord Strathmore ignored him. "What do you think your brother will say about all this?"

Her hands came to her hips. "I know what he would say to your suggested payment. It would be pistols at dawn."

"Are you sure? If you were my sister, I could not wait to get you off my hands. Your brother should have seen you married off years ago. Why are you not at home with babes at breast? No takers for a hoyden like you?"

"For your information, you imbecile, I have had plenty of offers. I'm simply not stupid enough to let any man gain control over me."

"You certainly need a firm hand."

"No man I have met is worthy of such a role."

"Wouldn't a prudent marriage make tonight's events redundant?"

"Not necessarily. I don't simply want wealth and security. I want it on my own terms. What if a husband objected to my breeding horses?"

"But that's the point, you silly woman. You wouldn't have to breed horses. Your husband could do it for you."

She stamped her foot, sending her cap flying and her hair falling free. "But I want to do this myself."

"Why, for heaven's sake?" he demanded in shock, as though he had not said those very words countless of times himself.

She lifted her chin, starlight on her hair. "So I can be free." She lowered her voice to almost a whisper. "I own nothing but my two horses. The estate I have slaved for eight long years to save goes to Daniel, nothing comes to me. I am at the mercy of a good marriage or a charitable brother. Would you be prepared to let others decide your fate, or would you take responsibility for your own life? Live it the way you want to live it?"

He almost sneered. Did she not realize no one's life was their own? It belonged to one's family, and Society's expectations. There was no such thing as freedom to do as you pleased.

"I don't intend to answer to anyone but myself," she declared as if the world would do as she said without extracting any penalties. "I don't expect you to understand. This is my life and I shall live it how I please."

"Your life," he echoed, feeling a pang of jealousy at her words. She stood before him so composed, so in command of her life, even when she was in the wrong. She had a choice in her destiny, which was more than he could say for himself. Since his father's death he'd controlled nothing. His path was chosen for him until he could find a way to atone for the past. A past he'd not created.

"Let me get this right," he said, his voice hiding his bubbling anger. "You want to be free but you'd break the law to do so, risking the very freedom you fight so hard for? The logic is missing from your words."

"I was not supposed to have been caught. Why couldn't you be inside drinking and eating with the other guests?"

"What and have missed out on this debacle?" He sighed, exasperated.

Jamieson stepped in. "My lord, no harm has been done. Caesar looks a picture of health. Perhaps the baron will simply agree to pay you in installments for the use of your stallion."

"Or he could agree to give me the foal once it's born."

"No." Rheda almost shrieked. "I would rather pay you."

"But you said you had no money. Are you playing with me? Come Stephen. Let us get Caesar in the stables and speak with the baron."

In a small voice she begged, "Please, do not tell Daniel."

The big, six-foot-four, solid wall of muscle folded his arms across his chest, his fingers tapping on his forearm. "Give me one good reason why I should not go back to the house and demand payment from your brother."

To add to her misery her eyes filled with tears. She did not want to cry in front of this man. In a strangled voice, she yelled, "My mares are mine, but he would sell them to pay you. I could not bear it if they were taken from me."

Without her horses, the women and children of Deal would be doomed. Deep in her heart, she knew Meg was right. Dark Shadow couldn't go on forever. She had to succeed with her horses. She couldn't walk away from the people who needed her help. She'd given them hope. They relied on Dark Shadow for survival. Now she was honor bound to ensure the help did not end.

The night became deadly silent.

A man almost as handsome as Lord Strathmore appeared out of the shadows, giving her a friendly smile. "No one is going to take your horses away from you, Miss Kerrich. I am sure Lord Strathmore is honored to have loaned you Caesar for the night. Is that not right, Rufus?"

Lord Strathmore snarled. "Not bloody likely. Stephen, this is not your business. Stay out of it."

Not one to miss an opportunity, she batted her eyelashes and pierced Lord Strathmore's friend with what she hoped

was a smoldering smile. "You are quite right, kind sir. No harm has been done. Caesar even enjoyed himself."

The man Lord Strathmore referred to as Stephen took the hand she held out and pressed a kiss to her fingers.

"Since Lord Strathmore is too rude to offer an introduction, may I present myself? I am Stephen Milton, Marquis of Worthington, at your service, Miss Kerrich. Forgive Rufus's bad mood. As a gentleman, I'm sure he'll overlook this misunderstanding."

She chanced a glance in his direction; his face was blank. A masculine Roman statue. The beauty not disturbed by any flicker of emotion. From his stoic continence, she had no idea how much trouble she was in.

"Stephen, let go of Miss Kerrich's hand and take Caesar back to the stables. Ask Ted to feed and water him. My stallion shall stay in the stables from now on." From his tone of voice, everyone present knew he would brook no argument. "You there, what is your name?"

Jamieson looked uneasily at her. She nodded her head. He removed his cap. "Jamieson, your lordship."

Turning toward the mares, Lord Strathmore said, "Take the mares home. I need to discuss this situation with Miss Kerrich. I will escort her home later."

Both she and Jamieson voiced their outrage instantly.

Rheda caught her breath. "I am not going anywhere alone with you." And she turned to walk to her mares.

The nerve of the man. He was not her lord and master. She answered to no man except, on occasion, her brother. The occasions becoming too regular for her own peace of mind. But that was different. Daniel was her brother.

"Then I shall have Lord Worthington fetch your brother."

His cold voice and impersonal tone halted her progress. His supreme arrogance vexed her.

She closed her eyes, fighting back the tears that threatened to flow. They dried up as her anger grew. Rage welled up inside until her whole body trembled. He had her cornered.

He knew she was at his mercy, and he would extract every ounce of payment.

She had let him know her one weakness—her horses.

Pivoting toward him she knew it would be useless to plead. The man was made of stone when it came to getting what he wanted. She knew why he wanted to talk with her alone. He did not want to seduce her, as Jamieson thought. He wanted information. Her moment of reckoning had arrived. He would use her love for the two mares against her and make her bend to his will.

Rheda's insides turned to ice. Her fear was as real as the stars above. She quaked right down to the soles of her brother's old boots. She did not fear being physically hurt; in fact that would be a blessing. Her fear went much deeper. She was going to have to choose—Dark Shadow or her dream of running her own horse stud. The villagers needed one or the other to survive.

Her fingers drummed on her thigh. *Or did she?*

He was a rake. He loved women. Would her charms be enough to sidetrack the man? She knew he found her desirable. With heat flooding her veins, she remembered the feel of his erection against her body.

Rheda looked deep into Lord Strathmore's dark eyes. *Let's experiment.*

Nervously, she ran her tongue over her lips and thrust her chest forward until her breasts parted her jacket, all the while watching his face. A smoldering response flared in his eyes. She couldn't resist letting a wicked smile play across her mouth.

If she was very clever, if she played Lord Strathmore very carefully, she might be able to talk Rufus into helping with her horse stud without having to reveal Dark Shadow's identity. After all, women were his weakness, and she intended to drive her own symbolic dagger directly to his groin.

★   ★   ★

She was up to something.

Rufus soaked in the delicate features of her pale face in the moonlight, watching the play of emotions. Sorrow followed by rage, followed by fear, and dash it all, hope. What was she thinking?

She understood the trap he had caught her in and what he would want from her. His mouth curved up in amusement at her apparent attempt at seduction. He looked forward to seeing how far she'd go.

Slice the knife home. You have the opportunity. Triumph similar to the pride he'd felt when he'd broken Caesar to saddle danced across his skin. He had Rheda at his mercy.

He had too much to lose by not pressing his advantage. She was their only lead.

She was far too young to remember anything about the night his father died, but he was certain she could lead him to Dark Shadow. The smuggler held not only the key to uncovering the traitor he and Stephen had been ordered to capture, but the spy may also know the truth about what happened to his father. Had his father really betrayed his class and country?

The sound of her soft voice giving Jamieson orders sent chills skittering over his skin. The older servant looked about as happy as a man facing the gallows.

Despite the fact that he'd already guessed her plan, seeing her here, with his stallion, shocked him to the core. Here was a baron's sister, a lady, dressed as a stable boy, caught in the wrong; yet she stood defiant, as regal as any princess. Unabashed at being caught thieving. She didn't even have the decency to fear him.

She had a lot to learn.

The horses and men left, leaving the two of them alone in the moonlit paddock. Even dressed as a young boy, she radiated sensuality. It poured from her in the flare of her hips, hugged by her breeches, the curve of her breasts bouncing

free of any corset, and the feminine pout of her luscious lips. Watching her from beneath hooded lids, he let his gaze follow the line of her breeches up to her tiny waist, onward over her full breasts to the white flesh he glimpsed at the open neck of her shirt.

His hands fisted at his side. They longed to stroke the curves so blatantly displayed before him. Like a man who'd suddenly lost his sight, her shape was imprinted on his brain. His inner voice screamed a warning, stay away from her, but with mounting anger at his weakness, he ignored it, tilting his head slightly as he watched her in increasing fascination.

With a quiet oath that reflected his self-disgust, he stilled his rush of desire. *Damn her, the maddening minx!*

The ruthless part of him wanted to end it now. Force her to comply with his demand and reveal the truth. He had the ammunition. *Would Father have done this? Would he have been as ruthless?* As always, his conscience warred—honor was his salvation and his curse.

His discomfort fed his temper. "Come here. I do not intend to shout our conversation across the field."

"Please."

He had the irrational urge to storm the short distance between them and put her over his knee. He had never met a more irritating woman. Or more tantalizing.

He bit his tongue and refused to rise to her challenge. He would not let her crawl any farther under his skin.

"*Please,* come here so I may converse with you."

Rheda slowly made her way toward him. His nerves began to sizzle as he watched her smugly smile and state, "There will be no kissing tonight. Now that you know who I am. If you do not behave like a gentleman I shall inform Lady Hale."

"Your point is?"

"She will expect you to adhere to the niceties of the *ton.*

If not you will find yourself betrothed. She's been trying to marry me off for years. I'm sure you won't want me for a wife—think of the Strathmore name—scandal follows me wherever I go."

"So I have heard. Society would not think anything less of me for a dalliance with the likes of you."

He watched a small frown form on her lovely face. "I am infamous? I have never even had a Season."

He was well aware of that, for he would have remembered. A beauty stands out, and Rheda was outstanding. "No. I don't know your name from London. Lady Umbridge was indiscreet tonight."

She drew herself upright. "Let me guess, Prince Hammed."

"Yes, that is how I began to understand your interest in Caesar."

She stood ramrod straight, staring him in the eye.

"Aren't you going to defend yourself?" he said quietly.

"I do not know what she said, so how can I?" She shrugged a shoulder. "Moreover, I do not really care. Those closest to me know the truth. That is all that matters."

He wanted to know. He wanted to know if she was a fallen woman. Wanted to know she was not a virgin. Wanted it so badly he wished the gossip were true. But then, why should he care? He had her trapped by her own behavior, and she was mistaken if she thought he was not ruthless enough to take advantage of it.

Every muscle in his body clenched. He hated how ruthless he'd become, but his job for the Foreign Office left him little choice. This was not the life he would have chosen. However, his father's traitorous behavior left him little alternative. He pulled at his gloves, trying to staunch the bitterness from seeping into his skin.

His father's death had opened his eyes to the hypocrisy of Society and its rules. Up until then he'd lived his life quietly, respectably for a young man of his breeding and wealth. He

had been content to let his father oversee the family holdings and investments knowing he was being given his freedom before he had to take his place beside his father at the head of the family.

As a young man finding adulthood, Rufus enjoyed the same pursuits as most gentlemen of breeding—gambling, the horses, and of course women, but he could easily have walked away. He couldn't wait to work at his father's side. He had hero-worshipped him.

Rufus knew what he wanted to do. Rheda and he were alike in this respect. He could understand her dream and her desire to breed horses. It was ironic really. He'd wanted to breed the finest racing horses in England. Still did. Unfortunately, fate saw to it that his dream of breeding Royal Ascot winners had yet to be fulfilled.

Even at twenty he would have been quite happy to settle down, live quietly, breed horses, and run the family home. The Strathmore estate, Hascombe, northeast of Cambridge, was not far outside Newmarket. He'd been engaged to the daughter of a duke, and life was wonderful.

Then his father died.

Shot himself, accidentally, while out hunting on this very estate—Hastingleigh. Accidentally, that was, until all the rumors started. Rumors insinuating that his father was a traitor. That he'd taken his own life rather than be caught.

Rufus could not find out how the rumors started, but they soon took hold until every door in the *ton* slammed closed to him and his mother and younger sister. Even Julie, his fiancée, who professed to love him more than her own life, deserted him.

His face hardened. Overnight his dream of breeding racehorse winners died. Who'd buy a horse or back the horse of a traitor's son? Worse was the impact on his mother.

Memories of the humiliation his mother endured during the first few years after his father's disgrace gave him the resolve to do what must be done. His mother staunchly de-

fended his father's innocence. So he'd avowed to prove her right.

Rufus pulled at his cuffs and swore under his breath. He was not about to let a wild, uncivilized native of Kent ruin this mission. Not when he might be close to the truth. He would clear his father's name at any cost. He owed Society, and this woman in particular, nothing.

Folding his arms across his chest, he let her suffer, the silence stretched out between them. Her pulse must be racing knowing he had her trapped. Deliciously trapped by her nefarious behavior.

However, his anger leaped when he observed her more closely. She stood, calm and cool, as if she had all night and it was his time that was a wasting. With the stupid cap hiding her curls, her delicate features took on a waiflike fragility in the moonlight. The masculine clothing hugging her curves delectably emphasized that she was indeed all woman.

A woman dangerous to his senses.

A distraction—two could play that game. "I would like the truth. I want the truth about how you came by the barrel."

Chapter 8

She wanted to laugh at his arrogance. As if she'd simply tell him. Instead, she crossed her arms over her chest and lifted both brows, regarding him in cool surprise, but inwardly her heart hammered with anger and fright. It was all she could do not to shrink back from his knowing gaze.

"What barrel?"

He frowned at her, looking irritated, then he angled his chin downward, staring at her as though she were a rodent under his foot.

"Who gave you the barrel?" he asked in an icy tone.

Her resolve began to crumble. Her arms slipped to hug her waist as if in protection. She would play dumb. Most men never considered she was smart enough to outmaneuver them.

"You want the barrel? Meg has the barrel, so I can't give it to you in payment for Caesar's services."

But then she'd forgotten he was not like any man she'd ever met.

Despite his best intentions, his temper cracked. His desire to conquer the woman before him was a powerful yearning inside him—he vowed he would crush any tender feelings for this infuriating vixen, beauty or not.

"Who gave you the barrel?" he suddenly bellowed without

warning. "The barrel I found you trapped by, on the cliff the other day."

Her green eyes were wide and filled with innocent shock. "Cliffs? I don't remember seeing you alone on the cliffs, ever." She paused for emphasis. "If I tell you about the barrel, I'll have to tell my brother and Lord Hale what you did to me. The whole truth . . ."

His mouth firmed. So this was how she would play it.

What started as a perfect lead in his quest to find a smuggler and subsequent traitor now resembled a Shakespearean tragedy.

Miss Kerrich was not a local wench he could accuse of lying. Nor would Lady Hale approve of his treatment of Miss Kerrich. Lady Hale had been so kind to his mother, he'd hate to disappoint her, or worse ruin his mother's relationship with her one true supporter. Without any evidence he had nothing to charge her with. His pulse hitched a notch. Miss Kerrich made a challenging adversary. She was a bright, intelligent woman, who for the past eight years had singlehandedly managed to hold a bankrupt estate together.

There was every possibility she knew Dark Shadow. Smuggling would seem the logical means to stay afloat in the wilds of Kent. Her estate's agricultural ventures would not have earned enough to save her.

Tonight was proof enough that she was not opposed to "taking" whatever she required. Her bold plan to use Caesar without Rufus's permission was all the evidence he needed.

He raised an eyebrow. "I see. Let's change the topic then. You seem keen to discuss payment for Caesar's services."

She wetted her lips with a nervous flick of her tongue. He was finally getting to her. "What do you suggest?" she asked.

"You should be nervous. I'm the one you'd better worry about now," he warned in a low voice. "Your mares' ownership is in my hands."

Rheda stared at him intensely as if weighing up what challenge he truly posed.

"I have no means of immediately paying you. If you could give me more time I will endeavor to come up with the money."

He stared at her. Running his eye over her body, watching her face flush knowing what he was seeing. "I'm not interested in money."

"You're disgusting," she snapped with a flash of renewed temper.

He swallowed a sharp retort and calmly stated, "A few days ago I'd hardly call your response as disgust. Quite the opposite in fact. You all but melted in my arms."

She looked wildly around her, as if trying to locate any avenue of escape. When she found none, her shoulders straightened and her demeanor changed. The tigress was back. Rufus couldn't help but be impressed.

The hellion in front of him clenched her fists and lifted her chin. "Stop playing with me. What is it you want? The sooner you get it, the sooner you can leave me alone."

"The last thing I'd like to do is leave you alone, sweet Rhe," he murmured, his tone deliberately low and silken.

Rheda took a step back.

He followed. It was time she became a little afraid. Her scent wafted up through the balmy night, and he simply had not been prepared for his body's response. In addition, the sight of her plump derriere had caused his groin to ache. All he could think about was taking her, bending her over the fallen tree trunk behind her, and possessing her body.

Bloody hell, he'd been driven to possess her from the first moment he laid eyes on her. Yet this incessant need to conquer, this lust, was more dangerous, more compelling than mere attraction. *Remember Marguerite.*

"You have courage, I'll give you that. You openly defy me, knowing the trouble you are in, and refuse to give me what I want." He smiled thinly, studying her, trying to judge

her next move. A suspicion flared. "Are you protecting someone?"

Her body tensed and she looked away. So she *was* protecting someone. Who? Her look became more mutinous. How far would she go to protect the source of her barrel? What would make her break? He had to find the key to her cooperation—soon. Until then he had to devise a way to keep this beauty in his sights. "You aren't going to tell me, are you?"

She gave a small shrug. "There is nothing to tell."

"I don't believe you. Until I find out the truth of how you came by that barrel, you and I are going to become very close friends."

"I . . . don't understand."

"Surely you can grasp my meaning. Your mind is like a steel trap." Rufus swore under his breath. Perhaps he was unwise to instigate the idea circling in his mind, but he could not afford to wait. He needed information, and fast. Time was running out. He was sure his plan would disturb him far more than it would her.

He caged his lust and, keeping his features enigmatic, said, "I require your services for the next month in lieu of payment for Caesar's pedigree."

"Very funny."

"I'm serious. I shall even agree to Caesar servicing your mares for as long as they are in heat. In return, you will be at my beck and call. Any time of the day or night I require your services, you will oblige me."

Her jaw clenched. He could almost hear her inner battle—the trade-off, her horse stud dream or her pride. The silence stretched into the approaching dawn. He could wait all night if he had to.

"You would force me to be your mistress? You'd ruin me." Her voice had risen.

He met her hot gaze levelly. "Only moments ago you informed me you had no reputation to ruin. Among other

things, I wish you to be my social secretary or hostess for the month. I am looking for property in the area, and I would like you to aid me in the search. If, in addition and by your own free will, you wish to share my bed, I would welcome it."

She gave him a scathing look. "I'd never willingly share your bed."

"I beg to differ. Only a few days ago I could have bedded you without too much effort."

"As I recall, I said no."

"But I didn't try very hard. You've yet to experience my more persuasive methods." He took a step toward her. "Care for a demonstration?"

She tensed and his body's natural response to her charms diminished. She still refused to admit her desire. Drawing a sharp breath, she took a step backward to a safer distance.

"Oh, no, you don't," he chided, seizing her around the waist as she tried to flee. She let out a small shriek and fought him as best she could, but Rufus was undeterred, easily restraining her.

He laughed. "Calm down. I'll make you a promise. I won't take you if you're unwilling. I give you my word." His lips nuzzled the soft skin of her throat. "At the moment I'm more interested in your knowledge of local matters than your acquaintance with more carnal topics."

Liar. With every rapid pulse kicking in his groin he wanted to sink between her thighs.

"It's simply that you have knowledge of the people and places around Deal. You have lived in the area all your life. You know everyone, and all the estates in the area. Men would not see you as a threat when discussing pricing. But I know differently. Your beautiful face hides a mind as sharp as a rapier's point, a most useful weapon for me to wield."

She struggled in his grip, her plump breasts pushing fully against his chest. He felt himself harden.

"And what exactly will my duties be?"

He bit his tongue to stop an unsuitable "duty" from slipping out. He moved his hips so she could feel the evidence of his arousal. After all he'd been through over the past few days she deserved to be frightened just a little, but he needed her cooperation. "Nothing that would cause your ruin."

She twisted and managed to flee his hold and back away from him, as if her life depended on it. "I would never have relations with you, even if it was my only chance of getting out of hell."

He strode after her, his thoughts turning more primal as he took in her swaying hips. There was a reason women did not wear breeches.

"Have you forgotten your brother is in the house behind us? One word would have him handing ownership of your mares to me."

She ignored him and continued walking.

"One month. One month is all I ask. I would like you to help me navigate the local gentry. I could call on you. It may even enhance your reputation."

"You rate yourself too highly, my lord. Your reputation is tarnished, too."

"Then help me out of the goodness of your own heart. Tell me who has estates to sell and the reasons behind the sale—which families were being forced to sell due to financial woes. Not much to ask considering what price the offspring of Caesar will bring you." He paused hoping to get a positive response, but Rheda merely sighed. He cleared his throat. "In addition, it would help me manage mothers with marriageable daughters in the area."

Rheda's laugh was filled with wry amusement. She halted so suddenly he almost tripped over her as she swung back to him. "You must think me simple. A man as skilled at dodging the parson's noose needs protection from local mothers with marriageable daughters? Hardly." She cocked her head.

"Still, I can see how when a man is trying to find a smuggler, mamas with marriage on the brain could be most annoying."

He clenched his hands at his side. She knew he wanted the source of her barrel and guessed it was to find a smuggler, yet she still refused to give him a name. She had to know who Dark Shadow was. He grew more determined to break her cool reserve.

"Has Mrs. Rathborne cornered you already? She's been trying to marry Mildred off to Christopher for the past twelve months." With a laughing gleam in her eye she added, "I bet Mrs. Rathborne was the first woman he persuaded his mother to invite to your welcome dinner."

Rufus found himself gritting back a reply. Christopher? Lord Hale's name on her lips sounded intimate. It shouldn't bother him in the least. Yet his body buzzed with jealousy.

"If you were to accompany me while I was in Kent, the implication would be there and I would likely not be bothered."

She gave a very unladylike snort. "I doubt that. You heard the gossip tonight. I have not a shred of respectability left in the district. A woman like Mrs. Rathborne would not see me as an impediment to marrying her daughter to Viscount Strathmore."

"And that would upset you?"

She looked like she was about to expand on that point but instead said, "Your wealth and status would overcome her objections to your behavior with Rheda Kerrich, the local fallen woman. She would assume a man of your status was simply engaging in a dalliance while in Kent. That would not advance my good character."

"Very likely. However, it can't hurt, either. Alternatively, tell me the truth about the barrel now and your help is not required."

"You're not listening to me, my lord." She looked away.

"Don't look at me like that. I'm immune to your charms, or have you forgotten?"

The tone of her voice, haughty and disdainful, left him in no doubt she would never help him unless forced to. "Your memory seems to be very selective. I can still recall how responsive you were in my arms." A fierce surge of heat flooded his body at the memory of her soft curves beneath his. "You were very tempting. I have never met a 'lady' who romps around the countryside dressed so inappropriately." He wanted to punish her. "Nor one who succumbs quite so readily to a stranger's seduction. So don't tell me you're immune. I know from experience that you want me."

She gasped, and he caught her hand before it reached his face.

"I wouldn't advise it. You have tried my temper to its limits tonight. My offer is fair. The price of Caesar's stud services are almost five thousand pounds. You're a smart woman. You'd be a fool to refuse."

He lowered her hand to her side, and she didn't fight him. In fact, she seemed to be seriously considering his proposal. He pushed his advantage.

"With the money you will make off just two of Caesar's progeny, you could buy more than a dozen mares."

Rheda shut her eyes. He watched her struggling with her dilemma. She opened them, and he saw his victory within their swirling depths.

She gave a strained smile. "But what good is a dozen or so mares with no stallion to service them?" She chewed her bottom lip; the sight sent more jolts of lust to his groin. "I will agree to your payment solution if I can have Caesar back to service the mares I buy from the first offspring."

His expression sobered. She was clever, very clever. So clever he wondered if he was doing the right thing. "You're agreeing to my offer?"

She shrugged her slender shoulders. "What choice do I

have? To save my dreams of owning a horse stud I have to make a pact with the devil. So be it. I'm a realist, Lord Strathmore. I'll get what I want, but I warn you, my lord, I'm sure you'll be left wanting."

He smiled at her sharp tongue. "I always get what I want, and right now, I'd like a kiss to seal the deal, Rheda."

He said her name softly, his tone almost a caress. His proposal was dangerous, but to call his bluff, to decline his offer, would mean untold suffering for all those she loved.

If she was discovered smuggling, Daniel's chance of a good marriage and restoring the de Winter name to prominence would be destroyed. Also without the horse stud, what would happen to the villagers of Deal once Dark Shadow was no more? What would happen to those who had nothing? Those she kept clothed and fed?

It did not signify that her reputation would be ruined. She felt honor bound to continue the financial help the villagers now relied upon. The pounding pain in her head struck her anew. She had no choice but to fall in with his plan. But she'd not make it easy for him.

"There is one more thing—Rufus." She gave in and used his name, wanting him relaxed for her next request.

He sighed. "What now? Is there more? Do you want me to tell Caesar to be gentle?"

She rolled her eyes. "You must promise me Daniel is never to know about our arrangement. It would destroy him. I may not care about my reputation, but he does. I'm the only family he's got."

He remained silent.

She pressed her point. "My brother shouldn't suffer for my behavior. So, before you get heady with victory, my lord, what do you propose to do about my brother?"

That wiped the smile off his face.

He tapped his fingers to his chin, and his eyebrows drew

together as he thought. He sighed. "I shall simply have to look as though I am courting you. I'm sure your brother would welcome such a suitable match given your reputation." She gasped, horrified. "It would not be any hardship to pretend to be captivated by your beauty," he added, his voice a husky entreaty.

"Daniel will no doubt read more into your proposition than you'd like. When you leave, he's unlikely to take your 'use' of me quietly. He's a marked swordsman, by the way."

"He's a mere boy, hardly a threat. You're right, though. I wouldn't want to cause your brother any further shame." He looked at the ground and tugged his cuffs. Finally, he turned back to her. "I shall ensure that I give you a very public reason to refuse my offer and to douse any expectations. The sin will be mine. Satisfied?" If he could clear his father's name, he'd not have to worry about a maligned courtship.

She heard him talk but didn't hear his words. Her gaze focused on his lips. He had a beautiful mouth, she thought. The very idea of kissing him sent her nerves fizzing.

"Now shall we seal our deal? With a kiss, sweetheart?" His smile full of teasing couldn't shock her out of her dreamy state. "I need practice in my courting skills." Caught in his hypnotizing stare, she stood as still as the night while he bent slightly to bring his mouth into delicate contact with hers. It was a mere brushing of flesh against flesh, barely that, and yet she felt the sensation like a burning brand. Abruptly she shivered.

When he lifted his gaze, she could see satisfaction in his warm brown eyes.

With a casual finger, he stroked down her back and over the crease where her trousers molded her bottom. She felt his finger all the way through her clothes.

"While I much prefer my women naked, you do look enticing in trousers. Remind me to make you wear them another time so that I may have the pleasure of stripping them

off you while I kiss down your long slender legs. You have the legs of a gazelle if I remember correctly." His voice was husky, a low caress.

Alarm rose within her; he was so sure of himself. So sure she'd succumb to his skills as a lover, and that was definitely not part of their deal.

She couldn't hide the tremble in her voice. "Have we finished here tonight, my lord?"

"Please, call me Rufus."

She ignored him. Already her heart raced with a mix of trepidation and excitement. She did not wish to become more familiar with this man—except on her terms. What her terms were, she hadn't quite decided.

Guilt raced through him. What was he doing? He'd never been this cold-blooded, this—dishonorable. Could he live with himself if he ruined her reputation irrevocably when she might not be guilty of anything but sharing a smuggled brandy barrel? For one moment a curl of doubt formed deep in his gut. But then he remembered Marguerite's face as she slid the knife into his side. He remembered the pain of his wound and the agony of Andrew's death.

He looked at the beauty before him and felt only loathing. She could be in league with an outlaw and mayhap traitor.

Yet, he could not lie to himself. Part of his desire to keep Rheda under his control was that he wanted her. He wanted her too much. He needed to remember to keep his mind firmly on the mission. He gave her one final concession.

"I will endeavor to be so convincing that Daniel and the rest of Kent's local inhabitants will believe my pursuit of you is honorable." So convincing, in fact, that the minx standing before him would give him the information he needed and end up in his bed.

She extended her hand. "We shall shake on it then."

He took the small delicate bones within his and lifted her hand to his lips. The touch of skin-to-skin sent another jolt

of desire pulsing through him. She watched him, and Rufus was satisfied when he felt her pulse speed up.

"I never shake hands with a woman." So saying he turned her hand and kissed her open palm, very pleased at the shiver of response she could not hide.

She snatched her hand away as if seared by a hot coal. She began walking backward out of his reach. He desperately wanted to stop her but knew if he touched her again, his sharp hunger for her might cloak him in dishonor. He would not follow in his father's footsteps and further tarnish the Strathmore name. Instead, he needed her off her guard, uncomfortable, and unaware of his intent to do whatever it took to pry her mouth open and reveal the truth. From the tales surrounding Rheda, her reference to Lord Hale as Christopher, and her response to his touch, he hoped she was more experienced in pleasures of the flesh than an unwed sister of a baron should be. For then her seduction would not see him galloping down a road to dishonor.

Guilty until proven innocent could be a costly stance to take. If she was innocent, her seduction would have consequences he didn't wish to face.

The tension of the moment was broken by a whinny and horses' hooves. Rufus looked to the tree line, and his jaw clamped shut. Jamieson had returned for her.

Rheda eyed her escape, needing no further encouragement. She turned and ran to safety.

Rufus raised his voice. "I shall call tomorrow morning. Have the mares ready."

He watched until he could see them no more, then he slowly turned toward the house. Stephen appeared from the shadows as Rufus entered the orchard.

"I am assuming you have a new plan. Did you get what you required from Miss Kerrich?"

Rufus inwardly admitted he had not. His body still throbbed with want, but instead he said, "Yes. She has agreed to a pretend courtship while I am in Kent."

"I say, Rufus—"

"A ruse only, Stephen." At least until he could ascertain the secrets she protected—was she innocent?

"And how exactly will that help us? I know how it might help you, but I am hoping the fact she's the baron's sister has not escaped your mind," Stephen added flatly. "Matrimony lies down that path. A fate worse than . . . well, you don't have to sacrifice everything for God and country."

Rufus did not speak again until they had reached the terrace. "I am going to keep my eye on Miss Kerrich. I shall get her to introduce me to everyone in the area, particularly the villagers of Deal, who we already know think she's a saint or else they would not have kept her identity a secret. I will wear her down, charm her, until she lets something slip or one of her accomplices does."

"Having met Miss Kerrich, I'd wager that could take a long time," Stephen replied mildly.

Rufus straightened his cravat. "Yes, well, I hope it won't take too long. Too much time in her company, and I am more likely to beat the knowledge out of her whether she knows anything or not. That woman is annoying."

"Then I suggest we find an alternative source of information. There must be others in the village that could be persuaded to talk. Greed can sometimes prove a better incentive than even your charms."

"I have already tried that and failed," Rufus said stiffly. "I have seen her with a barrel of French brandy. She knows something. And no slip of a woman will deny me."

"That was not a criticism, my friend." Stephen rushed to assure. "You did an excellent job finding the smuggler's location here in Deal. Because of you, we are one step closer to unearthing our traitor." The younger man hesitated. "But the Earl of Ashford will hang you out to dry if you get caught defiling an innocent. The Foreign Secretary will disown all knowledge of you, and the Strathmore name will be thoroughly tarnished for good."

They had reached the doors back into the dining room. Rufus hesitated before entering. "I am certain the woman knows who Dark Shadow is," he said grimly. "Lord Ashford wants the traitor caught. He won't care who I defile as long as it remains private. And I have no intention of letting a suspected smuggler stop me, regardless of whether she's a highborn lady or not."

The words fell easily but sat heavy on his shoulders. *This is not who you are,* a voice whispered inside his head.

He had a score to settle with his elusive enemy. Treason only headed the list of crimes. More personally galling was his father's rumored betrayal to the French and his subsequent suspicious death. He hoped the spy was the key to the truth. The spy might have heard the truth about his father. Did he work for the French? Did he betray the French aristocrats to the Revolutionary council? Rufus did not believe it. Why would his father have done so? They certainly didn't need the money.

Rufus would prove his late father's innocence to the world with his dying breath if that's what it took.

The dining room was empty. The men must have rejoined the ladies. They silently made their way to the drawing room.

Tomorrow could not come fast enough for Rufus. He had a smuggler to catch. Even so, he could not stop the thrill coursing through him at the thought of spending time in Miss Kerrich's company.

He wondered what their meeting tomorrow would bring. If she was involved in treachery, her beauty would not save her.

Nothing would save her.

Chapter 9

Upon rejoining the ladies, Rufus noted Rheda's brother, the baron, had already left. *How annoying.* However, he was relieved to see Mildred and her dreadful mother Mrs. Rathborne had also departed.

Still, he would have liked to ply the baron with questions about his estate. How was he able to remain solvent? Lord de Winter's answers would be most illuminating and perhaps would help ease his conscience. If Rheda was blameless of the crimes he suspected her of, and was in fact an innocent, there would be only one honorable course open to him if he was caught seducing her—marriage. That he prayed would not occur. He could not imagine Miss Kerrich sitting demurely at his family estate raising children and seeing to his household.

He smiled as an image of her dressed in male attire, speeding over his hills on a stallion, flittered into his mind. No she was no sedate young woman. Not suitable material for his future wife. But mistress . . .

He twirled his father's ring on his finger. His body hungered for her. Smuggling he could overlook, treason never. However, if she wasn't party to treason, then perhaps he would make her his mistress. If the stories of her affair with the Turkish prince were true, she would be experienced enough to satisfy him. Her fiery spirit bode well for her appetite in bed—wild and wanton, he'd guess.

He accepted a glass of brandy from Christopher and sank into a comfortable chair across from him.

"Miss Kerrich is very beautiful, is she not?"

Did Christopher know he'd met with her this evening? Was he in on her plan? No. Christopher did not have the gumption for it.

"I have only met her briefly the other day, but yes, she is." He raised a class in a silent toast. "You have not thought of making a match with her, given her brother's financial situation?"

"I'm hardly a catch, Rufus. I have proposed but to no avail."

Christopher's response stunned him and made him analyze his original deduction of Christopher's and Rheda's relationship.

Rufus blanched. "She refused you?" Why would a woman refuse an offer from a man like Christopher? It did not make sense. Given, he was nothing much to look at, but he was titled, extremely wealthy, and above all else—kind. A woman in Rheda's financial predicament would normally have grabbed such an offer with two hands.

Christopher laughed. "Several times actually, although I have not asked in the past year. The first time I proposed was just after her father died. She was left at seventeen with massive debts and Daniel to raise. He was only eleven."

Rufus's mind somersaulted, debts—massive. "Perhaps she was scared of too much change so quickly."

"Rheda scared? Unlike me, nothing frightens that woman. Her excuse was she had to keep Tumsbury Cliff safe for Daniel. I told her I would ensure it thrived, but she does not trust men easily. Given her father's moral bankruptcy, I am not surprised."

Christopher sat gazing into the fire, deep in thought. "I proposed again when she turned one and twenty. Daniel was fifteen by then and I thought quite capable of running the estate with an overseer. But again she declined."

"Her reason?"

Christopher turned to look at him, resignation in his eyes. "She did not wish to ever marry and become any man's property. Again, given her father's example, I can't say I blame her. The man was the worst sort of reprobate; brought whores into her home. It is little wonder Rheda has little faith in the male species."

Rufus experienced a flicker of unease. He felt for Rheda. Her father had lived his life not caring what Society thought of him, while his father cared too much. He did not know which was worse for a child to bear. Honor before all else or no honor at all.

Christopher continued, misery evident in his tone. "Mother cannot understand why I have not been pressing my suit for the last few years."

"You sell yourself short, old boy. You'd make a fine husband for Miss Kerrich. She would be lucky to have you."

Christopher's eyes became serious. "I don't have your looks or silver tongue, but I shall get Daniel's permission to marry her. Daniel is young and idealistic. He wants the family back into Society's good graces. He has decided to elevate the good name of de Winter. A marriage to the Earl of Hale would be most advantageous. I'm simply biding my time until the right moment."

Poor sod, he was smitten. Yet, Christopher was right. She was a surreal beauty. A beauty men would fight for, yet Rufus's instincts told him Rheda was not for Christopher. Christopher could never handle such a passionate woman. She needed a firm hand. A hand that Rufus could provide. He shook his head. No, if she wasn't for Christopher then she certainly wasn't for him, a tarnished Strathmore. Rheda was most likely mixed up in smuggling and perhaps worse, espionage. The Strathmore name was stained, a mark he had worked his life to atone for.

Along with capturing the traitor for his king and country,

there was only one way to redeem himself in Society's eyes. He must marry a lady of impeccable character and breeding. A woman whose reputation was, above all, spotless.

From what he had discovered of Miss Kerrich's reputation, it was covered in spots.

Feigning nonchalance, Rufus added, "I am surprised it has taken you this long, though. I would have thought with their financial situation, your offer would have been a godsend."

Christopher's manner changed immediately, and he eyed Rufus suspiciously. "I helped out where I could. I wanted to marry her, not put them in the poorhouse. With a little help the estate began to turn a profit."

"How magnanimous of you. You could have married her a lot sooner if you had applied the right pressure. Without your support she would have had to come to you for help."

Rufus could see the anger building in the man seated across from him. "I'm a gentleman. I didn't want to take advantage of a young girl's troubles."

Rufus almost smiled at that ridiculous statement. He'd never known Christopher to keep a mistress. He'd never been a rake of any sort—freedom? Christopher was trying to hide something. Why was he protecting her?

Christopher rose to stand next to the fire and looked Rufus up and down. "You seemed to have developed an interest in Miss Kerrich." Christopher's gaze hardened. "I would hate to think that after years of standing by you, our families could fall out over a woman. My father stood by your mother upon your father's death. Without our support your family would never have survived the scandal. My father made sure your father's death was recorded as an accident."

Rufus's head snapped up. "Ensured? Are you saying it wasn't an accident?"

Christopher coughed into his hand. "I am sorry, that was uncalled for. Yes, I was here when your father died, although I wasn't on the hunt with them that morning. I had crawled

into bed just before sunrise and wasn't in any condition to hunt. I am not really sure what happened." He shrugged. "It was a long time ago."

Twelve long years actually, but it seemed like only yesterday to Rufus. His father, the man he had looked up to all his life had died. The rumor was Lord Strathmore shot himself after being caught selling the escape routes of the French aristocracy to the Revolutionary Council.

Lord Hale, Christopher's father, ensured the shooting was recorded as an accident, and no charges were ever laid against his father, but the damage was done. Without the ability to defend himself, his father's name had been dragged through the mud. The Strathmore family became social persona non grata.

Something in Christopher's tone made Rufus think Christopher was lying. What was he hiding? "Then why bring it up?" Rufus asked lightly.

Christopher placed his glass of brandy carefully on the mantelpiece. "It was a reflex reaction. I have always considered Rheda mine. I've never had any competition, especially from a notorious rake like you. She has never been out of Deal and as such I have been able to wait for her with no other fitting suitors in sight. Your interest in her bothers me."

The smile no longer reached Christopher's eyes. Still, Rufus could not bring himself to give him everything he wanted. "What red-blooded male wouldn't be interested? I've a mind to court her myself." He could tell from Christopher's stance exactly how he felt about his statement. . . Well, he couldn't help that. It laid the groundwork for what was to come—the pretend courtship. Besides, Christopher was hiding something about his father's death, of that he was certain. The key to manipulating a man was to have something he wanted. Miss Kerrich's affections were worth cultivating simply for that, if not the smuggling. It seemed everywhere he turned, Miss Kerrich held the key to his past and his future.

He uncrossed his legs and swallowed. Using Miss Kerrich's affections was not without some risk. He hardened at the thought of her soft curves and silken skin. His body burned for her touch. To feel her long, graceful legs gripping his hips . . .

Rufus drained the remaining brandy from his glass. He knew what he had to do. Miss Kerrich was the lynchpin to succeeding in his quest. Not only might she help lead him to Dark Shadow, but she was the key to getting Christopher to reveal secrets of the past. Secrets that might help clear his father's name.

Partnering with Miss Kerrich was not for the fainthearted. She held the power to ensnare a man's heart. Rufus smiled into his empty glass remembering Marguerite's betrayal. As he made to retire for the evening he mused there was nothing fainthearted about Viscount Strathmore, which Miss Kerrich would learn to her detriment.

The candle flickered and spluttered, almost at the end of its wick. It didn't matter. The curtains weren't drawn and dawn was fast approaching. Christopher, still fully dressed, stretched his arms above his head and yawned. Even he had to sleep sometime, and after the excitement he'd had that night, this morning he would indulge himself and sleep well into the afternoon.

He flexed his shoulders and once more picked up his quill. The secrets hidden in the night gave him plenty to write about. His journal used to record the sins confessed and his desires yet to be fulfilled.

His desires. He had plenty.

He'd followed Rufus, and he'd seen Rufus with Rheda in the field. The little minx was up to mischief again. It looked as though she'd decided to borrow Rufus's fine stallion without his permission. Why wouldn't she? Caesar was a magnificent beast.

One more sin the lady had to atone for. She'd sinned

plenty over her short life. He'd recorded it all in his trusty journal. Recorded everything. He knew all her secrets, including the biggest secret of all. The one she didn't want the world to know.

His journals recorded each and every indiscretion involving the people in this town, including his own. He'd been writing his journals all his life, and many would quake in fear if they knew what he had written here. They were his most treasured possession. Leverage to use when the time was right.

He smiled. Let the world continue to overlook him, just as Rheda had done. She thought him a fool, and that would be her mistake.

He'd smiled and reassured her that he did not believe the rumors of her and Prince Hammed, when in fact he'd stepped back to wait and see if she grew round with child before he set his plan into action. He clenched his fist in anger. He didn't have to be the first, but by God he would be her last lover.

He knew he had to act soon. Rheda was a slut, and now that Rufus was here, she might take up with his friend as she had with the prince. Rufus was as magnificent as his stallion. Handsome beyond compare. Once Rufus left, Christopher did not want to have to wait months again to ensure she was childless before forcing her to be his bride. His mother was asking too many questions.

He'd been foolish to think that once her father died, Rheda would need his help to survive. Her damned smuggling operation had made it easy for her to decline his proposal.

He slammed his fist on the desk—decline him. An earl.

He clenched his teeth and gave a throaty laugh. Her smuggling would be her downfall. She would marry him or he'd see her and her brother transported to the colonies.

Soon she would not be able to overlook him. Soon he would have her right where he needed her.

Time was marching on. He was not getting any younger. His fortieth year was fast approaching, and his mother was demanding he marry.

He needed an heir. And he wanted Rheda to be the mother of his child. No other woman would do.

He closed his journal and stroked his hand lovingly over the leather. He didn't care that she was a whore. Whores could be kept in their place. This book provided him with the power to own her soul and soon—very soon—he intended to use it.

Chapter 10

Rheda moaned into her pillow, wishing the day away. Rolling onto her back, she dragged a hand across her face and yawned. Reluctantly she pushed herself up and swung her legs over the edge of the bed, blaming the humid night for her lack of sleep even though deep down she knew it was a lie.

Once on her feet she moved as if in a dream to the dresser where she poured water from the pitcher into the porcelain washbowl. Thoughts of Lord Strathmore continuously plagued her as she splashed the fresh, bracing cold water onto her skin. She tried to scrub the memory of his lips, hands, and caresses from her mind.

A few droplets of water slid down the valley between her breasts, just as she remembered his lips had done. Her body still hummed with need, remembering the soft trail of kisses and the way his mouth felt against her skin.

She shivered and kept toweling her face and chest dry. She hesitated before choosing her best day dress, denying it was for his benefit. Lady Hale deserved the effort.

The door to her room opened, and Penny, her maid, entered. "Daniel told me you were finally up." She gave her a searching look. "Late night was it?"

"I cannot keep any secrets from you." Penny was Jamieson's wife. Rheda was grateful to them both. They'd stayed with her even when she had no money to pay them.

With their help Tumsbury Cliff Estate had survived, if not quite blossomed. She would not be free without them.

"Miss Rhe, when will you learn, a husband can never keep anything from his wife. I make sure Jamieson tells me everything. It makes for a happy marriage."

For one fleeting moment Rheda reflected on the fact that perhaps not all marriages were to be feared. She shook her head. No. Penny and Jamieson were not nobility. They were free to marry for love, and had. In her world marriages were made like a diplomatic alliance—breeding, wealth, estates. That was what "marriage" meant. Women were nothing more than pawns in a game of chess. The weakest piece, expendable fodder.

Rheda shooed her foolish thoughts from her head. "Then you know what happened to our stunning plan."

"I'm not sure about stunning," Penny scoffed as she slipped a fresh chemise over Rheda's head. "But it appears Lord Strathmore is not as stupid as most gentlemen of the *ton*."

"No." As she opened a drawer and took out clean stockings, Rheda ignored the little thrilling flashes of memory, feeling his hands as they had massaged her deadened legs while she lay prone on the grass. Taking a seat before her mirror she rolled the thin white stockings up, remembering his strong, firm fingers stroking her legs, between her legs . . .

"Are you all right?" Penny asked.

She could only nod her head.

"Stop squirming." Penny began braiding her hair before securing it into a chignon. "Be careful. Lord Strathmore is dangerous. But my papa always told me to 'know thine enemy.' When is the next boat due in from France?"

"Soon." She shrugged. "It will be a new moon in only a few more days, when the summer skies are darkest, which makes it easier to remain hidden from the Revenue men."

Penny paused and studied Rheda's reflection in the mirror, a slight frown crinkling her weathered brow. "Then I would throw his lordship a ball, here at Tumsbury Cliff

Manor, to welcome him to Kent. Daniel wants to reenter Society. Then let us do it on a grand scale. I'm sure Lady Hale will help with the invitations."

Rheda returned Penny's frown, but only for a moment. Then a smile began to tug at her lips. "And who would suspect us of smuggling in the middle of entertaining? We would throw his lordship off our scent." She jumped up to hug her maid. "Thank you. That's a fabulous idea."

Penny pushed her out of her arms. "But you have to let Lady Hale propose it. Do not let Lord Strathmore know it was your idea."

She bit her lip. "What about Daniel? A ball will take money, and he is such a miser."

Penny walked to the door and turned before leaving. "Leave the baron to me. If he wants to fit back into Society, I will convince him a ball is needed." Penny giggled. "I will suggest it would be a good way to introduce you to the marriage mart. That should have him agreeing right quick."

Rheda rolled her eyes at her maid. Penny of all people knew she would never marry. "Don't you start. Daniel thinks Lord Strathmore will call to press his suit, and for now I would like to keep it that way."

Hiding behind the half open door Penny ventured, "You could do worse. He is rich, honorable, and exceedingly handsome. I'm sure sharing his bed would be delicious."

"I do not have to marry a man to do that," she replied dryly.

Penny frowned. "Your brother might have something to say about that." And she closed the door softly behind her.

"Not if he doesn't know," Rheda murmured under her breath.

She glanced at her bed. Images of Lord Strathmore naked, wrapped in her sheets, sent a curl of heat low in her belly. She wanted to splash her face with cold water all over again. She could not get the image of the powerful, tempting, and vexing Lord Strathmore molding his body to hers, his hands

demanding access to every one of her curves, out of her head. The thought of seeing him again made her slightly light-headed. No, it wasn't anything to do with Lord Strathmore. It was simply that she had not eaten since an early supper last evening.

That was all she needed, something to eat. As she made her way downstairs she knew she lied. Her ache wasn't in her stomach, it was between her thighs.

The next few hours saw her nerves stretched to the breaking point. Her body shimmered with one part excitement and two parts fear. Yes, she feared Rufus was a government agent seeking Dark Shadow. Doubtless her real gut-wrenching, cold, clammy-hands fear was her susceptibility. She dreaded testing whether she would be able to resist his powerful magnetism. Something about his lordship called to the woman in her. The woman she no longer wanted to deny.

Why did Rufus have to arrive in Deal just when her desires were surfacing? Meg told her she was a fool for holding on to her virginity as if it was a prize. Since her reputation was ruined, and she didn't wish to marry, Meg encouraged her to learn the joy of sinful pleasure. Seeing how happy Meg was with her lover, Rheda was tempted. Even more so, since she'd tasted Lord Strathmore's skills.

Rheda hadn't decided who would be her choice to introduce her into womanhood. A man who did not know her, a man passing through Deal would have been ideal. Unfortunately, now she couldn't imagine anyone other than Lord Strathmore. All other men of her acquaintance paled into invisibility next to him.

She batted away this maddening realization like a tiresome bee.

Just then, Jamieson entered. "The enemy's carriage is coming up the driveway."

She tsked. "It is Lady Hale as well. You had best go and get ready to show them in. Lord Strathmore should have

Caesar with him. He has promised me the use of his stallion to service my mares."

"In return for what?" Jamieson bristled with impatience. "I wish Master Daniel was here. I do not trust his lordship."

Her smile faltered. "There is no need to worry Daniel just yet. We are not even sure what his lordship wants."

Jamieson snorted. "I know what he's wanting."

Rheda felt her cheeks heating. "Don't be ridiculous. He has Lady Umbridge for that. Besides, I am not the sort of woman he would dally with. He might find himself married."

Jamieson glared. "A rakehell is not known for respecting boundaries. Why is he sniffing around your petticoats then?"

She glanced toward the door. "Daniel is not to know— you must promise me you will not tell him."

Jamieson's eyes narrowed. "Tell him what?"

Rheda swallowed and tried to look nonchalant. "I wasn't completely honest last night. I bumped into Lord Strathmore a few days ago."

Jamieson raised an eyebrow. "I know that. That is how you knew about Caesar."

"I happened to be rolling a cask to Meg's at the time. He seemed to be very interested in my barrel."

Jamieson's face paled. "Christ, this is even worse than I thought."

Rheda smoothed her ruffled gown of sprigged muslin and checked her hair coiled at her nape. "There is no need to panic until we ascertain just what he is about."

"And how do you intend to do that?"

She lifted her head. "By not telling Daniel for starters. You know what a hothead he has become. I need to keep our viscount busy."

Jamieson stood for a full minute staring at her as if she had gone mad. "The baron's not going to like it."

She gave him her most haughty look. "The baron is not going to know. Daniel actually thinks I should let Lord Strathmore court me. It seems Daniel wants to marry me off.

Let us ensure that is all Daniel thinks this interest in the viscount is."

Jamieson turned to go and admit the visitors.

"Do I have your word on this, Jamieson?" she pressed.

"It's dangerous. I do not trust Lord Strathmore. He's a man, like any other man, and his head will turn just as easily as every other man's when he's alone with you. Be careful." And he left Rheda to ponder on his words.

She tried to gather her composure as she tidied away her correspondence and locked her writing drawer. No one would think to look in a woman's writing desk for evidence of smuggling.

She moved to perch on the chaise. Her nerves were wound so tight she wondered if they would snap with a musical twang. She managed to take one deep calming breath before Jamieson announced, "Lady Hale and Lord Strathmore."

The scathing emphasis on Lord Strathmore's name earned Jamieson a quizzing look from Lady Hale, as Rheda rose to greet her.

"Rheda my dear . . . ," Lady Hale said as she accepted Rheda's kiss on her cheeks. "I am relieved to see you looking so well, but it is a shame you couldn't attend our dinner last night. Lord Strathmore was devastated at your absence."

She lifted an eyebrow at Lord Strathmore. He simply bowed over her hand. "Your presence was sorely missed, Miss Kerrich."

She withdrew her fingers before he could feel the slight tremble in her hands. Gone was the dashing pirate of the previous evening.

Today he was dressed with the casual elegance of a country lord at his leisure. His morning coat, a rich shade of burgundy, was worn over a single-breasted silk waistcoat with a high standing collar and fawn twill trousers. The effect was decidedly unsettling.

"Is Christopher not with you?" she asked. Rufus's smile diminished.

"No, he had urgent business at the last minute. He sends his fondest regards," Lady Hale added.

"Never mind, I will simply have to devote myself to Lord Strathmore." She noted his lordship's surprised look. No doubt he was trying to decide what she was up to. "I hope I have not taken you away from more important matters. I am quite recovered, Lady Hale. There was no need to trouble yourselves."

Staring at Lord Strathmore, she took two steps back and offered her visitors a seat. Rufus waited until Lady Hale was comfortable before he took the settee across from her. His large frame filled the piece of furniture.

He slid his long legs out in front of him and crossed one booted foot over the other, as if he was quite at home. One hand rose to tug at his cuffs.

Her words rushed out in fierce volley. "Where is your friend, Lord Worthington? He would have been welcome to join us."

Lord Strathmore's eyebrows knitted together.

Lady Hale answered. "The Marquis of Worthington has taken Lady Umbridge to see Jacob's Point. I did not know you'd had the pleasure of meeting Stephen."

Rheda sent a panicked look toward Rufus.

"Lady Kerrich gave us directions the day Lord Worthington and I arrived," Rufus said, coming to her aid, another lie. She flushed. Damn, she had almost given the game away.

"Oh, had I known I would have invited the marquis as well. You should have told me, Lord Strathmore."

"Please call me Rufus, ladies. I am quite certain we are past formalities."

"Charming. And you must call me Helen. Both of you. Lady Hale makes me feel older than my numerous years."

"Nonsense, you still look like a young woman, Helen."

"Isn't he the most wicked flatterer, Rheda?"

"So I am learning, Helen."

He slid Rheda a disarming smile. "Miss Kerrich, you do look a little pale. Did you not sleep well?"

She held herself stiffly. She was not about to invite any familiarity by letting him call her by her first name. "I slept well, Lord Strathmore. I trust you rested peacefully."

"Rufus," he taunted softly. "Well enough. I always do after a night of pleasant discourse." And he bestowed a winning smile on Lady Hale. Helen turned a girlish shade of pink, matching the roses in the vase on Rheda's writing table in the corner of the room directly behind Lord Strathmore.

"Rufus, perhaps Rheda would feel revived with some fresh air."

"Excellent idea. I have brought Caesar with me. Shall we see if he is in the mood to play?" His mocking gaze traveled over her body. "I hear you are after some servicing . . ." He paused before adding, "Your horses, that is. They were the topic of discussion last night. Perhaps I could see them?"

Gooseflesh rose on her arms. She did not want to be alone with him. He would ask her too many questions. She was not ready; her body was far too aware of him.

"We have not had any refreshments yet. I am sure Lady Hale would like some tea."

Rheda sank farther back in her chair, hoping it would swallow her and she would never have to get up. Folding her hands nervously in her lap, she watched for his next move, her heart pounding in her chest.

"Do not wait for me, dear girl. When a handsome man asks for a stroll on a sunny day, a young woman should accept with relish."

Rheda felt her face begin to heat. "I will ring for my maid; she can chaperone us."

"Nonsense, you do not need a chaperone. I trust Lord Strathmore implicitly. He is a fine gentleman." Lady Hale aimed a frigid stare in his direction. "Besides, your two mothers were my best friends. Rufus knows the penalty I

would extract for any inappropriate behavior, do you not, my boy?"

Rufus laughed, relaxing the tension in the room. "I shall consider myself duly warned." He offered Rheda his arm. "Shall we?"

She took his outstretched arm. Why did his simple nearness affect her so? It wasn't merely that he was handsome. She'd always considered herself immune to a handsome face. She was hard pressed to explain the deplorable effect that Rufus Knight, Lord Strathmore, had on her.

Conscious of Lady Hale's eyes on her she said, "I will show you to the stables. I might as well instruct Jamieson to put Caesar to work while you are here."

More likely it was the threat he posed. She kept looking straight ahead, ignoring the disturbing presence beside her. Whatever his attributes, they made her absurdly breathless and agitated.

As they made their way in silence across to the stable block, her excitement grew—Caesar. Today her dream began in earnest. No one could understand her driving need to implement her plan. It spelled the first step in her independence.

She was startled by Strathmore's smooth velvet voice. "Having your own horse stud means much to you, does it not?"

If she were honest with herself, she would admit it meant everything. Rheda gave a low laugh, which helped staunch the ache in her throat at the poignant memories she was trying to hold at bay.

This moment signaled the end of her constant and denigrating dependence on men. She would never accept her mother's life of servitude to a man. A piece of property to be bartered, a breeder, only taken out to either show off, or worse, to falsely charm so that her father could have his way.

She swallowed her disturbing memories. It was becoming extremely hard to bear that Daniel was beginning to think like most men.

She straightened her spine. She would rather go and live with Meg in her small cottage than be forced to marry, to endure as her mother had. She would soon have enough money to buy a few acres. She would use the land and her horses to make her own way in the world. Besides, she could always continue to use Dark Shadow. She did not really want to, but the alternative, the thought of relying on any man, even Daniel, was too scary.

"Does it not?" he repeated softy.

"Yes." She finally answered his question. "My horses mean everything to me."

"Everything or simply a means to an end? A way to build yourself some security. To ensure your life is your own."

She started and gave him a sideways glance. Bother the man. He was too perceptive by far. What else had he gleaned in their brief encounters? "Does that surprise you?"

His jeweled eyes glinted down from beneath perfectly arched brows. "No. Having seen you in action, nothing about you surprises me."

That honest observation won a reluctant laugh from Rheda. "I am nothing like the other ladies of the *ton* then?"

"You are a spitfire and a hoyden. A woman who goes after what she wants with dogged determination."

She raised an eyebrow. "That almost sounds like praise. Or perhaps envy. I thought men like you always did what you wanted, when you wanted . . ." She added dryly, "With anyone you wanted."

"You have experienced a lot of men then?"

"My father and his friends."

His eyes held hers as if trying to uncover all her secrets. "I can admire a person who chases their dreams," he said, his tone edged with respect.

Was he toying with her? "Is that why you are in Kent, my lord? To chase your dreams?"

His laugh was husky and charming—and quite disarming. "Perhaps you are my dream, Miss Kerrich."

"I think for a man such as you, seducing women is sport."

But not a bloodsport. She studied the viscount measuringly, as if she'd catch him out. He was a powerfully built man, broad chested and muscular. The top of her head barely came to his shoulder. Ordinarily, she was wary of powerful men. Yet surprisingly Lord Strathmore did not make her apprehensive. The few smugglers she'd met had a hint of violence about them. She had the measure of the man before her. His height and strength were not used to frighten; he had subtle weapons far more dangerous to a woman—his face and virility.

No, he did not physically frighten her. Her fear of him was seated on a deeper, more personal level. He tempted her. His aura of masculinity seduced her. She could feel her body succumbing to his presence as easily as a drunkard succumbed to free brandy.

"Come now, Miss Kerrich, not all men are like your father," Lord Strathmore observed, interrupting her intent perusal.

She caught herself before she stumbled over the cobblestones of the courtyard. Blast him. He really *was* too perceptive.

"My father is the only experience of men I have. I have yet to meet a man who makes me want to take a risk and test my knowledge."

Her uneasiness grew. Had he realized that statement was a lie? She did not want to admit her attraction to Lord Strathmore. He made her feel urges she had until recently successfully suppressed. She did not care for the sensations at all. Indeed, the sense of power, of vitality, about him was suffocating.

The sound of Caesar's neighing greeted them as they approached the stable. He was off to the left in the corral, the scent of the mares making him agitated.

They entered the stables together, Desert Rose calling out a welcome to her mistress. Jamieson appeared out of the shadows.

He nodded his head. "Your lordship. Miss Kerrich."

To her annoyance Lord Strathmore took over. "Jamieson, can you halter Desert Rose? We'll start with her since she seemed to take a fancy to Caesar last night." He turned to Rheda. "Did you wish to go back to the house and keep Lady Hale company? This is not an occupation for a lady to witness. Jamieson and I can take it from here."

She knew that she should do as he suggested. It was not proper. A proper young lady would never consent to watch animals mating. Besides, Lady Hale was alone. However, his manner of taking charge irked her. "I will stay. They are my horses, after all. I should learn the procedure for future reference."

His handsome mouth quirked. "I shall look forward to teaching you the ins and outs of breeding."

Her face heated. "I know what happens. I have seen it before."

"It?"

Her face was burning. "I have seen animals mating before."

His tone turned wry as he stripped off his jacket and waistcoat. He discarded his cravat and began rolling up his shirtsleeves. "You may wish to stand back. It can be a messy business."

She dragged her eyes away from the sight of his sinewy bare forearms, tanned and thick with muscle. The glimpse of smooth skin at the open neck of his shirt made her stomach flutter. She could see his chestnut eyes dancing with laughter. Stiffening her spine, Rheda opened her mouth to remonstrate, but he spoke again. "Caesar can smell Desert Rose. He can tell she is ready for him. A stallion is much like a man. Once he has his sights set on a mare, he will let nothing get in the way of having her."

"Then this mating should be a success."

Rufus turned to check that Jamieson was leading the mare out toward the corral. "Don't introduce them until I get there. We need to check the mare is still receptive and tease

the pair for a bit. It's essential that Caesar knows I'm fully in control, long before Desert Rose reaches him, because if the stallion suspects for one minute that I'm the weaker party, then he'll become difficult to control."

"Jamieson had no problems last night. I think you are making this seem more difficult than it is." And she moved to go around him.

His hand circled her upper arm and pulled her back. At her yelp of pain he dropped her arm as if he'd been burned. "I'm sorry. I did not think my grip was that firm."

She rubbed her upper arm. "It's not. My arms are tender from holding Desert Rose steady last night. Your stallion weighs a ton, and poor Desert Rose almost buckled under his weight."

A frown deepened on his face. "That is why I suggested leaving the task to men," he said gruffly.

"I am not disagreeing with you. Today I merely want to learn. It is my empire we are trying to build." She marched passed him out toward the corral.

She did not have to turn around to know his eyes followed her. She could feel the heat of his gaze like a caress.

As soon as they reached the fence Rufus took control of his stallion. "Caesar, here. He's experienced in breeding and will obey my command. Like all well-trained stallions, even if he is in the middle of copulation he would dismount if instructed."

The horse obeyed his summons even though Desert Rose was being tethered across the other side of the enclosure, well away from where Rufus stood. "Good boy. Are you ready to have some fun, Caesar? We have an audience today. A woman you must try to impress," he whispered loud enough for Rheda to hear. He was so transparent. He thought watching horses mating would make her uncomfortable.

He did not know her very well.

"Jamieson, are you ready?"

Jamieson nodded. Rufus put the lead on Caesar and

walked him toward the mare. "You always approach the mare diagonally from the side. Don't let the stallion come up behind her; he will often get too excited and make the mare nervous."

Rheda watched the stallion's approach in fascination.

"Notice that I am keeping Caesar far enough away from the mare so that all he can do is reach his neck over and nuzzle her hindquarters. I'm letting the stallion tease her for a couple minutes. To both further assess her willingness to allow him to mount her and to enforce to Caesar that I'm in control. If he knows I'm in charge he'll behave himself and he'll only mount when I give permission."

Keeping full control of Caesar, Rufus moved the stallion back behind Desert Rose. Caesar began prancing and snorting. On Rufus's command, "Up, Caesar," the big stallion mounted the mare. With cheeks flaming, Rheda squirmed upon seeing the size of the stallion's phallus as Rufus guided it into the mare. Her body flushed with heat. The act of copulation was very different from last night. It had been dark and she had been holding Desert Rose's head. She could not believe the size of the stallion. No wonder Desert Rose squirmed.

Rufus, damn him, noted her embarrassment. "Unlike people, horses do not thrust."

Instantly an image of Rufus thrusting inside her filled her head. He would be large, too. Everything about the man was oversized: his ego, his presence, the anatomy of his groin . . . What would it feel like? Would she enjoy it as her mare seemed to be doing? She raised a hand to her hot face.

"Hold her steady, Jamieson; it won't be long now."

Rufus was right. Suddenly, Caesar gave an almighty groan, and Rufus began to urge the large stallion to dismount. "The sound he made indicates he has ejaculated. Jamieson, walk Desert Rose around the stable yard for about quarter of an hour."

Jamieson nodded and moved off.

Rufus let Caesar off the harness, and the horse took off galloping around the enclosure. "He's pleased with himself." They walked in silence back to the stable. Jamieson was still walking the mare in the yard.

Once inside the dark and shadowy stables, Rufus walked deliberately toward her. She tried to move out of his way, but she wasn't quick enough and soon found herself up against the stable wall. Rufus's voice was soft and sensual, calling to her. "Men, too, can tell when a woman is ripe for the taking."

Rheda found her gaze riveted on his lips. Her heart began to pound in her chest. Her eyes swept across the rest of his face and froze at the expression that greeted her. He had gone quite still. There was soft fire in his eyes, and his gaze held her spellbound.

He reached up and slid his fingers behind her nape. Her breathing faltered altogether. Then shockingly, he lowered his mouth to meet hers in a feather-light contact.

Once again she was immersed in a rush of sensation at the exquisite caress. His lips were warm and firm, yet enticingly soft at the same time—and much too tempting.

Stifling a gasp, Rheda pressed her palms against his chest and pulled back her reeling head. "I am not a mare to be taken on your whim."

"So you admit you want to be taken. It is only a matter of when."

Anger flared, dousing her desire. She shoved him away from her and moved away from the wall. To her disappointment he did not even try to stop her. She stood breathing hard looking at his strong face, arresting and strikingly handsome in the dim stable light. He had a beautiful mouth; his lips were chiseled and generous, and they curved now in a knowing smile as he returned her regard.

"You are delusional," she scathingly stated.

"You have no idea what you are missing, sweetheart. Unlike animals, people experience passion."

"I am sure you would know."

He approached across the stable floor. Her legs were shaking too much to move away. He stood so close her breasts almost brushed his chest, but he did not touch her. "But do you know? Have you ever been so caught up in passion you forgot yourself?" His voice became husky. "I'd like to kiss you again."

She was trapped by the fire in his eyes. Rufus bent toward her, and his warm breath caressed her mouth. Rheda was powerless to move. His hand cupped the back of her head. He drew her close, and his other arm encircled her waist, pulling her roughly against his solid form. She was swamped by the strength and power of the man, yet not afraid. His lips began to play over hers with exquisite pressure. This kiss was slow and erotic and extremely thorough. Parting her lips, his tongue slid into her mouth, creating an intense yearning inside her.

The effect of his kiss had her reaching to grip his shoulders. His lips deepened the kiss, his tongue penetrating and swirling in her mouth, stroking her desire. The heady sensation he aroused was addictive.

She could not resist letting him continue.

Not when he was assailing her mouth with such silken roughness . . . molding, tasting, teasing, and ultimately conquering. All her senses felt pummeled as his tongue worked its magic provocatively against hers, playing a game she desperately wanted to win. But the winning strategy escaped her knowledge. Her body pushed hard against him, and a small moan of surrender escaped her lips.

In response, his kiss only deepened.

She raised her hand to his dark chestnut locks. They felt amazingly thick and silky. His hand that had been holding her head slid down her shoulder and moved to where the square décolletage of her dress exposed the pale skin above her breasts.

She was unprepared for the explosion of feeling that swept

her body when his knuckles skimmed the upper swells of her breasts. She gasped against his mouth, but he kept on kissing her, arousing with firm tender stokes of his tongue, slowly driving, deliciously plundering.

She wanted to move closer, to climb right in him and take that which had been denied her for so long. He shifted, and through her skirts she felt the pressure of his sinewy thigh against her femininity. At the same time his hand moved lower to mould and cup her aching breast.

Her moan was decidedly audible within the quiet of the stable, but she was beyond caring as the feverish surge of pleasure overwhelmed her. When his fingertips discovered her nipple through her bodice, fire streaked through her limbs, flooding her veins with shuddering heat.

She could feel the wildness stirring in her blood. It clamored for this captivating man's erotic assault on her senses. He was driving her mad, encouraging her response and taking her to a place she longed to go.

He was seducing her. And she was content to let him.

Yet, it was his tenderness that stunned her the most. She could feel how he was holding back his own strength and needs. Needs? She could feel the hard, extremely large evidence of his arousal against her stomach. Merciful heaven, what was she doing? A desperate voice protested in her head, more was dangerous.

He was dangerous.

Danger had never been more tantalizing.

Rufus lifted his mouth from hers. He struggled to get his breathing under control. "See what you do to me, Rheda? I'm as eager as my stallion."

"I'm not doing anything to you. From what little I know of your reputation you'd be eager for any woman. You are merely trying to seduce me."

"Yes. I am," he admitted, "and it's working."

He caught her blink of surprise at his admission and boast.

She cut her gaze away, and he stood mesmerized by the swallow of her throat. "Your touch . . . it does excite me." She turned to look into his eyes. "But a seasoned rake such as you knows that. The signs are there for your senses to see and feel."

Rufus shook his head to clear it of his driving need to possess her. He could take her, here and now. He knew it, and the beauty before him knew it, too. Yet, he felt dissatisfied. Where was the honor in her surrender? He was too skilled for her to resist, and having seen the primal mating of the horses, her blood was stirred.

Yet, he had to push her. Had to try and break down her resolve. He would not make love to her here even though his body hurt from his restraint. He wanted the first time with Rheda to be in a bed—his bed. Not in a stable reeking of manure and horses. He wanted to take his time, overwhelm her with pleasure, and ensure she fell completely under his thrall.

He would enslave her body. Make her crave his touch. Make her lose her mind in pleasure. Then perhaps she'd be more pliable. Perhaps she'd do anything to share his bed again, including letting her guard down and giving him what he really wanted—information.

The only problem was that each time he kissed her, what he wanted changed. Metamorphosed into something dangerous. Retrieving much needed intelligence began to diminish as his desire to claim her rose to a crescendo, beating loudly through his veins.

He lifted his hand and stroked the back of his knuckles along her cheek.

Her sweep of fair lashes lowered, fanning across her warm skin.

"I do wish to seduce you, sweetheart. But I also desire you. Far more than I would wish," he added in a ghost of a whisper.

She looked up at him, unblinking. "Do you always get what you desire, my lord?"

He answered with action. He lifted his hands to cradle her face, then stroked his thumb around the corner of her mouth and then across her sensuous bottom lip. He felt the plump swell of it quiver beneath the pad of his thumb. He leaned forward and skimmed his mouth along the shell of her ear. "Yes," he murmured. "Always."

With a soft growl he picked her up and walked a few strides and sat her upon some hay bales. He crouched at her feet, sliding his hands over her firm thighs, flat stomach, and cradled her breasts. He felt her nipples harden through the layers of her clothes.

He watched her face for any sign of denial. The sun shone through the open doorway, but the gloom of the stable caused the light to flicker over the fine bones of her face and the silken sweep of her eyelashes.

Rheda gasped faintly at his touch and trembled when he hooked his thumbs in the edge of her bodice. No corset. It was as if she welcomed his seduction. Her head went back to rest on the bales piled behind her, and with a deft tug he drew the fabric down, taking her chemise with it, until her pink nipples were exposed. The roaring in his ears increased—she was beautiful.

He hesitated, willing her to protest, but the snorts of the animals surrounding them was the only sound.

Rufus leaned forward to draw her left nipple between his lips; she gasped as his mouth suckled and gently nipped. He took that as a sound of approval. He drew her breast more fully into his mouth until she began to make small, breathy sounds of pleasure. Then he moved to the other breast, first circling the nipple with his tongue, teasing her as Caesar had teased her mare, then sucking at the very hardened tip as he gently nipped with his teeth.

Her murmurs grew more demanding. As Rufus cradled one breast and kissed her deeply, his other hand fisted in her skirts. Fleetingly, he knew he should be horsewhipped. He was not so lost in pleasure that he could not appreciate the

precariousness of their situation. Anyone could come across them—Jamieson, Daniel . . .

Instead he inched her skirts higher, then eased one hand between her thighs, touching her lightly in her most intimate place. He stroked her there, wanting to tease and tantalize. He played her with harmless little touches interspersed with the most unchaste caresses possible.

He drew back in order to feast on the golden curls at the junction of her thighs and breathe in the arousing scent of her.

Then he touched her intimately, and her small gasp made his blood flow molten in his veins. The silken skin between her thighs acted like a compass. All else, even her perfect breasts, were forgotten.

He touched the tangle of silken curls, and his body thrilled as he felt her wetness. "Oh, sweet Jesus," she murmured as he stroked her sensitive flesh.

He leaned forward and whispered "Beautiful Rheda" against her mouth before he stroked a finger deep inside her tight sheath. This time her gasp verged on something more.

She gave a little moan of surrender when he eased a second finger inside her. He wanted to give her pleasure. Exquisite, extraordinary pleasure. The kind of mind-clouding pleasure that might make her forget to be wary of him and divulge what he needed to hear.

With one hand fingering her taut nipple, he plunged his tongue deep within her mouth to match his fingers' ministrations. Her hips rose and she cried out again, but softly. A wither of a sound. Her breathing slowly grew raspier with each stroke of his thumb over her tightened nub, as he continued to penetrate her. Over and over he drew his fingers through the folds that guarded her pleasure until he could feel the little nub of her arousal, unmistakably firm and trembling.

"Rufus," she whispered, her hands clawing the bales of hay they sat upon.

He felt her climax inching near. She was murmuring his name over and over, and it fairly blew his head off. The endearment almost making him spill in his breeches, something he'd not done since a very young lad.

Her head jerked up, and her breath came on a rough cry. Her hips undulated with each stroke. He felt her begin to tighten around his fingers. She was passion personified. Beautiful. Wild. Sensual. With one finger and his thumb, he opened her wider, teasing her with quick, delicate strokes until she gave a strangled cry. And then she was shaking all over, her limbs stiffening as she shuddered with her release. He kissed her slender neck as she trembled and then nuzzled the frantic pulse at the base of her throat. Erotic. The sight and sound of her was so erotic it killed him.

He rose up and took her trembling lips in a searing kiss. He felt his heart flutter and engage in his chest. No. He forced the heady feelings down. He could not want to want her. His own needs must be denied. There was too much at stake.

Just then a commotion out by the corral made him draw back. He took in her flushed face. With a pang he realized he wished there could be more. Wished she wasn't who he knew her to be. A woman with secrets. A possible traitor. Never again would he let himself feel for a woman involved in his mission. He would have no more deaths on his hands.

He felt tarnished at the knowledge only her seduction and complete surrender would aid in the capture of the traitor. If he could he'd wish more for her.

He needed some fresh air. The scent of her was making him light-headed.

"It seems another female is impatient for her mate's touch. Please excuse me while I see to Caesar."

How could she have let that happen? Her body tingled in the afterglow of his skillful lovemaking, quickly followed by heated shame. He'd boasted of his skills as a rake, and he was

not wrong. The pleasure was indescribable, and to her horror it left her wanting more.

Worse. Wanting him.

Why did he unleash these strong feelings within her? He was a rake like any other.

Except, cried a tiny voice inside her, he is not like any other. His combination of beauty, wit, and brains had her in a scramble. She'd not met a man who matched her in intellect. Nor one whose outer beauty made her feel, and want, naughty, forbidden delights.

Rheda was still trying to make sense of what she'd let occur when Rufus moved to exit the stable. Turning with a shrug, he looked back at her. His face was all dark shadows as he blocked the light from the doors. It was a moment before he spoke. "When I'm done, I want you to show me Fraser's Landing."

Rheda stiffened. "You said you knew where it was."

He shook his head. She wished she could see the expression on his face. "I want you to show me exactly where you found the barrel." He turned to leave, calling over his shoulder, "Only then will I know if you deliberately lied to me."

This time a shiver that had nothing to do with delicious desire slid down her spine. How could he do that? It was as if the splendor of their intimate moment had never transpired. She was still tingling all over, while the warm yearning in her feminine center continued to throb.

Rheda's heart ached in her chest. God he was ruthless in his pursuit of the truth. And skillful. Her body still hummed. She tidied herself up, determined to remember that she could not let his seduction weaken her resolve.

"I lied, my lord," she whispered hoarsely under her breath. "And no matter how much you make my body sing, I'll never tell you the truth. But I'll play your game. I'll let you seduce me until I'm sated with pleasure." His seduction of her should keep him off balance and out of their business.

Chapter 11

It had been an exhausting day. As he'd thought, there was no way Rheda could have rolled the barrel up the slope at Fraser's Landing. Unless she had help. Rheda was either lying about where she found the barrel, or lying about being on her own.

Why did he not simply use his strength and power to overwhelm her? The growing desire to spank the truth from her had seen him send her home alone.

He'd spent the rest of the afternoon working with White Lily and Caesar. Near the end of the day Daniel arrived home and suggested a swim. He'd readily agreed. The scent of Rheda on his skin had driven him mad all afternoon.

Daniel invited him to stay for dinner, and the men had drunk into the early hours. Rufus took the opportunity of seeing if a little alcohol would loosen the baron's tongue. It had loosened but not about Dark Shadow, only his angelic sister. Daniel was taking the opportunity to push a match. If only he knew the truth. Rufus wanted only one thing from his sister—all right, two—her knowledge *and* her body.

Now, close to dawn, he rode into Hastingleigh and stabled Caesar himself. He'd enjoyed his dinner at Tumsbury Cliff Manor. Daniel was exuberant in his youth. It was fun to remember what he'd been like at Daniel's age. The only drawback was his body had been hard almost the entire evening. His awareness of Rheda annoyed him. He was old enough

and experienced enough with women to be able to ignore her appeal.

His body stirred once more. Tonight Miss Kerrich had obviously decided to play a very dangerous game with him. How like her to throw down a challenge. No doubt having Daniel in residence made her brave enough to flaunt her abundant charms.

Her attempts at seduction were successful; he was hard and hungry for more than food. Her dress had obviously been altered to show more of her stunning cleavage than was acceptable. Daniel, so caught up in his own excitement of having another male dinner guest, didn't seem to notice how she leaned over the table at every opportunity, her ripe breasts almost bursting free of the scanty material covering them.

Halfway through dinner it had been he who was praying. Praying he could hold fast to his determination not to throw her on the table and ravish her before the main course.

He needed a woman. Any woman would do. Any woman except a golden-haired goddess who, if she knew how much he craved a taste, would likely use it against him. Perhaps a quick trip into Deal was needed. A dalliance with young Lucy would see to his needs. He sighed out loud. He knew he didn't want any other woman. He wanted Rheda. He growled deep in his throat. Why did he desire the one woman he could not have?

He'd sworn that after Marguerite he would not get involved with any woman when on a mission. He could seduce when required but never lower his guard enough to enjoy or engage any feelings other than lust. Rheda made him feel too much—exactly like Marguerite. What was wrong with him?

Upon entering his bedchamber he crossed directly to the table to pour himself a large whiskey. He was too tired to ride into town anyway. Controlling his frisky stallion that afternoon had taken a lot of strength, and his patrol along the

coast on his way back, hoping to catch a glimpse of smuggling, had meant it was now almost morning.

He knew searching on his ride home would be a waste of time. Smugglers rarely operated on a cloudless, star-filled night. About a mile from Hastingleigh his warm bed had beckoned.

He took yet another sip of dulling alcohol and let it slide down his throat. Sinking into the chair by the dying fire, he closed his eyes. Immediately, Rheda's image flashed in his head. Her bare breasts, her nipples puckered and hard in his mouth. Her scent, her soft moans as he'd pleasured her. His groin throbbed. God, he was going to have to take matters into his own hand before he burst.

With his free hand he popped the buttons of his breeches. His erection sprang free. He wrapped his fist around his throbbing shaft, imagining Rheda down on her knees, her mouth hot and warm, sucking him dry. He groaned.

He continued to pleasure himself. The dream of her so real he swore he could feel her. God, her mouth felt good. His glass of unfinished whiskey dropped to the floor. He could feel her small hands on his thighs, her silken tongue running up the length of him. Her mouth teasing the head of his cock, until she sucked hard and drew him all the way into her mouth. He didn't want the dream to end. He was close to coming. His hips lifted in the chair. A woman's whimper of pleasure filled his hearing. Her moans sent him over the edge. He surged up and emptied his seed, his eyes flashed open, and to his horror Lady Umbridge was on her knees, her mouth drinking him dry. The whiskey began to rise into his mouth. He hurriedly pushed her off him and rose to his feet, fumbling to right his trousers.

He swung around to face her, humiliation burning his face. With anger building he watched her lick her lips and give a satisfied smile. "I've been dying for a taste of you for so long, my lord. I was not disappointed."

His voice matched how he was feeling, full of disgust, flat, and cold. "Get out."

She rose to her feet and let her robe slide to the floor. She stood before him completely naked. Naked in more ways than one. There was not a hair on her mound. Rufus had never seen the likes of this before. He'd read about the Arabs' preference for hairlessness, but he'd never known an English lady to indulge. He couldn't help himself. His body stirred at the sight of her woman's lips clearly visible to his eye.

She was a beautiful woman, and she knew it. He watched with revulsion rising as she made her way toward him. How could he feel such loathing for a woman and yet feel his body undoubtedly reacting to her exposed charms?

She stood before him, a smug smile masking her hard features. She took his hand and placed it on her mound. "Feel me. Have you ever seen or felt a woman who has been de-haired?" The skin was smooth, and he could feel and see all of her. He felt himself hardening against his will.

"When I sit on your face you'll feel like you're pleasuring a young girl."

He withdrew his hand as if she had leprosy. His desire withered, and he once again felt ill. He knew men who craved young girls and some even boys. The thought of tainting the innocence of one so young was abhorrent to him. "You disgust me. Get out of my room. In the future I shall have to remember to lock my door."

Her face darkened with anger. "You didn't seem to mind when I had my mouth wrapped around your cock. Your groans told me how much you enjoyed my attentions."

"I did not know it was you."

Her eyes narrowed. She spread her naked arms wide. "I don't see anyone else here."

He felt his face flush further.

"Ah, I see. You were dreaming of someone. Who?"

Rufus ignored her and moved to pick up her robe. "Put

this on and get out." He shoved the garment at her. "Before I summon Stephen."

Lady Umbridge gave him a knowing gaze. "Lady Hale said you'd stayed at the baron's for dinner. Your reputation with the ladies clearly indicates it is not the baron you were dreaming of, but he does have a sister." She pulled the garment on and covered her nakedness. "How interesting." At the door she hesitated. "You'd be unwise to make an enemy of me, Lord Strathmore. I could make your life very difficult"—she paused—"or very pleasurable. The choice is yours."

He refused to answer, but simply held her gaze.

She shrugged her shoulders. "Tomorrow night I shall come to your room. If your door is locked I will know what path you have taken." With that she slipped from his room.

Rufus moved and locked the door after her. He ran a hand through his hair and, appalled with himself, whispered, "It will be bolted."

Their secret pleasure room, tucked away in the old ruins, was suffocating with heat. The fire roared, and the manly scent of sweat, sex, and alcohol filled the air.

"No more boys for a while, Master. Once the villagers of Deal realize another boy is missing, they will ask questions."

Master—the name soothed his ego and filled his body with ungodly pride—how he craved the name. He watched his plaything bend and stoke the fire, the sight of open buttocks causing his sleeping manhood to stir. His sex slave had been with him for five years now, and must be getting on toward twenty. Perhaps it was time to replace him, but oh his mouth could do such wondrous things to one's body, and his appetite for perversity rivaled his own.

"*Mon ami,* don't worry your pretty head over such things." His French accent was more pronounced in his opium-induced haze.

Although the room was already hot, the young man

stoked the fire until they could've been sinners in the depths of hell. But to him it was heaven. For the added heat aided the body's absorption of the opium contained in the oil sleeking their skin.

His sex slave turned to face him. "Master, you should not have brought the boy here. It was dangerous. What if he were found here? What if they caught you? I couldn't bear to lose you . . ."

"Hush, my sweet. The boy is dead and gone. Come here."

His eyes greedily roamed over the young man standing naked before him, and his needs roared to life. His shaft hardened in an enticing offer. He loved watching the fragrant oil they rubbed all over their bodies glisten in the firelight. The young man before him looked like a Greek god: sleek, hairless, and more beautiful than any man he'd ever seen.

Except one. Rufus Knight, Viscount Strathmore.

Soon he would have the virile viscount at his mercy and when he did . . . He closed his eyes and let his imagination run wild. He felt himself grow harder as he pictured Rufus on his knees at his feet, his cock in Rufus's mouth.

His sex slave groaned.

He opened his eyes and watched the young man's eyes light with animal lust at the sight of his master's stirring member. God, he was lucky to find such a toy.

"*Veins m'aimer*—come love me, my boy—" He didn't have time to finish his sentence before a groan was torn from his lips as his plaything's clever tongue and mouth began servicing him with relish.

Chapter 12

Rufus awoke very early, with a very sore head. He'd drunk himself into oblivion following Lady Umbridge's distasteful visit. Taking a washcloth, he'd almost rubbed himself raw. His skin crawled remembering her mouth on him. Blast Stephen and his inability to keep his mistress under control. Perhaps he should tell him what occurred and let him deal with it. Why did he feel guilty when he'd done nothing to encourage the situation? He chose to remain silent. They didn't need any distractions while on this mission. He'd tell Stephen afterward.

Not wishing to face his friend, Rufus dressed and decided to ride into Deal alone to see if the villagers' tongues had loosened any since Stephen had thrown a large amount of coin around.

However, the gallop into Deal did little to shake the indecent thoughts of Miss Kerrich. The little devil sitting on his shoulder told him to take her—forget about seducing information—*claim her.* She was like a drug running rampant in his blood. If he did not have a taste and soon, the craving would race out of control.

She was becoming an obsession, like Marguerite. And *look how well that ended,* he growled to himself.

Marguerite had led him about like a bull with a ring through its nose, a dog on a leash, a stallion broken to saddle. She'd been his contact in Belgium. He'd fallen in love

with her at first sight, the word *angel* instantly popping into his head. She'd been small and delicate, a fair-haired waif whose decorum signaled perfection.

All his protective instincts had roared to life. He'd hated the fact Marguerite put herself in danger in order to help him and to aid the British government.

Fool. In Belgium the only person who'd been in danger was him. He'd been the one in need of protection. From her. From her treachery.

This time he'd not let Rheda get close. He'd not be fooled again. He'd take what he required from her, and he'd succeed in his mission regardless of the consequences to Rheda. She would have to face the penalties of her actions. He would not try to save her and risk his mission.

He set a fast pace, and Caesar rose to the challenge. All too soon, horse and rider rode into the main town square. There was little activity at the normally bustling port. Rufus could tell something was wrong. Decidedly wrong. The town felt even more morose than usual.

Deal was more like a den of iniquity than a thriving fishing port. The dock's abundance of sailors and smuggling cutthroats made the port town look like a version of hell.

Rufus handed Caesar over to the Bosun's Inn stable boy and, ducking his head, entered the somber enclave of the inn itself. Inside he found a mixture of sailors, local shopkeepers, and Revenuers—for once cohabitating without animosity.

They were all silent, with heads bowed, and no one seemed to notice his entrance. There was no sign of Lucy. He'd been half tempted to seek her out for some pleasurable relief. He refused to admit that only a golden-haired goddess with fire in her emerald eyes was the one he craved. It was business that stopped him dallying and nothing more.

His thoughts were interrupted when one of the men present began to speak. "I don't know how I'm going to break the news to his mother. Her husband, Harry, has only been gone six months. Now her Davy's been taken."

An older man, clearly a fisherman, shook his head. "Something's not right, I tell ya. I saw Davy come ashore last evening. He'd tied the boat up, and he was heading home-ward with a very respectable snapper." The man shook his head. "Davy wouldn't have gone out again. Not in the dark. What for?" He shook his head again and repeated, "Some-thing's not right."

Rufus's eyes gradually became accustomed to the dim light of the tavern. He focused on a bundle of white sodden rags on the table in the corner. A body. The body of a young child by the looks of it. He made to take a step closer when a hand landed on his shoulder. "It is not a pretty sight, Ru-fus. The rocks have cut the lad up pretty bad."

"Alex. What the hell are you doing in Deal? Not that I'm unhappy to see you."

Alexander Smythe, the Earl of Montford, was a close friend. Had been since they started their first year of school together. The boy with the face of a cherub turned out to hide the naughtiest temperament when it came to schoolboy pranks, and Rufus found himself being caned alongside Alex numerous times.

Upon adulthood, Alex's fair-haired air of innocence, coupled with chiseled aristocratic good looks, ensured they all—Rufus, Anthony, Richard, and Alex—were always sur-rounded with beautiful willing wenches.

"When we left London, you'd decided to escape to your hunting lodge with two perky actresses. I didn't expect you to emerge from your lair for at least a sennight. Alex, don't tell me you're so jaded that after only a few days you gave up your sweet treats."

"Don't be a bore. I did offer to share if I recall, but God and country came first. This atoning for the sins of your fa-ther is becoming tiresome. You're turning down all the fun and leaving a man with absolutely no competition when it comes to seducing willing wenches. The female battlefield is

far too easy with you forever leaving town to chase after villains."

Rufus's friend, although angelic of face, was anything but. Alexander was the most notorious rake in all of England, well—since their friend Lord Wickham's, Anthony Craven's, marriage.

"That's easy for you to say. Your father was a paragon of virtue. He must be turning in his grave at your exploits."

Alex mocked him. "Like you, there is no dishonor in my seductions." He paused and gave his trademark innocent smile that had many Society mothers fooled. "None that have come to light, that is. As it happens I am on a mission of my own. A damsel in distress."

Rufus couldn't help letting his lips curl into a smile, his tone equally mocking. "If you're in Southern England I assume it must be Miss Vanessa Thornton. We all know what she wants. You leg-shackled, married—to her. Be careful or it will be you who needs rescuing."

Alex ignored his jibe, his mouth firming into a hard line. "Don't start. I hadn't even had time to sample any of my guests' feminine delights before I was summoned. I had to dash back to London and set sail. Women! This is why a man shouldn't form any sort of attachments. But then you learned that lesson the hard way. Your last attachment almost damn well killed you."

Rufus pressed his hand to his side. "I'm lucky. I carry the constant reminder."

"I remember having to stitch you up. Sorry I didn't do such a bang-up job, but I'll wager the ladies smother you with sympathy when they see it."

Rufus swung away from his probing gaze and stared at the dead boy. "What are you doing here, Alex? Other than annoying me."

"Come," Alex said, and led Rufus to the back of the tavern. "It was my ship that pulled the body from the water. I

have to leave immediately for Portsmouth." Before Rufus could tease him further, Alex added, "The message from Vanessa was dire, and you know I promised her father I'd ensure her well-being while he is away. I owe him." Alex's mouth twisted, and he pointed to the body. "However, I can't leave without knowing someone will look into this death. I believe there is more to this than a simple drowning. The marks on the boy's body didn't just come from the rocks. He was found naked; even though the lad was pounded against the rocks, I would have expected some remnants of clothing."

"Was he beaten first?"

"I'm not sure, but there were bruises on his arms as if someone had held him in a vicelike grip." Alex choked on his words. "And there were teeth marks around his groin."

Rufus hit the wall with his fist. "Someone sexually used him? Is that what you think?" His anger now had a target.

"I don't know. It just doesn't look right. I've asked the locals. Too many *young* boys have gone missing over the last eighteen months for it to be coincidence. Boys no one would bother about. I can't stay to investigate, but you can." Alex leveled his gaze, and Rufus saw the anger churning within. "If you have time, can you look into this situation? Do it as a favor to me."

Rufus nodded his head. "No need to ask. I'll do all I can to help." When Alex was a young man of twenty, he was held captive by a Turkish sultan. Rufus did not know the details of his incarceration; Alex refused to talk about it and kept the worst of it from his friends. Suffering in silence.

There was no doubt that the anger Alex felt for this boy's death was real.

It also made Rufus feel sick to his stomach. He knew how important it was for Alex to fight for those who couldn't defend themselves. Rufus remembered several tales of young men, men of great beauty, men like Alex, being used as sex slaves by the perverted Turks. Turks thought nothing of men

with men, men with boys. Sodomy was rife throughout the Ottoman Empire. Perhaps that is why Alex thought he recognized it here.

It was no wonder his friend indulged in all manner of pleasure. Haunted by disturbing memories, Alex sought gratification in order to forget. Rufus did not blame him. It was an escape he used himself—frequently.

Rufus pledged his support. "I shall take care of this matter for you. I'll get some of my men to investigate. If anyone is preying on young boys I will find him. I give you my word." He hesitated to ask but he had to. "In return, could you do something for me?"

Alex remained silent but tilted his head slightly in assent.

"Some of your men must know people in the village. Your ships trade through Deal frequently. It was your tip that alerted me to Dark Shadow. Can you see if they know anything more about the smuggler—who he is? What cove he uses? Time is running out, and the good villagers of Deal appear to be stonewalling me."

"Is the infamous Strathmore charm failing you? Don't tell me you've been unable to seduce a local lass into giving you some information. You *are* slipping. Remind me when I get back to provide you with a demonstration in first-rate seduction."

Rufus frowned, not wanting to admit he'd found only one woman he wanted to seduce—information notwithstanding—but he couldn't. His churning feelings for Rheda were too similar to what he'd felt for Marguerite, and therein lay the danger.

Alex's smile died. "Good heavens. You *have* found a woman to seduce but"—his eyebrows furrowed—"let me guess, it's like Marguerite all over again." Alex shook his head. "Will you never learn? Remember what that evil bitch did to you. Her treachery got Andrew killed, and I thought I'd be giving you a burial at sea when I rescued you." He threw his hands up. "Christ, you stupid sap, you can't trust

women—period. You can't let beauty and soft curves cloud your judgment. Marguerite's weapons. Look how skillfully she wielded them. Women are not the weaker sex. They may not be as physically strong as men, but they have weapons that weaken a man's resolve—"

Rufus hissed. "Don't lecture me. I know damn well how deadly a pretty face and lustful figure can be. I'm guilty of the worst foolishness ever."

Alex's face grew serious. "It wasn't the knife wound that nearly killed you, it was the guilt. It ate you up from the inside until I thought there'd be nothing left."

"Don't—"

His friend did not spare him. "It was not your fault. You were not the hangman. Marguerite deserved her end—"

Rufus raised his hand and pointed his finger. He couldn't stop it from shaking. "No one deserves that end. It is barbaric. I'll never let another woman be hanged. Christ, Alex. You were not there. It took her almost an hour to die. If I'd had my pistol with me I'd have shot her to put her out of her misery."

"She was a murderer and a traitor—"

"Yes she was, but for almost six months she was my—everything. I loved her. I'd never loved any woman the way I loved her, yet I stood back and watched"—he swallowed the rising bile—"I had to watch her suffer like no human being should be made to suffer." His voice betrayed his raw state. "I'll kill a woman myself before I'd let her hang."

Alex raised an eyebrow. "I know you, perhaps better than you know yourself. I'm not sure you'd be capable of such an act."

"After what I've been through I'm not sure you'd know what I am capable of. Marguerite killed my friend. I was too blinded by her beauty to see the real her. It cost someone's life—how can I ever forget that?" His voice edged with steel, he added, "I won't let any woman come between me and my mission ever again—ever!"

"Is that why you won't seduce this woman who obviously can help you?" The two men stood glaring at each other. "Who is she?" Alex finally asked.

"I don't know what you mean . . ."

Alex's steady gaze indicated he did not believe him.

Rufus looked at the floor. "Miss Rheda Kerrich, Baron de Winter's older sister. She was in possession of an unstamped brandy barrel when I first met her. She knows something about Dark Shadow; I can feel it. She's hiding something. She's not as skilled as Marguerite." At Alex's smirk, Rufus scoffed. "At lying. I haven't bedded her."

Alex nodded. "Keep it that way. I didn't save you once, only for you to repeat your folly."

His voice heavy with bitterness, Rufus said, "I won't make the same mistake this time. Now that I am aware of women's treachery, I'll be the one doing the seducing, not the other way around."

"I see. Ignoring your true self has consequences—believe me, I know." Alex sighed as Rufus growled deep in his throat. "Don't listen then. Just remember I won't be here to pick up the pieces this time. Don't get involved with Miss Kerrich. Make her hate you. That ought to ensure she keeps you at arm's length." He waited for affirmation, but Rufus couldn't give it. Already he knew he was in too deep with Rheda. Something about her made him vow to ignore all of Alex's sound advice.

Sensing his defeat, Alex shook his head. "Be careful, Rufus."

"I have the truth on my side, and my blinders are off."

Alex's eyes softened. "Does that mean honor should be stripped aside for the greater good?"

Rufus's temper flared. "Don't twist my words. I'll not sacrifice honor to fight for what I believe in. That would make us no better than the French."

Alex leaned back against the wall and gave a low whistle. "Miss Kerrich has you tied up in knots." He put a hand on

Rufus's shoulder and squeezed. "If she is linked with this smuggler Dark Shadow, how honorable could she be? Dark Shadow is aiding a traitor. Deal with her and shut him down. Quickly."

Rufus ran a hand through his hair. He knew Alex was right. He had to end this inability to be ruthless where Rheda was concerned. It wouldn't matter how good she was in bed, he would ascertain all she knew and wash her out of his system. He gave Alex a shaky smile, resolving there, in the back of the tavern containing a boy's dead body, not to care about any punishment that might befall Rheda. Her actions alone would hold her accountable for whatever befell her.

Just then Alex's second mate arrived and whispered in Alex's ear.

"Sorry, old boy, but the tide's about to turn. I have to go. If she's involved in this you have to do everything in your power to find out. Seduce her and discover the truth. If she's guilty your honor is still intact. If your hunch is not correct, and she is in fact innocent of any and all knowledge about Dark Shadow, what's the worst that could happen?"

Rufus started to shake his head.

Alex laughed. "Let's face it. One lady is much like another where marriage is concerned. As long as they are not too hideous to look at, they know how to look after your household, and they provide children you know categorically to be yours, any female would do." Before he ducked under the door and left the tavern, Alex hesitated and added, "Careful, my friend. Women are dangerous in more ways than one. Let's have no repeat performances."

At Alex's departure, Rufus stood looking out of the empty doorway. Was he making a mistake? Was she innocent of involvement in treason or merely a good actress?

His mouth thinned into a grim line. Marguerite had been a brilliant actress. He'd taken her to his bed and, worse, to his heart. He thought he'd been protecting her against common

French enemies, when in reality she'd been working for them. He pressed his hand against his side, still vividly recalling the agony of her betrayal. A betrayal she'd found effortless.

He thought back to that terrible time. It was eight years ago, when he'd been working in Belgium tracing a stolen British gold shipment for the war office. He and Andrew Peters had traced the shipment to a manor near Marguerite's country estate.

They'd thought themselves so clever, planning the retrieval in a meticulous manner. Only they'd walked into a trap. As they were fired upon, Rufus couldn't understand how it had all gone wrong. It was as if—somehow they'd known?

It wasn't until he'd sprinted across the open meadow to ready the horses to make a last-minute dash to freedom that a sliver of unease pricked his skin.

Where had Marguerite gone? Andrew could take care of himself, but Marguerite was a woman.

For one terrible moment his world spun; he thought she'd been captured. Heedless of danger, he raced back to the house to rescue the woman he knew he could not live without.

He entered the house like a whisper. He could hear swordplay in the back room, and he made his way toward it. When he reached the room it was empty except for Andrew's body lying in an ever increasing pool of blood. He felt for a pulse—there was none.

He bolted to his feet. Marguerite. His heart thudded in his chest, and the pain under his rib cage, as if a fist was squeezing his heart, made him almost fall to his knees. Where was Marguerite? If she'd been taken . . . he felt sick knowing what they'd do to a woman of her beauty.

Then a small hand touched his arm, and she said in a voice filled with tears, "Is he dead?"

Rufus could only nod, his throat tight with emotion. He

pulled her roughly into his arms and held her tight. "Thank God you're safe. Come. We must hurry."

"Wait." She stopped him, and, rising onto her toes, she kissed his lips and thrust a knife in his side. Her laugh echoed through the deserted house. "When Napoleon enters England, I'll visit your family and tell them how you died in my arms. Died a lovesick fool."

Her ridicule still haunted his every waking moment, reminding him to never be a fool again.

He glanced skyward to the Kent sun and prayed for guidance. Marguerite had worn two faces. Did Rheda?

Chapter 13

Upon arriving at Hastingleigh, early, at a less than respectable hour, Rheda would've given anything to deny the spine-tingling awareness had anything to do with hoping to bump into Lord Strathmore. However, to her disappointment, she hadn't been shown into the breakfast room. She'd been left with a pot of tea in Lady Hale's drawing room. It was unlikely Rufus would stumble across her there.

As she sipped her tea, she pondered the man who, against all odds, was occupying her thoughts far too much. Not, sadly, because she wanted to know why he was here in Deal and what he was hunting, but because she could not forget how she felt in his arms.

Despite her vow to keep her feelings for him under control, Rheda felt a surge of desire whenever he was near. She freely admitted she was wilder than most young ladies, but to her shame she never realized she was a wanton. That had to be the reason why she longed for his soft caresses, ached for his dizzying kisses, and desired his experienced touch. His sensual magnetism haunted her no matter what time the day or night.

Putting her cup down, she sighed with longing.

"My, that was a big sigh. Only a man could elicit such feelings from a woman."

Rheda almost fell off her chair. She was no longer alone. A woman of such outstanding beauty that it made her breath

hitch entered the room. The first thing Rheda noticed was her snow-white skin, with not a blemish marring it. She fought the urge to touch the freckles she knew were abundant on her own face. She'd never before wished she'd worn a hat when outdoors.

The sophisticated woman—who looked older than Rheda—walked toward her and smiled. But it was a smile that did not reach her startling blue eyes. With a regal nod of her head, that didn't disturb the thick black tresses wound in a fashionable style about her head, the woman said, "You must be Miss Kerrich."

Rheda ran a hand over her own hair, trying to tidy the riotous curls. It was a hopeless cause. Wisps had escaped her clips on the gallop over here. She must look like she'd been thrown through a hedge.

The woman smoothed delicate, well-manicured hands over her stylish, deep lavender muslin gown covered with delicate lace insets, then took a seat opposite her. Rheda's hands itched to smooth the skirts of her well-worn riding habit, but she stopped herself. Why did she care what this stranger thought?

"You have me at a disadvantage," she responded.

"You know how to deflate a lady. I was sure your brother would have mentioned me."

Lady Umbridge. How could Rheda not have guessed? The widow was a startling beauty. The bitterness of jealousy scored her mouth. No wonder Lord Strathmore was not at all tempted by her behavior at dinner the previous evening. Rheda could never compete with a woman of such poise and beauty. "Pardon me. Of course I should have known who you were. Daniel has spoken of your beauty. He did not exaggerate."

"How kind of you to say so."

Rheda noted she did not return with a similar compliment. Why would she? Compared to this lady, Rheda looked like a farmer's daughter.

"You keep country hours I see, Miss Kerrich. I assume you are here to see Lady Hale." Her words were in contrast to her smile, which bordered on a smirk.

Rheda decided she'd had enough of being politely slighted. "Please, call me Rheda. Who else would I be here to see?" She made her tone as sweet as her shimmering temper would allow.

Lady Umbridge inclined her head. "You may call me Fleur." She indicated the tea pot. "May I?"

"Please. Help yourself—Fleur."

Fleur poured her tea and added three sugar lumps. "I adore sweet things. Now where were we? Oh, yes. We were discussing your reason for visiting so early in the morning. It would appear you are either trying to avoid someone or perhaps arranging a fortuitous meeting. I wonder which?"

Rheda fidgeted with an escaped strand of hair. How did Lady Umbridge know her motives? She'd been hoping to bump into Christopher. She wanted information. What did Christopher believe was the reason for the viscount's visit to the area? Rheda knew Lord Strathmore wasn't here to buy property.

"I can see by the guilty look on your face, it was not Lady Hale you'd hoped to see this early. Perhaps it was one of the guests, Lord Strathmore perhaps?" She lifted a straight eyebrow. Her blue eyes focused on Rheda. "I knew Rufus when he was younger. He was quite the boy." She paused. "Now he's become quite the man. All man."

Rheda couldn't help the heat that stole over her features. Without thinking she uttered, "I saw enough of Lord Strathmore last night, thank you."

Fleur sat back in her seat and smiled. "So he said on his return last night."

Rheda's head jerked up. Last night? He hadn't left Tumsbury Cliff Manor until well after three. Rheda had gone to bed earlier but had been unable to sleep knowing he was in their house. She'd not had time to warn Daniel. She hoped

her brother hadn't left the viscount alone. They had secrets that needed to remain hidden from an astute Lord Strathmore.

But Daniel insisted Rufus teach him how to play faro. They'd played well past midnight. It was close to three in the morning before she'd heard Caesar leave the stables. How was it that Fleur had talked with him so late? Her eyes flashed to Fleur and took in her raised eyebrows. Color flooded Rheda's face—there was only one way she would have known. He'd met with her on his return—early in the morning. Met with her for what?

Suddenly, the room grew as dark as if the sunlight had been sucked from the sky. *Stupid girl.* Her stomach gripped. She didn't want to know.

Fleur tried to feign innocence. "He did say how much he'd enjoyed your little supper. I believe the word he used was *quaint.*" The last word held hints of malice.

Rheda tried to hide the fury Lady Umbridge's words provoked. An image of them together, naked in Lord Strathmore's bed, discussing her lack of social skills, made her muscles seize with—no. She sucked in a breath. She was *jealous.* How could that be? She'd scratch his eyes out. Lord Strathmore might have an intellect she found stimulating and attractive, but as far as women were concerned, he was no different from any other man. He could arouse her passions, but that was merely physical. She had no emotional attachment to him. Except, of course, he could cause her a great deal of trouble if, as she suspected, he was here on His Majesty's business. Why did she care where he took his pleasure? Like every other man she'd known, he flattered to get what he wanted. Then he'd discard her just as easily. He'd lie to get his way and then indulge wherever and with whomever he pleased.

She stood, but she couldn't seem to get her legs to move.

Lady Umbridge gave a satisfied smile, fully aware of the inference generated by her conversation. "Leaving? So soon? But we have only just started to get to know each other."

"I was hoping to speak with Chris—Lord Hale—this morning. Have you seen him?"

"I have."

Rheda swiveled to stare at the doorway. Rufus. She cursed herself. His velvety smooth voice trickled over her like a summer shower.

"Lord Strathmore, do join us. Miss Kerrich appears to be in a hurry to talk with Lord Hale. Have *you* seen him?"

Rheda didn't want to look at him. She hated that she had to stand in the same room as his mistress and pretend that only yesterday he'd sworn that he'd die without a taste from her sweet lips. Men. They were all scoundrels.

She looked up to find Rufus studying her. She squared her shoulders and met his blatant stare. His full lips broke into a knowing smile. He could see her prickling with jealousy, and Rheda didn't like it. She did not want to care who warmed his bed.

But she did.

Unfolding his arms and pushing away from the doorway where he'd been leaning like a Greek god surveying his domain, Rufus sauntered into the room. He seemed to ignore Lady Umbridge and addressed himself directly to her. "Lord Hale is still abed."

Yet for all his cool composure Rufus seemed on edge.

"If you'll excuse us, Lady Umbridge, I shall escort Miss Kerrich for a stroll in the gardens until Lord Hale has risen."

"Darling, of course I don't mind. We saw enough of each other last night. Besides, I'm not hungry. Not hungry for food anyway." And she gave a giggle. "My hunger is more intimate in nature, if you remember. Last night only whet my appetite."

Rheda watched Rufus's lips tighten and his face redden. His eyes narrowed; his dark brows dipped low over his bold nose. He was livid.

"That's enough, Lady Umbridge. Do try to be less vulgar when in company." Rheda noted he had not attempted to

deny Fleur's statement. She could tell by the look of guilt flashing in his deep-brown eyes that he had indeed been with Lady Umbridge last night. The pain made her fingernails dig into her closed palms.

Something of her horror must have shown in her eyes because he took a step toward her, his eyes pleading. She inwardly cursed. She did not want him to know she cared.

Rheda tipped her chin up to an angle of defiance. Her features smoothed to a blank mask, the camouflage that was so much a part of her.

She'd survived her father's constant disappointments by facing bitter truths. She would not shy from them now. The truth was Lord Strathmore had been playing with her. He wanted to use her to gather information. He did not really desire her over and above a woman with such obvious experience. A woman who would know how to slake a man's appetites. A rake's appetites. Rheda wouldn't know where to begin. Rufus would find her lacking in comparison.

Rufus didn't know she was inexperienced in the arts of pleasure. He believed the gossip about Prince Hammed. He obviously thought a scandal-ridden spinster would be easy to seduce. From her response at their first meeting, he probably thought she'd tell him everything in exchange for a night in his bed.

She blinked away the welling tears. To think she'd almost decided to play his game. To let him teach her about passion. She shivered in revulsion. She'd not share a man with another woman. Not after seeing what it did to her mother.

He must have sensed some of her thoughts because he growled low in his throat, and with a firm grip on her elbow he all but propelled her out of the room as Lady Umbridge broke into peals of laughter behind them.

They were halfway toward the front steps leading down into the rose garden before Rheda realized where they were headed.

"Let go of me," she hissed. "I'll wait inside."

Rufus ignored her futile attempts to break free of his grasp. She felt the anger emanating from every inch of his hard, lean body. What had he to be angry about? Angry perhaps at being caught. *He* was the one seducing her while sleeping with another.

Rufus didn't speak until they reached the arbor. "My, my. Is the little wild cat jealous?"

"Why can't a man be satisfied with only one woman. Why can't he be true to her and only her?" She turned on him, her voice filled with scorn. "Why is one woman never enough?" He was exactly like her father. "Jealous? Hardly."

"It may surprise you, hellion, that some women do find me attractive and will do anything to share my bed."

"Lucky for me I'm not one of them. I'm not desperate enough to share."

He moved in close enough for her to smell the masculinity that clung to him. "Seethe your claws," he growled as if she were the one in the wrong. "If you were mine . . . I wouldn't share, either."

His grip tightened on her arm.

"I don't know what right you've got to be angry," Rheda said, her eyes darkening with pain. "I'm the one who's just been made fun of by your paramour. What delightful tales about me did you share with her?"

He fought to speak normally, but his voice emerged sharp and brittle. "Lady Umbridge is not my mistress. Not now. Not ever. She's the last woman I'd ever share a bed with."

"I see. Fancy that, a rake with taste." Rheda made a scoffing sound beside him. Her mouth straightened into an unhappy line. "I don't believe you. No wonder you found my feeble attractions wanting last night."

God, how wrong could she be? He'd wanted her with a hunger that made his stomach and every part of him ache to possess her. "Wanting? I've wanted no woman as much as I want you. I did not indulge my fantasy of ravishing you last night for several reasons. None of them involved worrying

about a relationship with Lady Umbridge. I have none. She is Lord Worthington's mistress, if you must know."

She shook her head and raised a hand to keep her wind-tossed hair from her eyes. "Why would Fleur intimate otherwise?" He couldn't mistake the disbelief in her face. She turned away. He cupped her chin and forced her to look at him. "It does not matter to me who you share a bed with." The wind whipped at her low words, so he had to lean closer to hear. A dizzying waft of her scent mixed with the fragrance radiating from the rows of flowers made his nostrils flare in response.

"Liar."

She gasped.

A torrent of words fought to escape, words that would tell her how much he desired her, how exquisite she was, how sensual and how addictive. He stifled them all. He had no right to pay compliments to a woman he could place in the hangman's noose. His soul grew colder than a frozen mountain peak. He'd known twelve years ago what clearing his father's name would cost him. What he'd not understood, could obviously never have comprehended, was that his pilgrimage would likely kill the last shred of his humanity.

He wanted it to be over. Wanted his task finished. He wanted his life back.

He would settle down and become the head of a respectable, scandal-free family. He would put aside his desires, his wants, and ensure the Strathmore name rose to prominence once again. He'd sworn it on his father's grave.

His cravat suddenly felt very tight.

The woman before him was everything he craved and everything he should fear. Beautiful, sensual, spirited, intelligent, and secretive. But was she deadly?

Rheda was like a drug seeping into his blood. In small doses he could control his need for her, but the more he saw, felt, and scented her, the stronger the craving became, until

he could all but forget his mission. He could feel his resolve not to bed her slipping like a set of whore's drawers.

Should he heed Alex's advice? Was he so coldly calculating that he could seduce, bed, and then arrest her? He looked down into vibrant eyes of ocean green. They were defiantly challenging, and his blood heated. He would not delude himself. The answer was yes.

He took a breath and felt like a sinner in confession. "I have never willingly indulged in any relationship with Lady Umbridge." He pressed on. "Yes, she was in my room when I returned from Tumsbury Cliff Manor last night. But not at my invitation. She's simply trying to cause trouble. She's the one who is jealous. She can sense my interest in you."

He saw Rheda's eyes flick over his face, and he steadfastly met her gaze.

"I want to believe you," she said at last.

He didn't understand why that was important to him. He advanced his course further. "There is one point on which I know we can agree. You want me just as much as I want you. Can you honestly deny it?"

She looked away, her bottom lip sucked between her teeth. When her gaze returned to his face he could tell she'd made a decision. "What does it matter? You would never want a marriage with the likes of me, and I'll not hurt my brother with any further disgrace. There can be nothing between us." She sighed in resignation. "Who you chose to sleep with is none of my concern."

He allowed anger to seep into his voice. "It is of no importance who I've slept with in the past, true, only who I now wish to sleep with." Lady Umbridge had pleasured him last night without his permission. He didn't want to inform her he had actually been dreaming of Rheda's mouth on him at the time. He pulled her to him like a fish on a line. "There is only one woman I want in my bed." He took her lips in a kiss, the taste of her rousing his need to boiling point.

Guilt assailed him. He shouldn't care about her, but he did. She was trying to do the right thing by her brother. He respected her for that. *Let her walk away*. But he couldn't let her demise stand in his way. Not until he knew whether she was involved with smuggling or worse, treason.

Rufus's heart clenched in his chest at the thought. A successful mission could mean her death. If she were guilty she'd hang. Not even he could save her.

He heard her wince. He noticed he was gripping her arms tightly and loosened his hold. He frowned. He couldn't let himself have any feelings for this woman. Not when he might have to arrest her—or worse—see her put to death.

Instead he turned his anger upon her. "Then let's end this before anyone gets hurt. Tell me about the barrel. What are you hiding? Who are you protecting?"

"Tell me why this information is so important. Then I might tell you. Can't you trust me—"

He released her and stepped away. "No. I don't trust anyone. Especially beautiful women." He pushed his coat aside and lifted his shirt. Rheda gasped as his torso came in to view. "A woman whom I trusted gave me this. A woman equally alluring as you. A woman who also asked me to trust her."

He was so beautiful. His chest and stomach glowed golden in the sun. Her hand rose to touch the sparse brown hair sprinkling his chest. Only when he was silent did she notice the jagged scar that sliced down his left side, destroying the perfection. She couldn't imagine any woman wanting to mar such beauty. She had to curl her toes up tight to stop herself stepping forward and planting kisses on the scar's jagged length.

"Who was she?" she asked in a quiet voice.

The pain drained from his eyes. He quickly lowered his shirt. "She is of no consequence."

"That's not true. She hurt you." She tentatively touched his chest. "Why?"

"Why?"

"Why did she knife you?"

He looked away, his mouth set in a firm line. "Because I was a fool."

"You're a fool if you judge all women by one bad experience."

He tugged at his cuffs. "Says the woman who judges all men by her father's standards of honor."

She turned away before he could see the pain in her eyes. "You did not know my father." Then she swung back to face him. "If you had you'd probably have liked him. He, too, loved bedding as many women as he could, while never engaging any other emotion than lust."

Rufus's lip curled up in disgust. "Lust is an emotion men cannot hide. A woman can see and feel a man's lust. On the other hand, women can fake lust as easily as they can fake every other emotion. That is what makes women so dangerous."

Rheda watched the play of emotions roaming his features. She saw hurt, pain, and something that looked a lot like guilt. "The woman who knifed you—you loved her." It wasn't a question. "You surprise me, Rufus. I never would have imagined a man like you being capable of love. Interesting . . ."

He narrowed his gaze. "I never make the same mistake twice," he warned. "Don't play games with me, Rheda. You won't like the outcome."

She moved until her hand pressed against his side where he had been wounded. "Only yesterday you were expertly demonstrating how pleasurable games could be. Why the sudden change of heart?" Her hand crept up his chest until she could feel a beat under her palm. She looked into his warm brown eyes and saw her answer. Her heart suddenly seemed to be trying to own all of her chest cavity. Did he have feelings for her? Was that why Rufus was determined that she believe he was not sleeping with Lady Umbridge? She could neither help nor hide her victorious smile. "Perhaps with me more than simply your lust is engaged."

She could feel the rapid rise and fall of his chest under her hand. His breathing increased, and his pulse raced. She licked her lips and stood on tiptoes to place a gentle kiss upon his sensuous mouth. He groaned and pulled her hard against him. Just as he'd stated, Rufus could not hide his lust for her. But was he hiding other feelings? She longed to find out.

Rheda took charge of the kiss. She plunged her tongue deep into his mouth, tangling with his tongue in a duel to control the rising taste of pleasure. She withdrew to stroke the inside of his cheek as he had done to her, before reissuing her challenge for dominance. She played with his tongue like an expert and won. He seemed to enjoy her occupation, if his escalating moans were anything to go by.

The kiss carried her away. She was lost in a swirl of desire. Her breasts ached for his touch, her belly churned, and she grew hot and restless. If he laid her down on the grass and lifted her skirts to sink between her thighs, she'd let him. The knowledge of her complete surrender should have frightened her, but instead it made her grow bolder.

She reached between them and ran her fingers over the hard ridge at his groin. His size was daunting and thrilling. What would he feel like when he drove deep within her? A wave of heat swamped her, and her fingers frantically fought with his trouser buttons, eager to free him to her touch. He lifted his head and roughly pushed her out of his arms. He stood looking at her with such heated longing it made her knees weak. His breath came in ragged pants, and he swallowed convulsively.

"What are you trying to prove?" he asked.

"You want me."

"I'm a man. Of course I want you. Any man would. Especially when you accost him like that."

She smiled and gave a laugh. "Then why did you stop?" He stood glaring at her. She pushed on, her smile vanishing. "You stopped because what you felt wasn't purely lust and you don't like it."

He snorted.

"I'm right, aren't I? A man simply consumed by lust, a man with no honor, would not have stopped until he'd thrown me to the ground and taken me."

"There is still time for that," he said dryly.

She nodded her head, studying their surroundings for a few seconds. Finally pointing she said, "Over here I think. The ground is dry and won't mark my riding habit."

His mouth softened yet his eyes still burned hot. "You enjoy riding. You could always ride me. If you sit atop me you'll not get one mark on your clothing."

She only just stopped her mouth from gaping open. Ride him? The idea intrigued her.

His smile widened, and he stepped toward her and ran a finger down her cheek. "What? No witty reply."

She shivered and tried to ignore his arousing touch. "I agree. A much better idea. If anyone came upon us my skirt would hide our joining."

His voice came in a low whisper that sent her heart racing after her pulse. "If you were riding me you'd not notice any visitor, I promise you that. Shall I demonstrate?"

Now it was Rheda's turn to swallow. Before she could answer a man sauntered through the trees. Davidson, Meg's brother.

"Excuse me, Miss Kerrich. I have an urgent message from Meg."

Rufus's eyes missed nothing. At the man's approach, even Rheda's freckles lost color as her face paled and she immediately began chewing her bottom lip. Her gaze swung back to him, and he could see fear in their green depths. Who was this man? And what was she afraid of?

With a swift nod in the man's direction she said to Rufus, "Please excuse me. It looks as if our—discussion—will have to wait until another day."

He took her hand on the pretence of kissing it, but he felt

her pulse; it was hammering. *Interesting.* "I hope our pleasant—discourse—has not been stopped by an emergency."

She pulled her hand from his, her flirtation finished, and produced a snippet of a smile—rather a strained smile. "No. I'm sure it is purely a domestic matter," she said, and made to leave.

As she hurried on her way with the stranger whispering in her ear, Rufus called, "I look forward to our future riding lesson." His baited sentence made no impact. Her concentration was honed on the man at her side.

Rufus stood watching as they left, heading toward the cliffs and Jacob's Point. He'd give them a few minutes before following them. The man was not one of Rheda's servants, so who was he and what did he want with Rheda? Was he Dark Shadow's messenger?

He tapped his foot, waiting until he thought it safe to follow. He couldn't tell if the buzz in his veins was excitement from anticipating a chance encounter with Dark Shadow or if it was the scent of Rheda still lingering in his nostrils. He absently pulled a rose off one of the bushes and put it to his nose. Rheda smelled infinitely sweeter, and her taste . . .

He dropped the rose in disgust and set off at a safe distance. It didn't take him long to catch up with them. The discussion between Rheda and the man was animated. He was gesturing up the coast and pointing to the sky. Rheda giving as good as she was getting. Her hands were on her hips, and she was shaking her head. Hidden behind the bushes, he couldn't quite catch what they were saying, their voices kept low.

A few minutes later his patience was rewarded when the man suddenly threw up his arms and yelled. "It's too bloody dangerous. Why won't you listen to me?"

Rheda swung her gaze along the cliff top, thankfully not pausing on where he remained crouched behind the foliage. "Shhhhh. Keep your voice down." They continued the discussion in quieter tones.

Rufus ignored the pain building in his cramping thighs and counted to ten. What should he do? Should he reveal himself and threaten this man, or remain hidden and follow him back to where he came from? If he had to force information from one of them, it would have to be the man. He knew he couldn't physically hurt Rheda. Anything physical with Miss Kerrich would be of a more pleasurable nature.

His annoyance made it difficult to remain still. He glanced sideways and was evaluating if he could make it to the tree on his right without being seen, when he saw the scruffy man give Rheda a piece of paper. She didn't even read it, simply shoved it down her bodice.

They separated and began to leave in opposite directions. Rufus tensed, frozen by indecision. He wanted to see what was in the note Rheda had tucked away, but the man leaving rather swiftly could lead him directly to Dark Shadow's hiding place. *Don't be ridiculous. The man would have to be stupid to go directly back to his leader.*

Rufus made his decision and stood, striding after Rheda. He picked up his pace. She was heading back toward Hastingleigh. He gave her a wide berth and went around and ahead of her so as to make it look as if he'd intercepted her rather than followed her.

As she approached the same rose garden where she'd issued her "riding" challenge, he stepped from behind a tree. "I'm happy to see you are in such a hurry to get back to me, my love."

Rheda took a big step backward, her hand going to her breast. "Rufus! You startled me." She made to go around him, adding, "And I am not your love."

Rufus's arm halted her progress, trapping her between him and a tree. "That certainly isn't the welcome I was hoping for, nor expecting. Not after our last conversation. I was eager to pick up where we left off. I believe riding lessons of an intimate nature were the topic of conversation."

"Let me pass. I haven't time for this."

"Why in such a hurry? Was the message he gave you of a dire nature?"

He watched her throat move as she swallowed. "No, it was nothing of note."

The pair seemed to have had a very heated conversation for "nothing of note." He stroked a finger down her cheek. He moved to stand in front of her, crowding her back against the tree. "I've been waiting with bated breath ever since you left. I hope you're not about to disappoint me."

Her breath faltered, long lashes swept up, and her wide-eyed gaze clashed with his. She licked her lips, and his body inwardly groaned, demanding action. He leaned forward and kissed her. She resisted for all of a heartbeat before opening for him. He took immediate advantage, claiming her mouth with a sweep of his tongue.

She didn't want the kiss to end. Rheda pressed intimately against him, his body as hard as the tree at her back. She sunk into the kiss, dueling with his tongue, stroking the rough inside of his mouth as he stroked hers.

A groan erupted from deep within his chest. His mouth on hers was warm and passionate, exploring her lips and molding them to his, tasting her thoroughly. The mutual tasting ignited a dangerous spark, and a fierce burn erupted between them.

Why did she react like a wanton at the touch of this man? This forbidden desire struck as quick as lightning and engulfed her. She was a mature woman of twenty-five. Why should she feel guilty experiencing that which her younger brother experienced whenever he wanted? The guilt wasn't over indulging in sins of the flesh; it was over who she was indulging with. This man could destroy all she and Daniel had built.

Her brain turned to mush as his hands tightened on her breasts, and this time the moan she heard came from inside of her. There was a delicious sense of impropriety about his

touch, a wicked wantonness that she entirely welcomed. Embraced.

His hands continued to fondle and explore her breasts; his fingers stroked the sensitive exposed skin, dipping beneath her bodice. One finger swept her cleavage and found her hardened nipple. She sighed, wishing it was his hot, wet mouth at her breast.

She felt him begin to undo the buttons of her riding habit. *Yes,* her body screamed. She wanted his mouth on her skin, her nipple in his mouth. With expert skill he had her jacket undone, and his nose was all but buried in her bosom; Rheda felt his warm breath on her skin, and she arched her back, wanting more.

To her disappointment he pulled back. Somewhere within the turmoil of sensation a cool voice said, "Where is the note?" Rufus's voice was strained, deeper than ever. "I saw him give it to you."

Her haze of heated desire cleared as if she'd been slapped. She pushed at his chest. "You are such a bastard."

He pushed her back against the rough bark. "And you, my dear, are playing a dangerous game. Don't push me, Rheda. I am capable of anything to get what I want."

She turned her head away so he could not see the devastation in her eyes. He'd tricked her with seduction, and to her shame she'd fallen for it. Fallen as easily as any other woman to his touch, his caress, his looks . . . She smacked her head back against the tree trunk. She of all women should know better.

He flicked her chemise with a fingertip. "I do so love this habit of not wearing a corset," he murmured. "It's liberating. So, imagine my surprise to find the note is no longer where I saw you tuck it." He reached and lightly squeezed one of her breasts. "They are plump enough to hold a note—so where have you hidden it?"

She shook her head.

He cursed. "I'm not letting you go until I read it," he said,

his jaw bunched tight. He leaned forward. "I wonder where on your person I'll find it."

"The note is private. Why should I have to give it to you?" she added with more bravery than she felt. If he read the note . . .

"He hardly seemed the type to be your lover."

Rheda felt as if she should protest the slander, but she'd run out of words. She hated the gleam in his eye—victory. No words would help her now.

She heard his breathy laughter and felt his hands lifting her skirts. She drew in a breath as she felt his hand brush lightly up her leg. She shivered in a combination of nervous fear and undiluted want.

"I seem to remember doing this once before," he murmured. "Legs of a gazelle . . ."

"You are despicable," she managed to say with a dry throat. Her hands clenching into fists.

His hands reached her bottom, and his touch turned impersonal, patting her undergarments, searching for the note as if she'd hidden it in her drawers. His hand moved toward her hips, and she knew that just a few inches higher and he'd find what he was looking for.

Through the maelstrom of conflicting sensations—one was certainly desire, the other definitely fear—she heard voices. Self-preservation finally tipped the balance on her need to be courageous. "Stop. Somebody's coming. You've searched me and found no note, now leave me alone."

Rufus looked down at his hands, hidden in the folds of her skirts, and he moved to cup her familiarly. A finger slipped in the open slit of her drawers and intimately stroked her moist folds. "Perhaps women can't hide their lust as well as I thought. If we had time I'd 'search' you until you once again came apart in my arms."

"Never." She squirmed, trapped between the tree and his body. The finger that had been stroking her, causing fire to spread deep into her belly, slipped inside her, and she moaned.

"I think the lady doth protest too much."

Fury erupted within her, and she pushed at his arms. "How dare you?" she managed, her voice trembling as much as her limbs. Reaching to rebutton her jacket, she said, "That's the last time you'll ever lay a hand on my—"

"In you, don't you mean? And it is not my hand that longs to be in you." There was something in his voice that her body reacted to. She grew wetter. "And I dare, Miss Kerrich," he warned. "To get what I want I'm a man who dares anything."

She looked into his eyes, hard and glinting in the sun. She slid away from him. He caught her wrists, easily restraining her. She tried to tug free, but he was too strong. The muscles in his shoulders and arms bunched, and she knew with frustration that he was using only a minuscule portion of his real strength. He was holding back so as not to hurt her.

"Fleur, I thought you said Lord Strathmore took Rheda for a stroll in the rose garden. Where are they?"

Both of them tensed at the sound of Lady Hale's voice.

"This is not over." His voice was a deep rumble as he slipped her arm through his and calmly turned to face Lady Hale and Lady Umbridge as they came into view.

Her inner voice made her start with guilt, because instead of being afraid at the prospect of a very personal search from this handsome rake, she was looking forward to it—minus any incriminating evidence of her smuggling activity.

Plastering a welcoming smile on her lips, she dug her fingernails deep into Rufus's sleeve, hoping they pierced his skin. She felt the muscles in his forearm tighten, and only then did her shoulders relax. She could feel the rough paper of the note rubbing her back where she'd tucked it into the waistband of her skirts.

Her confidence grew as the ladies approached.

"There you two are." Lady Hale's eyes ran over Rheda, and a small frown formed. "I hope Rufus has been behaving."

With suave timing, Rufus bowed. "Ladies. Miss Kerrich

had a slight fall. She tripped over some rocks near the cliffs' edge. If not for my swift actions she could have fallen."

Helen rushed forward and pulled Rheda into an embrace, while Fleur rolled her eyes behind the older woman's back. "Oh, my dear. No wonder you look so pale. Thank goodness you were in Rufus's safe hands." Fleur's smirk deepened. "Come. Let's get you a nice cup of tea. Katherine's coming for your fitting in less than half an hour." Turning to Rufus, she waved him away. "Haven't you something better to do, Rufus? Find Stephen and Christopher. Shoo. Leave us ladies in peace."

Rheda smiled sweetly at her nemesis. She could see him struggling to hold on to his temper as she silently goaded him.

"If you'd let me I'll escort you home once you have finished here. I need to check on Caesar's progress with your mares."

Fleur moved to his side and slipped her arm through his. "No need. The baron and his sister are staying for supper. Baron de Winter can escort his sister home." Fleur moved close to Rufus and almost purred, "If you are at a loss for something to do, why don't you escort me down to the beach. I love the lure of the sea."

Lady Hale's mouth firmed at the obvious flirtatious display. "Perhaps Lord Worthington would like to join you, Lady Umbridge." Dismissing the two of them, Lady Hale pulled Rheda toward the house. When they were out of Rufus's hearing she muttered, "Damn that woman."

"Lady Hale!"

"Sorry, my dear, but I want you to shine at this ball. If I can't persuade you to marry my son, then I shall look elsewhere. I promised your mother I'd see you married and married well. How am I supposed to spark Rufus's interest with a bitch in heat sniffing around him at every turn? It is bad enough she's got Stephen wrapped around her little finger—but Rufus."

Rheda laughed. "I hardly think Rufus would allow himself to be wrapped around anyone's finger."

Helen continued her path back to the house talking to Rheda over her shoulder. "Even though you are older than most debutantes, I forget how innocent you truly are. A woman of Lady Umbridge's low moral fiber and dubious talents can make a man do almost anything."

"A rake of Rufus's reputation hardly needs any encouragement to behave inappropriately. Why are you set on a match with him? If I were interested in marrying, which I am not," she added hurriedly, "how can you possibly believe I'd look twice at a man of his character, given the life my mother led?"

"That talk may work on your brother, but I know you, Rheda. I have seen you with Meg's children." Her voice softened. "The joy of holding your child in your arms is indescribable. Why do you think women are prepared to go through the pain of childbirth a second, third, or fourth time?"

"Or die . . ."

There was a slight falter in Helen's step. "Your mother loved you and longed for more children. She was aware of the price." She smiled and said hesitatingly, "Like mother, like daughter, I believe. I know how you long for a child. Don't forgo marriage based on your father's example. A life alone is a solitary state. You'd shrivel up and die."

Rheda's blood tingled with icy feeling. "I have Daniel."

Over the past twelve months she'd tried so hard to believe the lie she'd just spoken. Only now was she facing the truth that a life without a husband would almost certainly mean a life with no children. She'd not been prepared for the depth of her disappointment. She'd not understood how much of a sacrifice remaining childless would be. Some days it felt as if she was missing a limb. The pain was so overwhelming she'd even contemplated the concept of finding a "good" man to marry.

Only she knew they were as rare as gold doubloons.

Lady Hale stopped and swung to face her, studying her silently. "Daniel will create a family of his own. He will

move on with his life. Don't leave it until too late. Don't live your life alone. It will eat at your soul." She turned to continue walking. "With the right man you could lead a very contented life. A rich, full life."

Rheda could not have felt more shocked if Lady Hale had suddenly sprouted a second head. "Lord Strathmore is most certainly not the right man."

"There is more to Rufus than meets the eye." The older woman glanced over her shoulder and broke into a huge grin and winked. "Although what meets the eye is certainly desirable."

It was not the sun making her face hot. "On a cold day a fire is very inviting, but when you get too close—"

"I'm disappointed in you. You of all people should know better. Not all gossip is to be believed."

Rheda hung her head. Not once had Helen indicated she had heard or knew of the gossip surrounding Rheda's friendship with Prince Hammed. It pained her to think Lady Hale might think ill of her.

As if reading her mind . . . "I know you, Rheda, and I never once believed the spiteful things that were said." Helen shook her head. "Just as most of the stories surrounding Rufus and his family are grossly exaggerated. For example, his reputation as a rake—he's a healthy man and of course would indulge in the odd liaison. Any woman on her wedding day will thank him for his expertise. I suspect sharing a bed with Rufus would leave one quite breathless."

Rheda gave a quiet sigh. Helen had adored her husband and he her. Rheda, however, had seen what a marriage without love, or rather one-sided love, could do. She'd watched her mother's spirit die a little every day as her husband treated her as chattel. Something he owned and could do as he wished with, regardless of his wife's feelings.

Rheda's unease put a hitch in her throat. Admittedly her body reacted to the handsome rake, and that annoyed her. She inwardly justified her attraction to him—she *was* flesh

and blood after all, and his beauty beckoned like a succulent feast. The liberated part of her persona screamed at her—experience that which you crave to taste—passion. He'd be perfect. He'd no doubt introduce her to the delights of her body better than any man she would ever meet. Therein lay the problem.

Her heart beat faster, harder, with longing each time he was near. She was terrified of giving her heart and losing herself in a man who did not value her.

Lady Hale took her hand as they entered the house and began climbing the stairs to her drawing room. "He has a good heart. He has protected his mother and younger sister from the worst of the gossip. He refuses to hide from the scandal surrounding his father, but he declines to believe it. He has many powerful friends who have stood by him. Hardly the sign of a man with a suspect character."

Rheda felt trapped. She could hardly tell the woman who'd stood by her that Rufus demonstrated very little honor where she was concerned. He'd been trying to seduce her since they met, even after he'd ascertained she was in fact a lady. She pulled her hand free and gave Helen a hug. "I'm sure he'd make some woman a fine husband. Just not me."

"Don't be too hasty." Lady Hale waited for the servant to deliver the tea and leave the room. "Rufus is deeper than the face he shows Society. For instance, I know why he is really here in Kent."

Rheda almost dropped her cup. With shaking hands she lowered it to the saucer. She'd been correct—obtaining property was not his main objective. "He is not here to buy property then?"

"Goodness, no. He is trying to clear his father's name. He has been working to achieve that goal ever since his father's death."

Rheda frowned. "I don't understand. His father died almost twelve years ago. What does he hope to find?"

Helen lowered her voice. "I'm sworn to secrecy so I can-

not tell you too much. All I can say is Lady Strathmore, his mother, has high hopes that her son will shortly prove her husband's innocence."

Rheda frowned. What was Rufus up to? Her mind whirled with possibilities. What on earth did Dark Shadow have to do with Rufus's goal of clearing his father's name? She knew nothing of what occurred all those years ago. Lady Hale must be mistaken. Or mayhap Rufus was?

Her stomach tightened and nausea hit, making her palms sweaty. With so much at stake there was no way Rufus would give up his hunt for the smuggler, and that put the de Winter name at risk. Clearing his family's name could well tarnish hers. She didn't want Daniel to suffer the same fate as Rufus. If Rufus became thwarted in his goal, he might be angry enough to lash out at her family. Expose her smuggling and, worse, have her arrested. Even with the heat from the fire in the hearth, her blood ran cold. Rufus, if disappointed in his quest, might take his anger out on her. He could see her transported for crimes against the Crown.

She knew it was time to confess all to Daniel. It wasn't fair to keep her brother in the dark about the risk Rufus posed. Daniel's dream was to take his rightful place in Society, and Rufus had the power to destroy that. She hadn't sacrificed the past eight years to stand idly by and let that happen.

Perhaps it was time to turn the tables. Perhaps she should embrace Rufus's seduction. Let him believe she has fallen under his spell. That way she could keep him close and try to learn just what the handsome viscount was really doing in Deal.

From the sparks igniting within her, she knew she should be careful. She was far too excited by the prospect of allowing Rufus's seduction.

Knowing something of the man, she should be scared. Petrified. Frightened out of her wits.

She flashed Helen a congenial smile. "Perhaps I have been a tad hasty. To appease you, I shall reserve judgment on Rufus."

Helen clapped her hands in delight. "Wonderful. I promise I won't interfere." Rheda rolled her eyes. "Well, not much. It might also give Christopher the jolt he needs. It is high time my son found himself a bride. However, you, my dear, are more suited to Rufus." She sipped her tea before adding, "I can't wait to see their faces when they see you dressed for the ball. I'm certain you'll have the two of them fighting over you."

Rheda was certain she wouldn't. Christopher had never shown anything other than misguided duty in her. He had proposed on her father's death, largely because of pressure from his mother. He had honorably offered his hand in marriage as a way for him to help her out of the financial mire her father had left them in. Yet, he'd never once flirted with her, or tried to kiss her. She obviously did not ignite his passions. That was one of the reasons they were such good friends. If Christopher thought of her at all, it was as a younger sister, just as she thought of him as an older brother. They were both far too sensible to do anything to destroy their mutual friendship.

No. There would only be one man interested in her at the ball, and then only because he thought she could advance his cause. What exactly that cause was she was determined to find out. To that end she said cheerfully, "Then I'll need a dress to die for."

Helen simply chuckled. "For once I feel sorry for Rufus. I do believe you'll take him on a merry dance. I almost envy you."

"How so?"

She gave a wicked smile. "I still remember what it was like when you let a handsome man catch you."

A pleasant tingle raced down Rheda's spine. She sat up straighter in her chair. As long as the only catching Rufus did was for pleasure. She gritted her teeth and silently vowed he would not catch Dark Shadow.

Chapter 14

It was close to midnight when Rufus decided to pay an unannounced and secret visit to Tumsbury Cliff Manor. The baron could not afford a full complement of staff, and that, in all likelihood, would allow him to poke around the estate and outbuildings at his leisure. If he could only find illegal contraband, he'd have the proof he needed to arrest Daniel.

Part of him welcomed the chance to be caught snooping. He could do with a good fight to burn off his frustration—frustration at their limited progress in uncovering a simple smuggling network, and frustration at knowing the most beautiful woman he'd met in a long time was sleeping in the house he was about to visit. He'd love to instigate a personal search of her room, of her bed, of her person. He gave a silent curse.

He tethered Caesar a mile from the house—with mares in heat he couldn't afford to let Caesar come any closer—and began the walk to the manor pondering what he was going to do about Rheda. Stephen had suggested he talk with her about his mission. Explain to her why it was so important they find Dark Shadow. But he'd trusted a woman once before, and it had cost him his mission and his friend's life.

No. Until he found evidence of Rheda's innocence he could not afford to trust her.

He sidled into the stable and came to an abrupt halt, freez-

ing in the shadows. From somewhere within came the sounds of whimpering. He stood frozen against the wall. Who was up at this hour and why? He continued forward until he reached the first empty stall and stopped at the sight of a shape—a small shape. It couldn't be the baron. One of Meg's boys perhaps? The eldest helped with the horses. But surely they would be tucked up in bed by now.

He crept farther into the dimly lit stable, and as his eyes grew accustomed to the lack of light he recognized the shape—Rheda. She was leaning against the stable wall, her head buried within her arms—sobbing. He tried to stop his heart from lurching in his chest; he was helpless when it came to women's tears.

"What's happened?" he asked with barely concealed panic.

At the sound of his voice she swung round. "Rufus! Oh, Rufus!" She flew at him, grabbed his hand, and dragged him toward the stall at the rear of the building. "It's White Lily—please—you have to help me."

As they drew nearer Rufus could hear the mare's snorts of distress.

Rheda's tears continued to flow although her sobs had quieted. The sticky trails of tears on her cheeks testified to her anguish.

"Daniel is still not home, and Jamieson and Penny have been called into Seaton. Penny daughter's gone into labor." She gestured to White Lily who lay groaning on her side, legs thrashing, stomach heaving, froth covering her nose and mouth. "I can't get her to stand up. She's been lying down and standing up all day, but now she simply lies there panting and groaning. She's been fretting since early afternoon." Rheda's hands clenched and unclenched. "Caesar's mating hasn't hurt her—has he? He seemed so large . . ."

He shook his head grimly and began to take off his heavy overcoat. "She's got colic."

"Is the condition dangerous?"

"It can be." Trying not to show his anxiety, he ripped off

his jacket and began rolling up his sleeves. "How long has she been down?"

"This time? Not long." She started to cry again. "I tried to get her up, but I'm not strong enough."

He bent down and stroked the mare's nose. "Easy girl, we'll make you feel better, but you have to get up for me."

"What are you going to do?"

"I'm going to make her stand up. She could die if we don't get her back up and walking to ease the blockage in her gut."

"Will we have enough strength between us?"

"We don't need strength—I hope." He crouched next to White Lily's head. "You might want to stand clear. She may kick out." Then he took a deep breath and prayed this would work. If it didn't he was not sure he'd have the strength to pull the mare to her feet, even with rope. Besides, that method often hurt the horse even more. "Have you any cod liver oil in the house?"

"I'll go see. I'm sure we do." Rheda turned, and, lifting her skirts, she raced toward the house. He could hear her hurried footsteps on the cobblestones.

Quickly he bent to his task. He covered White Lily's nose with his hand and forced her mouth closed so she could not breathe. Immediately her legs started thrashing and she made to get to her feet. After an almighty struggle she stood, although she was still in palpable discomfort.

"Come on, we need to get you walking, young lady." And talking softly he encouraged the trembling mare out into the yard.

Rheda's squeal of delight made both the horse and Rufus jump. "You got her up." She slipped around him to walk on the other side of her mare, and she held up a container. "Cod liver oil."

Rufus nodded. "We are going to have to do this quickly because the minute I stop walking her, White Lily will try to lie down again. But we have to tip as much of the oil down her throat as possible."

Rheda nodded.

"I'll count to three. On three you pour the oil. One—two—."

Rufus pulled White Lily to a halt and opened her mouth. "Three!" as Rheda poured the oil.

The mare reared up at the taste but she stayed on her feet. The moment the oil had been administered, Rufus immediately had her walking around the yard again.

Rheda walked with them, patting the mare and whispering to her. "Why did this happen?"

"When did you last ride her?" he asked.

"The night we took her to Hastingleigh. She's been stabled since then."

"And before that? How long has it been since she was in a field, eating grass?"

"At least a week. Since she came into heat."

Rufus eyed Rheda over the horse's back. "The mare obviously has a tendency toward colic. She needs to be ridden every day. Every alternate day leave her in the field with no grain or hay. Let her eat grass. Too much grain will cause this condition. Less grain, more grass, and regular exercise should keep her colic at bay."

Rheda raised anguish-filled eyes to him. "It's my fault she's in such pain, isn't it?"

Rufus shook his head. "No."

She gave a sob and covered her face with her hands. "I thought I could do this. I thought I could run my own horse stud. But look what I've done to White Lily. She's in so much pain."

"If any woman can run her own horse stud it's you." Where had that affirmation come from? It made it sound as though he actually admired her. "She must have been showing symptoms for most of the day. Why did you not ask for help earlier? If I had been here I would have recognized the symptoms and it needn't have progressed this far."

Expression leeched from her face, as if shutters had come

down. "I find most men expect something in return for their help. I'm surprised you helped me without setting conditions."

Her quiet answer hit him like a physical blow. Was she right? Would he have used her distress to force her to confess? In a heartbeat. So why hadn't he? In the silence that followed, he held her defiant stare, afraid to face the reasons why he'd let this opportunity to force her confession slip by.

"I'm not like most men. One day you'll learn you can trust me. You can't live your life trusting in no one. Everyone needs help at some point."

But this beautiful cynic didn't believe him, though her faint smile seemed to express gratitude for his help. Her words came slowly. Carefully. "I am in your debt, Rufus. Thank you. White Lily's one half of my entire breeding stock. If I lose her—"

"Your dreams crumble?"

She nodded. "But what's worse, she is in such agony I can hardly bear it. How am I going to manage when something does go wrong and I lose an animal? It will happen at some stage, won't it—won't it?"

"You'll manage. You're tough."

"Like you?"

Rufus gave a hollow laugh. "I'm not tough. If I was, I'd not care what people said about my father." *If I was,* he added silently, *I'd not have sacrificed so much of my life running after the truth.* If his father was guilty, it would mean the man he'd called his sire was a stranger to him.

They continued to walk White Lily in silence. Around and around the yard.

He could feel Rheda's eyes on him, searching his face. Finally she broke the silence. "Were you at Hastingleigh when your father died?"

An arrow, dipped in guilt, hit him squarely in his chest. "No. I should have been."

Her eyes widened. "Do you think you could have prevented his death, or prevented his supposed treason?"

He eyed her sharply. "Supposed? You don't believe the rumors?"

She stroked White Lily's mane. "No, I don't. Christopher vigorously defends your father. He swears the late Lord Strathmore would never have sold out the French aristocracy."

The tight band encircling his chest eased slightly. "My father was a good man. He had many friends among the French nobility, and he would never have done anything to cause them harm." He paused and drew a breath. "The idea that he would sell their escape routes to the Revolutionary Council is ludicrous. We certainly didn't need the money. That was the first thing I noticed, when, on his death, I reviewed the account ledgers. Even if I'd never earned anything off our assets ever again, there was enough money to last several lifetimes."

"Then how did the rumor start?"

He pulled on White Lily's halter as she tried to momentarily slow down. "I have no idea. Lord Ashford found a document in my father's pocket. I still firmly believe it was planted there."

"I don't understand. Who would want to implicate your father?"

He raised an eyebrow. "The real traitor, for one. I have only recently learned that was the reason Lord Ashford was at Hastingleigh on that fateful day. He'd had a tip-off. Of course he wasn't the Foreign Secretary then. He was with British Intelligence."

Her eyes narrowed, and her lip slipped between her teeth as she pondered his words. "Is that why you are here in Kent? To hunt for your father's killer. It happened so long ago. What do you hope to find now?"

He smiled. Rheda lifted her chin, standing like a marble

Aphrodite, glimmering in the moonlight, impervious to the dangers lurking around her, daring him to answer. He tenderly reached across the mare and tucked an errant strand of curl behind her ear, his voice oddly gruff. "I am looking for the truth, Rhe. Will you help me find it?"

Would she? Could she? The terrifying thing was how much she wanted to do so. The obnoxious, belligerent rake was easy to resist. But this side of Rufus, the generous, tender side, frightened her.

She could never repay his kindness from tonight. He could have ruthlessly forced the truth from her—he knew how much her horses meant to her. But he was behaving honorably, and at no small inconvenience to himself, he was helping her.

Even worse, his vulnerability when he'd talked about his father made her want to cradle him to her bosom, as she did with Connor after a bad dream.

Now he was talking to her as if she were his equal. He wasn't demanding, bullying, or seducing her. He was simply asking for her help.

They continued around the yard in silence. She couldn't stop stealing breathless little glances at him, tall and virile in his rolled-up sleeves and open-collared shirt. His face was a mask of concern for her mare, making her wish for just a moment that his soft whispers and gentle caresses were not only for White Lily.

The very air became rife with tension—her body alerted to his masculinity, while the woman in her responded to his pain.

Her father had caused her pain, too. But Rufus's pain stemmed from losing someone he loved and respected. Of seeing that name tarnished without proof. Rheda's father had needed no help in tarnishing his own name. He reveled in it, enjoyed the scandal, and did not care how it affected her or Daniel.

Rufus might not think so, but he was lucky to have had a father of that caliber for even part of his life. Perhaps the son of such a man was someone she could trust.

As if he'd heard her thoughts he looked up, and they gazed at each other. It was as if the stable yard and the mare did not even exist. She opened her mouth to speak, but could she trust a man? This man?

"You'll find I am a much better friend than foe, Rheda."

She had no doubt about that. She nodded her head. "I'm sure that's true. Quite frankly, I can't afford either."

He had the audacity to laugh. "You, my sweet, are too clever by far. It's the one thing that makes our verbal sparring so enjoyable. Perhaps that is why I refrained from blackmailing you tonight. I am enjoying the cut and thrust far too much, and I don't want it to end."

"Then I shall have to let you win the verbal battle while ensuring I win the war."

His voice took on a husky quality. "I know what I wish to win, and it isn't only information. To sample the pleasures of your body, a man would fight and win a dozen wars."

She sighed. "Just when I finally thought a man was unique enough to see past my beauty to what was underneath, you prove otherwise. Men think with the member between their legs more often than their brains. Thankfully, it makes them easy to predict."

"Don't be naive. Your intelligence enhances your beauty. Why is that a bad thing? Your beauty gives you many advantages."

Why did men see beauty as an advantage? "Name one," she snapped. Beauty fades. Beauty hides a multitude of sins.

Rufus coughed. "Well, men are more likely to offer you the protection of their name. Beautiful women are assured of procuring a husband."

"And what advantages does marriage bring to a woman? I see how a wife advantages a man, but how does it benefit a woman?"

"How!" he said. "You'd be taken care of. Provided for . . ."

Seeing his expression of disbelief, Rheda almost shook her head in despair. "So, let me get this right. A woman of my intelligence—your words—should be content to marry simply to be provided for." Her tone edged toward thunderous, but she didn't care. "A woman of my intelligence couldn't possibly provide for herself. Is that what you are implying? What do you think I'm doing out here at three in the morning walking a horse?"

He had the decency to look sheepish. "You, my delicious Rhe, I'll grant you, are the exception. Perhaps that is why I find you so captivating."

His soft tone was her undoing. Her body's battled response slipped away, and a desire to make peace took its place.

Trust him, a small voice whispered. *Tell him Dark Shadow won't aid his father's cause.* But she couldn't. Not yet. She needed more proof before she'd allow herself to trust a handsome man. She swallowed guiltily. Did she have double standards? Would she trust Rufus if he was not so damn handsome?

"I swear I'll earn your trust. When I do I pray it is not too late." His voice was low and lulling. "Now off to bed with you. You need some sleep if you're to relieve me in a few hours. I'll take the first watch. There is one thing you can't dispute. I'm stronger than you. It's best I am here in case White Lily tries to go down again."

She walked around White Lily and on impulse leaned in to him and kissed his cheek, a light lingering press of lips. "Thank you. I realize you could have used White Lily for your own ends." She drew back. "Your actions have spoken to me louder than any seduction ever could. I will think about your request."

She was almost to the door when he called softly, "Don't think too long. A man of my position and nature is not known for his patience."

She looked at him—really looked at him—and noted the lines of despair etched behind his eyes. Discovering the truth about his father meant as much to him as her need for independence did to her. His quest weighed him down as much as her lack of freedom smothered her.

"I'll give you my answer after the ball. The ball is Daniel's night. I won't risk anything spoiling it."

He nodded curtly. "I can settle for that. I'll hold you to it."

Chapter 15

The night of the ball seemed to arrive sooner than Rheda had anticipated. Her heart hadn't stopped racing all day. Her dreams hung on the success of this night. Unlike other young women, she was not worried about the success of the ball. Rather, she was on tenterhooks about the final shipment under Dark Shadow's leadership. If the landing went to plan, she'd give up smuggling and concentrate on her horses.

After her talk with Daniel, about Lord Strathmore's likely purpose in Deal, her brother finally conceded that retiring Dark Shadow was sensible. When she explained her worries about the villagers' plight, he agreed to help build her horse stud to ensure her independence, and to provide the villagers with a legitimate income. He saw the advantages of selling Caesar's offspring and creating a breeding herd.

Both siblings recognized that they'd pushed their luck too far. With Rufus ferreting information about Dark Shadow, it was time to retreat and protect what they had built.

Rheda felt confident the night would be well received by their guests. Lady Hale and her servants had been in residence for the past four days seeing to the house's preparations. Rheda had been too busy organizing the goods manifest to worry about the arrangements. Daniel, however, embraced the ball as if this one engagement would secure his place in Society for eternity.

She hoped it didn't secure his place in infamy instead.

Concerned at Daniel's high hopes, Rheda warned her brother not to be overconfident. They mustn't take any risks tonight or try to be too clever.

She'd explained why it was important to be wary of the viscount. Daniel threw a tantrum when Rheda suggested changing the night's final run. After much arguing and threats, Rheda finally saw the sense in continuing with their plans to land a shipment on the night of the ball. For once it would provide both of them with an alibi.

The ballroom would be filled with over one hundred guests who could vouch for their presence for the entire evening.

Daniel organized for Davidson to see the boat in and instructed his team to use the northern cavern entrance.

She bit her lip and looked out the window. Her eyes filled with concern as she noticed the darkening sky. She could feel the change in the air. There'd likely be a storm tonight. That should move the odds in their favor despite making the landing more difficult. Revenuers were reluctant to take to the sea in a storm. They didn't know the coast and deadly rocks. Those born in Deal could sail these waters blindfolded.

As she made her way to her room Rheda knew she should be helping with the last-minute preparations, but she still had tasks of her own to complete.

She entered her bedchamber and looked at the dress Penny had arranged on her bed. It was perfect. That's when her mind took flight.

Rufus was fixated on seduction in order to pry out her secrets, but she knew he also wanted her. He had to be kept busy tonight. Just thinking about giving rein to her own desires turned her blood to liquid fire.

But the question was how? Unlike Rufus, the infamous rake, she had limited sexual knowledge. She knew the rudiments, but how to entice a man of such experience was beyond her. Her previous fumbling attempts hadn't even warranted a raised eyebrow from Rufus.

She picked up the dress and held it against her. She

frowned. If she didn't know better she'd think Penny had altered the neckline. It seemed to have dropped a few inches.

She stood swaying, watching her reflection in the mirror. She could always ask Meg, but it was getting late and Meg had already left. She put the dress back on the bed and sighed. There was no time to indulge her appetite for carnal knowledge. Perhaps she should simply entice Rufus and let him lead her.

Then she remembered something—something she'd seen at the cove a few months ago—she put her hands to her face to try to cool the hot flush—something she'd tried hard to forget.

One day, over a month ago, she'd agreed to accompany Lady Hale to Margate, but the older woman came down with a headache and cried off. The day had been extremely humid, and on the way back from Hastingleigh, Rheda had decided to pop to her private cove for a swim.

She was halfway down the path when she spotted the couple on the beach. Daniel and his lover, Sarah, naked and engaged in lovemaking. She knew she shouldn't watch, but they looked so beautiful together. Their naked bodies, almost lost against the backdrop of sparkling sea water, were intimately joined on the white sand.

She'd watched transfixed as Sarah straddled her brother and made love to him with her mouth. She'd never seen anything so erotic. Daniel's groans filled the air as he sunk his hands in Sarah's hair. She'd watched transfixed as Sarah's tongue, lips, and mouth worked their magic.

A picture of Rufus naked on the sand flashed in her head. Rheda imagined straddling Rufus the way Sarah had her brother. She closed her eyes. She could almost feel his roughened skin beneath her lips—almost taste his manhood in her mouth. She let out a dreamy sigh. She found herself growing warm. Her breasts began to tingle, and she pressed her hands to them, remembering Rufus's hot mouth suckling her.

Rheda smiled to herself, opened her eyes, and began to get ready for the ball. Suddenly, she longed for the opportunity to cross swords with Rufus. She'd like a chance to play with one sword in particular—his rather large sword. When she got him alone, she'd show him that she was just as expert at seduction. At least long enough to ensure tonight's shipment landed without a hitch.

Of all the nights for a ball, this had to be the worst. There was a storm coming and it was almost a new moon. Rufus's suspicious soul screamed that this evening was not simply about introducing him to Kent. Rheda was too smart to let such an opportunity go by. A storm, a ball to keep him busy, and a nearly new moon. The perfect night for smuggling.

His carriage trundled its way through the darkening Kent night, rocking violently in the rising wind. Black rolling clouds had turned the evening's dimming light to gray earlier than was usual in late summer. A warning splatter of rain drummed on the carriage roof.

He knew both Revenuers and smugglers alike gave thanks for the fine weather they'd experienced over the past week, but they had known it wouldn't last forever. Rufus had hoped it would last at least one more night. Once again he was disappointed.

As if to prove its point, the threatening storm issued a flash of lightning that lit the dim interior of the carriage. It was followed by thunder rumbling in the distance. The two distinguished gentlemen occupying the carriage viewed the storm's arrival with increasing anger. Although they were dressed in formal evening attire, they looked as if they were off to war rather than the baron's ball. The carriage bristled with pistols and swords.

"Blast it all," Stephen muttered. "It looks like we are in for a squall. That won't help."

Rufus glanced at his friend. "No moon. Storm clouds. No light at all. Daniel could not have planned the night better."

The two men continued their journey in silence. Rufus knew no one would suspect the carriage carried two of England's best spymasters. The baron was in for a surprise. Smugglers always used the new moon because it kept the night dark and did not illuminate the coastline.

Lady Hale had confessed it was Rheda's idea to hold the ball when Rufus tried to cry off attending.

He leaned back against the squabs of his carriage, closed his eyes, and tried to ignore the adrenaline pumping hot and fast through his veins. His plan would work. His men were in place. The trap was set. The preparation had been meticulous, and he did not expect any problems. His Revenue men were hidden on Baron de Winter's cliff tops near the reported landing area.

Rufus's finely honed senses suggested the baron, young Daniel Kerrich, was Dark Shadow. Who else would Rheda vigorously try to protect. That was obviously why she was so staunch in her refusal to provide him with information until after the ball.

Tonight all they needed was to catch the baron, with his smuggling gang, in the act. Then the man would have no choice but to lead them to the spy, whether he liked it or not.

"Are you sure about tonight's plan? The baron appears to be far too young, and Miss Kerrich has told you nothing?" Stephen liked to double-check everything; that's why Rufus favored working with him.

"We paid a lot of money to learn that he was the likely candidate."

Stephen continued, "Informants have been known to take the money and flee, especially if they are mistaken."

Uncrossing his legs, Rufus dryly responded, "Ardale is one of Alex's men. He makes his livelihood from selling information. Trust me, if he says the baron is Dark Shadow, then he is."

With a wan smile, Rufus knew the ball they were on their

way to would be the perfect diversion. The baron sought to distract them by holding a reception in Rufus's honor. With a wry smile he welcomed the opportunity to keep an eye on their target. However, the baron probably had other plans. Perhaps even to divert a notorious rake with womanly charms.

He pulled at his cuffs, refusing to admit that a certain woman added to his already tight-as-a-drawn-crossbow nerves. Since their previous interlude he could not get Rheda out of his head. He could still taste her.

He shifted uncomfortably on his seat and reminded himself that she was party to smuggling, and worse, treason. Besides, she was far too forward and opinionated. He pictured her delicate face and feline eyes. Yes, she was too much of a wild cat.

His mouth set. He shouldn't be thinking of Rheda. Nothing and no one came before his mission of restoring his family's honor.

As if reading his thoughts, Stephen interrupted, "It's Miss Kerrich I am concerned about. We have been unable to ascertain her situation in all of this. Still, I think it hardly likely that a young woman would be involved in smuggling."

Rufus let out a mild oath. "Do not underestimate the woman. You of all people must have noticed she is not your conventional demure lady. There is something uncultivated and uncontrollable about her. And even more dangerous than that, she has a brain."

Why a woman so bereft of life's social graces should set his pulse racing at the mere sight of her confused him. He was not immune to a woman's beauty—far from it. He would admit to bedding countless women over the years, but only those who knew the game—no innocents or unmarried young ladies. And self-preservation meant he avoided any woman who might make him forget who he was and how he should conduct himself.

A woman like Miss Kerrich.

Rufus played with his cravat, his finger pulling at his neck. It seemed awfully tight tonight.

Stephen chuckled. "I agree Miss Kerrich is not your usual young lady. Few resounding beauties reached the age of five and twenty unmarried. Not for want of offers, either. Did you know she has declined several marriage offers from Christopher over the past eight years? And, given her younger brother's purported need for funds, I find that very intriguing."

In the dark interior of the carriage Rufus replied dryly, "Miss Kerrich's perfectly capable of looking out for herself. Who do you think raised the young baron after their father's death? Holding on to his inheritance until he came of age has no doubt meant she has ended up a bit unconventional."

"Well, I never thought I would see this day—the honorable Lord Strathmore making excuses for improper behavior! I wonder what has caused this mellowing in your standards. Her beauty perhaps?"

"Don't be ridiculous."

"She has got to you!" Suddenly, Stephen's voice grew serious. "Don't get so caught up in her at the ball that you let the vixen sway you from tonight's mission. I know what a woman of such comely charms can do to a man's senses. And you of all people know the danger."

Rufus gave a wicked laugh. "Stephen, I carry the scar from the only woman I was naive enough to let deceive me. If Rheda is involved in this treachery, I won't raise a hand to save her."

"You have been spending a lot of time on a woman you have no interest in saving."

"It was for the mission," he said gruffly. "I was trying to learn about her brother, see if she would let anything slip. But she was far too clever for that."

Stephen replied, "Of course, I am sorry. Here I was thinking she had turned your head. I should have known after

your last mission you'd be well able to resist even such a delectable temptation as our Miss Kerrich."

Rufus could not see the smug smile on Stephen's face, but his friend's tone indicated his concern. Under his breath Rufus declared, "A woman is of no importance tonight. Even Daniel's barony won't save him if Ardale is correct." He rechecked his gun. With a voice as cold as the steel in his hand he added for Stephen's benefit, "I will capture him, and he will tell us what I need to know."

The carriage came to a halt in front of Tumsbury Cliff Manor. Stephen opened the door to a steady torrent of rain.

"Damn, we shall get wet through before we even get inside. We shall have to run."

Before Rufus could respond, Stephen donned his thick coat and ran for the entrance.

Rufus's mood darkened further as he acknowledged his own eagerness at seeing the totally unsuitable Miss Kerrich.

His mouth set. Enough foolishness. His mother depended on him to restore their good name. Only then could he give up the life of espionage and, for once, consider his own dreams and desires.

What worried him was that he couldn't remember what they were.

Fighting to control his emotions, he stood for a moment, perched half out of the carriage, the rain forgotten, tugging his cuffs down and straightening his coat. Then he alighted and walked slowly up the steps and through the door.

The rain ran off his coat, and once free of the garment, he shook away the remaining dampness from his clothes. He handed his coat to the doorman and heard Rheda's voice. The soft husky tones sent a shiver down his spine. As he moved closer to the receiving line he caught glimpses of apricot silk draping seductive curves. The night's earlier restlessness returned. He must remember that tonight was not about the pleasure of being in a woman's company. It was about redemption—for him and the Strathmore name.

★ ★ ★

Rheda's heart was pounding so hard she felt sure the ladies next to her would hear it. Lord Strathmore was sinfully handsome in his formal evening wear. The task she'd set herself tonight made her stomach churn in a heady mixture of fear and desire.

She followed his movement around the room over the top of her open fan, which she waved violently, trying to cool down. She swallowed. She knew in all likelihood there would be only one way to ensure she had his undivided attention. She closed her fan, not wishing to advertise her hand's tremble.

How far would she have to go to save her brother? Would she have to sacrifice all of herself to hold his attention? Her pulse tripped. She knew she shouldn't feel this way, but she hoped so. She wanted to make love to the handsome viscount.

She glanced around the ballroom. Her nerves were making her look for a way to escape, but her path was set for the night. Her brother was unaware of the risk she would take to keep their secret. If Daniel found out, she could have her plan backfire, giving her brother just the ammunition he needed to see her betrothed. He would love to see her married to a viscount. This viscount.

Deep in thought, she did not notice Jamieson at her side until he spoke. "Excuse me, Miss Kerrich, your brother requests a private word in the library."

She gave a convincing smile, concealing her disquiet from her guests. "What now, Jamie? Has he lost his cheroot case again?" With a toss of her gloved hand, she exclaimed to her friends, "And they call us the dizzy ones! Please excuse me while I see to my brother's latest non-emergency."

Her heart skipped a beat as she hurried Jamieson out of the ballroom. They climbed the stairs to the library, to the strains of the minuet echoing throughout the house.

She quietly hissed to Jamieson following behind. "What

trouble has my brother got into now? It has to be urgent—
Daniel told me to keep an eye on Lord Strathmore. I can
hardly do that if I am not in the ballroom."

Jamieson responded calmly. "We have a spot of trouble. I
will let his lordship explain." And he pushed open the library
door.

She crossed the threshold and saw Daniel pacing the new
Persian carpet, fists clenched at his side and his face set like
the grim reaper. Upon seeing her, Daniel walked over and
gripped her hands with his.

"Rhe, we're in trouble."

Although she saw the makings of a disaster in his eyes, she
tried not to show her distress. Slipping her hands free, she led
him to the settee by the fireplace, calmly sat down, and mo-
tioned for him to do the same. "Now, tell me what the problem is."

"Davidson's fallen off his horse and broken his leg. He
cannot organize the run tonight. I am going to have to slip
away and bring the boat in."

She pressed her hand against her stomach. "Is it too late to
cancel?"

"Yes. The boat will have left France already. Damn,
tonight of all nights. This was supposed to prove we weren't
involved. I was to be in full view of Lord Strathmore. If he
notices I am missing our carefully laid plan is all for nothing."
Daniel stood and moved to the fireplace and gripped the
mantelpiece. Glanced at the clock. "What should I do, Rhe?"

She closed her eyes so she could concentrate. After a moment she opened them, took a breath, and said, "You will
proceed as planned, but use the tunnel to the beach so you
can move about unseen. Until you leave I suggest you pretend to have drunk too much. If anyone misses you I can always say you have gone to lie down. Can you signal the boat
to move farther down the coast?"

Daniel nodded.

"Good, then I suggest we use the southernmost cavern. If

anyone is waiting for you, they won't expect that—they will think it is too rocky to land there in a storm. There is less chance of being seen."

She rose and moved to the library's huge window to draw back the drapes. "The storm is picking up. Daniel, please be careful. I cannot lose you."

He walked to the window and hugged her. "I will be as quick as I can. Will you be all right here on your own? I have to take Jamieson with me."

"Of course." She gave him a reassuring squeeze and a bright smile. "I have some business to attend to. I must ensure Lord Strathmore is looked after." Now it was doubly imperative she did not let the viscount out of her sight. Her brother had to remain safe. She would have to keep Lord Strathmore busy.

Although Rufus smiled politely, bore his share of dances with no sign of ill humor, and never exposed his true churning state of mind, his temper was rising from simmering to boiling point. Now he could not find the baron anywhere; had they lost him?

He approached Stephen and said, "Worthington, a private word if I may?"

They withdrew a small distance from the throng.

"Have you seen the baron?" he asked. "He has been gone for over an hour."

"He left to oversee some preparations on the estate due to the weather, but he should have been back by now." Stephen hesitated. "I knew the storm would be trouble."

Rufus had checked everywhere in the manor except the bedchambers. He lifted his head upward, assessing the likelihood of the baron being above. "Stay in the ballroom. I will see if I can find him above stairs."

The thought of Rheda's bedchamber made his rake's instincts flare to life. He knew he should be focused on the trap he and his men had set tonight, but in truth, the moment

he'd set eyes on Rheda in that gown, an ache of desire fiercer than any he'd ever felt throbbed in his groin and overrode all common sense.

Standing next to her brother in the receiving line, she'd looked like an angel. He'd almost forgotten to breathe. God, he wanted her the minute she'd smiled a warm welcome.

Rheda. Rheda had looked like a shimmering goddess, dressed in pale apricot. Her lustrous fair hair glinted as the candlelight caught the threads of gold in her chignon piled high on her head, emphasizing her long slender neck. Tonight she looked like any other refined lady of the *ton*. Only a thousand times more beautiful.

His fingers itched to touch and stroke the fine, milky perfection of her skin. And the need to press his lips to the pulse he saw racing at the base of her throat almost overwhelmed him.

He remembered her pliant from the cliff top and sated in his arms. No simpering girl, Miss Rheda Kerrich was definitely a woman, definitely all woman—but definitely not for him.

Tonight she'd been the perfect hostess, witty, engaging, and demure, with an air of unconcealed confidence about her. Was she playing in her brother's deadly game? Was she being used to unbalance and distract him from his true mission?

If so, her plan was working. Awareness of her coated his skin like a fitted glove. His highly developed senses for members of the opposite sex were galloping out of control. She looked more demure, completely virginal, the perfect English rose. Yet he knew her, understood her character, and wouldn't underestimate her brain. He'd do well to remember even roses had thorns.

Steeling himself against the desire racing through his already on-edge body, he unlatched her door and stepped into her bedchamber.

The room was stifling. The only light came from a fire roaring in the grate. At first glance the room appeared

empty. Rufus made to back out and close the door when a movement in the shadows to his left stopped him in his tracks.

"I thought you'd never find me."

Her voice was soft, sweet, and teased over his skin like a feather, exciting every inch of him. He should have retreated, but it was too late now. He stepped farther into the room and closed the door, forgetting everything except the silken-clothed vision before him.

She moved toward him until her breasts pressed his chest directly where he felt his heart pounding. He looked down her gown into the valley between her breasts and desire erupted. She rose up and brushed her lips over his, her fingers twining in his hair, and he let her have her way, powerless to stop her.

Her eyes locked with his, and he couldn't understand the message flashing in their emerald depths. All he could do was drink in their sparkling splendor.

He was so enchanted that he was completely unprepared for what happened next. She began maneuvering him toward the fire. He felt his boots stumble against something on the floor, and before he could blink, she gave his chest a firm shove. He landed on his back, atop fur throws, with Rheda straddling his thighs; her dress was rucked up her legs, her breasts tantalizingly close to his mouth.

His libido went off like a cannon, powerful and punishing, and before he could think better of it he reached for her and dragged her more firmly atop him for a mind-blowing kiss.

Yet, he was to be denied. Rheda sat up, straddling his waist, her hands holding his wrists in her gentle but firm grip.

"If I remember correctly, you were eager to teach me to ride," she said, her voice a whispered aphrodisiac. "Tonight it is my turn to have my wicked way with you. You're not the only one who wishes to seduce for information." She let

go of one wrist and stroked a finger across his lips. "Why for instance are you really in Deal?"

Rufus opened his mouth to answer, and her finger slipped inside. His traitorous mouth responded by clamping around her small digit, drawing it in farther and sucking firmly. She wriggled atop him, and his judgment clouded.

Excitement avalanched down his spine, and his body, already eager, leaped more prominently to attention. He could overpower her and stop her game at any time, but right now he preferred to play. He longed to see what she was up to and how far she'd go.

He relaxed back against the throws and let her finger withdraw from his mouth. He gave her a dazzling smile. "I find Deal an immensely pleasurable town."

"We aim to please, my lord. Shall I demonstrate how accommodating we Dealites can be?"

She began to undo the buttons of his jacket and waistcoat. She indicated he should help, and he rose enough for her to slip the garments off his shoulders and pull them off his arms. Then she tugged his shirt over his head. Her gaze fastened on his bare torso, and she tentatively raised her hand to brush her fingers lightly over his chest, tracing the curve and dip of bone and muscle. His stomach clenched as he tried to hold still, tried to stop himself from reaching for her. He almost broke when with a slight moan she bent her head and let her tongue taste him.

He refused to give in to her torment. Closing his eyes he lay back, more than willing to indulge her. He was a consummate rake. He could control his passions when needed. At anytime he could reverse their positions.

He inwardly smiled at her tentative strokes over his skin. She seemed fascinated with his ribs and stomach, her touch almost like she was worshipping him. He'd give her a few more strokes, then he'd switch places.

He drew in a deep breath as her fingers grew bolder and

trailed lower to pluck at the placket of his breeches. Despite his previous thought of taking control, he shifted to accommodate her small hand. He grew harder, if that was possible, and he wasn't surprised when he felt air on the head of his lengthening shaft. With a mind of its own, there was no way it would not escape the confines of his clothing in its quest to be touched.

She mocked his very thoughts. "Someone is keen to let me play." One hand slipped inside the opening and touched him. He surged into her palm on a deep groan. Her other hand pushed and pulled his breeches apart. He lifted his hips to help her, all pretense of resisting gone under her arousing fingers.

She smiled saucily and leaned forward until he felt her hot breath on his skin. He reached up and pulled the pins out of her hair, threading his fingers through the silken mass to let her tresses glide over his sensitized skin. His body was on fire. He burned for more.

And she gave it. He came up off the floor as her lips touched the tip of his cock. She ran her tongue down the length of him and took one of his sacs into her mouth, rolling it around and licking it with her tongue. She nibbled back up the hard length of him, and he heard his own breathing grow louder.

"Christ that feels so good. Take all of me—please . . ."

She lifted her head and gave him a victorious smile. There was something so erotic about her expression, with her lips glistening and puckered. He wanted to drag her down and kiss her senseless, but he'd rather she kissed another part of him altogether.

"I like the taste of you. Hmmm, all man." And she licked her lips.

It was too much. Rufus cried out, arching up from the floor. "You're driving me mad, Rheda. Please put me out of my misery, I'm begging you."

She hesitated for a split second, and he thought that per-

haps she'd meant to only tease him. That she'd not meant to let her supposed seduction go so far.

Then she bent and licked the tiny bead of moisture escaping from the tip of his member, and he was no longer capable of thought at all.

Rheda reveled in the power she held over this strong, virile man. He didn't appear to notice that she had no idea of what she was doing. She was simply giving in to her desires. The reality of the doing was very different from being a voyeur. It was infinitely more arousing.

She let her mouth move over his skin, trailing kisses over his hip and down his thigh. She ran her tongue up the inside of his leg. He had a small mole near where his thigh joined his groin, and she kissed it tenderly.

He was warm and alive under her mouth and more beautiful than anything she'd seen. Rheda sensed the raw power and strength of the man beneath her, and it thrilled her to her core knowing she was in control. He was at her mercy and loving every minute of it.

The fact he wanted her was more exciting than she could have imagined. She swirled her tongue around the head of him. He was big, and he seemed to grow bigger with each touch of her lips. She had to open wide to take him completely into her mouth.

His groans were intermingled with his rapid pants, and the more she suckled and caressed him, the hotter grew her own desires. She could picture stripping off her gown and pressing her hot skin to his roughness. The urge to make love with him, his hard length powering into her, giving her pleasure while taking his own, was all consuming.

Only now did she fully understand why Daniel enjoyed "fishing" so much. For the first time she understood the command of lust and how it could be between a man and a woman. She was eager to partake in the feast.

All thoughts of keeping him occupied until the shipment

landed fled. She was on a knife's edge, and at any moment she hoped to lose her balance and spiral out of control. All she wanted was him. And she was going to have him.

Bliss. Pure unadulterated bliss. Pleasure like he'd never known before. Rufus was lost.

How he'd ever thought of her as innocent . . . Her skills were being clearly demonstrated. Each touch, each lick, each suck, almost unmanned him.

He prayed for control. He felt her breath on his rigid shaft enticing his overheated and sensitized skin. She teased, playing him like an undisputed maestro. He wondered if he'd last much longer.

She continued stroking with her tongue, delicate little licks, like a cat, before her hot, wet, mouth swallowed him whole. Her mouth was strong and purposeful as she suckled him.

He was losing control, and he was normally always in control. He should put a stop to this and tumble her beneath him. Once on top he'd be the one driving her mad.

He gave a loud groan as she took him deeper into her mouth. Involuntarily, Rufus's hips left the floor. Oh, yes, this is what he needed. He forgot all about dominating. He forgot all about finding her brother. All he focused on was pleasure. Just pleasure, pure and simple.

Rheda knew she was approaching the point of no return. She was on the verge of combusting. The urge to rip her own clothes from her body and join with him was like a dose of poison ivy. The insistent need to scratch was tormenting her, but she'd only itch more once she let herself indulge.

She was supposed to be in control. This craving wasn't what she'd meant to happen.

Was this how he'd felt as he'd given her pleasure? Wanting her while denying himself more. He'd had the strength to walk away. Would she?

God, he was disciplined. She hoped she carried the same trait.

Please, she prayed, let him finish before she gave in and lifted her gown and straddled his pulsing member.

She knew he was close. His groans were escalating. His jaw was taut, and the pulse at his temple pounded. Rufus's hips lifted, and he thrust himself deeper into her mouth. She clamped her lips firmly around him and suckled hard.

His hands sunk deep in her hair, pulling tight. She ignored the pain as he gave one loud bellow, while trying to sit up and pull out of her mouth, but Rheda wouldn't let go. She wanted to taste him. Wanted all of him, and she felt his hot seed pulse deep in the back of her throat—salty and delicious.

Rufus collapsed back onto the throws, his eyes closed and his breath ragged in his throat.

She pushed up off him with trembling hands. She licked her lips and swallowed. She'd won. She'd made him lose control while maintaining her own. If only it was as easy to make him divulge what he'd do to Dark Shadow if he found the mysterious smuggler. Would Rufus understand?

She sat beside him, soaking in the beauty of him as he lay replete. His trousers were hanging open, his chest was covered in a fine sheen, and his stomach muscles contracted with each deep breath. She couldn't help herself. She reached out and ran her fingers over his damp chest.

As she moved her fingers lower he grabbed her wrist. "Give a man a minute to recover," he whispered hoarsely. "Then I'll make love to you until you faint from the pleasure. I promise you."

Where would be the harm in that? her mind screamed. He looked like a god—he'd be heaven. The thought of his hands on her skin, his mouth on her breasts, she didn't want to deny him. *Why should I?*

The wild, unconventional Rheda Kerrich answered to no

one. She'd taken risks plenty of times, but she shook her head, knowing to give into him would be reckless and dangerous.

She looked into his eyes and recognized the gleam within. She didn't respond fast enough. He moved like lightning, and before she could blink she ended up flat on her back with a very large aroused male above her.

"Did you think I'd let you leave without a seduction of my own?" He laughed quietly beside her ear. He ground the evidence of his recovery against her stomach. "I'm going to pleasure you until you beg me to let you come. Or, until you confess the identity of Dark Shadow. Then and only then will I let you climax."

How did such a threat feel like a promise? Rheda almost begged him to do his worst . . . which would more likely be his best.

Her feverish brain was on fire. Her lips parted on a sigh, and she couldn't help herself. Her hips rose to push against the hard length of him, and he chuckled deep in his throat. "This shouldn't take too long."

"It's late. I should be getting back to my guests," she whispered against his chest.

"I didn't start this liaison, siren. From the minute I entered the room you were bent on my seduction. Here I am— more than willing."

He knew he should leave. He had other places to be, other business to attend to. With a muted curse he decided Stephen could handle the baron. He'd use this blatant opportunity to try to break Rheda. They'd have leverage over Daniel if Rheda confessed to her brother's black market activities.

Worry knifed through him because whatever her scheme, Rufus had to admit, it seemed to be highly effective. He was hard and tempted beyond sin. When he should be continuing his search for the baron his mind was focused on more personal desires.

He wanted her. The dam had burst, and under the torrent of desire his ability to resist had been swept away. He could no longer forgo the pleasure he'd find within her body. The skill she'd shown moments earlier, her mouth hot and tight on his aching shaft, had him wanting more. His body was fit to burst, and he no longer had the strength to deny himself.

For a long moment he met her emerald eyes. Was that fear or desire he saw reflected in their jeweled depths? What was she hiding? Who was she protecting? It would almost be a relief if it was Daniel. The thought of her protecting a lover sent his mind into a dark hole. He didn't like the idea of her being another man's lover. That should have sent icy fear down his back. He was getting too close.

Whether from fear or desire, he was mesmerized by her body's response to him. He leaned down and took her mouth. She opened to him, absorbing the slow, penetrating motion of his tongue.

As the tentative thrust of her tongue met his, Rufus groaned, "I've wanted you for so long."

She moaned and moved restlessly beneath him.

"I know your body craves my touch. Your breasts ache, your belly tightens, and the place between your thighs grows damp." She was making small sounds of pleasure deep in her throat, and she gasped as his hands freed her breasts and his fingers tweaked her hardened nipples. "I shall ask a question, and for each correct answer you will be rewarded with a stroke from one part of my body."

To demonstrate, he kissed her again, his tongue stroking deep within her mouth. He tangled his fingers in her silken hair, remembering the feel of it on his bare torso—scorching. He drank from her sweetness, but instead of dimming the fire, it caused the desire to ignite and erupt in a blaze of heat and need.

In the flickering firelight he could feel her hapless gaze search his face. She licked her lips, and his member jerked against her stomach. "We shall see who breaks first. I think

you want me more than you're admitting. I'm sure I can last longer than you." To prove her point she lifted her hips and rubbed herself intimately against the hard ridge of his erection.

He gave a husky laugh. "I love a challenge." He drew back. "Fair's fair, my love. You had a taste of me, now it is my turn." With those words he slowly swept his hand down her body, feeling every soft curve through the silk of her gown before pausing at the juncture of her thighs. He felt her shiver under his hand.

His eyes held hers for a moment as he raised her skirts to bare her delectable flesh, but she made no protest. Her thighs parted on their own accord as his palm stroked along the warm satiny skin.

Rufus lowered his mouth to her puckered nipple, suckling her as his hand rose higher on her thigh, and he fingered the soft folds at their damp apex.

She was wet silk between her legs, aroused as much as he. Yet, even as his body screamed to take her, he ruthlessly controlled his savage need. He wanted her dripping, begging him to take her, and then he'd demand to know her secrets.

He rose on all fours and swept his gaze over her. She looked beautiful beyond words. Her breasts gleamed milky white in the firelight. Her skirts bunched up at her waist allowed him a perfect sweeping view of her gazelle-like legs and the honey-colored hair that surrounded his prize.

"I know your brother is Dark Shadow. However, he was too young to have set up the ring. Who is he working for?" Rufus was certain the mastermind behind the ring must be the spy he sought. It was the perfect cover. Put a young pup in charge of the operation so if he were caught, everyone would assume all that was transacting was simply smuggling by a young nobleman in need of funds.

She stiffened at his words. "Ring? What ring?" she uttered breathlessly.

He moved slowly, placing kisses down her slightly

rounded stomach until at last he could breathe in the heady scent of her desire. As he sat between her thighs he gave a knowing smile. "Are you ready for this, Rheda? Can you imagine what my tongue will feel like upon you?"

She squirmed, lifting her hips in a silent plea.

He bent and set his tongue to her, lapping lightly before drawing back. "A name. Give me a name, and I'll give you more. You'll find the bliss even deeper when I'm sheathed deep within you and we are fully joined."

Her voice so soft he almost didn't hear her, said, "Pleasure is not a good enough reason to betray a trust. Not even pleasure with you."

He nodded and ran his finger between her silken folds. "I can offer so much more. My desire for you is not faked. With your skills you'd make me a fine mistress. I can offer you security." He slipped a finger inside her. "I can offer you your dream—horses. I'd help you establish your stud."

His offer was the slap she needed. The passion swirling around her, through her, all but vanished.

Reality hit home like a cold wind off the sea. A lock snapped open deep inside her chest, and her worst nightmare was revealed. There was no passion without love, not for her. She didn't want passion, she wanted—love. She wanted to scream out a denial, but her heart betrayed her. It bled at the thought of letting a man who did not love her have sex with her. For that is what it would be, nothing more. It would not be making love, and that is what her heart wanted.

She closed her eyes lest he see her weakness. This meant nothing to him. She meant nothing to this man except a source of information and pleasure.

She could never give herself to a man who would not value the gift she bestowed.

Fury fed her strength, and she rose to push at his chest, knocking him backward, and he hit the floor at her feet.

"Your offer is insulting."

His eyes glinted anger in the dim light. His jaw was tight and his fists clenched. "Insulting? You should be grateful for such an offer. The scandal-ridden sister to a penniless baron. A woman who gave herself to a Turkish prince for two horses." He rose to stand on his feet, towering over her as she lay stunned on the throws from his vicious verbal attack. "Perhaps you think to know your own worth and expect me to pay more. Marriage? Is that what you are after?" He leaned down until his nose touched hers. "Never. Never to the likes of you. I wouldn't taint the Strathmore name."

She hid the pain his words sliced into her heart and hit back. "From what I have heard your father did a good job of that all by himself."

A hiss escaped through his clenched teeth. "If you weren't a—lady—I'd kill you for that remark."

He stood and retrieved his shirt. "If you didn't want me buried between your thighs, what was this scene all about?"

She couldn't look him in the eye. She had wanted him. But he'd killed that desire with his callousness. She refused to be a man's plaything. Her mother had suffered the agony of being in thrall to a man who did not love her, and Rheda knew her heart was becoming engaged. She vowed she would not let a man have that power over her—ever.

Thank goodness she'd learned in time that Rufus had no feelings for her. Real feelings. Lust was not love. If her mother hadn't taught her this, Rufus's actions surely had.

However, the night had not been a complete waste. She glanced at the clock. The boat should have made shore by now. Rufus caught her glance, and she watched a muscle in his jaw tighten.

"You were the distraction. Bravo, my dear. I've never enjoyed a distraction so much. You were truly magnificent." He immediately pivoted for the door. Before he stepped through he threw a further insult over his shoulder. "Your brother must be so proud."

Chapter 16

He did up his jacket on the way down the stairs. He'd left his waistcoat on the bedchamber floor and wouldn't risk going back for it. Risk his temper exploding and him taking his anger out on her—in her.

Christ, he tugged a hand through his hair. The woman was going to drive him insane. How could he feel anything but loathing for such a woman? His stomach clenched and his blood froze—but he did.

The hunt for his father's salvation was obviously clouding his judgment. There was just too much going on in his mind, too many questions requiring answers, too many restless doubts. And there was also something else that wouldn't let him alone—something kicking and screaming in his chest with every breath he took. Perhaps that's why he'd allowed himself the temporary luxury of just enjoying her seduction. Now that Rheda had opened the door to carnal delights, what reason was there to stop him from taking her—willing or not?

His honor—that's what. He still had a smidgeon of honor left. Marguerite hadn't destroyed it completely.

Strange, all Rheda needed to do was flash a smile and he was eager to have her. It was as if she reached deep into him and teased a part of him he tried to keep buried. He was helpless to resist her, eager to forget everything deadly she could unleash.

Betrayal, agony, hurt, and worse. She could drag the Strathmore name so far down in the mud nothing would ever clean it. But he still wanted her, desired her—Christ, he closed his eyes and admitted that he didn't want to hurt her. Why should she suffer because of her brother's lawlessness?

He of all people knew how unfair being tarred with another's brush was. He finally admitted what he'd been trying to fight. He admired her. He admired her loyalty to her family and her ability to not give a damn about what people thought of her. Wasn't she trying to protect her brother just as he was protecting his mother and sister? He'd shown that he was quite prepared to do practically anything to ensure their happiness.

His thoughts were interrupted by one of his men. "Lord Worthington requires your presence on the cliffs. The baron left the house over an hour ago."

With grim determination forcing thoughts of Rheda from his head, Rufus grabbed his great overcoat and left the house.

Cursing under his breath, he struggled to make headway against the howling wind. Visibility was limited to the arc of his lantern, about three feet in front of him. He'd fallen at least three times, slipping in the wet muddy grass as he battled the windy conditions. He concentrated on keeping his footing on the slippery stones near the cliff top.

Stephen materialized out of the darkness on his right, soaking wet in his thick overcoat. "You're late," he yelled into the wind.

"Apologies. Something came up." He did not want to elaborate on exactly what part of his anatomy had come up. His friend would be furious.

Stephen moved close and spoke in Rufus's ear. "Damn, this storm. The men cannot see a thing. I'm sure they'll not land a boat tonight in these conditions."

Rufus flicked his dripping fringe out of his eyes and pulled his hair back, tying it at the back of his neck. He knew they

would. Rheda's seduction was all the proof he needed. Why else would she have offered herself to him?

"They'll come." He said. "This storm hit suddenly, too late for the French to turn back. They'll anchor out to sea and row the cargo in."

"Are you sure? It would be bloody dangerous with waves of this size; they might break up on the rocks."

He glanced across at their men, huddled with their backs against the elements like a herd of cows sheltering from the rain. Turning back to Stephen he said, "I'm sure they've landed in these conditions before. It's more trouble than it's worth for the Revenuers to catch them in a storm."

"Well, my men have been scouring the cliff tops since early evening and have not spotted anyone. Now it's almost impossible to see anything in this weather. The smugglers have the advantage over us."

Rufus pointed down the cliff. "We need to get the men on the beaches. They have to land the cargo somewhere."

Stephen shrugged his shoulders. "It's like finding a needle in a haystack, there are so many coves and caves in the cliffs around the coastline. Where do you want to position the few men we have?"

Rufus rubbed a hand across his forehead and tried to ignore the water streaming down his face. "South is too rocky in this weather. Take the men and split them into groups of three. Let's search cove by cove. Start up north by Hallow Cove, the men can work in threes, two men down on the beach and one man on the cliff top to signal us if they find anything. We'll work down the coast back to this point. Get the men to signal with their lanterns if they see anything suspicious."

"What are you going to do?" Stephen eyed him worriedly.

"I am going to have a quick check south. They just might be stupid enough to try and land at Sholden Bay."

"Be careful, Rufus, you'll only have two shots; one from

each pistol. The gunpowder is likely to be too wet to re-load."

He gave a grim smile. "I have my trusted sword." He stepped back and offered Stephen his hand. "Good luck, my friend. Keep safe."

"And you." Then Stephen hurried over to the drenched men and barked out his orders.

Rufus swung around to stare at the southern coastline. It was savage in its beauty. The waves were white foam, crashing against black rock. Spray, falling like snowflakes, was drifting inland on the wind.

Two cold, wet, and miserable hours later, Rufus finally admitted to himself they'd missed their prey. He pulled his watch out of his pocket, fingers fumbling, numb from the cold; he struggled with the catch to lift the watch's lid. Close to three in the morning. They would have unloaded and sailed back to France by now.

He closed his eyes, bitter in his defeat—and his head dropped back, the rain lashing at his face. Pulling himself together he straightened and stood, head held high once more, fists clenched. He would not give up, and he shook himself, trying to rid the stink of despair he could smell on his body. He strode slowly back toward the rendezvous point, knowing Stephen would've signaled him if the men had found anything. His face remained expressionless as he renewed his vow to catch Daniel, come what may.

Ahead of him loomed Jacob's Point, a massive rock formation believed by some to be haunted by a young lad named Jacob who, having climbed the rock to avoid his drunken father's beating, had fallen to his death in the sea fifty feet below. They said that on misty nights, the young ghost was often on the outcrop, his arms outstretched as if pleading with his father. The stories were more likely to be due to an excess of gin.

He came to an abrupt halt. About two hundred yards away two eerie figures seemed to hug the rocks, and the hairs on his neck rose. For a moment he thought he was looking at young Jacob and his father. Then his instincts roared into life. They were men, not ghosts. Men—very much alive.

Drawing his pistol he advanced on them. The wind made his approach soundless, and they hadn't yet seen him. They were too engrossed in their conversation. He took one steady step after another, trying not to squelch in the mud. "Good evening, gentlemen. No sudden movements if you please."

He still could not clearly make out the men's features. Then, just as he was about to advance closer, his knees buckled; his head felt like it had split in two. He landed face first in the mud, the fall broken by the softness of the soaking wet ground. Someone had hit him from behind.

He looked up from the mud, blinking furiously, trying to get the grit out of his eyes. The two startled men turned to flee; one of them glanced his way, and he thought he saw concern in the man's eyes. He raised his pistol and managed to fire one shot at the fleeing men. With a satisfied smile he slumped back down, certain he'd hit one of them. He let a wave of nausea and black spots swamp him before succumbing to total darkness.

He awoke to firm hands turning him over in the mud.

"Are you shot, Rufus? Can you hear me?"

He winced. Stephen's concerned voice sounded like a ship's foghorn in his ear.

"I'm fine, stop fussing, I haven't been shot." He took Stephen's outstretched hand and let himself be pulled to his feet. He stood gripping Stephen's arm for a few seconds as he cleared his groggy head. He gingerly felt the back of his skull. No blood, good, the skin hadn't been broken. All he could feel was a large bump.

"I take it you ran into trouble," Stephen said. "The men have checked along the beach, but there is no one about. God damn it, we've missed them."

"I came across two men. Then someone hit me over the head from behind. I did manage to get a shot away. I'm sure I hit one of them; I think it was Daniel."

Stephen turned and called to his men. "You two, Gregory and Carter, organize the men to search the grounds. If he's wounded he cannot have gone far."

Rufus tried to clear his throbbing head; his skull felt as though it wanted to explode. He rested his head in his hands. Was it Daniel he'd seen, or did he desperately want it to be him just so he could use the baron as an excuse to despise Rheda? If Daniel was innocent then Rheda's words would be true and he'd have to admit feelings for her that he had no right to indulge.

Rheda. He turned so quickly another bout of dizziness swamped him.

"Are you sure you are all right?" Stephen asked. "You have a nasty bump on the back of your head."

"I am fine. I have to get back to the manor; if it was Daniel he'll go to Rheda."

"Are you sure?"

Rufus realized he wasn't really. He shrugged his shoulders. "There's no point standing here in the howling wind and rain. The men are searching the grounds; we should search the manor."

Chapter 17

Rheda tensed at the sound of the purposeful footsteps approaching her room. Her stomach, already a twisted snare of knots, lurched, and she swallowed the bile rising into her mouth. There was no turning back. The scene she was enacting would probably seal her fate. But it was Daniel. Her brother. What else was she to do?

Luckily, Rufus's shot had only winged her brother's arm. Barely a scratch. She'd been able to quickly patch him up, and now Daniel was safely hidden in the caverns below the manor.

The blazing fire, and the warmth from her bath, couldn't keep the chill from pervading her bones. She drew in a deep breath and slowly exhaled, willing her racing heart to calm down. He'd see right through this charade.

She knew Rufus would come for her. All games would be over. Time for the much needed reckoning had arrived.

Her door flew open with such force it almost came off its hinges. She flinched at the unrefined power and beauty of the man filling the doorway. Raw vitality emanated from his body, buffeting her senses. It was a very dangerous yet seductive combination.

His dark brown eyes disquietingly familiar did not even start at the sight of her lying naked in the copper bathtub. So much for the idea that her bodily charms might disarm him;

after her actions earlier this evening, he was impervious to her nudity.

His broad shoulders filled the doorway, subtly reminding her there would be no escape. She allowed her gaze to travel up the hard lean length of him. His presence dominated her bedchamber. Her mouth went dry. She briefly closed her eyes and offered up a silent prayer. "Where is he?" Rufus's voice was as cold and imposing as the rest of him. Although she knew what was coming, this Rufus frightened her.

Rheda steeled herself against his dark insolent beauty and snapped, "Lord Strathmore, what is the meaning of this intrusion? I am bathing. Kindly remove yourself, sir, or with one scream I'll summon help and have you removed."

Cold and arrogant, Viscount Strathmore raised a sardonic brow. "Not a very convincing performance, Miss Kerrich. The only help a scream will likely summon is my men, and I'm sure they'd love to witness Miss Rheda Kerrich in all her natural beauty."

He moved farther into her bedchamber with surprising grace for a man thrumming with tension, then stood before the fireplace, surveying her with a cool, raking glance.

Rheda shivered under his slow, deliberate stare; he made her feel tarnished, unworthy, but she lifted her chin and studied him with the same cool insolence he was giving her.

He was worth the attention. His hair that had flowed freely over his shoulders in the ballroom just hours earlier was now plastered to his head; water dripped onto his collar below. The threads of copper that ran through the rich, chocolate-colored hair glinted in the firelight, flashing danger.

"I won't ask again." The timbre of his voice, low and cultured, flowed like velvet but with an edge of steel. "Where is your brother?"

Rheda felt herself flush, but she kept her gaze steady, gesturing with one wet arm, around the room. "You can see my chamber is empty. I have no idea where he is." She

paused, raised an eyebrow, and continued, "Do you think he's hiding in the bathwater?"

As soon as the rash words were out of her mouth she wished she could take them back, for he moved deliberately toward her until he stood towering over her at the tub's edge. His scathing perusal swept the water, searching its dark depths before moving over her half-exposed breasts and up farther until their eyes met.

"You do not even seem surprised I am looking for him. Why is that, I wonder?" His questions held an edge of wryness.

Rheda dreaded having to respond. Whatever she said would only deepen the trap he was setting for her. Feigning indignation, she countered, "I am flustered, my lord. I have never before had a *gentleman* barge into my chamber while I was bathing."

He dropped to a crouch next to the tub, his black breeches pulling tight across the powerful muscles of his thighs. With elbows resting on the tub, he leaned his chin on clasped hands. "Ah, but then my beautiful Rheda, earlier tonight you didn't want me to be a gentleman."

She swallowed, her traitorous body reacting to his husky murmur, the scent of sandalwood and masculinity surrounding him.

The wicked rogue slowly reached out and with one finger traced a droplet of water from her right shoulder diagonally across her exposed breasts until his finger rested on her now hardened left nipple hidden just below the waterline.

Her breath quickened. She desperately tried to ignore his touch, but her body grew hot with desire at the feel of his finger slowly circling her areola. His smile widened at her body's obvious response.

His head turned and his seductive smile froze. Straightening, he moved to the corner of the room. A towel lay crumpled there, a scarlet stain visible on one small corner.

Rheda's stomach knotted.

He swiveled to face her, no amusement or softness in his steely gaze. He stepped closer, grim anger scoring his mouth, but then he visibly repressed it. "Not seen him? Then where did this blood come from? I know I wounded him. If you are cut, show me. He has been here, hasn't he? Where are you hiding him?"

"You misunderstand, my lord." Rheda lowered her head, allowing her embarrassment to flame into her cheeks. "It's my blood. My monthly courses have just started."

Men, she knew, did not discuss such topics. She held her breath, hoping that would unsettle him. But his next statement made her choke on her own words.

"Stand up. We'll see how truthful you are."

Her head came up. "I beg your pardon?"

"I said stand up. If what you say is true it shouldn't take long for the evidence to appear."

Rheda's fear was replaced with sparks of anger. Her teeth set and her voice changed. All pretense of softness and femininity gone. She snapped, "How dare you? Get out of my chambers, *now!*"

With arms folded across his chest, he commanded, "Either stand up or I will call my men to help you out of the tub. Your choice."

Rheda closed her eyes, feeling a spell of dizziness. Lord Strathmore had her trapped by her own lies. She chewed her bottom lip, trying to decide what to do. She had to delay the excise men as long as possible. Long enough for Daniel to escape. Lifting her head, she squared her shoulders and, with great dignity, complied. She gracefully stood up, naked, proud and tall in the tub, water streaming down over her curves.

There was a bleak satisfaction at the reaction her emergence from the water provoked. Longing flared across the finely chiseled features.

He swore softly under his breath before flashing a mock-

ing smile. "Rheda means goddess in ancient Anglo-Saxon—did you know that? You are aptly named, for you truly are a goddess among women."

His gaze swept from her ankles, still hidden by the water, up her legs, halted at the thatch of fair curls at the apex of her thighs, continued over her stomach, and lingered again at her breasts, until finally resting on her face. Heat stole through her body and pooled in her loins. She noted his obvious arousal and the look of lust lighting his brown eyes. It was all she could do not to jump from the tub and flee.

Rheda kept her palms flat against her thighs, willing them not to try and cover her. She wouldn't give him the satisfaction of knowing her embarrassment. Above all she did not want him to realize that he was the first man to ever see her naked.

But God help her, he did not stop there. He slowly circled the tub until she could no longer see him—he was somewhere behind her. She trembled in discomfort. It was unnerving not being able to see what he was looking at, or read the expression in his eyes. With her back to him, Rheda felt more exposed than ever, but she refused to turn around and face him.

The quiet seemed to stretch on, the only sound being the water dripping off her nude body into the tub. Each passing minute increased her body's tremors. Soon she'd be unable to hide her distress.

Rheda closed her eyes and took a deep breath.

He spoke again, harshly and with ragged breath. "I see you lied."

She started, almost falling forward out of the tub. She hadn't heard his silent approach. He was close enough for his soft breath to caress her damp skin.

"This isn't a game. A game where you think I'll see your heavenly charms and forget what I am after. I want the whereabouts of your brother, and I don't care how I get it."

Regaining her composure and taking several large gulps of

air, while still not looking at him, Rheda replied, "I'll not let you hurt my brother."

His only response was a touch. A seductive slide of his warm finger down her spine. Rheda tensed, waiting for the molten pressure from his finger to continue its downward path. But his finger stopped its seductive trail once it reached the end of her spine, leaving a sudden chill in its place.

"Does your brother know the lengths you go to protect him? Earlier this evening you seduced me so that he could carry on his smuggling business immune from capture. Your scheme did not work."

"I don't know what you mean."

"I grow tired of your lies. I can leave you standing here in all your glory as long as it takes. I'm finding the more I know you the more I grow immune to your abundant charms."

His very stillness sent a shiver through her. "Your desire was not faked."

Rufus gave a harsh bark. "Neither was yours."

"That's true. I do desire you. But tonight I learned something about myself. I want more, and we come from different worlds. You'd never understand mine, and I certainly wouldn't want to live in yours. It would be far too restricting."

Rufus moved to stand in front of her. Time stretched between them as his gaze bored into her. Her nerves pulled taut. What would he do with her?

One perfect eyebrow rose. "Desire me? Truly? Are you lying, sweetheart? If, once again, I were to offer you a position as my mistress in exchange for saving Daniel, would you take it?"

"You're the one who'll pay." The anger infusing his face told her she'd said the wrong thing. He thought she was agreeing to his offer.

"You'd trade your body to save your worthless brother. Perhaps I should indulge in sampling your delights before I decide whether to save Daniel or let him rot."

Rheda hugged herself. He sounded so defeated. So tired. As though this situation pained him as much as it pained her.

She'd driven him to this.

She'd not meant to, but she'd used the only weapons she had—her looks. The weapon had backfired. She'd pushed too far. If he followed this path, Daniel and Lady Hale would likely require him to do the honorable thing. Marriage to her would hurt him and his family even more. "No. Stop. That is not—"

He moved before she had time to finish her sentence, cutting her words with a kiss. He swept her up in his arms and walked with her to the bed, dropping her down on the soft bedding before slowly following her down and covering her body. The feel of his soaking-wet clothes wasn't the only thing sending a chill through her. There was no softness in his touch this time. No gentleness.

Rheda struggled in earnest. Anger hummed around them. He was a man simply going through the motions of sex. This was no longer about pleasure; it was about teaching her a lesson. If he wanted to hurt her he couldn't have found a better way. This was not how she'd imagined her first time would be—certainly not her first time with him.

His mouth took hers in a bruising kiss. His tongue probed her tight lips, forcing his way in. Invading. Punishing.

Rheda knew she deserved to be chastised. She'd teased this man. Pushed him to do something she knew he'd never forgive himself for. Or her.

If Rufus discovered he'd raped an innocent, it would destroy him. He had no idea who she really was. No idea that the rumors about her and the prince were false. She had never professed her innocence. Now he was going to pay the price for her pride.

She had to help him. Perhaps if he understood she truly wanted him, he'd not feel so guilty over what he was about to do. She might even be able to hide her virginity from him if she made it plain she welcomed his ravishment.

She stopped fighting him and kissed him back. She let loose her passion and took control. She pushed her tongue into his mouth and moaned low in her throat. She bent her legs to hug his hips and let him sink between her thighs. She could feel his rampant erection through his clothing.

On a groan his kiss softened. His hands gentled, and he let go of her wrists so he could stroke her body.

Would he stop if she asked? Could she reason with him now, or would he think it still a game?

For some reason she could not get the words out.

She watched with willing fascination as he shrugged rapidly out of his clothes.

He was fully aroused, and the magnificence of his nude body took her breath away. The muscles of his chest and torso rippled and flexed, and her fingers longed to trail every inch like the shadows from the fire dancing over his naked skin.

Her eyes roamed over him in a thorough assessment, taking in the hard contours, the robust swell of his arms, the flat ridge of his abdomen, the flesh, thick and rampant between his legs . . .

"No more teasing, Rheda," he urged, gripping her wrist and pulling her up on her knees. "You set this in motion, and now I can't—I don't want to—stop. Damn the consequences."

His face was still hard and emotionless, but his eyes burned with intensity as he bent her over his arm and laved her nipples. "I want you. God help me I've wanted you since the first day I saw you on that damn cliff with that barrel."

She gave him a small smile. "I think I have wanted you as much. That is why I have fought you so hard. It scares me. This power you have over me."

"Power! I've felt powerless since I met you." Raw desire darkened his husky voice. "I want your softness clenching and shivering around my hardness."

His mouth, hot and moist, licked the space between her breasts, sending heat searing to her very core. Rheda gripped

his shoulders for strength, but she knew he wouldn't let her fall. He licked and kissed, whipping her into a frenzy. When his delicious mouth grazed one jutting nipple, she arched more. He parted his lips and took the puckering bud into his hot, wet mouth, and she all but collapsed back onto the bed. Nothing had ever felt this amazing. The pleasure was almost more than she could bear. Every nerve ending screamed for more.

Turbulent emotions came bubbling to the fore. All her feminine instincts took over, and she found the courage to slide her hands over the skin she'd been hungering to explore. It was firm, hard, yet sensual.

She was conscious of his hand sliding lower. Rufus flicked his tongue over her nipple and then drew it fully into his mouth. He sucked at her breast while cradling her mound in his palm. Any thought of resisting him had gone from her mind. She didn't want to stop him.

But he broke away from her, leaving her bereft. Her breasts felt raw and ravished from his delicious ministrations. If he asked her questions now, she might break. She yearned for his lips and hands on other parts of her, too.

As if sensing her every desire, he let her nipple slip between his teeth, and he turned his ravenous attention to her belly.

Hot lips pressed a trail against her taut skin, over her hips and down her thigh, branding her in the most wicked way. Her entire body trembled with the knowledge of what was to come—hoped was to come. She knew where this would end, and she couldn't regret it. Her legs parted to make his access easier—faster.

She dragged in a deep breath as his hand went between her thighs, burning her skin.

"I still have the taste of you imprinted on my brain," he ground out, his voice rough and turbulent, the tension of his restraint evident.

He parted her legs farther. The flesh tingling and exposed

to him—he needed no encouragement to take eager advantage.

His fingers parting the curls at her junction, Rufus, holding her gaze, lowered his head. The heat in his eyes blazed, and she closed her eyes at his first lick.

She arched and cried out as his hot, slick tongue lapped the sensitive area. Her fingers curled in the sheets, and she let out a deep and guttural groan as pleasure so intense—soul-wringing pleasure—raced over her.

He lapped her dewy folds of flesh, softly, almost reverently, then flicked the tip of his clever tongue over the delicate hardened nub, causing her to sob and cry out. "Oh, Rufus."

His lips kissed through her folds expertly in fluid strokes, stirring a welter of emotions in her belly, making her thighs flex and her hips lift in unrestrained longing.

A tight bolt of lightning began to unfurl in her stomach, and she couldn't help grinding herself against him. His tongue stroked faster, and just when she couldn't stand another second, he plunged his tongue deep inside her and she shattered. Shooting stars clouded her mind, and she floated in a haze of sensation.

When she finally brought her emotions under control it was to find him leaning over her, his stormy brown eyes tinged with gold, so dark and smoldering that she shivered at the intensity reflected in the deep chocolate pools.

She wanted him so badly, it hurt. An ache deep within her belly that only he could appease.

He kissed up her body and rose onto his thick, muscle-bound arms to stare at her with a force of need that humbled her. He lowered his head, fingers threading through her hair, spreading it out on the pillow beneath her. His mouth softened, its beautiful lines stark and sensual.

Rheda fought back a moan as his lips began to caress hers. She could feel his passion. Feel it matching hers.

"I shouldn't want you like this. Be consumed by you. But I can't deny my need for you . . ." His whisper filled her

mind and stirred a quickening deep within her. His touch felt so right . . . Even though he was her enemy. He could take everything she loved away from her. His tone deadly calm he added, "Once this is over, once I capture Daniel, I can't promise to protect you, but I'll try."

Before she could respond, giddiness made way for panic as she felt his turgid manhood nudge her entrance. She knew she had to relax. Meg told her it would hurt more if she didn't. If she was to try and hide her innocence she mustn't react. How painful could it be? Just looking at him hurt more than she could bear.

He withdrew and slipped a finger into her wet passage. "You're so tight," he breathed.

She took a deep breath and tried to get her unused muscles to loosen. She concentrated on Rufus's clever fingers; another finger had joined the first, intensifying the pleasure, evoking first a resigned sigh at the pain to come, and then a low, whimpering moan at the gratification he was stoking deep within her. Perhaps it wouldn't be too bad.

He kept up his sensual assault, egging her on, until she warmed and softened and surrendered to the dark magic he commanded. Rheda threaded her arms around his neck, pressing closer. She desperately wanted him, and a whimper of need escaped, begging him to ease the inexplicable hunger.

His fingers left her, and she didn't protest when she felt his thick, velvet-smooth shaft pressing against her thigh. Her breasts swelled beneath his luscious mouth, while her body quivered at the promise of that thick, rigid flesh giving her pleasure.

The tip of his shaft pierced her slick passage. She arched her back and lifted her hips instinctively seeking, and he thrust inside her to the hilt. Pain tore through her, and she couldn't stop crying out in shock, digging her nails into his shoulder as she gasped and whimpered.

Rufus stilled above her. "Christ." His eyes widened, and his face filled with fury. "You're a virgin." He struggled to

get his breathing under control; sweat beaded his forehead. "More deceit. What did you hope this sacrifice would bring? I won't be forced into marriage with you—and even if I were I won't save you if you are guilty," he growled.

"I tried to tell you on the cliff top that I'd had no lover. I've never had a lover. Tonight, would you have listened to me if I'd pleaded my innocence?"

His hair had fallen forward and shielded his eyes. Already she felt him tense with guilt.

He was still embedded inside her, but he held still. The pain was easing. Tentatively she moved, lifting her hips, drawing him deeper within her.

He shuddered above her. "Don't, Rheda. I shouldn't have done this . . ."

She moved again and lifted her torso off the bed to lick his nipples. "Let go of your guilt and make love to me. I've waited a long time to experience passion. Please make it special. Don't let me have wasted my . . ."

At her breathy entreat, she felt his body surrender to her.

"I know this is wrong, but it feels right. You feel right. I can't stop," he groaned, voice rough. His fingers trailed down and moved between their bodies, softly stroking the sensitive bud of nerves at her apex. Then he bent and took her lips in a kiss so full of feeling her heart melted.

She wanted him. Far too much. He would be her first lover. God, she wanted him to be her only lover . . . To fill her, to teach her about—love. Her eyes welled with tears. There would be no love—he would despise her when he realized who she was—Dark Shadow, the smuggler he sought.

Then he moved within her, and Rheda closed her eyes and forgot everything except for the hard lean body above her. She took the newfound comfort of his tender kisses and caresses. But as he began to stroke inside her, all thoughts of tenderness flew out the window.

He withdrew slightly, then thrust back into her. Slow at first, he eased himself from her sheath, then pushed back in-

side—all the way in—in a relentless plundering that made her feel more than she ever thought possible.

More painful than losing her virginity was the knowledge that Rufus would never look upon her with anything other than disdain once the truth came out.

For a long moment Rufus didn't move. He was caught up in the enormity of what he had just done. Could he be wrong about everything?

If so, this night would cost him.

Soon he could feel her softening, warming around him, feel her virginal tightness become wetter with her increasingly renewed arousal. Finally, she moved her hips beneath him. He heard her breath catch in a startled gasp of pleasure as his powerful length filled her.

Sheathed tightly inside her, he began to move, withdrawing and thrusting again, forcing himself to go slow, to hold back, to restrain the excitement flaring through his senses. She was moist and hot and insanely inviting. Yet her instincts, too, were quickly driving him to completion.

She wrapped her legs around him and lifted herself to match his rhythm, but he felt her innocence. Calling on all his willpower, he began to coax a sexual response from her. When Rheda's thighs parted to accept more of him, Rufus clenched his teeth, fighting the scorching hunger of his body.

This was the space between heaven and hell. A scorching hunger singeing every part of her. The heavy, burning ache inside her was growing, melting the pain in her heart.

Rheda felt the heat and desire. Her entire body throbbed at the feel of Rufus's hard flesh joined with hers.

His hot breath seared her nipple just before he took it deep into his mouth. The twinges of pleasure sharpened. She tried to press closer, molding her skin to his as she felt the hot, coiling tension rise, spiraling through her body; her need was ravenous. She opened wide to him. In reward, he

sank deeper. She whimpered, pleading, needing . . . He thrust harder, faster, and Rheda suddenly erupted in a blinding flash of stars.

Rufus captured her wild cries with his mouth. When she shattered, rigid and lost in her release, he followed, shuddering and spilling his seed deep within her in a burst of explosive need, his hoarse groans mingling with her cries as he convulsed against her.

For a long while afterward he lay there, breathing harshly, shock waves still pulsing, his face buried in the riot of curls surrounding her face.

She moved slightly beneath him, and he rolled onto his back, his skin layered with a sheen of sweat from their wild lovemaking.

He cursed his own weakness. Guilt ate at his soul. Not only had he taken her virginity, he'd knowingly done so when Rheda knew she was all but a prisoner.

She'd stripped him of his honor as easily as a whore raised her skirts. She proved exactly what sort of man he really was.

He stood and picked up his trousers. Unable to look at her he said, "You will get dressed and join me in the library. We have much to discuss."

She sat up, a look of startled surprise on her beautiful face. She gathered the sheet tightly against her breast to cover her nakedness.

"Do not keep me waiting long or I'll send my men to get you, whether you are properly dressed or not."

Then he was gone.

Rheda pictured him fierce and angry, striding down the hall with each heavy footstep thumping the boards. He probably hated her with a vengeance right at this very minute.

She ran a hand through her tangled hair. She must look like a wanton. She cringed. What had she done? This was her fault. She could have stopped him. If she'd struggled

harder he would have stopped. He would never have taken her against her will. Deep down she knew that.

She was the one who'd behaved appallingly. She'd behaved selfishly. She'd wanted him, so she'd had him.

In the dim firelight she searched the room for her clothes. She hesitated in her dress. What a mess. She sunk down to sit on the end of the bed, her heart heavy. She thought about all that had happened over the past few weeks. All of it she had caused. It hadn't started the day she'd disobeyed Daniel and rolled the barrel to Meg's. No, it had started long before that. It started when her father died and left her with a mess to clean up.

A tear seeped out of the corner of her eye. She'd selfishly decided to make her own way in this world. Turning down Christopher's honorable offer of marriage and setting up a smuggling ring—what had she been thinking?

And there was the problem. She didn't think. She was so full of pride and scorn for the world of men that she thought of no one else but herself.

Oh, she'd pretended it was Daniel's inheritance she was saving. It would have been saved if she'd married Christopher. No, it wasn't Daniel she was thinking of. She did it for herself, and no one else.

Shame and disgust racked her body, and she let out a sob, quickly stifling it with the back of her hand. She was responsible for Daniel being chased and shot by the Revenue men. All because she wanted—she wanted—she wanted . . . The words kept echoing in her head.

She stood and rinsed herself in the cooled bathwater before slipping her dress over her head. She could only reach some of the hooks at the back, and the bodice gapped open. She didn't care. She had a more pressing problem—Daniel. How could she protect him from the scandal she was about to unleash.

Once she'd donned her stockings and slippers, she tidied her hair.

She didn't even hesitate when leaving the room. Rheda made her way determinedly down the stairs. She knew what had to be done. She had to clean up the chaos she'd instigated, and damn the cost to herself. She'd do what she should have done several years ago, and she prayed it would not be too late for Daniel.

Chapter 18

Rufus refused to notice the shaking in his fingers as he poured himself a stiff brandy. He could barely swallow the liquid past his guilt.

Had he learned nothing? He'd let his rampant desire for a woman cloud his judgment for a second time. Upon entering her room and seeing her lying naked in the tub, he should have immediately turned around and escaped. He should have let Stephen retrieve her. Could have, should have, would have . . . But one step into the room was all it took for his resolve to crumble, for his driving need to possess her rise up from the ashes like the phoenix and burn every other thought out of his head.

His gut swirled in agony as the fiery liquid hit. He clenched his fist tightly around the glass. The thought of Stephen seeing Rheda's nude body, touching her body—he wanted no other man to see her, or have her. The words, *you're mine*, pounded through his brain.

She was certainly his now. He'd taken her virginity. He didn't want to focus on the implications his bedding Rheda wrought. Finding Daniel and capturing the spy had to come first. He'd deal with the aftermath later. He hadn't even withdrawn. What if he'd gotten her with child.

He took another swig of his drink.

Tonight had been an unmitigated disaster all around. He'd let Daniel slip through his fingers. He'd been knocked un-

conscious. He'd let smugglers escape, and worst of all he'd taken great pleasure in deflowering Miss Rheda Kerrich.

There would be a price to pay for each of his failures.

With a grim smile he recognized which one of his mistakes would demand the worst punishment. Rheda.

On the heels of his disparaging thoughts, the door opened and Rheda swept into the room. The fresh scent of orange blossom sent his senses reeling.

"I am here as you commanded, my lord," she said, her tone sweet and slightly mocking. Then she curtsied deeply, almost to the floor.

For a moment he could not respond, deafened by his own heartbeat. Rheda's spirited beauty made speech impossible. He gazed, riveted, upon that perfect heart-shaped face, sleekly framed by her long golden tresses spilling over her shoulders like a silken waterfall.

The golden flecks in her tawny green eyes sparkled with anger. Her tall, slender, and luscious body was once more fully clothed, but now that he'd seen the delights that lay underneath, Rufus's memories became feral.

It took a supreme effort of will to pretend a casualness he did not feel. His pride and the raging hunger to take her again made his voice sound harsher than he'd intended. "Do you know what the *Crown* does to traitors? Have you ever seen a man hanged?"

The smile left her delicate features, to be replaced with a confused frown. "Traitor? I am not sure I understand you, Rufus. What is it you think my brother has done?"

Needing to dominate the proceedings, Rufus remained standing, leaning against the mantelpiece, one hand in the pocket of his jacket. A bitter smile twisted his mouth. "Your brother is the infamous leader of the Deal smugglers. They call him Dark Shadow, do they not?"

Rufus watched his beautiful prey, and he caught the flicker of fear passing over her delicate features.

A discreet cough came from a chair behind them. Rufus had purposely asked Stephen to join them. He couldn't trust himself in Rheda's presence. The urge to protect her rather than interrogate her overwhelmed him.

Stephen stood to reveal his presence. "Miss Kerrich, I would advise cooperating with Rufus. Your brother is in serious trouble." Stephen's words made Rheda's bottom lip tremble, and she tilted her head in acknowledgment.

Stephen remained standing, as did Rufus. "I repeat. Your brother is the infamous leader of the Deal smugglers. I am not asking you, I'm telling you. I shot him tonight, at Jacob's Point."

Rheda rolled her hands in her lap. "I swear to you on my mother's grave, Daniel is not Dark Shadow."

Rufus moved to her chair, bending down until his hands rested on the arms, trapping Rheda in her seat. He looked directly into her eyes. "This is gone way past a game, Rheda. Men could get hurt—killed. Daniel could have been killed tonight."

She gasped.

Rufus cursed and moved to the sideboard containing the much needed brandy.

Stephen spoke up. "If he is not Dark Shadow, then he certainly knows who he is."

Rufus caught the glint of truth flash in her vibrant eyes. Rheda hung her head. Time ticked past, the silence almost deafening in the room. Finally, she roused herself. "You want me to betray—a confidence. I at least deserve to know why? Why is Dark Shadow so important to you?"

It was Stephen who answered her. "Not important to us, to the Crown."

Rheda frowned. "The Crown?"

"The Crown believes Dark Shadow is aiding a French spy. The spy is using his smuggling ring to send England's secrets to Napoleon."

Rheda jumped to her feet in horror and cried, "No." She vehemently shook her head. "That cannot be true." Her face drained of color, and she began to sway on her feet.

"Rufus, brandy," Stephen called as he caught Rheda before she hit the floor and laid her on the settee. Rufus pushed his friend aside and brought the glass to Rheda's lips. Rufus made her drink until the color began to creep back into her cheeks.

She pushed Rufus's hands away and made to sit up. "I'm fine. Stop fussing." Rufus remained on his knees beside her. "I'm fine, Rufus. Really." He held her gaze for what seemed like eternity before, with a curse, he stood and moved to the fireplace.

She swung her legs over the side of the settee and took in the grim faces of the men before her. She'd been such a fool. All this time they had been trying to aid England, and she'd thought only of the shame her illegal activities would bring down upon her brother. What about all the soldiers whose lives were in jeopardy because of her selfishness and arrogance?

Before fear made a coward out of her, she quietly said, "Daniel is not Dark Shadow. I am. Daniel helps occasionally, but the smuggling ring was my invention and I control it. Daniel would rather fall on his own sword than commit treason." She paused. "As would I."

Stephen let his breath out on a whoosh. "Heavens. I didn't see that coming."

Under his breath Rufus said, "I should have known."

Rheda held her palms up. "When my father died, I was seventeen and penniless. I was so alone. Daniel was only eleven and did not understand the consequences of our impending bankruptcy."

"Why did you not accept Lord Hale's offer of marriage? A far more sensible thing to do." Stephen's words were filled

with censure. She could not bring herself to look at Rufus, afraid of seeing the same disapproval on his face.

"I thought about it. Seriously. I thought about it so much my head almost burst. But have you ever felt trapped?" She wrung her hands, not waiting for confirmation. "One night I couldn't sleep so I went for a walk along the cliff tops. That's when I spied them—smugglers." She hesitated, then defiantly added in a rush, "If they could do it, why couldn't I?"

"Christ." Rufus rubbed his hand across his face. "Who helped you? One of them must be the spy."

Rheda shrugged her shoulders. "I doubt it. The ring is mostly run by the women in the village. I admit Jamieson and Meg's brother Davidson helped me in the beginning. They set up the contacts. But it is the women who decide what contraband we buy and what gets sold back to the French. We were very clear, no coin was to exchange hands—because we didn't have any to start with. We had to trade."

The men looked even grimmer, if that was at all possible. Rufus would barely look at her. Her stomach churned. She wanted to beg him to understand, but with Stephen in the room she kept up the polite charade as if Rufus and she, only an hour earlier, hadn't shared the most intimate act two humans can share. With a sickening lurch the truth hit her. Perhaps what they shared meant nothing to him. Why would it? He'd bedded countless women. Seduced to get what he wanted. She breathed in, trying to suck her pride back up off the floor.

Rufus slammed a quill and paper in front of her. "I want the names of everyone who 'trades' through your outfit."

She eyed him suspiciously. "You won't arrest them or hurt them? The women have children, families. Who would look after them? I know it is not one of my gang."

Rufus's face became a mask of anger. "You think a woman cannot betray?" He lifted his shirt; her pulse hammered not

out of fear, his polished skin beckoned for her to touch. "I know exactly what women are capable of. I told you a woman did this to me. On a previous mission, a lover betrayed me, killed my friend, and damn well near killed me." His voice shook fury. "In my profession trust is a commodity that can see you dead. A sweet smile, a luscious body, a beautiful face no longer works on me. I'll not be fooled again. I trust no one—it's safer that way."

She saw the truth of it in his eyes, and her heart cracked. She could never be more than a bedmate to this man. He would never trust her. Not now.

She swallowed, understanding a man with his past would not listen to reason. The women of Deal would never be traitors. They simply wished to survive and feed and clothe their children. "You haven't answered my question. Will they be harmed?"

"Not if they are innocent of treason."

Somewhat pacified Rheda added, "I'm not sure what my list will tell you. They are all locals who have lived their whole lives in Deal. There is not a Frenchman among them."

Stephen said coldly, "One of the locals is our spy. It can be no one else."

Stephen gave her a suspicious look. "If Rheda is Dark Shadow and yet she really knows nothing about the spy, we have a bigger problem. How is he slipping the messages through the smuggling ring?"

Both men turned steely gazes her way. They doubted her innocence. She flushed with a mixture of fear and anger. "I am not a spy. All I wanted to do was get enough money to save Tumsbury Cliff and build my own horse stud."

Rufus studied her face. She could see him weighing up her guilt or innocence. She had no idea how she could persuade him of her blamelessness. When he was in this mood, a cold, calculating aristocrat, she knew better than to appeal to his emotions. He had them too under control.

"I want a list of everybody involved in your operation—buyers and sellers," growled Rufus, turning away from her.

It took her almost half an hour to write. The list was fairly extensive. It included most of the wealthy families of Deal and the surrounding area, as well as those among the lower ranks. During this time Stephen and Rufus talked quietly over by the window. "I've finished."

Stephen crossed the room and took the paper from her hand.

Rufus chastised her. "Your silly games have cost us precious time. I pray we catch the spy before the latest intelligence is in Napoleon's hands."

Rheda felt her back stiffen. "If you'd tried talking to me like a human being instead of trying to lord it over me or seduce me at every turn, this could have been sorted out much sooner."

"She's got you there, old boy."

"I don't trust anyone." Rufus's face flamed with color, and he steadily approached until he was towering over her. "Stephen, I need a private word with Miss Kerrich." His tone indicated his friend had better not refuse.

At Rheda's panicked face Stephen chortled. "I shall not go far. Scream if you need me."

"I won't need any help, thank you," she softly replied.

Stephen's mouth twitched. "I was speaking to Rufus." His mouth broke into a huge grin as he closed the door behind him.

With shaky breath Rufus withdrew to the hearth. "You have some explaining to do."

"How so? I have told you all I know."

Was she telling the truth? He clenched his teeth, disgruntled and frustrated at the predicament he was in. And he was furious with himself. He'd vowed he would keep away from the baron's sister until he knew categorically she was not an innocent. He'd let his cock override his innate good sense.

"You let me ravish you without telling me the truth. Why? Now that your smuggling operation has been discovered, it will come to an end. Did you hope my honor would elicit an offer of marriage in order to replace the business you have lost? Did you hope to gain a silk purse?"

Rheda stared speechlessly at him. "I have never wished to marry," she replied coldly.

"You kept your virginity a guarded secret. Letting me think the scandal with Prince Hammed was true."

"I believe I indicated when we first became acquainted that there was no scandal."

"You never denied the allegation," he stated flatly. "You knew I was trying to seduce you. Why didn't you tell me the truth? Your behavior during the night was not exactly what one would call circumspect. In fact, I'd say you deliberately led me to believe you were other than an innocent miss." He turned away, unwilling to face the unsettling knife cut of hurt her using him had slashed deep into his chest.

It wasn't simply his pride that was battered. His heart felt like it had been attacked with a club. She'd played him. She'd let him think she was a fallen woman. His honor was her backup plan. Now she had him trapped by his need to avoid bringing further shame on the Strathmore name. He could not father an illegitimate child.

He moved toward her, his shadow slipping over her. She looked more delicate than he remembered, and her bottom lip trembled. "I want the truth. Why the devil did you let me compromise you?"

What could she say—*because the mere sight of you sets my insides on fire? That I burn for your touch until I ache? That even now all I can picture in my head is your powerful physique, all rippling muscles and chiseled strength? That the thought of your sensuous mouth on me makes me wet between my thighs . . . ?*

Rheda kept her lips tightly closed least they spill her most intimate secrets.

"Tell me," he demanded. He swung around to face her. "Tonight, did you or did you not purposely set the tub scene to distract me? Did you use your body to entice me into bedding you, knowing I'd ruin you?"

She could not hold his icy gaze. In a way she had used him. "Not exactly."

"Then, what exactly?"

Her cheeks flooded with crimson. She took a deep breath. "Yes, I wanted to distract your search, but I had not planned to be compromised. I thought your honor would prevent things going so far . . ."

Rufus's jaw tightened till the muscles stood out in rigid relief. "What did you expect me to do when you rose from the tub like a water nymph? I may be a gentleman, but I am not a saint." He walked and poured himself another drink.

Rheda shivered. The brandy seemed to have done little to improve his mood. "I did not anticipate you making me get out of the bath."

"Well, your plan backfired. Unlike Prince Hammed, who obviously gave you the horses before you had to sacrifice your virginity, I was stupid enough to succumb to your abundant charms." His mouth thinned. "We will discuss the situation we find ourselves in once I have completed my mission." Rufus took a deep breath. "It would seem I have no course open to me but to offer you marriage—"

"Marriage!" Rheda jumped to her feet and cried. "Don't be ridiculous. There is absolutely no need for that—"

His mouth twisted bitterly. "What if you are with child?"

Rheda felt trickles of perspiration run down between her shoulder blades. "Then I will raise him or her on my own like many women are left to do."

He moved quickly and gripped both her arms in a vice-like grip. "I will not have a child of mine born a bastard. There has been enough scandal in my family. I will not tolerate more."

Rheda stared down at his hands until he released her, but

he did not step back. She felt his virility humming around him, and despite herself couldn't help the flare of response simmering in her belly.

"I suggest we wait and see if I am with child before we rush into matrimony. You certainly do not wish to marry a woman like me, and I have no wish to tie myself to a man who will forever despise me."

Rufus stepped even closer. His chest brushed against her breasts, and she clenched her fists at the immediate response of her nipples puckering under her dress.

"I assure you, marriage to a woman of your ilk was not my plan. I have been striving to restore the Strathmore good name for over ten years, and I am not about to undo all that work for your convenience," he softly uttered, a hint of bitterness edging his tone. "You will become my wife, and you will deport yourself as a married lady of nobility should. Do I make myself clear?"

"What, pray, does that mean exactly? What of my horse stud?"

Rufus threw his head back and laughed. "I did not realize that respectable ladies bred horses. They leave that to their husbands." His smile vanished as quickly as a rabbit down a rabbit hole. "There will be no horse stud, no smuggling, nor any other illicit activities of any kind. You will at all times honor the Strathmore name. Your home will be my country estate near Cambridge, where you will reside with my mother. You will be my viscountess, and I demand you behave like one."

He never raised his voice, yet his words seemed more unequivocal than if he'd shouted at her. His tone was dark, while something hard and unforgiving in his eyes seeped like ice into her soul. He sounded like he hated her. Really hated her.

She swallowed back threatening tears. She would not let him know how much his words hurt her. Knowing how he felt about her, she could never marry him. But he was right.

Her behavior was scandalous and once known would tarnish his reputation. She did not care about her own. However, Daniel would also suffer. She couldn't allow that to happen.

"I believe you have made it very clear what your orders are, my lord. If you don't mind, I think I shall retire. It has been a very long night."

"I have placed guards outside your room—"

"To keep you out or me in?"

He ignored her inflaming comment. "Later today, you will summon Daniel for questioning. Only then will we formally announce our engagement." He drained his glass, then turned away to refill it.

He dismissed her as if she were a servant. It was the humiliation, as much as the coldness in his eyes, that cut her to the quick. Yet she blinked back the sudden tears that blurred her vision and lifted her chin, vowing that she would do what she should have done eight years ago.

She needed to slip free of her captors and find Lord Hale.

Chapter 19

Rheda sat quietly in her room waiting for the right moment to escape. It came shortly after the guards at her door removed her breakfast tray.

"If you don't mind I shall take a nap. I have been up all night. Please tell his lordship not to disturb me until I have had a few hours sleep." She hesitated. "Not unless he wants a swooning female on his hands."

All the guard did was nod and close the door firmly in her face.

Rheda quickly drew the drapes and arranged the pillows as if someone were sleeping in the bed. The room was dim enough that anyone looking in to check on her would believe she was abed. She glanced at the clock on the mantel. She would have probably no more than three hours at the most to get to Hastingleigh and back.

A sharp pain sliced through her stomach. If her plan worked she wouldn't have to come back. She wouldn't have to see Rufus again. That's where the pain came from. She couldn't fool herself. Even now she wanted very much to see him. To beg his forgiveness and to explain that she had not used him.

The appeal of allowing herself to grab his offer of matrimony drove her. It would be all too easy to agree. To picture herself living as his wife, sleeping in his bed, bearing his children. Yet, it would be her mother's situation all over

again. A woman in love with her husband. A husband who had not an ounce of love for his wife. Rufus's likely infidelities would destroy her.

She knew she would never survive in a one-sided relationship. She could not allow herself to be forced into one now.

The pain of their shared pleasure ripped through her chest until it felt hollow. She recalled every imprint of the lean, hard length of him. She wanted to be naked and wrapped in his arms again. But once she'd spoken to Christopher that could never happen. She did not know how she would get the taste and feel of Rufus out of her mind. It would be unfair to bring him to her marriage bed. Christopher deserved better.

With a sigh she crossed the room and found the hidden latch to the secret panel. Almost every room in the house had secret doors down to the tunnels and caverns beneath Tumsbury Cliff Manor. Remnants from when her great-grandfather had been a smuggler. One of the other reasons she'd seen no harm in indulging in free trade. If it was good enough for her ancestors, it was good enough for her.

Instead of following the tunnels to the caves down by the cliffs, she turned right and headed to the entrance that emerged about half a mile behind the stable block, pointing directly inland to Hastingleigh.

The day was humid with fluffy clouds filling the sky, the miscellany of the storm that had blown through last night. She was pleased she'd slipped on her cotton dress. She could feel the warm breeze on her back where her dress still remained unhooked. She smoothed her skirt and hoped she looked more acceptable than she felt.

She kept to the tree line, just in case any of Rufus's men spotted her. They were still out hunting Daniel. Would he disown her when he heard of her disgraceful conduct? She wanted to explain, to beg his forgiveness.

She pushed the coming scene with Daniel out of her mind

and focused on her proposition. Would Christopher still want her? She could marry Christopher because it didn't matter that he didn't love her. She didn't love him. It was the thought of marrying a man she loved, but who would never return her love, that frightened more. Love gave a person the power to hurt.

She hoped her appearance wouldn't put him off. Telling Christopher she was no longer innocent already had her stomach churning. But she would swear to him that she would be faithful and never look at another man. Or at least one man in particular—Rufus—ever again.

That would be her worst punishment for her selfishness. She would never again know the joy of Rufus's touch, his kisses, or the feel of his muscled strength against her bare skin. She would never see his eyes darken with desire when he looked at her, and she would never feel her body warm and soften when he delivered one of his sensual smiles that melted her from the inside.

Tears blurred her vision and she stumbled over a tree root, falling to her knees. A cry of anguish escaped before she could stop it. She didn't know what hurt more, her grazed knee or her heart.

"I say, Rheda. Are you all right?"

Christopher. The concern on his dear face made her sob even louder. He didn't deserve to have her foisted on him. She shouldn't have come. Her idea was even less noble than enticing Rufus into dishonor.

She sank to the ground. "Oh, Christopher. I've made such a mess of things," she sobbed.

He crouched down on his haunches and gently wiped the tears off her face. "I am sure you've done no such thing, my angel—"

"But I have," she wailed.

"What has upset you, Rhe? I was on my way to see you."

"I'm not all right. I've been so selfish. Thinking I could

do it all on my own. I should have accepted your proposal long ago, but my fear wouldn't let me."

He pulled her into his arms, and she felt the softness of his plump body. Instantly, she compared it to Rufus's hard, lean frame and found it wanting. He took off his gloves, something he rarely did due to the large red birthmark on his hand. A mark he preferred to keep hidden.

He gently stroked her cheek with his gloveless fingers. It did not even kindle one tingle of awareness that a simple touch from Rufus ignited. She pulled away in disappointment and shame.

"You know you never have to fear me. I'd never hurt you."

Rheda nodded. "I don't fear you."

He cupped her cheek. "Then why did you decline my proposals? Am I that repulsive?"

She lowered her head. "No. It's just I didn't love you." She rushed on, "I do love you, but more like the love I feel for Daniel. Like a brother. I didn't think that was fair to you."

He gave a barked laugh. "Look at me, Rheda. I know I am not a prime catch, but I would have cherished you for the rest of your days. I still will if you'll let me."

The strength seemed to drain out of her at his words. She sagged against him and thought how easy it would be to let him take care of her. She whispered, "It's too late now. I'm ruined."

Christopher didn't say a word, but she felt him stiffen at her words. "Do you still keep a journal?"

She nodded.

"I do, too. Do you know what I believe?" He did not wait for her answer. "I believe that my journal is a private confession between me and God. He sees everything I have done, and by writing the words, by letting him see my sin, he washes me clean. God is merciful and forgives everything. If you are truly repentant He forgives you. Just as I always will forgive you."

"What if I have done such wrong he—and you—can never forgive me?"

There was only a slight hesitation before he stroked her hair and said, "I suggest you tell me everything, Rhe. There are not many things a man like me cannot fix."

So, like a sinner in a confessional, Rheda told him everything. She confessed that she was Dark Shadow, about Rufus's hunt for the smuggler to catch a spy, and about her fall from grace last night in Rufus's bed because he'd thought the scandal with Prince Hammed was true. And finally about how much she loved Rufus and how she had to set him free so he could restore the Strathmore name. "Now he wants to do the honorable thing and marry me, and I can't let that happen. It will ruin him. Imagine me in London, pretending to be a lady."

Christopher had gone as still as one of the statues decorating his extensive gardens. His arms had tightened around her until she could barely breathe. So she was not sure how he'd taken her confession of sharing Rufus's bed. She couldn't bring herself to look at him.

They sat in silence for what seemed like hours but must have been only moments.

"You never did tell me why Prince Hammed gave you your Arab horses. I suppose it doesn't really matter now."

She pressed Christopher's hand against her cheek. "I shall never forget that you believed in me when everyone shunned me." She took a deep breath. "He gave me the horses as a gift for saving his sister's life. She almost drowned while swimming, but I happened along and managed to save her."

Christopher laughed and pulled her to her feet. "I never doubted you then, and I don't doubt all you have told me now. If you really don't wish to marry Lord Strathmore, although I would be remiss if I didn't point out what a catch the man is, then I would still be honored to make you my wife." And he bent and placed a chaste kiss on her knuckles.

Rheda frowned. Why would a man of Christopher's

breeding and wealth wish to marry a woman who was no longer pure, could be pregnant with another man's child, had no dowry, and confessed to love another?

She shook her head vigorously. This was wrong. Her idea was despicable. She was caught, and dishonor would be the outcome either way. Rufus's family would suffer if he married her. And Christopher would be lumbered with a wife who loved another. There had to be another way.

"I can't let you sacrifice yourself for me, either. I seem to be sadly lacking in honor today. I think the best thing would be for me to simply slip away. If I disappear, eventually the scandal will die down, and Daniel could go on to marry well and succeed in his dreams for his barony. He's is still young, and marriage can wait a few years."

"But what of me, Rhe? What will I do without you?"

She finally looked at him. His face was solemn and his pale blue eyes seemed so sad. She couldn't help cupping his cheek. "Christopher, you underestimate your charm. You are a wealthy earl and could have your pick of young debutantes. You don't want me."

He gave her a wan smile. "I know what I am, Rheda. The bumbling idiot, that's what you all call me."

Rheda felt heat flush her cheeks. She did think of him as a bit of a buffoon. "You are the gentlest and kindest and most honorable man I know—"

He became very animated and pulled her close to whisper in her ear. "Then marry me. Can you imagine me being happy with a young debutante? You know I am a man of simple pleasures. I don't like London. We may not have a burning passion for each other, but we have a strong friendship and mutual admiration." He placed a gentle kiss on her lips. "I wouldn't want you to change in any way when you become my wife. I'd take you as you are. That's the Rhe I know and love."

Her eyes welled with tears, so overcome with his heartfelt words. She stepped back out of his embrace. Perhaps he was

right. Perhaps friendship and mutual admiration would be enough. At least Christopher was not ashamed of who and what she was. He'd take the good with the bad. Unlike Rufus who expected a paragon of virtue as a wife.

Rufus—why did she have to love a man who would never love her? A man who wanted a perfection that did not exist. Could she marry and share Christopher's bed while her heart belonged to another. Her head pounded from lack of sleep, and the confusion that assaulted her body made her nauseous and weepy.

"Thank you, Christopher, for your honorable offer. I will seriously consider it, but I need to talk with Daniel first."

"I am sure Daniel would welcome the match."

"What about your mother?"

Christopher smiled, and his eyes lit up. "Mother adores you. She need not know the circumstances behind your acceptance. If I am happy, Mother will be happy. And if you marry me, I'd be the happiest man alive."

Impulsively, she reached up and kissed his lips. To her surprise he stiffened and pulled back. If she'd kissed Rufus, he'd have pulled her hard into his embrace and kissed her until she had no breath and could barely stand. They would both have been caught up in a wild passion that neither could deny.

She backed away, immediately feeling ashamed of her boldness. "My apologies. I am too impulsive sometimes."

He pulled her roughly back into his arms and kissed her. "Never apologize to me. You took me by surprise that is all." He let her go and turned her toward Tumsbury Cliffs. "Go. Find your brother. I shall go and prepare to deal with Rufus and his men. I may be a bumbling idiot, but I think I know how to handle Revenue men. We shall ensure your smuggling activities do not see the light of day."

Her mind was whirling as she made her way back to the manor. Was she doing the right thing? Christopher had seemed so earnest, but she'd always sworn she'd never marry

a man who did not love her. Was Christopher's admiration enough?

She was too tired to think. One minute she wanted to do the right thing and set Rufus free, the next she wanted to grab his offer of marriage and every other part of him, and damn the consequences. Having any small piece of him in her life would be better than never seeing him at all.

But would it? He despised her and had all but admitted he would lock her away. He would continue his life as if nothing had changed. The thought of him with other women . . . women sharing his bed, a mistress sharing his life, while she was punished and shut away, hurt so much she almost collapsed on the ground.

Think, Rheda. What is the best outcome for all concerned? For her brother? Daniel wouldn't care who she married as long as she did. However, she hoped he'd prefer Christopher as it would keep her near to him.

Rufus would probably drop to his knees and thank God if she chose Christopher. She squeezed her eyes shut, refusing to cry.

What of Christopher? He seemed very sincere.

What do you want, Rheda? popped into her befuddled brain. She was too tired and too hot to understand why the thought of giving up Rufus seemed the worst course of action when she'd sworn never to marry a man who did not love her.

With a sigh she rubbed her aching temples. What she really wanted right now was to cool down. She turned toward the cliff tops. A swim. She needed a brisk dip to clear her mind. Then she'd find Daniel.

Rufus moved toward the cliff, wanting to clear his mind and body of the scent, taste, and memory of Rheda. She needed a chance to sleep. Besides she was well guarded and would be waiting for him on his return. He'd left the manor

and headed to the coast. He did not know what he hoped to find, but surely the smugglers would have left some imprint, some clue to where the boat had landed.

He had just made it back up to the cliff tops from one of the smaller coves when his eye caught a splash of blue. He ducked behind some bushes and waited to see who was about.

"What the bloody devil . . . ?" He cursed under his breath. It was Rheda. Without any escorts. Where were his men?

A crafty smile broke over his lips. She thought she'd given everyone the slip. He would follow her and see who she met. With any luck she'd lead him directly to Daniel. He refused to admit that the tension invading his frame was fear. Fear she was meeting someone a lot worse than Daniel—a spy. A man whose relationship would see her pretty neck stretched on the gallows.

Could he live with the knowledge he'd sent her there? He almost dropped to his knees with the pain that lanced his chest. He couldn't bear the thought of Rheda being hurt. He wanted to protect her. His name could do that. He had to marry her.

Rheda did not appear to be in a hurry. He made sure to keep a distance between them so she would not see him. He trailed her to the cliff tops. Then she suddenly seemed to vanish into thin air.

His heart leaped into his throat, and a cold chill skittered down his back. Had his frigid demeanor pushed her too far? Had she thrown herself off the cliffs? He raced to the cliff's rim just in time to see her winding her way down a hidden path to what looked like a small cove below.

He'd found her secret swimming hole.

His blood heated, and his body reacted to the thought of a naked Rheda swimming in the sea. Her body glistening wet, her nipples hard from the cold sea water. His groin throbbed with the desire to see this goddess in all her natural beauty once more.

He did not even hesitate to follow her. What harm could there be? His mood brightened at the thought of being able to catch her vulnerable and naked.

He found a ledge a short way down the winding path and settled in to enjoy the view. He felt like a voyeur, yet something drove him to remain hidden. A woman had fooled him in the past, and he wanted to see if she was playing him false. His honor meant he would overlook her smuggling, but treason—never. Not with his father named as a traitor. He could not afford to have his name linked to another suspected spy. He'd never prayed so hard. Not treason. Please, not treason.

He sat with his back against the cliff, his long legs out in front, one foot crossed over the other, feeling the tension tightening his shoulders. There was no way she was going to escape him. This path was the only access from the cove. When he'd looked his fill, he would join her on the sand and . . . He drew a deep breath and tried to calm his roaring libido.

Every nerve ending hummed as he soaked in the wild natural beauty before him. The sand was pristine, the color of dried hay in midsummer, a polished gold. The sea as smooth as glass, the color reflecting the light blue of the sky, with sparkling, sun-induced diamonds dancing across the sleek surface.

But what truly drew his gaze with ardent fascination was the fair-haired nymph standing like a pagan goddess at the water's edge.

Ripples of tiny waves were lapping at the bare feet poking from beneath her light muslin gown, while her slippers dangled from the fingers of her tiny hand. Rheda's opulent tresses fell in ringlets down her back, her head lifted as if in worship to the sun.

She looked so—young. So innocent in her freedom. He could almost believe she was not party to treachery. That she was not the renowned smuggler aiding England's enemies.

If he lived to be a hundred, Rufus knew he would never fully come to know this woman. It left him wary. Her energy, drive, and audacity knew no boundaries. She'd managed to set up one of the most successful smuggling operations in Southern England, aiding not only her but the women of the village, while avoiding selling herself in marriage. She'd remained her own person, bound to no one and proud of it. She didn't care that she'd given up her position in Society. She could have taken London by storm, making an excellent match for herself and aiding Daniel, but freedom meant more to her.

He understood that desire more than anyone. The freedom to be oneself. How could he fault her for achieving the one thing he'd dreamed of most of his adult life?

For one short moment jealousy ate at his soul. He envied her the simplicity of her life. He couldn't afford such luxury. He had a mother and a sister to protect. If not for them he would have been free to pursue his desires, even pursue a woman like Rheda . . .

He almost let out a startled gasp. Like Rheda—he'd never once in his life thought of a woman as being perfect for him. Something had changed. Women had simply been vessels for enjoyment, satiation, and pleasure. He always knew eventually he'd marry in order to produce an heir. He'd marry for duty and to protect his family name. Never once had he let himself have false hope that a marriage would be more. Hope of finding that one special woman—a woman who made his soul sing and his heart soar.

He thought back three months ago to Anthony and Melissa's wedding day. The couple appeared radiant as they stood at the altar, engrossed in each other. As Rufus watched the service, he'd never seen a man so content and a woman so loved.

Rufus hadn't understood the feeling churning in his gut as they'd said their vows. He hadn't realized that it was envy streaking through every fiber of his being, followed by in-

tense regret that he'd never find such bliss with Clare. He'd marry for his family, and the unfairness of that had almost been more than he could bear.

Rheda bent to run her fingers through the waves. A fierce need ripped through him as he watched her. *She was his.* He'd been her first lover, and a possessive hunger to be her last sank deep into his heart, branding him deep in his soul.

He admired her inner strength. To save a bankrupt estate, singlehandedly, from the age of seventeen was a feat most men could not achieve.

A warm pride flowed through his bloodstream at the thought he'd been the first man to unleash her passions. Yet the scene she'd set for him in the bathing tub was worthy of an experienced courtesan. His fists clenched thinking of how he'd lost control and with no thought to the consequences to his family, he'd taken what his body craved.

Five years ago Marguerite had bedazzled him, too. His own vanity coupled with her beauty and apparent desire fooled him into believing she loved him. Yet all the while Marguerite was working for the French. He'd been such an easy target, so desperate to learn anything of his father. So eager to have someone love him despite knowing of his father's sin.

Rufus closed his eyes on the haunting memories. His gullibility had cost the life of his friend and partner. He vividly recalled Andrew lying dead at his feet, while all he'd been able to do was sink to his knees, gripping the dagger stuck in his own side. Marguerite's final insult had been to blow him a kiss as she galloped off.

Three years' work destroyed because he could not see past a sweet face, soft words, and pretty lies.

The hackles on his nape flexed. Never again would he let a woman trifle with him.

Use him. Humiliate him. Betray him.

Never.

He would not become bedazzled by Rheda. Damn the

minx. He did not want to have this burning heat and desperate need inside of him.

He stood and took a steadying breath. He stepped down onto the sand. He would not lose. Not again.

As he made his way across the sand he heard a sound that froze him in his tracks. Her shoulders were hunched and her body shook. Rheda was quietly sobbing.

He stood motionless . . . a woman's tears.

Rheda sank to her knees and began sobbing in earnest. Loud wrenching sobs that caused his chest to contract.

"Don't cry." He spoke before he could stop himself.

She looked up through wet eyelashes and tried to stifle a sob.

He knelt down next to her and wiped the tears from her cheeks. "Everything will be all right. I give you my word. Daniel will come to no harm if he is as innocent as you say."

Chapter 20

She closed her eyes wearily. "Everything is such a mess. I only needed until the end of summer and I could have finished with Dark Shadow for good. No one would have been the wiser. Now . . ."

"There is no need for anyone to know about Dark Shadow. All I want is the spy."

She swallowed hard. "What if you don't find the spy?"

"I'll find him." His voice held a savage edge. "I'll not stop looking until I do."

"You'll need Dark Shadow's help until he's caught. Won't you?"

He sat on the sand beside her, his arms resting on his bent knees. He was silent, staring out over the water for what seemed like ages. Would he answer her?

"I never wanted to work for the government."

"Then why do you?"

"As you are learning, life is full of consequences."

"What did you wish to do with your life?"

He gave a wry smile. "We have something in common. Remember? I told you. I wanted to breed the finest race-horses in all of England."

She ran her fingers through the sand. "I'd loved to have done that, too, but they won't let women enter horses in the General Stud Book at Weatherby's. So breeding cavalry horses was my only choice. What stopped you?"

He ran his hand through his hair. "My father's death."

She stared long and hard at Rufus. "Finding this traitor is personal to you, isn't it?"

A muscle in his jaw clenched. "The spy could be my salvation."

"I don't understand. How?"

"I'm hoping the spy can reveal the truth about something that occurred many years ago, or at least tell me who would know."

She sat up and declared in wonder, "You want to prove your father innocent."

His head lowered and he sighed. "Yes. But it's also about me. I need to atone for my failure. I should have been with him on the day he died."

She put her hand on his arm. "The late Lord Hale, and indeed Lady Hale, always spoke so highly of your father. They did not believe he was guilty of aiding the French. Is that not enough?"

He ground his teeth, as if striving for control. "I just need to know the truth. Was the father I worshipped a traitor? Was my upbringing a complete lie? It's the not knowing that kills me."

She saw the despair in his eyes. She laid her hand over his heart. "You know the answer to that. Deep inside, you know."

His gaze flew to hers. He sucked in an audible breath. "God, you're right." He thumped the sand. "I know he was innocent, and I owe it to him to expose the perpetrators of such a lie."

"I can't imagine spending so many years of my life chasing a truth I already know to be true. It seems such a waste—"

He started to rise, but Rheda grasped his arm, detaining him. "Would your father have wanted you to fritter away your life on this pointless quest? Revealing the truth won't change anything. Whatever you uncover, your father will still be dead."

"But my family will be free," he growled. "Not everyone

is content to live in the backwater of Kent. My mother's life was taken from her. She was shunned by many whom she called friends, and she lives her life too ashamed to show her face in Society, the only world she had ever known. Now Madeline, my younger sister, is due for her come-out. What sort of husband will she find with a traitorous father? It is not always about oneself, Rheda. I have responsibilities. Others to take care of."

Rheda hung her head in shame. "I'm sorry. You've uncovered my worst sin—selfishness." A surge of anger shot through her. Anger at herself. She picked up a stick and threw it in the sea. "It's entirely my fault. All of this," she said softly. She looked at him and pleaded, "I'm sorry."

"Why didn't you simply tell me the truth, Rhe?" He looked at her, his eyes reflecting openness instead of his normal distrust.

She knew he meant about the barrel. "At first it was because I couldn't take the risk. You might have arrested me, and the further shame would taint Daniel. Then it was because your arrogance annoyed me—"

"You mean if I'd asked you nicely you'd have told me?"

She smiled. "Maybe." She gave a small chuckle. "No, that's a lie. I didn't want to tell you because"—she took a deep breath—"I knew you'd despise me once you knew I was Dark Shadow."

His eyebrow rose, and he cupped her chin in his hands so that she had no choice but to look at him. His eyes probed the secrets hidden within her. Finally he asked, "Why was that important to you?"

She tried to pull away. She didn't want to face the answer to his question. His very nearness sent a shiver through her.

"Tell me," he insisted.

"I—that is—I was attracted to you. I'm sure most women are," she added hurriedly.

"Attracted?" He gave one of his bone-melting smiles. "Is that all it was—attraction? You promised no more lies."

She pushed at the hand holding her chin. "All right, damn you. I have feelings for you, even though I tried desperately not to."

He believed her. Her face flushed with color, and she squirmed in embarrassment. She wasn't telling him this to mollify him. She already knew he'd protect her, he'd offered her his hand in marriage. She would be safe.

"Then why did I find you crying?" Women. He'd never understand them.

"Because I can't marry you," she said on a heavy sigh. "For all the reasons you mentioned. The scandal surrounding me, the sacrifices you have made for your . . ." She rose to her feet, and he followed. He stood behind her as she looked out over the sea. Finally, she turned to face him. "I think I have a way out for you."

He was intrigued. "A way out? Perhaps I don't want a way out."

Her pretty eyes filled with unshed tears. "I am trying to be noble. To do the right thing. To be selfless."

"Which is?"

"Christopher has offered for me. He has always wanted me. I could—"

He grasped her arms in a biting grip. Fury like nothing he'd ever known swept through him. *She was his.* "No. You will not marry another." She gasped, her face a mask of shock. "You're mine." And with those words he pulled her hard against him and took her lips in a kiss he hoped would drive the thought of any other man from her mind.

Rheda stiffened until suddenly she softened against him and they were kissing with frantic intensity, as if the truthful conversation just witnessed wiped the past week's battle of wills clean.

His hands slid up her back to twist in her hair, while her arms wrapped around his neck in a tight embrace. She clung

to him. Their tongues mated in a fever of need, and she was making hoarse sounds of pleasure.

In a blinding flash, he realized this woman was perfect for him. He would never be satisfied with pious and dull. He wanted a woman with wild, uncontrollable passions.

Her confession about her feelings for him made him hope for more. If it was possible, they would have a marriage with mutual affection, if not love . . .

As the kiss grew more feverish, Rufus's restraint shredded. While keeping his lips locked to her, he shrugged out of his coat. Picking her up in his arms, he made to lay her on the garment, when something near the rocks on the left of the cove caught his eye. Someone was struggling in the water. He heard a small cry, and he set Rheda on her feet, ripped off his boots, and dove under the waves.

In a few long strokes he reached a boy struggling in the water. It was Connor. "Okay. I've got you. Don't panic. Put your arms around my neck. Not too tight or I won't be able to breathe."

The lad did as he was told. Rufus could tell he was near complete panic. The boy was shivering so hard, Rufus could hear his teeth chattering.

As Rufus waded in to shore the boy cried out, "Rhe," and promptly burst into tears. Rheda held out her arms, and Rufus gently lowered the boy into them.

"Connor. Hush now, you're safe." But the boy just kept sobbing, drenching her dress with tears.

Rheda whispered, "I've no idea what he's doing trying to swim around the point. The rips can be very dangerous. He knows better."

Rufus looked at the young boy shaking and crying in Rheda's arms. "Something has frightened him. A near drowning maybe, but there was no rip and he was still swimming strongly when I reached him."

★   ★   ★

Rheda couldn't take her eyes off Rufus as she held the sobbing boy in her arms. Her body flamed, very conscious that Rufus's torso was still bare. She watched entranced as a trickle of water ran down the side of his neck, disappearing into the black hairs on his chest. She reached out and caught the next one with her fingertip. His chest muscles flexed under her touch.

She jerked her hand away. Rufus remained crouched next to her. His eyes held hers, and she nearly forgot that she held Connor.

She sat gently rocking him, and gradually his shaking subsided and his cries subsided into sniffles. "What happened, Connor? Why were you swimming around the point? You know it's dangerous."

Connor pressed his cheek into her chest. "I had to get away from the man."

Rufus started at his words, and she noted his hands formed into fists so tight his knuckles turned white. "Did the man hurt you, Connor?" he asked gently.

The boy shook his head and clung to Rheda even harder.

Rufus cursed under his breath.

"What man? Why would a man want to take you, Connor?" Connor did not answer her; he merely turned his face away and buried it in her dress.

"There have been several young boys who have gone missing or turned up dead over the last twelve months," Rufus said. "My good friend, Lord Alexander Montford, asked me to investigate while I am in Deal."

Something in his grim tone alerted her to the fact that she would not like the answer to her next question. "Why would a man want to take young boys . . . ?" Her words petered out when Rufus raised his eyebrow and shook his head. She gasped. Her father's lifestyle meant she'd been privy to an education in the seedier aspects of life. She hugged Connor tighter. "How many boys have gone missing?" she asked, sick to her stomach.

"Six—that we know of. The last one only a week ago." Rufus gently pried the boy's head out from between her breasts. "Connor, we want to stop this man. Can you tell me who he is?"

Connor shook his head, his eyes wide with fear. "He wore a black leather mask, but he had a French accent."

Rheda and Rufus exchanged glances, horror and hope lighting their eyes. The spy.

Rufus's voice held a more urgent note. "Where did he take you, Connor?"

Connor hiccupped. "He grabbed me at Jacob's Point and dragged me back toward Dead Man's Cove. I bit his hand and managed to break free. Then I ran into Harding's Wood. I lost him for a while, but when I emerged he found me again. So I dived into the sea and swam. I knew about this cove because I helped you and Mother ferry the goods ashore. All I had to do was make it to the caves, and I could make my way into the manor through the tunnels."

"Ah!" Rufus said. Rheda flushed with color. He knew her secret. He shook his head before standing and pulling on his shirt.

"Can you get the boy up to the house and alert Stephen and the men? I'd use the tunnels just to be safe. I'm going to try and track him. It's the best lead we've had so far. Tell Stephen to send some of the men to Harding's Wood and the rest to follow the cliffs south of Jacob's Point."

Rheda bit her lip. "Why don't we all go up to the house and you can take the men with you?"

"There's not enough time. Connor's abductor probably won't search for him for too long, not wearing a mask. I have to go now." He bent down and sweetly kissed her lips. "Tell Stephen to hurry."

Then he raced up the hidden path to the cliff tops. Rheda and Connor watched until he was gone. "Can you walk, Connor?"

The boy rose to his feet but clung to her hand. Together

they made their way across the warm sand to the boulders hiding the entrance to the cavern system that ran under Tumsbury Cliff Manor.

Rheda tried to hurry, but Connor's strength was waning. Then out of the shadows Daniel appeared. "Daniel! I'm so pleased to see you. Pick up Connor; we have to hurry."

"What's happened?"

"There is no time. I'll have to explain when we get to the house."

Rheda paced the drawing room. Connor lay wrapped in blankets on the settee, being warmed by the fire. Penny had let him have a thimble of brandy in a warm cup of tea and fed him scones. He seemed to be recovering well from his ordeal. Jamieson had gone to fetch Connor's mother and siblings.

Rheda had wasted no time informing Stephen and Daniel what had occurred and where Rufus had gone. Stephen and his men left immediately to start the hunt. They had taken Daniel with them. Stephen had not wanted to let him out of his sight.

"Stop pacing. You'll wear the rugs out," Penny scolded.

She crossed to kneel at Connor's side. "I just wish I could do more. Connor, can you remember anything else? Anything at all about the man that took you? Just close your eyes and try to recall . . ." She reached out and brushed his hair out of his eyes.

He grabbed her arm, his eyes opening wide. "His hand. When I bit him, I bit him really hard. He took his glove off to wipe the blood, and I saw it. He had a horrible growth on his hand—"

"Do you mean a birthmark?" Rheda asked, waves of fear beginning to crash over her until she could barely swallow.

"I don't know. It was red and covered almost all of the back of his hand."

Rheda gasped and sank back onto the floor. Her hand hovered over her mouth. She felt like she was going to be sick. Under her breath she uttered, "Oh, God. What have I done?" Icy chills were not kept at bay by the log fire directly behind her. "I don't believe it. It can't be . . ."

Penny stopped buttering a scone and with her knife in hand asked, "What's wrong?"

She raised anguished eyes to Penny. "I know who took Connor." Hurriedly she got to her feet. "He's in trouble. I've told him everything. I have to warn him—"

"Warn who?" Penny grabbed her by the arms. "Stop for a moment. You're not making sense."

Ignoring Penny, Rheda said to Connor, urgency underpinning her words, "In what direction was the man taking you? It's very important. Think hard. Lives are at risk . . ."

"Stop it, Rheda. You're frightening the boy."

"Think, Connor. Please . . ."

He sat up and looked out the window toward the northern coastline. "We were heading toward Kingsgate Bay. I'm sure of it because I remember thinking that if I couldn't escape before we left Harding's Wood, I'd try and lose him in the caves just before Kingsgate."

Rheda took his head in her hands and planted a big kiss on his head. "Thank you." She turned and raced for the door.

"Where do you think you're going?" Penny asked, hands on hips.

"I haven't got time to explain. When Jamieson returns with Meg, tell him to get word to Stephen and his men. Lord Hale took Connor. I think he's at the old ruins at the entrance to Kingsgate Bay." And before Penny could stop her, Rheda raced for the stables. It took her longer to saddle White Lily than it should have because she fumbled in her haste. She took a deep breath to try to calm her nerves.

Rufus was in terrible danger. Christopher would be ex-

pecting him. She'd told Rufus's enemy everything. She needed to find one of Stephen's men before it was too late.

If Christopher captured Rufus . . . She couldn't bear to think about it. This was all her fault. With her heart pounding louder than White Lily's hooves thumping on the ground, Rheda prayed she'd get to Rufus in time.

Chapter 21

Pain. . . .
    Pain everywhere.

Now Rufus knew what it felt like to be stretched on the rack, waiting to be drawn and quartered. Every muscle in his body was on fire. The chains pulled taut; his joints screamed, wanting to pop from their sockets.

He tried to raise his head, but each tiny movement caused nausea to erupt deep in his gut and he fought the urge to vomit.

Rufus closed his eyes and stayed his head, trying to focus through the pain. His pride was in tatters at having let the enemy sneak up on him unawares and render him unconscious with one simple blow. He knew he'd been taken, but to where, and by whom?

He forced his eyelids to lift and waited for the haze to clear. He kept his body still, hiding his return to consciousness from anyone who might happen to be in the room. Like a fox testing the poacher's trap, he evaluated his position.

He was chained in the middle of what looked like a dungeon. A well-fitted-out, comfortable dungeon. The slate stones beneath his feet were covered in Persian rugs. The wall to his right displayed an opulent wall hanging of Christ's last supper; he hoped that wasn't an omen. To his left stood a day couch covered with opulent fur throws.

A fire crackled behind him. He knew because the flames

flickered shadows across the wall in front of him, and he could feel its heat on his back.

He looked down his body and his skin crawled.

Christ, he was naked. He jerked on his chains, the metal manacles cutting into his skin. *Stay calm. Fear is your enemy.*

He swallowed his terror and flexed his muscles, assessing the damage. He clenched and unclenched his fingers and rolled his shoulders. Nothing appeared to be broken. But his shoulder joints felt as if they were about to explode. His arms were spread above his head, extended and pulled tight, chained to the ceiling. His legs, too, were spread wide, and he was shackled to the floor by the ankles, suspended in the shape of a cross.

If his enemy wanted him open and exposed, he'd succeeded.

The room was quiet. Deathly quiet. Sensing he was in fact alone, Rufus gingerly lifted his head to survey his prison. With the ringing in his ears and the haze clouding his brain clearing, he began to notice more. The room smelled musky. The air clinging to the inside of his nose was salty and damp against his bare skin. They were near the sea. There were no windows in the room, even though it was luxuriously furnished. Lighted candles licked the cold stone walls, casting an eerie glow around the chamber.

The owner of this place was obviously a wealthy man, and a man with perversions. His gaze landed on the grotesque stone statues positioned in each dank corner, and with frightening clarity Rufus understood who'd captured him. The man who "used" this room was an abuser of young boys. Connor's kidnapper.

The bile he'd been keeping at bay rose into his throat. Rufus was certain he'd been found by the man responsible for the disappearance of the boys.

Fear grew to unimaginable proportions. He yanked on the chains with all his strength. The chains did not break.

His head drooped down to his chest once more, defeat a crushing weight. Without Rufus's protection the degenerate responsible for Connor's capture would go after the boy to silence him. His gut clenched in horror. That would lead him straight to Rheda.

He raised his head. He would not give up. Never. He had to escape. To save Rheda and Connor. Rheda. Adrenaline surged; his mind blocked the pain. He looked up at the ceiling and began to pull his arms down as hard as possible. If he could just slip his hands out of the manacles . . .

Soon his arms shook from the strain, and blood dripped down his arms from where his skin had split against the iron bands.

"I'd stop trying to get free. You'll break your wrists, very painful, and you still won't be able to escape."

Rufus's head jerked to the right, and he swallowed in disgust. A man stepped through a stone door, closing it softly behind him. He wasn't very tall. His head was sleeved in a black leather mask that had slits for his mouth, nose, and eyes. It tied at his neck.

The hood didn't frighten Rufus. More disturbing was the fact the enemy before him was naked below his mask. His lithe body was covered in oil and gleamed in the candlelight. As he moved closer, Rufus realized his body was devoid of any trace of hair. Not that he wanted to look, but he was agog, as there appeared to be a chain running from a ring in the man's foreskin to his scrotum.

Rufus could face many things. He could take a vicious beating, and had on many occasions. He had been whipped to within an inch of his life but . . . but the thought of this "thing" touching him was a perversion he'd never had to face before. He hoped he had the strength to endure. The strength to escape.

The hideous vision reached out and stroked Rufus's chest. Rufus jerked back, his nausea returning in force.

"My master was right. You are beautiful. Like a Greek god." He began to walk around Rufus, lightly touching him. "I'm honored that my master has chosen me to prepare you."

"Touch me again, and I swear you're a dead man."

From the pitch of his voice Rufus had no doubt the "thing" before him was a young man. A boy really.

His tormentor stopped in front of him once more, and in reply to his threat simply reached out and cupped Rufus's balls in his hand and lightly squeezed. "Magnificent."

Rufus fought against his bindings, trying to escape his touch but to no avail. He swallowed the bile in his throat.

With a sigh the boy turned and walked toward the chest along the stone wall. "But you are not for me." He glanced over his shoulder, and the mask split as he smiled. "Not yet anyway. My master is the only man allowed to initiate a new pleasure toy." He took out a bottle. "But if I am very good, if I prepare you well, I get to play once he is finished with you."

Rufus's heart was pounding in his chest, sweat peppered his skin, and he thought he was going to vomit. The thought of the boy touching him terrified him. As the boy approached him, with his hands covered in liquid, he tried not to let his fear show.

"Who is your master?"

The boy began by sliding his hands over Rufus's chest, working the oil deep into his muscles. The pungent oil made his nostrils flare, and he gagged. The smell was sickly sweet.

Opium.

The oil contained opium. They were trying to drug him.

"Patience. Don't worry. There is not enough opium in the oil to render you unconscious. It's simply the master's way to help you relax. To make you more receptive to his touch . . ."

The boy worked quietly but earnestly. He moved around behind Rufus and worked the oil all over his back, from his

neck all the way down both his legs. Working it into every crevice of his body.

Rufus struggled against the chains, but it was hopeless. He screwed his eyes closed, trying to imagine himself anywhere but here. Trying to imagine he was not being molested. He could not help the automatic reflex to clench his buttocks against the invading hands.

Once his back was covered, the boy moved to stand in front of Rufus, and Rufus knew what he was going to do. Bile threatened to choke him. He swallowed. "When I get free, you'll wish you'd killed me when you could."

The boy ignored him, coating his genitals in the oil, stroking him intimately all over. The boy's voice was breathy. "Once all the opium seeping into your skin begins to work, you'll have no choice but to enjoy it."

Rufus gritted his teeth and tried to disassociate himself from the feel of the boy's hands on him.

He could feel the opium beginning to work. He tried to tell his brain not to respond to the stimulus. But the boy knew what he was doing. Rufus pulled on his metal cuffs. The pain of the metal chaffing his skin kept him from succumbing to the drug's numbing effects.

He could hear the boy's ragged breathing as he grew more aroused in his work.

"That's enough, Samuel," a voice growled from the door.

Rufus's head swung around to the sound of a familiar voice. His taut muscles relaxed with hope, only a few seconds later to begin trembling when he saw the apparition before him.

His revulsion turned to horrified surprise.

"Ah, Rufus. I do wish you'd stop fighting your body's natural response to stimulation. I suspect that like the rest of you, your erection will be splendid."

Lord Christopher Hale stood before him. But not the Christopher he knew. This man was dressed in a gentleman's

dressing robe of deep blue silk, and he was obviously naked underneath. His pupils were dilated, and the skin at the V of his neck glistened with oil, too.

Christopher took another step toward him and whispered, "The veins in your neck look as if they are about to burst, you're trying so hard to resist." He reached out and ran a finger from Rufus's chest to his groin. "That can't be good for you. Let me tell you, my fine friend, not even you will be able to withstand the opium's effects for long."

Rufus couldn't control the tremors racking his body, but he fought not to let his horror show, willing every muscle in his face not to flinch. The touch of Christopher's finger revolted him, yet his body and mind almost welcomed the chance to focus his anger.

"Aren't you a clever one?" His voice strangled in his throat. "But not that clever. I found your lair. If I can, then my men won't be far behind."

Christopher merely smiled and cupped Rufus's cheek. "Your men do not know where you are. I saw you leave Rheda with the boy on the beach. I will think of you when I take her to the marriage bed. Did she tell you she'd practically begged me to marry her?"

It took all of Rufus's skill not to shudder at the deep knife wound of betrayal spurred by his words. "You lie," he said, but heard his own conviction waning.

He refused to flinch when Christopher whispered in his ear. "She told me all about you, Rufus. How you ruined her and how you are here in Deal hunting for a spy. Why would she do that unless she did not want you?"

Christopher was likely playing with him, but how did he know about Rufus's mission? He couldn't, unless someone had told him.

Cold ice spears struck. Betrayal, Rheda's betrayal, cut him to the bone. She'd been in league with this monster, an abuser of children, all along. Her treachery hurt more than anything this man could do to him. His body went rigid

with anger. His gaze cold, he looked at the monster in front of him and said, "You can have her. I came for you, and now I have found you."

Christopher laughed. "Bravo. No, my sweet thing. I've found you. How like your father you are. He was a beautiful man, too. But alas, like father like son. He did not understand the pleasure to be found between men. I killed him for it. Just as I will kill you."

Suddenly, Christopher grabbed Rufus's head with both hands and kissed him violently. It was not a kiss of passion. It was hard and brutal. Rufus tasted blood as the man ground his teeth against Rufus's dried and cracked lips.

When Christopher let go and stepped back, Rufus jerked on his chains and spat the blood from his mouth.

"But unlike your father, I intend to initiate you into my erotic world before I kill you. I have been salivating over tasting you since you were a young man."

Rufus blocked the images his words evoked. "You killed my father? Why? How?" The shock and the opium had numbed his brain, slowed his reactions. Only now did he see that Christopher had begun to untie the cord to his robe.

"If you behave I might tell you—just before I kill you." Christopher moved in close and licked Rufus's nipple.

Rufus counted to ten and forced himself to ignore the threat standing before him. "You've fooled us all, Hale." He gazed at his captor. "You've been wearing a disguise. Padding I assume. There is not an ounce of fat on you."

Christopher preened. "So nice of you to notice." He ran his hand down over Rufus's chest, stomach, and around to his buttocks. "My body is not as magnificent as yours. Yours is all gleaming, solid muscle." He sighed and stepped back, then turned his palms up, his robe falling open. "I deemed a disguise necessary. In case anyone witnessed a boy being taken. No one would suspect me. As an overweight, wet fish, mummy's boy, I'm inconsequential. I'm overlooked, ignored, and never a suspect in any wrongdoing."

"You appear to be well versed with wrongdoing, *traître.*"

Christopher laughed. "Oui. I knew the boy had heard me speak in French. A pity that. The boy has to die." His eyes flashed with anger. "As now will Rheda. You really should not have involved her. Your seduction of her upset my carefully laid plans. Although I take no pleasure in women, they are essential for one thing only—an heir."

Rufus shook his head. He was missing something here. "Why kill Rheda? She works with you." It did not take long to understand. It was silly what a rush of relief did to his spirits when he was still chained and in danger of being raped. "She doesn't work for you. She doesn't know who you are. She came to you for help, nothing more—"

Christopher moved quickly and yanked Rufus's head back by his hair and whispered into Rufus's ear. "She has already agreed to marry me, fool. She's how I found out that you work for Ashford."

Rufus kept his face expressionless, but his heart bloomed in his chest. Rheda hadn't betrayed him.

"She came to me and told me everything. A bumbling idiot is never suspected of wrongdoing. She had no idea that I was anything other than what she saw."

Relief flooded through Rufus, quickly followed by guilt. Rheda would never align herself knowingly with evil. Yet, Rufus couldn't help his question. "Why on earth would she come to you?"

Christopher gave a satisfied smile. "To beg me to marry her so she could save you from your honorable sacrifice. She didn't want to see you involved in further scandal by being forced to marry her. The silly girl loves you."

Rufus closed his eyes against the anger. Anger at himself. If he'd not been such a coward and hidden from his true feelings for Rheda, she would never have sought Christopher out.

"I saw her go to the cove and watched you follow her. So I set up a trap. Connor was a very convenient tool. You, of

course, raced to his rescue. It was too easy. Soon, Napoleon will be victorious and I shall be free to carry on my life. Rheda was to have been my wife. When *I* was ready. Why do you think I encouraged her smuggling operation? For leverage, of course."

"Rheda knew nothing of your treason. How do you use her to send the communiqués?"

"I exchanged wool for brandy. She never suspected anything. The odd bale here and there. She thought it quaint that a rich earl would risk free trading for brandy." He laughed. "Little did she know that I'd woven messages into the bale's warp and weft. This war will be over soon, and the French will win."

"I hate to pour cold water on your fantasy, but Napoleon is never going to win."

"That is what your father thought twelve years ago. France has never been stronger. Napoleon is on the verge of a great victory."

At the mention of his father, Rufus's heart thudded against his rib cage. His father had died at Hastingleigh. Knowing what he did now about Christopher, this could no longer be a coincidence.

"How does an English earl's son become France's deadliest spy?"

Christopher moved close, his mouth inches from Rufus's lips. Rufus refused to flinch, refused to show how much his erstwhile friend now sickened him.

"You are not stupid, *mon ami*. A man with my tastes—my distinct appetites—is easy to exploit. I was careless in Paris in my youth. I found myself caught in a morally bankrupt position. I'm sure you can guess to what I'm inferring." He placed a fleeting kiss on Rufus's lips. "The French had enough evidence to have me imprisoned for 'the rest of my unnatural life' if I did not cooperate. For the future Earl of Hastingleigh, that would never do."

"What has my father got to do with any of this?" All of his

body felt cold, even with the fire blazing behind him, and he cringed at the thought of what he might hear.

Christopher's mouth curled back in an evil smile. "Nothing. That's the joke, nothing. The added bonus to killing your father was watching you fall apart." He moved behind Rufus and began running his hands over his back, buttocks, and legs. "You put on such a stoic front when rumors of your father's treason arose." Warm lips pressed against his skin, and Rufus realized what it meant to have your flesh crawl.

"I didn't plan to frame him for treason. Lord Ashford was at that time a field agent, and he was closing in. I had to turn his suspicions in another direction. When Lord Strathmore's gun accidentally went off in our struggle, I immediately grabbed the opportunity presented. I planted a minor communiqué into his pocket. Nothing that would see him found guilty but enough evidence to raise doubt in Ashford's mind and throw them off my scent."

"So you killed my father for convenience. So heroic."

Christopher moved slowly around to face Rufus, his hand trailing over Rufus's skin like a cold reptile. "No. I killed him because he was going to expose me—expose my 'unnatural' predilections to my father. He'd caught me with a young stable lad. He'd threatened to go to my father unless I left England immediately. I could hardly do that when the French already owned me."

Rufus's head lowered, and he let out a breath he didn't know he'd been holding. His father was innocent. Now all he needed to do was capture Christopher and get him to tell Lord Ashford the truth. Fear slithered away as blood-surging determination to escape seized every inch of his body. His muscles tightened and flexed.

If he could clear his father, the Strathmore name would be all about honor once more. He yanked on his chains. He could perhaps gain a little of his life back. If he still had one by the time Christopher was finished with him.

He would survive. When he did, he'd be free to make his

life what he wanted. What did he want? He sucked in a breath. He wanted—Rheda . . .

Averting his eyes he gulped down his fear as Christopher slipped the robe from his body.

"You may leave us, Samuel," Christopher whispered, desire hitching his voice.

"I want to watch."

Christopher moved to the boy and kissed him passionately through the mask. "You may play with our new toy later. Once I have finished."

Rufus's insides turned liquid. He prayed he'd have the strength to endure. Stephen couldn't be far away, unless—his breath faltered—unless Christopher had captured Rheda and Connor before they'd reached Stephen. He closed his eyes. Sweat trickled down his back, and yet he'd never felt so cold.

A warm hand on his chest made him open his eyes and brought him back to reality. The hand traveled toward his groin. He would not be this man's plaything. He shifted his head back. "Christopher . . ."

Christopher moved his face closer. Rufus sent his head crashing forward, but the effects of the opium slowed him down. Christopher pulled back, and Rufus's head found only air as his chin slammed into his own chest.

Christopher gripped Rufus's chin in his large hand. "I shall enjoy taking you. I've dreamt about having you for years." Christopher fondled him intimately and began to pepper kisses down Rufus's stomach as he dropped to his knees. Rufus was like a caged wild animal, fighting his bindings, fighting to avoid Christopher's disgusting mouth. His eyes screwed tight, not believing what was happening to him.

Suddenly, the door at the side of the chamber burst open. "Get your mouth off him, you pervert!"

Rheda.

Chapter 22

Equal parts fear, embarrassment, and relief swept through him as she stepped into the room and closed the door softly behind her, a pistol pointed directly at Lord Hale. Rufus ran his tongue over his swollen, bloodied lips. He tried to keep his voice steady so Rheda wouldn't learn how close he'd come to breaking down.

"Find the keys and release me from these chains."

Christopher turned so he stood facing Rheda. Rufus saw the blush sweep up Rheda's neck and onto her face as she saw the condition Christopher was in.

Christopher slid his hands down his body. "I'm happy for you to search me. However, being naked it is rather difficult to hide a key on my person." Christopher stepped toward Rheda.

"Keep away from her—"

"It's all right, Rufus. If he takes one more step, I'll ensure he can't molest anyone ever again." She lowered her aim from Christopher's chest to his groin, bravely staring the other man down. Christopher halted, a snarl curling his lip.

Rheda knew she shouldn't think it, but Rufus looked magnificent. His split lip the only sign that he'd been hurt, although from what she'd seen when she'd thrown open the door, she wasn't sure of what he'd had to endure. Terrible

thoughts polluted her mind. He was alive; that was all that mattered.

She swallowed back a cry. But if Christopher had . . . It would be her fault.

It was then she caught the first waft of the sweet sickly smell. What was it? It was a pleasant odor, but one that sent unease skittering down every inch of her spine. She shook her head. She had to concentrate.

Before her stood a trim Christopher she did not know; one with no softness to his form or his eyes. His pale blue eyes glinted cold and deadly in the candlelight.

Her voice shook with rage. "I want the keys to unlock his shackles." Christopher made to move. "Don't move. Just tell me where they are." He pointed toward the sideboard at the back of the dungeon. She made her way toward the keys, her eyes never leaving Christopher's face. She scooped them up and made to throw them to Christopher. "Release him."

"No. You do it, Rhe. I don't want him near me." She'd never heard Rufus plead before, and her heart constricted in agony. What had Christopher done to him? No. She'd done this to him. She'd betrayed his confidence, thinking as always that she knew better, and had sent him straight into a trap.

Would he ever be able to forgive her?

She managed to get the shackles at his ankles unlocked, but with growing horror she realized she couldn't reach the manacles about his wrists. She tentatively touched his chest and looked deep into his eyes. "Rufus, I can't reach," she calmly uttered.

Her voice and touch seemed to soothe him. She could physically feel his body gather itself. He nodded, his expression murderous. She hated to think what he was planning to do to Christopher once he was free.

No doubt the same thought had occurred to Christopher. He would be getting desperate. She needed to watch him like a snake watches its victim before it strikes.

She beckoned Christopher closer and tossed him the keys. "You do it. If you touch any part of him except the chains, I'll make you wish you'd never been born."

Christopher approached Rufus as timidly as a deer advancing into an open field. At Rufus's side he hesitated.

"Get on with it," she ordered, trying to keep her voice firm when inside she was shaking like a leaf.

She knew the last lock had been released when Rufus swung his fist around and connected with Christopher's chin. Christopher went down on his bare behind with a thud. Rheda would have smiled had not Rufus followed him to the floor, his legs buckling beneath him.

Without thinking, she rushed to his side. She tried to grip his arm, but her hand slipped on his oiled skin. The pungent smell was very strong; it dawned on her the sickly stench came from his skin.

"Opium," he croaked. "I can't get my limbs to function properly. I'm about as useful as an inebriated sailor in a storm." He tried to smile as if his condition was not important, but she knew they were in trouble. She didn't have the strength to carry him.

"If I wipe the oil off would that help?"

"It couldn't hurt. It will at least stop the opium from continuing to soak into my bloodstream."

"Take the gun." She shoved it into Rufus's hand. Then she hurriedly crawled across the jagged slate stones to Christopher's discarded robe, and, trying to ignore the beauty of Rufus's body, she rubbed as much of the oil off his skin as was possible.

Although conscious, Christopher had not moved. He sat watching her rub Rufus down, his expression that of a beggar who suddenly finds himself a chest of gold. She tried not to look at him, the man she had considered a confidant and friend. However, as she bent down to rub Rufus's legs, Christopher groaned. She glanced over, and her stomach heaved. Christopher was fully aroused and enjoying her

ministrations to Rufus's body. She stood quick and turned her back on Christopher and his disgusting condition. She handed the robe to Rufus. "Put this on."

Rufus flushed. He also seemed mortified at Christopher's condition. He, too, could not look at the man. Or at her.

He took the robe from her without glancing up. But the material had barely left her fingers when Rheda suddenly found herself jerked backward off her feet by her hair. Pain slashed at her scalp, her hair almost ripped out at the roots. Too late she understood their mistake. Christopher had wanted to distract them. He'd wanted Rufus to be self-conscious in front of her.

Christopher pulled her tight against his nakedness, wrapping one arm around her, pinning her arms to her sides, while the other gripped her neck so tightly her eyes began to water.

"Drop the pistol. You know I have the strength to break this pretty neck."

Rheda whimpered as his fingers dug into her flesh.

"If I drop my weapon, Rheda is as good as dead." Rufus cocked an eyebrow. "As am I."

"Then we appear to have a stalemate. One that I shall win. All I have to do is wait for Samuel to return. He shouldn't be long. Allowing him to prepare you has made him anxious to play. Your superbly masculine body was almost too much for him. I've never seen him so excited before. Not even for my attentions."

Rufus would not look her in the eye. His steely gaze was fixed on Christopher. Rheda had never seen such hatred blazing from their depths. Something stirred in her chest—hope. He was beautiful beyond imagining, yet his countenance screamed rage, an avenging angel. He would not let Christopher win.

She listened to the venom as it flooded his rich baritone voice. "I am perfectly aware of what your lapdog wants with me."

★ ★ ★

Rufus lifted the pistol and aimed it at Christopher's head. "But I insist on disappointing you."

Damn. Rufus cursed under his breath. Christopher moved so that he was more firmly shielded by Rheda's body; Rufus couldn't get a clean shot.

"I don't know why you are so eager to dispatch me to the underworld. I'm the only one who can clear your father's name."

Out of the corner of his eye he saw Rheda's head lift. "I know the truth. That is all that matters." He hoped the lie did not reverberate in his voice. He needed Christopher alive. He needed his confession in order to once and for all squash all the rumors. Without Christopher's testimony, all he'd have to convince a society that viewed him as little more than dirt under its boot was his word. It would not be enough.

"What has Christopher got to do with your father?" Rheda asked.

Christopher's hold tightened on her neck. "Don't talk, my sweet. This is between Rufus and me." Christopher kissed the top of her head. "Do behave. I have plans for you once Rufus is dead. I want an heir. I'll keep you locked away until you give me a son. You wouldn't wish the authorities to know your brother is Dark Shadow."

The thought of the bastard forcing his attentions on Rheda made Rufus's gut crawl. It was bad enough knowing the monster had his filthy hands on her now.

"Rufus, shoot him. You have the gun. All you have to do is wound him, and he'll drop. You don't have to kill him."

Rufus hesitated. What if he missed and shot Rheda?

"You won't miss."

Christopher raised an eyebrow. "But you won't risk it, will you, Rufus?" Rufus watched helplessly as Christopher tightened his grip on her throat. "Honor won't let you sac-

rifice her for the cause. You'd rather let me go than have an innocent woman's blood on your hands."

Rufus growled low in his throat. He was right. Christopher wasn't worth Rheda's life. He slowly lowered the gun. "I've caught you once; I can catch you again."

Christopher, still with his hand wrapped tightly around Rheda's throat, edged toward the door. "A deal then? You let me go and I'll let Rheda live."

"Once through that door you'd best leave her behind, or I'll kill you."

Rheda began to struggle. "Don't do this. You can't let this monster go."

Rufus held Christopher's victorious gaze.

"Rufus! My life is nothing compared to stopping Christopher."

"Don't struggle, Rheda, please . . ." Rufus raised the gun again as Rheda tried to break free of Christopher's hold.

"He knows the truth about your father—you can't let him escape. I'll not let you." Her words were a scratched cry as Christopher's fingers began choking her in earnest.

"Shut up, bitch. You're ruining everything."

Rufus watched with his insides tearing apart. "He killed those boys," she gasped. "You can't let him go free, he's a monster. You can't . . ."

Anger tightened like a fist in Rufus's gut as he watched Christopher's face twist in a mass of fury. Both his hands were now squeezing the life out of her. If Rufus didn't act soon, Christopher would snap her neck like a twig and escape through the door.

He pointed the pistol, but Rheda was struggling so much he was scared that if he fired he'd hit her instead of Christopher. Horror like he'd never known almost paralyzed him as her body went limp. She was dying in front of his eyes.

He pinched himself hard. He had to stay alert. He wasn't about to let the woman he loved die.

With a roar, he threw himself at Christopher, knocking Rheda sideways and onto the floor and driving Christopher back against the stone wall. *His* fingers wrapped around Christopher's throat.

Remorselessly, Rufus squeezed with all the strength he had left, but with all the oil on Christopher's body he couldn't maintain his hold. Christopher's right knee lifted and kneed him in the groin.

Their fight raged around the stone. Each time Christopher tried to go for the pistol that lay next to Rheda's inert body, Rufus drove him back. As Christopher's desperation grew, his face twisted into a mask of rage and hatred.

Rufus's arms began to tremble with effort. He felt his strength wane. Christopher landed a solid punch on his chin, and his legs buckled. His knees hit the slate floor. Luckily, the intense pain cleared his mind of the opium's numbing effects. With a sudden lunge Rufus rolled on his back, scrabbling for the pistol. Snatching it off the floor, he turned and fired.

Christopher crumbled to the floor, blood trickling down his naked chest, a bullet hole over his heart.

He shook his head to focus. Christopher was dead, but they weren't out of danger yet. The pistol held only one shot, and they had to escape Samuel.

His heart constricted with terror as he registered the prone form of his beautiful, gallant, unconscious love. *Get up!* He snarled to himself. On hands and knees, he crawled across the cold stone chamber to Rheda. She was so still. Tentatively, as if he didn't want to feel the truth, he gently touched her neck, checking for a heartbeat. The cold knot in his stomach eased as he felt a flutter under his fingers. Her pulse was erratic, but she was alive.

Gently, he cradled her face. "My love, wake up." His voice sounded gruff and angry in the stillness.

She did not stir.

He gently shook her. "You have to wake up. I can't get us

out of here on my own. I'm not strong enough without you. I need you." His plea echoed around the chamber.

He swallowed hard, his heart pounding as if it would break. He smoothed the hair off her ashen face and whispered, "Come on, you little fighter. Don't give up on me now." Emotion pricked behind his eyelids.

She had to live.

Then he heard the footsteps running toward the chamber. He tried to pull Rheda up onto her feet, but they both sagged back to the floor in a jumble of arms and legs. Steeling himself, he rose to his knees and levered his body between the door and his love. He would protect her with his last breath if that was what it took. He raised the empty gun, hoping it might halt the enemy's advance.

Chapter 23

The door crashed inward. Stephen stood in the doorway with Daniel peering over his shoulder. Rufus dropped the pistol in relief.

"Please help her" was all he could manage before he sagged back onto the cold slate floor, energy draining from his drugged body.

"Rhe." Daniel pushed Stephen aside and raced toward her. His fingers found the pulse point in his sister's neck. "She's alive, thank God." He swept her up in his arms. "I'm taking her up to the house and calling the doctor." And without a backward glance he strode out of the dungeon.

Stephen crossed to Christopher's body. "He is very much dead I see. Was he our spy?" And shrugging out of his coat he walked and handed it to Rufus.

Rufus nodded.

Stephen sniffed the air. Softly he asked, "Are you all right?"

Rufus could see the question in his eyes, and he swallowed his embarrassment. "I will be once I've had a dip in the sea and several mugs of strong black coffee." Stephen did not ask more.

Rufus held out his hand. "Help me up." Stephen helped pull him to his feet and held the coat while Rufus slipped it on.

Rufus asked, "How many men do you have with you? We

need to search the ruins. Hale has an accomplice—a young man called Samuel. We have to find him."

"What does he look like?"

Rufus closed his eyes momentarily. "I don't know. He was wearing a full-head, black leather mask."

Stephen gave him a blank look, then blinked. Walking to the door he called one of the men over. "Get the men and search the ruins. We are looking for a man—young. Hold any you come across until Lord Strathmore can interrogate them."

"Yes, my lord."

Rufus joined Stephen at the door.

His friend asked, "What now?"

"I'm going for a swim, and then I'm going up to the house to put my life in order."

"She'll be fine, Rufus. She's alive and she's strong."

"You should have seen her." Rufus let the emotion he barely held in check flood his voice. "She was fearless. She saved me from a fate worse than death—"

"Miss Kerrich is quite a woman," Stephen said softly. "Congratulations."

"Don't congratulate me too soon. I still have to convince Rheda."

Stephen laughed and clapped him on the back. "The biggest mistake you could make from this mess is to let her escape." Stephen sobered. "I've never met a woman more right for you, Rufus. Don't let foolish pride stop you from finding happiness."

Rufus felt his mouth twist in a wry smile. "One thing my father's disgrace taught me is that pride is a useless emotion. Speaking of pride, I think I'm going to need your help to make it down to the beach."

A strong steady heartbeat thudded beneath her ear. Muscular arms held her tight against a solid chest. The masculine scent of sandalwood. Rufus.

As the mist on her brain continued to clear, she realized she was being carried and that they were moving at a fast pace. Heavy booted footsteps crunching on gravel. Her senses focused. Sun warmed her face and fresh sea air filled her lungs.

They were free of the dungeon.

They had survived.

The rush of relief gave her the strength to open her eyes. The world appeared fuzzy and distorted. Light temporarily blinded her; she reached up and cupped the face above her and tried to get her throat to work. Each swallow caused hot, raw pain and brought tears to her eyes. The sound that came out was croaked and muffled; she hoped Rufus understood. "I knew you'd save us," she managed.

"We cut it a bit fine," he said. "It took Jamieson too long to find Stephen. We were down by Fraser's Landing."

Daniel? Not Rufus. Daniel. Rheda's heart almost stopped.

"Where's Rufus?" she croaked, struggling in Daniel's arms. Was he hurt? Throat forgotten, she closed her eyes and gave a silent prayer. Was he dead? She couldn't remember anything except Christopher's fingers squeezing the life out of her. She pummeled Daniel's coat with her fists. "Put me down. I have to go to him."

Daniel simply held her tighter. "Calm down. Rufus is fine. He has a few cuts and bruises and of course his body is under the influence of the effects of the opium, but it's nothing that a bath and a stiff drink won't fix."

Rheda slumped back against his shoulder. Thank God. She forced her words out even though it felt like she'd consumed a hedgehog. "Where are you taking me?"

"I'm taking you to Hastingleigh. It's closer than Tumsbury Cliff. I want the doctor to look at you."

"If you put me down I can walk. It's Rufus who needs a doctor. He could hardly stand."

She felt the chuckle rumble deep in Daniel's chest. "He was strong enough to kill Christopher and save you both. I don't think he's at death's door."

Christopher was dead? Rheda bit her lip. Poor Lady Hale. Her son was her life. How could she face the woman who had always been her friend, knowing she'd helped kill her son?

Christopher was dead! Her mind cartwheeled. Despair seeped into every pore. If Christopher was dead, that meant Rufus would never be able to clear his father's name. Rufus would only have his word as evidence. Would that be enough? Given Society's tendency to believe the worst— definitely not. It was little wonder Rufus sent her away with Daniel. He wouldn't want to see her. She'd cost him everything; her stupidity had made him a captive, had caused him to suffer terrible indignities, cost him his pride, and, worst of all, destroyed his only hope of clearing his father and restoring the noble family name of Strathmore.

She didn't blame him if he never wanted to see her again.

And she wanted him. She wanted him so much. The truth sizzled across her heart like a lightning bolt streaking across the sky.

All her life she'd believed it was marriage she'd feared. Giving a man so much power over her. Only now did she realize her fear wasn't a husband—or children. The monster of her nightmares was marriage *to the wrong man.*

She was petrified of making her mother's mistake and choosing a man who did not love her. Her mother desired to remain near her childhood friend, Helen. This formed the basis of her marriage, and as she'd watched her husband's character weaken and degenerate over the years she'd regretted her choice.

Regretted it deeply.

Rheda refused to take the same path. But how was she to judge if a man would make a good husband? She'd had limited exposure to men, other than the sycophants and leeches who surrounded her father.

Except for Rufus. At the thought, it was as if someone dashed a bucket of cold water in her face. Rufus was noth-

ing like those men. Nothing like her father. He had strength of character. He wouldn't blame his wife and tenants for his financial troubles. He wouldn't hit out at his neighbors or curse his wife for dying in childbirth and leaving him with two children to raise. He wouldn't drink and gamble their inheritance away and leave them destitute.

He wouldn't be so selfish.

Unlike her. The horror of her actions—her selfish actions—made her tremble in Daniel's arms, made her retch into her hand. She'd been behaving like her father. She'd taken the easy way out—smuggling. Using the help she could give the villagers as an excuse to condone her behavior.

But Rufus had never taken the easy way out. There *was* no easy way out for him. In the face of his father's death and supposed treachery, Rufus could have turned bitter. He could have slunk away and lived his life at Hascombe and not given a damn for what others thought. With his wealth he could have lived a life of idleness and debauchery.

But he hadn't. He'd stood proud and faced Society's scorn. He'd risen above his shame to serve his country, trying to atone for his father's actions even while believing him innocent. He'd put his family obligations ahead of his own desires.

For twelve years he'd believed in his father, in his family's honor, and in himself. He was never going to give up when he had a sister and mother to care for and protect.

He was an honorable man—even to saving her life at the expense of his own honor and his family's vindication. The thought of his sacrifice tore a sob from deep within her. His family.

Family. No wonder a man of his moral fiber would suggest marriage. He'd taken her virginity, and in his eyes there was only one honorable outcome—marriage. Especially if she was with child.

She touched her stomach and reverently rubbed her palm

over it. Rufus's child. The warmth of the image of their child swept away the last vestige of the cold dungeon.

Nevertheless, marriage did not guarantee fidelity, and family didn't mean love between husband and wife.

She needed time to think through all the options, weigh up the risks, and finally talk with Rufus.

Her breath seemed to be stuck in her damaged throat. What did Rufus truly desire? Once she knew his heart, she'd be able to make a decision.

She was so lost in her thoughts and fears that Rheda wasn't aware of her surroundings until Daniel gently laid her on a bed.

Then reality flooded back. "We're here? At Hasting-leigh?" She tried to rise, but Daniel pushed her back down.

"Stop it, Daniel. I need to go to Lady Hale. Her world has just imploded. She needs me."

Daniel shook his head. "Dr. Caxton has given her enough laudanum to make her sleep through the night. You need to get some rest, and I want the doctor to look at your throat. You can barely speak, and the bruises need treat-ment." He wrinkled his nose. "And you need a bath. What is that smell?"

"Opium." She instantly recalled wiping it off Rufus's naked body.

"I'll arrange for a bath to be brought up." At the door he hesitated. "You realize I will be speaking with Rufus. You must know you've been compromised. You were found with a naked man." She started to speak, but Daniel held up his hand. "I'll brook no argument. I allowed your last escapade to ruin you. You saved the princess's life and carried the shame for something not of your making. I'll not see you ru-ined again." And he left, closing the door with a sharp click.

Rheda collapsed back on the bed and shut her eyes. Her throat burned, and she was desperate for a drink. As if read-ing her thoughts, there was a knock on the door and one of Lady Hale's servants entered carrying a tray.

"Lady Umbridge thought you might like some refreshment. I've set your bath in the dressing room, through the door." The girl pointed to the open door to her right. "Do you need help undressing and getting into the bath?"

"No," she managed to croak out.

"Cook's prepared a hot honey drink to ease your throat. Dr. Caxton's orders."

Within half an hour Rheda relaxed against the back of the tub. The hot drink helped to ease her throat, just as the heat of the water was easing the scrapes and bruises on her body. She had scrubbed the traces of the dungeon from her skin, but she could not block them from her mind.

She hoped Rufus was resting. She wanted him refreshed before tackling the difficult conversation to come. The scented soak in the bathtub had been illuminating.

She did not yet have all the answers, but one thing was very clear in her mind; she loved Rufus Knight with all her heart. And if his name and his bed were all he could offer her, then she would take it gladly, for to be the object of his desire was—quite frankly—worth any price she'd have to pay.

"How is your throat, Rheda?" asked a voice so empty of concern it caused the hairs on her arms to raise.

She opened her eyes and took in the haughty beauty entering the room. Lady Umbridge glided closer and, gathering her skirt about her, sat on the stool beside the bathtub.

"Much better if I don't talk, Fleur."

"Fine. I'll do all the talking then, shall I?" Fleur said acidly. "I must admit I was not overly surprised when I heard the tale of Christopher's double life. I suspected he was odd long ago, upon my first visit to Hastingleigh as a young bride. He was the only man who never tried to seduce me."

"Perhaps, in some things, he had good taste?" The snarky comment slipped out without any thought.

Fleur's eyes flashed, and she drew herself up. "I see the

time for pleasantries is past. I have something you, or should I say Rufus, want. No. Need."

Rheda sat up straighter in the tub. "What?"

The other woman's teeth showed white in a parody of a smile. "I have your attention at last." She leaned forward. "I admit Christopher intrigued me when I learned what had occurred. So I searched his room. It's amazing what one can find when one snoops. I found some reading material that was very enlightening."

The moment the words left Fleur's mouth, Rheda remembered her last conversation with Christopher, and the water seemed to turn to ice. He'd told her he kept journals. Why had she not thought of it? "Christopher's journals."

Her smile widened. "You know of them. Then you'll comprehend what is in them." She paused, delicately. "*All* of them."

Rheda kept her face calm, her expression politely interested. "Why tell me? Why not simply hand them to Stephen?"

The woman leaned forward. "Because you have something I want. Something that is to be mine."

Under the water, hidden from view, Rheda's toes curled. "I cannot fathom what you're—"

Fleur cut her off. "Oh, I think you do. Six feet three inches of virile masculinity. He belongs to me, and I want him back."

"I've had a very trying day. What exactly is it that you want?" She managed to keep her voice steady, yet inside her body tightened like a bowstring before it was fired.

"That's better. Let's at least try to be grown up about our situation." Fleur settled back on her stool. "I want you to refuse Rufus's proposal—I know there will be one, so don't pretend otherwise. His honor would call for nothing else."

Rheda inclined her head. "He has a strong ally in my brother. Even if I wanted to I'm not sure either will allow me to decline."

"You're a smart woman, Rheda. A woman who set up and successfully ran a smuggling ring should have no trouble extricating herself from a simple marriage proposal." Lady Umbridge ran her hand over her hair. "I'd hate to have to destroy Christopher's journal containing the truth about Rufus's father or allow the journals about your smuggling—and affair with Prince Hammed—see the light of day. Think how the scandal would damage the Strathmore name. It would certainly seal their social demise."

Rheda took two slow, cleansing breaths. When she spoke again her voice was deathly calm. "My declining Rufus's offer won't ensure your suit."

"Leave the seductive manipulations to the expert. I, too, am a clever woman. I'm pretty sure he'll do what he needs to do in order to procure the journal."

"You'd blackmail a man to your bed?"

Fleur made a rude sound. "Not just any man and not to my bed. I'll force him to marry me."

Before she could censor her thoughts, Rheda blurted out, "That won't do much for his honor."

Fleur surged to her feet, the stool crashed to the floor, and the woman's palm cracked across Rheda's cheek in a stunning slap. "I'll not need 'other entertainment' when I have a man of his stature in my bed. You have until tomorrow morning to dissuade him. If Rufus does not wash his hands of you by then, Christopher's journal, with the evidence of the late Lord Strathmore's innocence, goes in the fire, and the journals about you will be sent to the local magistrate and perhaps the *Times*."

She stood staring down her long arrogant nose, as if Rheda was an insect. In the most vicious tone she said, "If you truly love him you know there is only one course of action open to you. I promise I'll—satisfy him." She smiled and licked her lips. "More than you ever could."

The echo from the door closing sounded like the lid being slammed on Rheda's hopes for the future. As her dreams

disintegrated her tears welled. She tried to stem them but couldn't. For once in her life she had no idea what to do.

She let go and sobbed against the cruel hand of fate. She sobbed so loudly that she didn't hear the door open and didn't realize anyone had entered the room until Meg pulled her into her arms.

"Shhh. Don't cry. Everything will be—"

"No. It won't," she wailed.

Meg gently wiped the tears from Rheda's eyes. "There is nothing women cannot do or overcome. You told me that."

"I was wrong." She hiccupped.

"Emphasis on the *women*—two heads are far better than one. Tell me what the problem is."

And it all came out. During Rheda's story Meg paced the bathing chamber, hands clenched at her sides. "What a bitch. I hope you told her to go to Hades."

"You know I can't do that. She's right. I can't destroy Rufus's life goal or his family's future in Society. It would be selfish, and I've sworn to start afresh and to think of others first."

"But what of Rufus? He's asked you to marry him. He has feelings for you. Are you prepared to destroy that?"

"Feelings? Desire is easily replaced. Another pretty face, and men are content." Rheda dried herself with the towel. "What else am I to do? If you have another suggestion I would gladly hear it."

"We could beat her until she tells us where they are."

It was a tempting thought. "With her thick skin, it would probably only tickle."

The two of them fell silent, remaining so while Meg helped her dress.

"I need more time," Rheda said finally, not expecting any brilliant reply from her friend.

Meg shook her head and finished lacing up Rheda's gown. "We have until morning to come up with a cunning plan, so don't do anything rash. If we can't think of a solution by then . . ." Meg clapped her hands together.

Rheda's heart leaped up and into her throat. "What?"

Meg shrugged her shoulders and looked away. "You could pretend to run away like a dog with your tail between your legs, then when she gives the journal to Rufus come back and unmask her treachery."

She sighed. "My selfish self already came up with that idea, but Fleur holds the trump card. She has the journals about my exploits. I can't walk into Rufus's life when he's finally been cleared of scandal only to burden the Strathmore name with my own disgraces."

Meg dropped her gaze to the floor. "We'll think of something. I know we will."

Would they? Perhaps she was deluding herself, thinking she could outmaneuver a slippery eel like Lady Umbridge.

Rheda inwardly scoffed. Rubbish. She'd dealt with cutthroat smugglers, saved Tumsbury Cliff, faced down a French spy, and she wasn't about to let a vicious whore of a woman take everything that was important from her. She'd find a way.

She had to find away.

If she couldn't . . . She'd have to walk away—for now.

Pushing the thought of failure from her mind, she said, "You're right about one thing, though. I have until morning, and I am not going to let that woman destroy what might be my one perfect night."

She welcomed Meg's embrace and hugged her back as hard as she could, as if doing so would keep the pain from invading another inch of her skin. She had one night left to spend with the man she loved, and she would not waste it on "what could be."

Pushing out of Meg's hold, she made for the door. Meg's words following her.

"You helped save Rufus from Lord Hale. I suggest you confide in Rufus and let him save you from Lady Umbridge. You don't have to do everything on your own."

She hesitated at the door, a small smile on her face. "Oh,

I don't intend to spend this night alone. *Nor ruin it by causing Rufus any further distress.*"

She'd give herself to Rufus. Immerse her body, heart, and soul in his passion. She'd create memories to last a lifetime. Only then, if she had no other option, would she have the strength to leave. Only then would she have the strength to walk away. To end up empty—like before.

Chapter 24

Rufus sat quietly before the fire in his bedchamber, drinking a glass of warming brandy. It wasn't a cold night, yet he welcomed the alcohol's burn. He'd discarded his cravat and jacket, and undone his waistcoat. His legs stretched out toward the hearth. He could feel the heat from the fire on the soles of his Hessians.

Since escaping the dungeon he'd not been able to rest or have a moment to himself, and he needed to think through the implications of all he'd learned today—both about his father and about himself.

The swim had refreshed him and restored his senses, but the aftermath of Christopher's death and the revelation Hale was indeed the spy had meant he'd had a busy afternoon.

His men found no trace of Samuel. Tomorrow they would widen their search. He'd promised Alex, and even though Christopher was the likely perpetrator in snatching the boys, Samuel could well follow in his footsteps. The only problem was no one knew Samuel's identity. Samuel's mask obscured his features. He could be walking about Hastingleigh estate as any one of the servants.

But Samuel wasn't the only person on his mind. Rufus had already summoned his mother. Lady Hale would need a friend. His worst pain came from the knowledge he'd hurt Helen, a dear and loyal friend to his family. His mother's grief would be as deep as his own.

Rufus would keep Christopher's treason a secret from the world at large. Since he could no longer give evidence as to the innocence of Rufus's father, there seemed little point in dragging Lord Hale's name through the mud. It would hurt only Helen, and she was the innocent party in all of this.

Stephen had agreed to his plan. The public story would be that Christopher died trying to stop a smuggler—Dark Shadow. They would tell only Lord Ashford the truth. The spy had been dealt with, and that had always been the goal.

His lips curved in a warm smile. His father would be proud of him. Proud, not because he'd done what he'd aimed to do. No, his father would be smiling down on him because one moment's clarity revealed to Rufus what was truly important in life. Life was meant to be lived, with and for the living, and he'd stupidly spent his life chasing the dead. It didn't matter what Society thought. He knew that now. His friends and family. All that mattered was what kind of man he was in the eyes of family.

Shame gnawed at his empty stomach. His living family. He couldn't remember the last time he'd had a conversation with his mother or his sister. Madeline—she was about to have her coming out, and he couldn't remember spending any quality time with her over the past six years. What were her dreams, her hopes? What kind of woman had she developed into? He did not know the answers, and that saddened and embarrassed him.

Then there was Rheda. He took a deep breath. He didn't quite know what to think of her situation, but she was the most amazing woman he'd ever met. And she'd captured his heart.

He knew that he'd never want any other woman. Rheda had challenged him from the first day he'd met her. She'd brought out the best and worst in him, and still she'd come to his aid at great risk to herself. He gave a sigh and felt his body quicken. Did she love him?

The door opened, and, as if she heard his silent call, she

was there in his room. His heart sped up. She looked beautiful. His fists clenched in his lap at the sight of the bruises developing around her slender throat.

When she walked into the center of his room and smiled, his world lit up and his head started to swim.

"Are you all right?" she asked shyly.

I am now, he wanted to say, but her beauty held him speechless. Seeing Rheda safe . . . In answer he rose, and in one long stride reached her, caught her up against his chest, cupped her chin, and slowly lowered his mouth to hers.

Rheda closed her eyes, slipped her arms around his neck, and accepted his tongue into her mouth in warm, loving invitation. He tasted of warm brandy. He tasted—like the man she loved.

Rufus pulled back and rested his forehead against hers. He was breathing heavily. "My wild and reckless Rheda. I should put you over my knee for risking your pretty little neck. What were you thinking coming to that hell hole on your own? You take too many risks."

Her head was so light, her blood so hot, she barely heard his soft censure. "I thought only of saving you." And she threw herself back into the embrace, kissing him with feverish urgency as if tomorrow would sneak up on her before she'd taken her fill of him. She had a lifetime of memories to live in just one night. The thought spurred her actions.

A groan emitted from deep in his chest as she ran her hands over his body, all the while edging him back toward his large canopied four-poster bed. When they came to an abrupt halt, hitting one corner post of the bed, she pressed him back against it, grasping the flaps of his unbuttoned waistcoat.

For once in her life she was glad of her reckless nature, for his kisses made her boldly impatient to see him in all his glorious nakedness.

She broke their kiss and daringly rained butterfly-light

licks and nibbles down his throat until she could part the V of his shirt to slide her hands inside. Her fingers sought his nipples, and she raked her nails lightly over his skin.

He hooked his finger inside her gown at the shoulder and followed her décolletage down to the front, grazing her sensitized nipple as his touch passed over her breast.

"I want you naked," she panted, feeling her nipples instantly harden.

Never one to be denied that which she wanted, Rheda tore her hands from his chest and pushed the waistcoat off his shoulders and down his arms. She reached and pulled his shirt from his trousers, running her hands seductively up his chest as she helped him to pull the garment over his head.

"You set my world on fire, siren." He grasped her hips and pulled her closer until she could feel the evidence of his desire hard and pulsing against her belly. More brazen still, she cupped him through his breeches, and he moaned and dropped his head back against the post behind him.

She ran her questing fingers up the length of his arousal, then up his flat belly to his chest. Finally she curled her fingers around his nape and stared at him. He no longer looked like the composed and elegant lord she'd first met on the cliff top. He looked as wild as an unbroken stallion. She pressed a kiss to his chest. He looked at her in tormented ecstasy.

"Life is full of risks," she whispered. "You once promised to show me such pleasure I'd scream until I was hoarse. I'm not sure my throat is up to screaming, but my body is willing to risk the pain to experience all the pleasure you can give it."

The wicked smile he gave her sent a thrill all the way down to her toes.

Without hesitation he swung her up into his arms and rounded the bed to gently lower her to the mattress. She lay back and felt her body quicken as he bent down and stole her breath with his kiss, petting her breasts through her gown.

He stepped back.

She shivered in anticipation. He slowly began to unbutton the placket of his trousers. She licked her lips as hungry desire consumed her. She feasted on the breadth of his wide shoulders, the clean sweep of his taut waist, and the sculptured planes of his chest, the marble-like skin covered with sparse brown hair.

She rose to her knees, kissing his tantalizing skin, stroking his fine velvety flesh, exploring with mouth and hands his powerful chest and rippling belly. Her fingers traveled over his skin reverently. She luxuriated in the feeling of his broad shoulders and the rock-hard curve of his biceps and strong forearms.

He gripped her wrists and removed her hands from his body, pushing her gently back onto the bed. "Enough, my wild beauty. I want to last long enough to render you speechless."

Her body thrummed with impatience as he bent to remove his boots. Then her mouth dropped open as he pushed his breeches and the rest of his clothing down over his slim hips. Her breath hitched as she took in his naked body. Her gaze stayed riveted on his enormous jutting erection. "You are a . . . magnificent specimen, Lord Strathmore," she whispered.

He laughed softly, lifted his lashes, and captured her as she reached to stroke him. He wove his fingers through hers and pulled her into his arms. "You've seen me naked far more often than I've seen you, and I'd like to rectify that anomaly."

Her cheeks filled with heat, but she boldly turned around and lifted her hair out of the way, eager for him to proceed. His fingers set about unfastening her gown in the back. She felt her gown gape open, and he ran a finger down her spine.

"I do love your trend of not wearing a corset."

His husky words sent her heart racing out of her chest. He gently slipped the gown off her shoulders. She moaned as his hands skimmed over her shoulders and he molded his palms to her breasts, his thumbs flicking over her hardened nipples.

Impatient, Rheda wriggled out of her dress and watched with delight as Rufus tossed it on the floor, his eyes never leaving hers. Like a sinful Madonna she rolled onto her back, adoring the way his eyes caressed every inch of her exposed skin.

His warm, sure hands moved up her calf, and he fumbled in his haste to remove her stockings and garters. Once he had her completely naked he stood back, his chest heaving with desire. Under his lashes his chocolate-colored eyes devoured her, and she rose onto her elbows, crooking her finger and beckoning him.

He stood silent for a moment, continuing to drink her in before slowly joining her on the bed. As he moved over her, Rheda discovered the powerful aphrodisiac of skin against skin.

"I can't believe you're mine," he whispered. "I thought I knew the type of woman that was perfect for me. A quiet, pious lady to honor my family's name. But you—you, my golden temptress—have shown me I desire, and deserve, so much more. I want you and only you. My wild and irrepressible goddess."

She drew in a sharp breath as the pain and irony of his words almost destroyed her. She'd won his devotion only to lose him due to her past sins. But he was not the only person with honor. She, too, could be truly selfless and do what was right. What was best for him.

She watched as his head lowered to her breast, as he opened his mouth. When he took hold of her and began to suckle, Rheda closed her eyes and blocked out everything but his touch, his kiss, his body, hard and unyielding above her.

He moved and spread her open with his massive thighs. He rose onto his hands above her; she opened her eyes and watched him—watched them, their bodies joining and separating. He teased her to the edge of insanity with the tip of his cock, moving in short, provocative little strokes.

She lifted her hips, begging for more. "Yes, Rufus. Take me—God that feels so good."

"All good things come to those who wait, little hellion." But his ragged breath told her she was not the only one on the very edge.

Moving down over her body, he bent his head and tortured her woman's petals with his clever tongue, laving and flicking and sucking her rigid nub until she was mindless. He was relentless in his quest to bring her pleasure. Again and again his wicked mouth brought her to the sheerest edge of climax, but when her moans heralded her oncoming release, he stopped, returned, and slipped the tip of his enormous member just a little bit deeper than before.

He teased her mercilessly. Letting her scale the cliff face but never fly free. Wildness beat its drum in her blood, and she arched uncontrollably against him, her legs wrapping around his hips.

"Please, Rufus, for the love of God," she groaned, tightening her arms until his hard chest chafed against her aching breasts.

In one swift movement he plunged deep within her, and she felt him quiver above her. "So tight, so hot . . ."

Closing her eyes at the feel of him filling her so completely, she moved her hips, willing him to go deeper.

He needed no further encouragement. He kissed her lips and began to withdraw and reenter her wet sheath in a quickening pace. She joined in, her hips matching his powerful thrusts, the frenzy of their desire shaking her very soul. She could not help the budding cries sounding from within her battered throat. Just when she felt her climax start he slipped from between her thighs and lay back pulling her atop him. He paused, panting hard. "Take me, siren. I want to witness your complete abandonment. I want to hear and feel my wild wanton ride me to completion."

Rheda couldn't think of anything more pleasurable as he lifted her hips and guided her down over the full length of

him. He was deep inside her, buried to the hilt, and she felt every hard inch of him. His strong hands grasped her hips as she began to ride him. When he slipped a finger between their joined bodies to touch her throbbing center, she shuddered and dropped her head back, quickening her pace.

"You're so beautiful," he gasped, watching her with dark, glittering eyes.

He reached up, caught her bouncing breasts in his hands, and then with a ripple of stomach muscles, surged up and took one peaked nipple into his mouth. The feel of his rock-hard muscles rubbing against her mound tipped her over the edge, and she abandoned herself to her shattering climax, heedless of the pain radiating from her throat as she screamed his name over and over and over . . . Then she was conscious of nothing except the exquisite feel of him deep within her—touching the edges of her womb.

Before her cries of passion had started to ebb, he gave a rough growl and rolled her beneath him only to possess her again. He grabbed her wrists and entwined her hands with his as he drove into her like a wild beast. She relished his frantic coupling, and she opened her legs wide and took everything he had to give. His muscles corded and tightened in his neck as he cried out and pulsed deep within her—he shuddered—and collapsed sated in her arms.

"I'm not the only incorrigible one now, am I, Rufus?"

He opened one eye. "Did I hurt you?"

She shook her head and stroked back his damp hair that covered his face.

"Thank God." He sounded almost shaken. He laid his head on her breasts, his body still joined with hers, and pressed a single, tender kiss to her skin. He rolled on his side and pulled her tightly against him. Wearily he said, "Just give me a minute," he muttered, "and I'd love to pleasure you again." Only moments later he fell into an exhausted sleep.

She lay watching him sleep. He looked younger and more vulnerable with his face relaxed and happy. Her heart felt full

seeing that he slept with a smile on his face. Rheda decided he deserved to always look happy. No more shouldering life's trials on his own. She wanted to be there to help him.

She *would* be there to help him. To love him. To protect him.

She thought on the situation with Lady Umbridge, and slowly a plan formed. Rheda was not opposed to being underhanded. When fighting an opponent no better than a gutter rat she had to think like one.

She inwardly chuckled so as not to wake Rufus. She knew what to do. She'd use the fact that Fleur had no idea who Meg was.

Rheda would disappear, pretending to flee as per Fleur's instructions. Fleur would think she'd won and perhaps let her guard slip. Meanwhile Meg would follow the bitch's every move and steal back Christopher's journals.

Rheda pressed a light kiss to Rufus's cheek. He didn't even move a muscle, his exhaustion seeing him sleep like the dead. "Please don't think I've given up," she whispered into his ear. "I'll be back, and we will have our happy ever after. No one is going to stop us, certainly not a desperate, oversexed slut."

She slipped carefully from the bed, pulled on her clothes, and went in search of Meg.

Chapter 25

The sunlight streaming in through the windows woke him. Like the big bad wolf in the tale of Little Miss Riding Hood, he thought all the brighter to see the beautiful woman beside him. One part of his anatomy was certainly big and wickedly hard. Damn his exhaustion last night. He'd wanted more than that brief encounter.

He rolled to face Rheda, his groin throbbing at the prospect of making love to her again.

But the space beside him was empty—the outline where her head had rested on the pillow and her lingering scent on his sheets the only evidence that she had ever been in his bed.

A sense of unease gripped him before his rational mind told him she'd probably been called to see Lady Hale.

He rolled away to look out the window, and a lingering flicker of doubt became a certainty. The sun was only just over the horizon. It was too early to have been summoned anywhere.

He tossed back the bedcovers and collected his clothes. Where the hell was she? He should have stayed awake last night and talked. There were things that needed to be said. Thanks for saving his life. Assurance he would honor his proposal . . .

His rejuvenating sleep seemingly forgotten, Rufus dressed

and strode to the bedchamber Rheda had been assigned. It was empty, the bed not slept in.

Downstairs the breakfast room, too, lay empty. He stopped Lady Hale's butler and inquired if her ladyship was awake and was told she had been given another dose of laudanum during the night and would likely sleep until midday.

"Has any of the staff seen Miss Kerrich?"

"No, my lord. Not since last night. She may have taken an early-morning stroll. I saw her brother, Baron de Winter, out near the stables."

"Thank you." Rufus almost ran down the steps and across the stable yard.

Daniel looked up from saddling his horse as Rufus approached. "Well met, Rufus. Stephen's asked me to ride into Deal and request more men to help search for Samuel, but I need to talk with you urgently."

"Have you seen Rheda?" he asked.

Daniel's eyebrows rose. "I visited her room just now and it was empty. She'd obviously not slept there last night. I assumed she was with you." The young baron gave him a thin smile. "Actually, it is of Rheda which I wish to speak."

Rufus held up his hand. "I am marrying her, Daniel, if that sets your mind at rest." He paused. "If she'll have me. Her opinion of marriage and of men in general is not high."

Daniel's face relaxed, and he laughed, his grin infectious. "Rheda taught me that nothing worth having comes easy. I'd love to be a fly on the wall when you propose." He gave Rufus a shrewd look. "I'm counting on you to convince her. I'll not stand by and see her suffer a further scandal when, once again, she is the innocent party."

"I intend to lock her in a room with me until she says yes."

"If I know my sister, that could take a while. I hope you have plenty of provisions." Daniel laughed.

Rufus looked around the yard. "I have to find her first."

Both men shifted uneasily.

"You don't think anything has happened to her? Daniel voiced Rufus's deepest fear. "We still haven't caught Samuel."

In unison they turned and ran for the house.

"My goodness, where's the fire?" Lady Umbridge called as she descended the stairs, a vision in layers of lavender silk.

Daniel's mouth fell open, but Rufus found himself totally unaffected by the bountiful amount of flesh on display. "We're worried about Rheda. She appears to be missing, and with Samuel on the loose . . ."

The woman flashed Daniel a dazzling smile, and the boy gazed at her like a lovesick calf. "Rheda left a short while ago. The poor child felt awkward at having to face Helen when she woke."

She's lying, thought Rufus. With calmness he did not feel, he asked, "Did she say where she was going?"

"Why, home to Tumsbury Cliff of course," Fleur replied with an easy smile. "I'm famished." She took Daniel's arm. "Come. You men need sustenance. Why don't you keep me company for breakfast?" And this time the look she focused on Rufus told him food was not what she hungered for. It made the thought of eating repugnant.

"You keep Lady Umbridge company, Daniel. I must find Miss Kerrich."

He was already halfway down the steps before Daniel called, "Of course, Rufus. I'll expect an announcement later this afternoon."

An hour later he stood outside the baron's house rubbing the back of his neck and trying to get the mixed emotions of panic and anger under control.

Jamieson swore she wasn't at the manor and that he hadn't seen her. Rufus believed him only because he, too, seemed to grow concerned when he learned that Rheda was no longer at Hastingleigh.

"Where else would she go?" he asked the man. "Where would she go if she had some issues to think about?"

Jamieson's eyes narrowed, and he frowned. "Meg. She'd go to Meg."

Rufus swung up onto Caesar's back before Jamieson finished the sentence and was galloping down the drive a few seconds later.

He pounded on Meg's door like a knight besieging the castle, rescuing the damsel in distress. It only took a few thumps before the door was thrown wide, and Meg stood there wiping her hands on her apron.

"Is Rheda with you?" he demanded.

"Good morning, my lord."

Her greeting tempered his impatience, and he gave her a proper greeting, adding, "My apologies. It's just Rheda has gone missing and with Samuel still at large, I'm worried."

"Rheda hasn't gone missing." Meg hesitated before adding, "She felt it appropriate to leave."

"She's confided in you? Appropriate?" He captured Meg's wrist as she made to close the door. "What are you not telling me?"

Her gaze flicked to his hand wrapped around her wrist, then up to his eyes. She glared at him until he let go. "Rheda doesn't wish to see you. I think it best you leave." And she shut the door in his face.

Rufus stood staring at the door in shock. How could she have given herself to him with such tenderness, such passion, and then coldly walk away?

He tried to tamp down the flare of panic inside him. It was quickly replaced with anger. How could she give up on them before they had a chance to . . . ?

He sunk down on the doorstep. He'd never told her of his love for her. Or how much he admired her.

But he couldn't rid himself of the sick feeling squeezing his heart. Perhaps she had meant every word she'd thrown in his face. Perhaps marriage was an institution she would never contemplate entering. What filled him with overrid-

ing dread, however, was the thought she had never loved him. That perhaps, all along, her true goal had been to protect her smuggling operation.

Abruptly he rose and mounted Caesar. He had every intention of establishing the truth—no matter what the cost.

As Rufus stalked to his horse and galloped off, Rheda's breath let out in a rush. She'd had visions of him forcing his way into Meg's house and carrying her off. That would destroy their plan. She didn't want Rufus to know the truth; he'd likely strangle Fleur and rise to Rheda's defense, destroying any chance of the Strathmores taking their rightful place in Society.

She was a tad disappointed that Rufus had so little faith in her ability to aid his endeavors. He should realize that she wouldn't run away.

Meg filled the kettle and sat it on the fire. "A cup of tea is in order," she said over a lot of banging and clashing of kettle, cups, and saucers.

"I take it you're cross with me, Meg."

Meg's lips thinned, and she ignored Rheda's question until she'd placed a cup in front of her. Then she snapped, "You should have told him the truth. He's a grown man and can make his own decisions. Besides, look at the worry you're putting him through."

Rheda looked up through eyes welling with tears. "How could I put him in that position?" She wiped her cheeks. "No. I've done the right thing. I've caused this mess, and I'll fix it. For once I'll help someone else—selflessly for a change."

Meg sighed. "The two of you need your heads banged together. You'd probably deal with Fleur quicker with Rufus's help."

Rheda kept her silence. But what if Rufus told Fleur to go to hell, which he likely would? If he lost his only chance of redemption, would he come to resent her? When he looked at her in years to come, would the fact he gave up everything

for her destroy the love he had for her? She couldn't risk it. Not when this plan would work. A little while later, after the two women had almost finished clearing the plates from the boys' midday meal off the table, there was more pounding on the door. Rheda looked at Meg and shook her head.

Wiping her hands on her apron, Meg moved and opened the door. Before she could react the door was pushed open and Lord Worthington and one of his men entered. His narrowed gaze latched on to Rheda. "You're to come with me, under orders from the king."

Meg pushed between Stephen and Rheda. "On what charge?"

"Smuggling."

Rheda gasped, and then fury overtook her common sense. She'd underestimated her foe. "But I did exactly what Lady Umbridge said—" she began.

Stephen's gaze swung from Meg's angry face to Rheda and asked incredulously, "What has Fleur got to do with this?"

Rheda open and closed her mouth. Perhaps this had nothing to do with Lady Umbridge. "Nothing, I don't know what I'm saying."

"This is a mistake." Meg tried to pull Stephen's hand from Rheda's arm. "Let her go. What does Lord Strathmore have to say about all this? When he finds out that you've manhandled Miss Kerrich . . ."

Stephen looked down his nose at them. "Who do you think sent me?"

Pain like that from a festering boil grew and throbbed as Rheda heard Rufus's title. Was this his revenge on her for leaving him? Did he have so little faith in her? In their love? At the first fence he'd faltered. Rufus still didn't trust her, and the knowledge made every hollow in her body ache.

To her dismay, Stephen and his men escorted her like a common criminal back to Hastingleigh, and she soon found herself locked in her bedchamber.

Quite some time later, when her nerves were stretched to

breaking, she heard the sound of heavy footsteps nearing her door and knew instinctively whom they belonged to.

This time it did not crash open; he simply unlocked the door and stepped inside, quietly closing the door behind him. Rheda scrambled up from where she was sitting on the edge of the bed, her mouth open to berate him. Instead she froze, made speechless by the raw anger in Rufus's eyes.

Her tone hardened. "I don't deserve this."

"Don't you?" Rufus answered, his tone clipped.

"I can explain—"

"Can you? Last night was one of the most unforgettably passionate nights of my life. I woke eager for more, only to find you gone. What was last night to you? Was it supposed to stop me from arresting you for smuggling? If so, it appears to have backfired."

His scathing tone caused a hot flush to spread up her neck and flood her cheeks. "You don't trust me. After all we have been through you still don't trust me," she said, utterly bereft.

"Trust?" He gently raised her chin, and she saw the stormy tempest of his eyes had softened. "What is this all about, minx?"

She jerked her head away from his touch. "I'm not sure you deserve to know after this behavior."

"What has Lady Umbridge got to do with this?" he demanded.

His grip on her chin stopped her from averting her gaze. *Blast.* She was a terrible liar, always had been. "I'm sure I don't know what you mean."

"Stephen mentioned you'd thought Fleur had something to do with your arrest. I want to know why?"

Feeling the sting of unwanted tears, she cried, "Can't you just trust me?"

"Not if it means I lose you," he swore furiously.

"For once in my life let me do the right thing. Please don't force the truth from me."

He rubbed his thumb over the corner of her mouth and

leaned in close. The scent of him sent her pulse ricocheting to every corner of her body. "The right thing is to tell me you love me, too, and that you'll gladly become my wife," he whispered against her ear.

Her breath faltered. What was love without trust? Is that why she felt dampness on her cheeks?

"I do hope they are tears of joy."

When she remained silent, he prodded her in the ribs. "Are you not going to give me an answer?"

"No."

"No, you won't answer? Or no *is* your answer? I warn you, the answer better be yes or I'll strip you naked, lay you on this bed, and make mad passionate love to you. Then I'll tell your brother. You know he'll insist we marry. I'm sure he'll be ecstatic at our union."

Would he ever trust her? And if he couldn't, what would that do to his love over time? She wouldn't end up like her mother, married to a man who despised her. Rufus sat back and ran a hand through his hair. "I'm not wrong, am I? You do love me. I know who you are, Miss Rheda Kerrich, and the Rhe I know and love would not have made love to me last night if she didn't love me. She wouldn't have rushed to save me at her own peril, and she would not be sitting here letting her world fall apart." He leaned in until their noses almost touched. "Would she?"

She felt like screaming at him, "When will you understand I have a plan?'

She saw a shade of uncertainty in Rufus's eyes. His self-doubt tore at her heart, but she shook her head gravely. "Rufus, you once accused me of being selfish, and you were right. But watching you—seeing how you put everyone before yourself—made me realize that love means sacrifice—"

"Marrying you won't be a sacrifice. Come here, sweetheart." Rufus pulled her into his arms, and she was too weak-willed to resist. "Is this about your being a smuggler?"

"I know you've worked all your life to clear your father,

and I destroyed that when you had to kill Christopher. I won't see the chance to prove your father's innocence taken away from you again."

He crushed her against his chest. "You're wrong. I've been so pigheaded. The past is for the dead. The future is for the living, and I want my future to be with you. I love you, Rheda. I love everything about you. Your spirit, your courage, and your selflessness. Nothing would make me prouder than having you by my side, as my wife, my lover, and my true partner."

At her shocked silence he drew back, his mouth curving into a glorious smile. "If you are trying to be noble because of Christopher's journals, the ones Lady Umbridge found, don't be. They are in Stephen's safekeeping. All of them."

She threw back her head and laughed. "Meg was right. I've worried everyone for nothing." She pushed at his chest. "However, I'm not sure you know me at all. How could you think I'd simply let Fleur win? I had a plan. A good plan. But you couldn't trust me to sort her out on my own."

He hugged her tightly. "It wasn't that I didn't trust you. I was goddamn worried about you. Samuel is still out there. All I wanted to do was find you to ensure you were safe."

"Oh."

Relief and longing warred in Rheda's chest, but she forced them away. She stepped out of his hold. It was time for some straight talking. She had to ascertain if this was more than obligation on his part.

"Are you sure that you want to marry me? I know how important your family's standing is. I can't possibly be your countess. I wouldn't know where to begin. I've never been to London. What if my past became known? What if the scandal with Prince Hammed arose? I'd shame the Strathmore name all over again. You'd be universally condemned for your whore of a wife."

"Don't say that. Don't ever say that," he said, anger scoring his words. "I was your first lover, and goddamnit I in-

tend to be your last. If the past few weeks have taught me anything, it's that the only opinions that should matter are those of my family and friends. You taught me that."

He pulled her into a tight embrace. "I don't give a damn what Society thinks anymore. You've opened my eyes to true honor. You gave up a real chance to be a darling of Society in order to keep Tumsbury Cliff safe for Daniel—"

"You're wrong, I wasn't selfless. I did it for me, too. I was so afraid of ending up like my mother. In love with a man who would never love her—"

"Well, you haven't ended up like your mother. The man before you loves you more than life itself and always will."

"That hardly makes me qualified to be a countess."

"But your love is all I require. I've let Society dictate the man I have become, but I swear no more. Once we marry I intend to retire to my estate—with you—and breed racehorses. And my wife will breed the finest cavalry horses for the army." He took her hand and placed an intimate kiss on her palm. "We'll be so wrapped up in our family we won't give a toss about Society."

The turmoil in her heart still raged, but as she searched his face a flicker of hope began to burn.

"You're sure you won't care if my past raises its ugly head. If I marry you there is no guarantee someone—Lady Umbridge for instance—won't take pleasure in disparaging me and therefore your family. What will your mother think?"

"My lovely, wonton, and reckless Rheda cannot be frightened of my mother? I would not have thought it," he teased. "If you must know, Mother is here and she's dying to meet the woman who saved her son's life." His voice softened, and the tender notes made her want to weep again. "My mother has only wanted me to be happy. That is what true love means, putting someone else's happiness before your own and not caring about the consequences. And I won't be happy, I won't be whole, without you by my side."

When she didn't reply, he leaned closer, the earnestness in

his eyes growing more intense. "I know I'm asking you to risk everything, to give yourself to me in marriage, but I promise on my father's grave that I will love you, cherish you, and revere you until the day I die." He bit his lip and dropped to one knee. "You've taken risks all your life. Will you take one more? Will you trust me with your heart, Rheda? Will you have the courage to love me back? Marry me."

Risk? He thought being his wife was a risk to her? "Oh, Rufus, loving you, marrying you, is no risk. More than anything it would be my dream come true."

With a raw sound, he rose to his feet and hauled her into his arms. His kiss was fierce, consuming. He twisted his hand in her hair and held her still as he plundered her mouth with relish.

He gazed over her shoulder to the bed. "I intend to lay you down, remove your clothes, worship every inch of your skin, and ensure that your brother is fully aware of what I do. I intend to make it so you can never leave me."

Rheda cupped his face in her hands. "You don't need to do that. I will gladly be your wife. I love you, Rufus. I love the man you are. I love that you love me and that you love your family above all else."

"We'll make a bigger family—together. Wild little hellion children who will challenge us every day." He lifted her hands to kiss her fingertips ardently. "Say it again—tell me you love me."

"I love you, Rufus. Now and forever. I only hope," she murmured, "the price you pay for marrying me is not so high you live to regret it."

"There is no price to pay. You've taught me that love is the only true measure of a man's worth." He laid her on the bed and kissed her sweetly. "I must be the richest man in the entire world, for I have found a love that surpasses anything I've known before."

He stood up. "Excuse me for one moment." He strode and opened the door to the bedchamber and murmured to

someone waiting outside. On his way back to the bed he began removing his jacket, a half-smile playing on his lips. "I gave your brother the good news. I thought that when I ravish my wife to be, I'd like a bit of privacy. I want to pleasure you all the way down to your soul, siren, and I want you free to make as much noise as you like."

"Promises, oh, promises," she murmured, stretching seductively like the true siren she was.

His slow smile curved into a huge grin. When he had stripped down to his breeches, he called huskily, "Come and get me." And he almost melted as he saw the brilliant sparkle of her emerald eyes and felt lust and love surge through him.

Rising to her knees, his siren, his heart, crawled to the edge of the bed. She ran a finger down his chest until it came to rest on the waistband of his trousers. "I'll undress you, if you undress me."

His grin widened.

Within minutes they were both naked and breathing heavily. He lowered her down onto the bed, her riotous curls cascading wildly around her naked breasts. He buried his head in the tresses and breathed deeply. Her fragrance was that of the rambling roses that grew along the cliff tops.

He finally lifted his head and swept his gaze over every tempting curve of her body. His hands and mouth burned with the need to touch her, claim her, mark her as his.

"Mine. My love. My wild and wicked siren."

Her soft smile held an erotic allure. "You make me wild. Wild with want. Wild with love and desire."

He flashed a roguish smile. "Then it's my duty to help unleash all that wildness."

"One kiss and I'm wild. Wild for you," she responded, reaching up to slip her arms around his neck.

He leaned down and kissed one hardened nipple. "I intend to keep you permanently wild."

His touch was a flame against her skin. Her limbs tightened, and she made no protest when his hands slowly stroked

down her body. He watched her, totally absorbed in her reaction, a wicked sensuous smile lingering on his mouth.

He caressed her inner thighs until her skin erupted in a blaze of heat. Rufus lowered his head to kiss her, and she felt the wildness deep inside rise and take her over. He boldly possessed and claimed her mouth.

His tongue stroked the inside of her mouth while his questing fingers delved into the wet heart of her, and her world erupted into scalding white heat. His long, talented fingers surged deep within her, and his mouth captured the cries his ravishment drew from her. She was almost mindless in his loving. She clutched his thick, chestnut hair, her hips lifting in a silent plea for release.

Yet he did not allow her fulfillment. He brought her to the brink of climax and drew back, a teasing light in his eyes.

"Rufus . . . ," she begged. "Your siren may well be about to claw you."

He lifted slightly off her, his muscled arms holding his weight above her as he bent to kiss and lick her sensitive breasts until she thought she'd lose her mind. "I'd enjoy you scoring my back, marking me as yours," he whispered against her heated skin. He moved to his side.

Dazed by the erotic warmth in his voice, she gritted her teeth, savoring the way his hands drifted back up over her stomach, his fingers questing and shaping the sensitive mounds of her breasts. He rolled one peaked nipple between his thumb and forefinger, and she cried out.

Her hands gripped the sheets as his flaming tongue swirled over her breasts. The deliberate attack on her senses caused her to moan and arch up off the bed, opening her thighs wide so Rufus could position himself between them.

Rheda loved the feel of him against her—his rippled stomach, the sparse curls on his chest brushing her skin, and the rigid rod of his arousal, thick and pulsing between her thighs. She almost climaxed as he suddenly thrust home, shuddering as she fully absorbed his swollen length.

"There is nothing as thrilling as feeling you deep inside me," she murmured, her voice choked with love. "God, I love you . . ."

"As I love you, Rhe." His gaze locked with hers, and he flashed a look so filled with love her heart almost burst from her chest. Then his grin turned cocky. "Let's see exactly how wild I can make you."

She shivered at the promise in his voice and in his touch. "Yes," she panted. "Give me everything you've got to give."

He drew back and surged inside her, impaling her with his thick, pulsing shaft. "Like this," he said, and he took one of her peaked nipples deep into his mouth.

"Oh, yes, Rufus . . ."

Rheda welcomed his growing fever and locked her legs around his hips, clinging to him, meeting him stroke for powerful stroke. She felt his composure fraying, and their joining turned frantic, the rhythm building to unleashed wildness.

His thrusts were relentless in his quest to pleasure her. Rheda held on, wanting them to explode together. Her fingernails scored his back where she clung tightly, her body tightened, and they climaxed in an explosion of convulsive pleasure, his harsh groans louder than her crooning cries.

She felt Rufus's seed pulse deep within her before he collapsed spent and languid from the force of their fierce lovemaking.

"Was that wild enough for you, my love?" he panted.

"It will do for a start, my lord," she said, still trying to catch her breath. With strength she didn't know she possessed she rolled Rufus over until she lay on top of him, the delicious aftermath of love echoing in their racing heartbeats. "Once you've recovered I intend to thoroughly teach you about wildness." She smiled and then ran her hand down over his chiseled chest and rippling stomach to lightly cup his flaccid member.

To her surprise she felt it stir to life.

"You've taught me so many things already, my beautiful, generous Rhe. Perhaps, for this next lesson, I'll be a slow learner. After all, you have a lifetime in which to teach me. And I have a feeling I'm going to enjoy every lesson."

As she bent and took his mouth in a searing kiss, she felt him harden between her thighs and realized he wouldn't need any teaching. He was already wild enough for her.

Rufus, her perfect mate. Rufus, exactly the man she wanted.

And, she finally realized, the man she deserved.

Epilogue

R heda made her way down the long corridor toward the top of the stairs. Even the shadows seemed to be judging her tonight. She drew a deep breath and prayed she would not fail. This was her first public appearance as Rufus's wife.

They had married by special license in the chapel at Hastingleigh almost a month ago. Rufus's mother, Susanne, and Lady Hale had seen to everything.

Rufus had refused to use the journals to expose Christopher's treason to the world and vindicate his father. He could have done so and used Christopher's guilt to elevate himself in the eyes of Society, but had chosen to spare Helen the pain he and his family had endured all his adulthood. His sacrifice only made Rheda love him more.

Of course Lord Ashford had been told the truth, and he did everything in his power to raise the Strathmore's standing, even arranging for the Prince Regent to bestow an earldom upon Rufus for services to the Crown.

Rufus had received his new title from Prinny that morning. He was now the Earl of Hascombe, the name of his family's estate near Cambridge. The title did not come with additional property or added wealth, neither of which Rufus needed, but it elevated Rufus and firmly restored him to his rightful place in Society. His mother and sister could stand with their heads high.

Tonight's ball at Lanwades House, the Strathmore's London home in Mayfair, might not have yet commenced, but already it was the talk of the season. The unexpected rise of the Strathmore name, coupled with his marriage to an unknown baron's sister, meant the cream of London Society would be here tonight, no doubt to appease their curiosity and—more stomach-churning in Rheda's mind—to judge.

Her nerves buzzed like dragonflies—dragonflies with large wings and fiery breath.

Madeline, Rufus's sister, appeared beside her. "Nervous?"

"I feel sick to my stomach."

Maddy, as she had asked Rheda to call her, laughed. At nineteen, Maddy was more excited about tonight's events than scared. There was no mistaking Maddy as Rufus's sister. She was stunningly beautiful, like her brother, with the same glowing auburn hair, and warm and inviting chocolate-colored eyes.

"Me, too. It is my first proper ball and my first introduction to Society." Maddy gave her a small smile. "Let's slay them together. We Strathmore women must stick together."

Rheda laughed and hugged her new sister. The girl's smile lit up her face, and Rheda knew Maddy would be the one slaying hearts tonight.

"You make it sound as if we are about to do battle."

"We are." Maddy laughed.

They made their way together to the entrance of the ballroom. The women spied Rufus at the bottom of the stairs, and Rheda's breath caught in her throat. He looked so handsome. His formal attire hugged his wide shoulders and emphasized his lean waist and narrow hips. A stiff white cravat gleamed at his throat, making the black-on-white look less severe. His chestnut hair glinted in the candlelight, and his chiseled face drew her longing gaze. But it was the fiery approval and possessive love she saw shinning within his eyes that made her heart flip.

Maddy took her arm and nodded at Rufus. "You at least have your knight to defend you."

Rheda felt herself quake. She was to descend the stairs alone, all eyes on her. Rufus sent her a quelling look that gave her courage and calmed her. She had run a smuggling ring for many years, dodging Revenue men and worse. She was not about to let a room full of Society matriarchs intimidate her.

She raised her head, and, keeping her eye on Rufus waiting for her proudly at the bottom of the stairs, she began her descent.

"Isn't my wife the most radiant woman you've ever seen?" were the soft words that greeted her as she safely reached the bottom.

"Second most radiant," said a now familiar voice at her husband's side. Anthony Craven, the Earl of Wickham, gazed with adoration at his wife, Lady Melissa, who stood proudly beside him.

Melissa flushed and came forward to tuck her arm through Rheda's. She began drawing her away from the two men, who proudly watched like the love-struck husbands they were.

"I hope you are not going to hover all night, dear husband. This is my first engagement since the birth of our son, Harry, and I mean to enjoy it." Melissa blew Anthony a kiss. "Shoo. I have important ladies to introduce Rheda to."

For a moment panic assailed her, until she felt the firm squeeze of her arm and Melissa whisper, "I know what it's like to be the talk of the *ton*. Come, let me introduce you to Lady Horsham. Once we have that formidable lady's support, you will have arrived. No one will dare spread any gossip."

Rheda smiled at her new friend. She still missed Meg but understood why Meg did not wish to leave Deal.

She was thankful that Melissa and Anthony had welcomed

her enthusiastically into their lives. Melissa had even asked her to be Harry's godmother when Anthony asked Rufus to be godfather. "Thank you for being here. Your support means the world to me. Knowing Rufus's friends accept me is all I really need."

Melissa stopped and pressed a kiss to Rheda's cheek. "Not accept—love. A woman who has won Rufus Knight's heart wins ours, too." She laughed gaily. "I have a terrible soft spot for Rufus. He did help save me after all. I'm so very happy he found the perfect woman."

Rheda looked back through the crowd at her dashing husband and saw his eyes were still upon her. She didn't think she could get any happier.

Melissa followed her gaze and smiled at Anthony. "Come. Stop gawking. The two of them are much too pleased with themselves as it is. Anthony especially so, now he has his son."

They turned and continued across the large ballroom toward Lady Horsham. Rheda patted her stomach. Son. How she'd love to have Rufus's child.

"If Rufus is anything like Anthony, I'm sure you'll be with child soon."

It was with a blush staining her cheeks that Lady Rheda Strathmore was introduced to Lady Horsham.

She'd survived. Several hours later Rheda had finally begun to relax.

She smiled when she spotted Daniel across the room, dancing with a duke's daughter. He'd taken to London Society like a duck to a pond. He had them all utterly charmed. The handsome baron, who no one had heard of, had many of the mothers with unwed daughters in a swoon.

She glanced across at her husband. One more thing to thank Rufus for. And Stephen. The two men had worked tirelessly to hide any evidence of her former career as Dark Shadow. Yet still the terror of being exposed haunted her.

She could still hurt Rufus and his family. Knowing her past, knowing what exposure would cost those she loved, she found it difficult to relax in such company.

Everything went swimmingly until she turned to find Lady Umbridge's hostile gaze and cold smile focused her way.

The woman made a beeline for Rheda, obviously intent on causing trouble. Her skin prickled and went ice cold. This was precisely what she dreaded: a person who had the ability to expose her past and hurt all the work Rufus had done for his family.

"Lady Strathmore," Lady Umbridge said with poisonous sweetness. "So nice to see you again. You must have enjoyed meeting Prinny today. After all, I know you have an intimate fondness for princes."

Rheda's face flooded with heat, her mouth dried, and she felt as though she would be sick.

Struggling to respond, Rheda sensed a change behind her. Her husband suddenly appeared at one elbow, taking her hand and giving it a reassuring squeeze. Maddy materialized on the other side.

"My wife knows how to mix well in all company, even with those not worthy enough to be in the same room." The direction of his harsh gaze and his cool words left the other guests in no doubt as to his meaning.

Before Lady Umbridge could utter a retort, Rufus leaned in close and whispered in her ear, "I have *all* of Christopher's journals. There is an interesting chapter on your visit to Hastingleigh many years ago as a young bride, and your abortive attempt to seduce my father. Apparently you made quite a spectacle of yourself chasing after a happily married man. I suggest you leave this ball, and if I ever hear any lies concerning my wife and a certain Turkish prince I will take pleasure in publishing your sordid tales to the world."

For the space of three heartbeats Lady Umbridge stood white-lipped, shaking with what could have been fear or

fury. Then she turned in a swish of skirts and headed toward the exit.

"Nicely handled, Brother," Maddy whispered, rising on tiptoes to press a kiss to her brother's cheek before disappearing back into the crowd.

Rheda gazed up, her love shining from her eyes focused totally on the man she'd had the good sense to marry. "Thank you," she whispered. "Thank you for risking loving me."

He brushed her mouth tenderly with his lips. "No. Thank you. There is no reward without risk, and the prize of your love is greater and more desirable than I ever could have imagined."

The orchestra struck up a waltz, and Rufus drew her into his arms. "Now, the new Earl of Hascombe intends to dance with his wife to show the world she belongs to him."

Samuel kept to the shadows of the ballroom, careful to keep his expression bland and drawing limited attention to himself.

He longed to destroy the man who'd taken his master from him.

At first he'd wanted to enact his revenge against Rufus's lover, in the same way Rufus had killed Christopher. Samuel would rip Rheda from his arms and cause Rufus to suffer her loss for all eternity.

But death for Rheda was too merciful. She had played an equal part in Christopher's demise and the destruction of Samuel's world. She should suffer as deeply as her husband. He could think of nothing better than forcing Rheda to watch her husband live the rest of his life consumed by guilt and grief.

It wasn't until he'd followed the couple back to Hascombe, the Strathmore estate, that his plan for revenge formed and crystallized.

Now with heightened anticipation he watched the young, dark-haired beauty rise on tiptoe, kiss her brother's cheek, and, with a gay laugh, flounce away to join her friends.

Madeline. Rufus had a sister. A sister he protected with a ferocious and all-consuming fervor.

Madeline. A cold, cruel smile curved Samuel's lips.

Revenge would never taste so sweet.

Did you miss Bronwen's first book, INVITATION TO RUIN?

One Good Lady Is About to Go Bad . . .

The only thing Miss Melissa Goodly has ever wanted out of a marriage is love. But any hope of that dissolves one wild night, when she loses herself in the arms of the most irresistible—and unobtainable—man in all of England. For when they are discovered in a position as compromising as it is pleasurable, she has no choice but to accept his proposal.

Avowed bachelor Anthony Craven, Earl of Wickham, never meant to seduce an innocent like Melissa. Yet now that the damage is done, it does seem like she'd make a very convenient wife. After all, she is so naive he won't have to worry about ever being tempted. Or so he thinks, until the vows are spoken and they are left alone—and his new bride reveals a streak just as brazen and unrestrained as his own. . . . .

GREAT BOOKS,
GREAT SAVINGS!

When You Visit Our Website:
www.kensingtonbooks.com
You Can Save Money Off The Retail Price
Of Any Book You Purchase!

- **All Your Favorite Kensington Authors**
- **New Releases & Timeless Classics**
- **Overnight Shipping Available**
- **eBooks Available For Many Titles**
- **All Major Credit Cards Accepted**

Visit Us Today To Start Saving!
www.kensingtonbooks.com

All Orders Are Subject To Availability.
Shipping and Handling Charges Apply.
Offers and Prices Subject To Change Without Notice.